BLACKBERRY WINE

Joanne Harris

BLACK SWAN

BLACKBERRY WINE
A BLACK SWAN BOOK : 0 552 99800 1

Originally published in Great Britain by Doubleday,
a division of Transworld Publishers

PRINTING HISTORY
Doubleday edition published 2000
Black Swan edition published 2001

1 3 5 7 9 10 8 6 4 2

'God's Garden' by Dorothy Frances Gurney
reprinted courtesy of Burns and Oates Publishers.

Typeset in 11 on 13pt Melior by
Hewer Text Ltd, Edinburgh.

Black Swan Books are published by Transworld Publishers,
61–63 Uxbridge Road, London W5 5SA,
a division of The Random House Group Ltd,
in Australia by Random House Australia (Pty) Ltd,
20 Alfred Street, Milsons Point, Sydney, NSW 2061, Australia,
in New Zealand by Random House New Zealand Ltd,
18 Poland Road, Glenfield, Auckland 10, New Zealand
and in South Africa by Random House (Pty) Ltd,
Endulini, 5a Jubilee Road, Parktown 2193, South Africa.

Printed and bound in Great Britain by
Clays Ltd, St Ives plc.

To my grandfather, Edwin Short:
gardener, winemaker and poet at heart.

Acknowledgements

Many thanks go to the following: Kevin and Anouchka for bearing with me, to G. J. Paul, and the Priory Old Boys' Club, to Francesca Liversidge for her inspired editing, to Jennifer Luithlen, to my splendid agent, Serafina Clarke, for showing me the ropes, but not giving me enough to hang myself with, and to Our Man in London, Christopher Fowler. To all my colleagues and pupils at Leeds Grammar School, goodbye, and good luck. I'll miss you.

1

WINE TALKS. EVERYONE KNOWS THAT. LOOK AROUND YOU. ASK
the oracle at the street corner; the uninvited guest at the
wedding feast; the holy fool. It talks. It ventriloquizes. It
has a million voices. It unleashes the tongue, teasing out
secrets you never meant to tell, secrets you never even
knew. It shouts, rants, whispers. It speaks of great things,
splendid plans, tragic loves and terrible betrayals. It
screams with laughter. It chuckles softly to itself. It weeps
in front of its own reflection. It opens up summers long past
and memories best forgotten. Every bottle a whiff of other
times, other places; every one, from the commonest
Liebfraumilch to the imperious 1945 Veuve Clicquot, a
humble miracle. Everyday magic, Joe called it. The trans-
formation of base matter into the stuff of dreams. Layman's
alchemy.

Take me, for instance. Fleurie, 1962. Last survivor of a
crate of twelve, bottled and laid down the year Jay was
born. 'A pert, garrulous wine, cheery and a little brash, with
a pungent taste of blackcurrant,' said the label. Not really a
wine for keeping, but he did. For nostalgia's sake. For a
special occasion. A birthday, perhaps a wedding. But his
birthdays passed without celebration; drinking Argentin-
ian red and watching old Westerns. Five years ago he laid
me out on a table set with silver candlesticks, but nothing
came of it. In spite of that he and the girl stayed together.
An army of bottles came with her – Dom Pérignon, Sto-

lichnaya vodka, Parfait Amour and Mouton-Cadet, Belgian beers in long-necked bottles, Noilly Prat vermouth and Fraise des Bois. They talk, too, nonsense mostly, metallic chatter, like guests mingling at a party. We refused to have anything to do with them. We were pushed to the back of the cellar, we three survivors, behind the gleaming ranks of these newcomers, and there we stayed for five years, forgotten. Château-Chalon '58, Sancerre '71 and myself. Château-Chalon, vexed at his relegation, pretends deafness and often refuses to speak at all. 'A mellow wine of great dignity and stature,' he quotes in his rare moments of expansiveness. He likes to remind us of his seniority, of the longevity of yellow Jura wines. He makes much of this, as he does of his honeyed bouquet and unique pedigree. The Sancerre has long since turned vinegary and speaks even less, occasionally sighing thinly over her vanished youth.

And then, six weeks before this story begins, the others came. The strangers. The Specials. The interlopers who began it all, though they too seemed forgotten behind the bright new bottles. Six of them, each with its own small handwritten label and sealed in candle wax. Each bottle had a cord of a different colour knotted around its neck: raspberry red, elderflower green, blackberry blue, rosehip yellow, damson black. The last bottle, tied with a brown cord, was no wine even I had ever heard of. 'Specials, 1975,' said the label, the writing faded to the colour of old tea. But inside was a hive of secrets. There was no escaping them; their whisperings, their catcalls, their laughter. We pretended indifference to their antics. These amateurs. Not a whiff of grape in any of them. They were inferiors, and we begrudged them their place among us. And yet there was an appealing impudence to these six freebooters, a hectic clash of flavours and images to send more sober vintages reeling. It was, of course, beneath our dignity to speak to them. But oh I longed to. Perhaps it was that plebeian undertaste of blackcurrant which linked us.

From the cellar you could hear everything that went on in the house. We marked events with the comings and goings of our more favoured colleagues: twelve beers Friday night and laughter in the hallway; the night before a single bottle of Californian red, so young you could almost smell the tannin; the previous week – his birthday, as it happened – a half-bottle of Moët, a demoiselle, that loneliest, most revealing of sizes, and the distant, nostalgic sound of gunfire and horses' hooves from upstairs. Jay Mackintosh was thirty-seven. Unremarkable but for his eyes, which were pinot noir indigo, he had the awkward, slightly dazed look of a man who has lost his way. Five years ago Kerry had found this appealing. By now she had lost her taste for it. There was something deeply annoying about his passivity and the core of stubbornness beneath. Precisely fourteen years ago Jay wrote a novel called *Three Summers with Jackapple Joe*. You'll know it, of course. It won the Prix Goncourt in France, translated into twenty languages. Three crates of vintage Veuve Clicquot celebrated its publication – the '76, drunk too young to do it justice, but then Jay was always like that, rushing at life as if it might never run dry, as if what was bottled inside him would last for ever, success following success in a celebration without end.

In those days there was no wine cellar. We stood on the mantelpiece above his typewriter, for luck, he said. When he'd completed the book he opened the last of my companions of '62 and drank it very slowly, turning the glass round and round in his hands when he'd finished. Then he came over to the mantelpiece. For a moment he stood there. Then he grinned and walked, rather unsteadily, back to his chair.

'Next time, sweetheart,' he promised. 'We'll leave it till next time.' You see, he talks to me, as one day I will talk to him. I'm his oldest friend. We understand each other. Our destinies are intertwined.

Of course there was no next time. Television interviews, newspaper articles and reviews succeeded each other into silence. Hollywood made a film adaptation with Corey

Feldman, set in the American Midwest. Nine years passed. Jay wrote part of a manuscript entitled *Stout Cortez* and sold eight short stories to *Playboy* magazine, which were later reprinted as a collection by Penguin Books. The literary world waited for Jay Mackintosh's new novel, eagerly at first, then restless, curious, then finally, fatally, indifferent.

Of course he still wrote. Seven novels to date, with titles like *The G-sus Gene* or *Psy-Wrens of Mars* or *A Date with d'Eath*, all written under the pseudonym of Jonathan Winesap, nice earners which kept him in reasonable comfort for those fourteen years. He bought a computer, a Toshiba laptop, which he balanced on his knees like the TV dinners he made for himself on the nights – increasingly frequent now – that Kerry worked late. He wrote reviews, articles, short stories and newspaper columns. He lectured at writers' groups, held creative-writing seminars at the university. There were so many things to occupy him, he used to say, that he had scarcely any time to do any work of his own – laughing without conviction at himself, the writer who never writes. Kerry looked at him, narrow-lipped, when he said this. Meet Kerry O'Neill – born Katherine Marsden – twenty-eight, cropped blond hair and startling green eyes, which Jay never suspected were coloured contact lenses. A journalist made good in television by way of *Forum!* a late-night talk show, where popular authors and B-list celebrities discussed contemporary social problems against a background of avant-garde jazz. Five years ago she might have smiled at his words. But then, five years ago there was no *Forum!*, Kerry was writing a travel column for the *Independent* and working on a book entitled *Chocolate – a Feminist Outlook*. The world was filled with possibilities. The book came out two years later, on a wave of media interest. Kerry was photogenic, marketable and mainstream. As a result she appeared on a number of lightweight chat shows. She was photographed for *Marie Claire*, *Tatler* and *Me!*, but was quick to reassure herself that it hadn't gone to her head. She had a house in Chelsea, a *pied-à-terre* in New York and was considering liposuction on her thighs. She had grown up. Moved on.

But, for Jay, nothing had moved on. Five years ago he had seemed the embodiment of the temperamental artist, drinking half a bottle of Smirnoff a day, a doomed, damaged figure of romance. He had brought out her maternal instincts. She was going to redeem him, inspire him and, in return, he would write a wonderful book, a book which would illuminate lives and which would all be due to her.

But none of that happened. Trashy sci-fi was what paid the rent; cheap paperbacks with lurid covers. The maturity, the puckish wisdom of that first work, had never been duplicated, or even attempted. And for all his brooding silences Jay had no temperament to speak of. He had never given in to an impulse. He never really showed anger, never lost control. His conversation was neither brilliantly intelligent nor intriguingly surly. Even his drinking – his one remaining excess – seemed ridiculous now, like a man who insists upon wearing the outmoded fashions of his youth. He spent his time playing computer games, listening to old singles and watching old movies on video, locked in his adolescence like a record in a groove. Maybe she was mistaken, thought Kerry. He didn't want to grow up. He didn't want to be saved.

The empty bottles told a different story. He drank, Jay told himself, for the same reason he wrote second-rate science fiction. Not to forget, but to *remember*, to open up the past and find himself there again, like the stone in a bitter fruit. He opened each bottle, began each story with the secret conviction that *here* was the magic draught that would restore him. But magic, like wine, needs the right conditions in order to work. Joe could have told him that. Otherwise the chemistry doesn't happen. The bouquet is spoiled.

I suppose I expected it to begin with me. There would have been poetry in that. We are linked, after all, he and I.

But this story begins with a different vintage. I don't really mind that. Better to be his last than his first. I'm not even the star of this story, but I was there before the Specials came, and I'll be there when they've all been drunk. I can afford to wait. Besides, aged Fleurie is an acquired taste, not to be rushed, and I'm not sure his palate would have been ready.

2

London, Spring 1999

IT WAS MARCH. MILD, EVEN FOR THE CELLAR. JAY HAD BEEN working upstairs – working in his way, with a bottle at his elbow and the television turned on low. Kerry was at a party – the launch of a new award for female authors under twenty-five – and the house was silent. Jay used the type-writer for what he thought of as 'real' work, the laptop for his science fiction, so you could always tell what he was writing by the sound, or lack of it. It was ten before he came downstairs. He switched on the radio to an oldies station, and you could hear him moving about in the kitchen, his footsteps restless against the terracotta tiles. There was a drinks cabinet next to the fridge. He opened it, hesitated, closed it again. The fridge door opened. Kerry's taste dominated here, as everywhere. Wheat-grass juice, cous-cous salad, baby spinach leaves, yoghurts. What he really craved, Jay thought, was a huge bacon-and-fried-egg sand-wich with ketchup and onion, and a mug of strong tea. The craving, he knew, had something to do with Joe and Pog Hill Lane. An association, that was all, which often came on when he was trying to write. But all that was finished. A phantom. He knew he wasn't really hungry. Instead he lit a cigarette, a forbidden luxury reserved for when Kerry was out of the house, and inhaled greedily. From the radio's scratchy speaker came the voice of Steve Harley singing 'Make me smile' – another song from that distant, inescapable summer of '75 – and for a moment he raised his voice to sing along – 'Come up and see me, make me smi-i-i-ile' – forlornly in the echoing kitchen.

Behind us in the dark cellar the strangers were restless. Perhaps it was the music, or perhaps something in the air of this mild spring evening seemed suddenly charged with possibility, for they were effervescent with activity, seething in their bottles, rattling against each other, jumping at shadows, bursting to talk, to open, to release their essence into the air. Perhaps this was why he came down, his steps heavy on the rough, unpolished stairs. Jay liked the cellar; it was cool, secret. He was always coming down there, just to touch the bottles, to run his fingers along the dust-furred walls. I always liked it when he came to the cellar. Like a barometer, I can sense his emotional temperature when he is close to me. To some extent I can even read his thoughts. As I said, there is a chemistry between us.

It was dark in the cellar, the only illumination a dim light bulb hanging from the ceiling. Rows of bottles – most negligible, chosen by Kerry – in the racks on the wall; others in crates on the flagstones. Jay touched the bottles fleetingly as he passed, bringing his face very close, as if to catch the scent of those imprisoned summers. Two or three times he pulled out a bottle and turned it in his hands before replacing it in the rack. He moved aimlessly, without direction, liking the dampness of the cellar and the silence. Even the sound of the London traffic was stilled here, and for a moment he seemed tempted simply to lie down on the smooth, cool floor and go to sleep, perhaps for ever. No-one would look for him here. But instead he felt very wide awake, very alert, as if the silence had cleared his head. There was a charged atmosphere in spite of the stillness, like something waiting to happen.

The new bottles were in a box at the back of the cellar. A

broken ladder had been laid across the top of it, and he moved this aside, dragging the box out with an effort across the flagstones. He lifted out a bottle at random and held it up to the light to decipher the label. Its contents looked inky-red, with a deep layer of sediment at the base. For a moment he imagined he saw something else inside there, a shape, but it was only sediment. Somewhere above him, in the kitchen, the nostalgia station was still tuned to 1975 – Christmas now, 'Bohemian Rhapsody', faint but audible through the floor – and he shivered.

Back in the kitchen he examined the bottle with some curiosity – he had barely glanced at it since he brought it back six weeks before – the wax seal at the neck, the brown cord, the handwritten label – 'Specials 1975' – the glass grimed with the dust of Joe's root cellar. He wondered why he had brought it back from the wreckage. Nostalgia maybe, though his feelings for Joe were still too mixed for that luxury. Anger, confusion, longing washed over him in hot-cold waves. *Old man. Wish you were here.*

Inside the bottle something leaped and capered. The bottles in the cellar rattled and danced in reply.

Sometimes it happens by accident. After years of waiting – for a correct planetary alignment, a chance meeting, a sudden inspiration – the right circumstances occasionally happen of their own accord, slyly, without fanfare, without warning. Jay thinks of it as destiny. Joe called it magic. But sometimes all it is is simple chemistry, something in the air, a single action to bring something which has long remained inert into sudden, inevitable change.

Layman's alchemy, Joe called it. The magic of everyday things. Jay Mackintosh reached for a knife to cut the seal.

3

IT HAD WITHSTOOD THE YEARS. HIS KNIFE SLICED IT OPEN AND THE cork was still intact beneath. For a moment the scent was so immediately pungent that all he could do was endure it, teeth clenched, as it worked its will on him. It smelt earthy and a little sour, like the canal in midsummer, with a sharpness which reminded him of the vegetable-cutter and the gleeful tang of fresh-dug potatoes. For a second the illusion was so strong that he was actually *there* in that vanished place, with Joe leaning on his spade and the radio wedged in a fork in a tree, playing 'Send in the Clowns' or 'I'm Not in Love'. A sudden overwhelming excitement took hold of him and he poured a small quantity of the wine into a glass, trying not to spill the liquid in his eagerness. It was dusky-pink, like papaya juice, and it seemed to climb the sides of the glass in a frenzy of anticipation, as if something inside it were alive and anxious to work its magic on his flesh. He looked at it with mingled distrust and longing. A part of him wanted to drink it – had waited years for just this moment – but all the same he hesitated. The liquid in the glass was murky and flecked with flakes of brownish matter, like rust. He suddenly imagined himself drinking, choking, writhing on the tiles in agony. The glass halted halfway to his mouth.

He looked at the liquid again. The movement he thought he saw had ceased. The scent was faintly sweetish, medicinal, like cough mixture. Once again he wondered why he had brought the bottle with him. There was no such thing as magic. It was something else Joe had made him believe; one more of the old fraud's trickeries. But there was something in the glass, his mind insisted. Something special.

His concentration was such that he didn't hear Kerry come in behind him.

'Oh, so you're not working.' Her voice was clear, with just enough of an Irish accent to guard against accusations of having a privileged background. 'You know, if you were planning on getting pissed you could at least have come to the party with me. It would have been a wonderful opportunity for you to meet people.'

She put special emphasis on the word *wonderful*, extending the first syllable to three times its natural length. Jay looked back at her, the wineglass still in his hand. His voice was mocking.

'Oh, you know. I'm always meeting wonderful people. All literary people are wonderful. What I really like is when one of your bright young things comes up to me at one of these wonderful parties and says, "Hey, didn't you used to be Jay somebody, the guy who wrote that wonderful book?" '

Kerry crossed the room, her perspex heels tapping coolly against the tiles, and poured herself a glass of Stolichnaya.

'Now you're being childish as well as antisocial. If you actually made the effort to write something serious once in a while, instead of wasting your talent on rubbish—'

'*Wonderful*.' Jay grinned and tipped the wineglass at her. In the cellar the remaining bottles rattled boisterously, as if in anticipation. Kerry stopped, listened.

'Did you hear something?'

Jay shook his head, still grinning. She came closer, looked at the glass in his hand and the bottle still standing on the table.

'What is that stuff, anyway?' Her voice was as sharp and clear as her icicle heels. 'Some kind of cocktail? It smells disgusting.'

19

'It's Joe's wine. One of the six.' He turned the bottle around to see the label. 'Jackapple, 1975. A wonderful vintage.'

Beside us and around us the bottles were in gleeful ferment. We could hear them whispering, singing, calling, capering. Their laughter was infectious, reckless, a call to arms. Château-Chalon muttered stolid disapproval, but in that raucous, carnival atmosphere his voice sounded like envy. I found myself joining in, rattling in my crate like a common milk bottle, delirious with anticipation, with the knowledge that something was on the way.

'Ugh! God! Don't drink it. It's bound to be off.' Kerry gave a forced laugh. 'Besides, it's revolting. It's like necrophilia, or something. I can't imagine why you wanted to bring it home at all, in the circumstances.'

'I was planning to drink it, darling, not fuck it,' muttered Jay.

'What?'

'Nothing.'

'Please, darling. Pour it away. It's probably got all kinds of disgusting bacteria in it. Or worse. Antifreeze or something. You know what the old boy was like.' Her voice was cajoling. 'I'll get you a glass of Stolly instead, OK?'

'Kerry, stop talking like my mother.'

'Then stop behaving like a child. Why can't you just grow up, for God's sake?' It was a perpetual refrain.

Stubbornly: 'The wine was Joe's. I don't expect you to understand.'

She sighed, exasperated, and turned away.

'Oh, please yourself. You always do. The way you've fixated on that old bugger for all these years, anyone would think he was your father or something, instead of some dirty old git with an eye for little boys. Go on, be a mature adult and poison yourself. If you die they might even do a commemorative reprint of *Jackapple Joe*, and I could sell my story to the *TLS*—'

But Jay was not listening. He lifted the glass to his face.

The scent hit him again, the dim cidery scent of Joe's house, with the incense burning and the tomato plants ripening in the kitchen window. For a moment he thought he heard something, a clatter and glitzy confusion of glass, like a chandelier falling onto a laid table. He took a mouthful.

'Cheers.'

It tasted as dreadful as it did when he was a boy. There was no grape in this brew, simply a sweetish ferment of flavours, like a whiff of garbage. It smelt like the canal in summer and the derelict railway sidings. It had an acrid taste, like smoke and burning rubber, and yet it was evocative, catching at his throat and his memory, drawing out images he thought were lost for ever. He clenched his fists as the images assailed him, feeling suddenly light-headed.

'Are you OK?' It was Kerry's voice, resonant, as if in a dream. She sounded irritated, though there was an anxious edge to her voice. 'Jay, I told you not to drink that stuff, are you all right?'

He swallowed with an effort.

'I'm fine. Actually it's rather pleasant. Pert. Tart. Lovely body. Bit like you, Kes.' He broke off, coughing, but laughing at the same time. Kerry looked at him, unamused.

'I wish you wouldn't call me that. It isn't my name.'

'Neither is Kerry,' he pointed out maliciously.

'Oh well, if you're going to be vulgar I'm going to bed. Enjoy your vintage. Whatever turns you on.'

The words were a challenge which Jay left unanswered, turning his back to the door until she had gone. He was being selfish, he knew. But the wine had awakened something in him, something extraordinary, and he wanted to explore it further. He took another drink and found his palate was becoming accustomed to the wine's strange flavours. He could taste old fruit now, burnt to hard black sugar, he could smell the juice from the vegetable-cutter and hear Joe singing along to his old radio at the back of the allotment. Impatiently he drained the glass, tasting the zesty heart of the wine, feeling his heart beating with renewed energy, pounding as if he had run a race. Below stairs the five remaining bottles rattled and shook in a frenzy of exuberance. Now his head felt clear, his stomach level. He tried for a moment to identify the sensation he felt and eventually recognized it as joy.

4

Pog Hill, Summer 1975

JACKAPPLE JOE. AS GOOD A NAME AS ANY. HE INTRODUCED HIMSELF as Joe Cox, with a slanted smile, as if to challenge disbelief, but even in those days it might have been anything, changing with the seasons and his changing address.

'We could be cousins, you and me,' he said on that first day, as Jay watched him in wary fascination from the top of the wall. The vegetable-cutter whirred and clattered, throwing out pieces of sour-sweet fruit or vegetable into the bucket at his feet. 'Cox and Mackintosh. Both apples, aren't we? That must make us nearly family, I reckon.' His accent was exotic, bewildering, and Jay stared at him without comprehension. Joe shook his head, grinning.

'Didn't know you was called after an apple, did you? It's a goodun, an American red apple. Plenty of taste. Got a young tree meself, back there.' He jerked his head towards the back of the house. 'But it's not taken that well. I reckon it needs a sight more time to get comfortable.' Jay continued to watch him with all the wary cynicism of his twelve years, alert for any sign of mockery.

'You make it sound like they've got feelings.'

Joe looked at him.

'Course they ave. Just like anythin else that grows.'

The boy watched the rotating blades of the vegetable-cutter in fascination. The funnel-shaped machine bucked and roared between Joe's hands, spitting out chunks of white and pink and blue and yellow flesh.

'What are you doing?'

'What's it look like?' The old man jerked his chin at a cardboard box lying by the wall which separated them. 'Pass us them jacks over there, will you?'

'Jacks?'

A slight gesture of impatience towards the box: 'Jack-apples.'

Jay glanced down. The drop was easy, five feet at the most, but the garden was enclosed, with only the scrub of waste ground and the railway line at his back, and his city upbringing had taught him wariness of strangers. Joe grinned.

'I'll not bite, lad,' he said mildly.

Annoyed, Jay dropped down into the garden.

The jackapples were long and red and oddly pointed at one end. One or two had been cut open as Joe dug them up, showing flesh which looked tropically pink in the sun. The boy staggered a little under the weight of the box.

'Watch your step,' called Joe. 'Don't drop em. They'll bruise.'

'But these are just potatoes.'

'Aye,' said Joe, without taking his eyes from the vegetable-cutter.

'I thought you said they were apples, or something.'

'Jacks. Spuds. Taters. Jackapples. *Poms de tair.*'

'Don't look like much to me,' said Jay.

Joe shook his head and began to feed the roots into the vegetable-cutter. Their scent was sweetish, like papaya.

'I brought these home from South America after the war,' he said. 'Grew em from seed right here in my back garden. Took me five years just to get the soil right. If you want roasters, you grow King Edwards. If you want salads, it's your Charlottes or your Jerseys. If it's chippers you're after, then it's your Maris Piper. But these' – he reached down to pick one up, rubbing the blackened ball of his thumb lovingly across the pinkish skin – 'Older than New York, so old it doesn't even have an English name. Seed more precious than powdered gold. These aren't just potatoes, lad. These are little nuggets of lost time, from when people still believed in magic and when half the world was still blank on the maps. You don't make chips from *these.*' He shook his head again, his eyes brimful of laughter under the thick grey brows. 'These are me Specials.'

Jay watched him cautiously, unsure whether he was mad or simply making fun.

'So what *are* you making?' he asked at last.

Joe tossed the last jackapple into the cutter and grinned. 'Wine, lad. *Wine.*'

That was the summer of '75. Jay was nearly thirteen. Eyes narrow, mouth tight, face a white-knuckle fist closing over something too secret to be examined. Lately a resident of the Moorlands School in Leeds, now with eight weeks of holidays stretching strange and empty till the next term. He hated it here already. This place with its bleak and hazy skyline, its blue-black hills crawling with yellow loaders, its slums and pit houses and its people, with their sharp faces and flat Northern voices. It would be all right, his mother told him. He would like Kirby Monckton. He would enjoy the change. Everything would be sorted out. But Jay knew better. The gulf of his parents' divorce opened up beneath him, and he hated them, hated the place to which they had sent him, hated the gleaming new five-speed Raleigh bike delivered that morning for his birthday – bribery as contemptible as the message which accompanied it – 'With love from Mum and Dad' – so falsely normal, as if the world wasn't coming softly apart around him. His rage was cold, glassy, cutting him from the rest of the world so that sounds became muffled and people were walking trees. Rage was inside him, seething, waiting desperately for something to happen.

They had never been a close family. Until that summer he

had only seen his grandparents half a dozen times, at Christmases or birthdays, and they treated him with dutiful, distant affection. His grandmother was frail and elegant, like the china she loved and which adorned every available surface. His grandfather was bluff and soldierly and shot grouse without a licence on the nearby moors. Both deplored the trade unions, the rise of the working class, rock music, men with long hair and the admission of women into Oxford. Jay soon understood that if he washed his hands before meals and seemed to listen to everything they said he could enjoy unlimited freedom. That was how he met Joe.

Kirby Monckton is a small Northern town similar to many others. Built on coal mining, it was in decline even then, with two of the four pits shut and the remaining two struggling. Where the pits have closed, the villages built to supply them with labour died, too, leaving rows of pit houses staggering towards dereliction, half of them empty, windows boarded up, gardens piled with refuse and weeds. The centre was little better – a row of shops, a few pubs, a mini-market, a police station with a grille across its window. To one side, the river, the railway, the old canal. To the other, a ridge of hills reaching towards the feet of the Pennines. This was Upper Kirby, where Jay's grandparents lived.

Looking towards the hills, over fields and woodland, it is almost possible to imagine that there have never been any mines. This is the acceptable face of Kirby Monckton, where terraces are referred to as mews cottages. At its highest point you can see the town itself a few miles away, a smear of yellowish smoke across an uneven horizon, with pylons marching across the fields towards the slaty scar of the open-cast mine, but the hollow is relentlessly charming, shielded by the ridge. The houses are for the most part larger, more elaborate here. Deep Victorian terraces of mellow Yorkshire stone, with leaded panes and mock-Gothic doorways, and huge secluded gardens with fruit-trees en espalier and smooth, well-tended lawns.

Jay was impervious to these charms. To his London-accustomed eyes Upper Kirby looked precarious, balanced on the stony edge of the moor. The spaces – the distances between buildings – dizzied him. The scarred mess of Lower Monckton and Nether Edge looked deserted in its smoke, like something during the war. He missed London's cinemas and theatres, the record shops, the galleries, the museums. He missed the people. He missed the familiar accents of London, the sound of traffic and the smells. He rode his bike for miles along the unfamiliar deserted roads, hating everything he saw.

His grandparents never interfered. They approved of outdoor pastimes, never noticing that he returned home trembling and exhausted with rage every afternoon. The boy was always polite, always well groomed. He listened intelligently and with interest to what they said. He cultivated a boyish cheeriness. He was the cleanest-cut comic-book schoolboy hero imaginable, and he revelled sourly in his deception.

Joe lived on Pog Hill Lane, one of a row of uneven terraces backing on to the railway half a mile from the station. Jay had already been there twice before, leaving his bike in a stand of bushes and climbing up the banking to reach the railway bridge. On the far side there were fields reaching down to the river, and beyond that lay the open-cast mine, the sound of its machinery a distant drone on the wind. For a couple of miles an old canal ran almost parallel to the railway, and there the stagnant air was green with flies and hot with the scent of ash and greenery. A bridle path ran between the canal and the railway, overhung with tree branches. Nether Edge to the townspeople, it was almost always deserted. That was why it first attracted him. He bought a packet of cigarettes and a copy of the *Eagle* from the station newspaper stand and cycled down towards the canal. Then, leaving his bike safely concealed in the undergrowth, he walked along the canal path, pushing his way through great drifts of ripe willowherb and sending clouds

27

of white seeds into the air. When he reached the old lock, he sat down on the stones and smoked as he watched the railway, occasionally counting the coal trucks as they passed, or making faces at the passenger trains as they clattered to their distant, envied destinations. He threw stones into the clotted canal. A few times he walked all the way to the river and made dams with turf and the accumulated garbage it had brought with it: car tyres, branches, railway sleepers and once a whole mattress with the springs poking out of the ticking. That was really how it began; the place got a hold on him somehow. Perhaps because it was a secret place, an old, forbidden place. Jay began to explore; there were mysterious raised concrete-and-metal cylinders, which Joe later identified as capped pitheads and which gave out strange resonant breathing sounds if you went close. A flooded mineshaft, an abandoned coal truck, the remains of a barge. It was an ugly, perhaps a dangerous place, but it was a place of great sadness, too, and it attracted him in a way he could neither combat nor understand. His parents would have been horrified at his going there, and that, too, contributed to its appeal. So he explored; here an ash pit filled with ancient shards of crockery, there a spill of exotic, discarded treasures – bundles of comics and magazines, as yet unspoiled by rain; scrap metal; the hulk of a car, an old Ford Galaxie, a small elder tree growing out of its roof like a novelty aerial; a dead television. Living alongside a railway, Joe once told him, is like living on a beach; the tide brings new jetsam every day. At first he hated it. He couldn't imagine why he went there at all. He would set out with the intention of taking a quite different route and still find himself in Nether Edge, between the railway and the canal, the sound of distant machinery droning in his ears and the whitish summer sky pushing down the top of his head like a hot cap. A lonely, derelict place. But his, nevertheless. Throughout all that long, strange summer, his. Or so he assumed.

5

London, Spring 1999

HE WOKE UP LATE THE NEXT DAY TO FIND KERRY ALREADY GONE, leaving a short note, through which the disapproval showed like a watermark. He read it idly, without interest, and tried to remember what had happened the night before.

> *J − Don't forget the reception at Spy's tonight − it's very important for you to be there! Wear the Armani − K.*

His head ached, and he made strong coffee and listened to the radio as he drank it. He didn't remember a great deal − so much of his life seemed to be like this now, a blur of days without anything to define them from each other, like episodes of a soap he watched out of habit, even though none of the characters interested him. The day stretched out in front of him like an empty road in the desert. He had a tutorial that evening, but was already considering whether to miss it. It was all right; he'd missed tutorials before. It was almost expected of him now. Artistic temperament. He grinned briefly at the irony.

The bottle of Joe's wine was standing where he had left it on the table. He was surprised to see it still over half full.

Such a small quantity seemed too little to account for his pounding hangover and the dreams which finally chased him into sleep as dawn bled into the sky. The scent from the empty glass was faint but discernible, a sweetly medicinal scent, soothing. He poured a glassful.

'Hair of the dog,' he muttered.

This morning it was only vaguely unpleasant, almost tasteless. A memory stirred at the back of his mind, but it was too distant to identify.

The door rattled suddenly and he turned round, feeling obscurely guilty, as if caught out. But it was only the post, half pushed through the letter box and spilling onto the mat. Through the glass door a square of sunlight illuminated the top envelope, as if marking it for his special attention. Probably junk mail, he told himself. Nowadays he rarely ever received anything else. And yet, by a trick of the light, the envelope seemed to glow, giving the single word stencilled across it a new, brilliant significance: 'ESCAPE'. As if a door could be opened from the London dawn into another world, where every possibility remained to be played out. He stooped to pick up the bright rectangle, opened it.

His first thought was that it was indeed junk mail. A cheaply produced brochure entitled HOLIDAY HIDEAWAYS, GREAT ESCAPES, blurry snapshots of farmhouses and *gîtes* interspersed with blocks of text. 'This charming cottage only five miles from Avignon . . . This large converted farmhouse in its own grounds . . . This sixteenth-century barn in the heart of the Dordogne . . .' The pictures were all the same: rustic cottages under Disney-coloured skies, women in headscarves and white *coiffes*, men in berets herding goats onto impossibly green mountainsides. He dropped the brochure onto the table with an odd sense of disappointment, feeling cheated, as if something as yet unknown had passed him by. Then he caught sight of the picture. The brochure had fallen open at the centre page, a double-page spread of a house which looked curiously familiar. A large square-built house, with pink-ish, faded walls and a red-tiled roof. Beneath it, the words, 'Château Foudouin, Lot-et-Garonne.' Above it, in red, like a neon marker, 'FOR SALE'.

The surprise at seeing it there, so unexpectedly, made his heart lurch. A sign, he told himself. Coming now, at this moment, it had to be. It had to be a sign.

He looked at the picture for a long time. It was not exactly Joe's château, he decided after some scrutiny. The lines of the building looked slightly different, the roof more sloping, the windows narrower and set deeper into the stone. And it was not in Bordeaux but in the next county altogether, a few miles from Agen, on a small offshoot of the river Garonne, the Tannes. Still, it was close. Very close. It couldn't be a coincidence.

Below stairs the strangers had subsided into eerie, ex-pectant silence. Not a whisper, not a rattle or a hiss escaped them.

Jay looked at the picture intently. Above it the neon sign flashed relentlessly, enticingly.

FOR SALE.

He reached for the bottle and poured himself another glass.

6

Pog Hill, July 1975

THAT SUMMER MOST OF JAY'S LIFE WENT ON UNDERCOVER, LIKE a secret war. On rainy days he sat in his room and read the *Dandy* or the *Eagle* and listened to the radio with the volume turned right down, pretending he was doing homework, or wrote blisteringly intense short stories with titles like 'Flesh-Eating Warriors of the Forbidden City' or 'The Man who Chased the Lightning'.

He was never short of money. On Sundays he earned twenty pee washing his grandfather's green Austin, the same for mowing the lawn. His parents' brief, infrequent letters were invariably accompanied by a postal order, and he spent this unaccustomed wealth with gleeful, gloating defiance. Comics, bubble gum, cigarettes if he could get them; anything which might have incurred the disapproval of his parents attracted him. He kept his treasures in a biscuit tin by the canal, telling his grandparents he put his money in the bank. Technically this was not a lie. A loose stone by the remains of the old lock, worked carefully free, left a space maybe fifteen inches square, into which the tin could be slotted. A square of turf, cut from the banking with a penknife, concealed the entrance. For the first fortnight of the holiday he went there almost every day, basking on the flat stones of the jetty and smoking, reading, writing stories in one of an endless series of close-scripted notebooks, or playing his radio at full volume into the bright sooty air. His memories of that summer were illumined in sound: Pete Wingfield singing 'Eighteen with a Bullet', or Tammy Winette and 'D.I.V.O.R.C.E.'. He sang along much of the time, or played air guitar and pulled faces at an invisible audience. It was only later that he realized how reckless he had been. The dump was easily within earshot of the canal, and Zeth and his gang might have come upon him at any time during those two weeks. They might have found him snoozing on the bank or cornered in the ash pit – or worse, with the treasure box left carelessly open. Jay never considered that there might be other boys in his territory. Never imagined that this might *already* be someone's territory, someone tougher and older and altogether more streetwise than himself. He had never been in a fight. The Moorlands School discouraged such marks of poor breeding. His few London friends were distant and reserved, ballet-class and pony girls, army-cadet boys with perfect teeth. Jay never quite fitted in. His mother was an actress whose career had dead-ended in a TV sitcom called *Oooh! Mother!* about a widower caring for his three teenage children. Jay's mother played the part of the interfering landlady, Mrs Dykes, and much of his adolescence was made hideous by people stopping them in the street and yelling her screen catchphrase, 'Oooh, am I interruptin' somethin'?'

Jay's father, the Bread Baron who made his fortune with Trimble, a well-known slimmers' loaf, had never quite made enough money to make up for his lack of pedigree, hiding his insecurity behind a façade of bluff, cigar-smoking cheer. He, too, embarrassed Jay, with his East-End vowels and shiny suits. Jay had always seen himself as a different species, as something hardier, nearer to the raw. He couldn't have been more wrong.

There were three of them. Taller than Jay and older –

fourteen, maybe fifteen – with a peculiar swing to their walk as they strolled along the canal towpath, a cocky strut which marked the territory as their own. Instinctively Jay snapped off his radio and crouched in the shadows, resentful of the proprietary air with which they lolled on the jetty, one crouching to poke at something in the water with a stick, another popping a match against his jeans to light up a cigarette. He watched them warily from the shadow of a tree, hackles pricking. They looked dangerous, clannish in their jeans, zip-up boots and cut-off T-shirts, members of a tribe to which Jay could never belong. One of them – a tall, lanky boy – was carrying an air rifle, slung carelessly into the crook of his arm. His face was broad and angry with spots at the jawline. His eyes were ball-bearings. One of the others had his back half turned, so that Jay could see the roll of his paunch poking out from beneath his T-shirt, and the broad band of his underpants above his low-slung jeans. The underpants had little aeroplanes on them, and for some reason that made Jay want to laugh, silently at first into his curled fist, then with a high, helpless squawk of mirth.

Aeroplanes turned round at once, his face slack with surprise. For a second the two boys faced each other. Then he shot out his hand and grabbed Jay by the shirt.

'What the fuck *thar* doin ere?'

The other two were watching with hostile curiosity. The third boy – a spidery youth with extravagant sideburns – took a step forwards and poked Jay hard in the chest with an extended knuckle.

'Ast thee a question, dinty?'

Their language sounded alien, almost incomprehensible, a cartoonish babble of vowels, and Jay found himself smiling again, close to laughter, unable to help himself.

'Atha deaf as well as daft?' demanded Sideburns.

'I'm sorry,' said Jay, trying to pull free. 'You just came out of nowhere. I didn't mean to scare you.'

The three looked at him with even greater intensity. Their

eyes looked the same non-colour as the sky, a peculiar shifting grey. The tall boy stroked the butt of his rifle in a suggestive gesture. His expression was curious, almost amused. Jay noticed he had tattooed letters on the back of his hand, one letter pricked out across each of his knuckles to form a name or nickname: ZETH. This was no professional job, he understood. The boy had written it himself, using a compass and a bottle of ink. Jay had a sudden, startling vision of him doing it, with a dogged grimace of satisfaction, one sunny afternoon at the back of a maths or English class, with the teacher pretending not to see, even though Zeth wasn't bothering to hide. It was easier that way, the teacher thought. Safer.

'Scare us?' The bright ball-bearing eyes rolled in counterfeit humour.

Sideburns sniggered.

'Astha gotta fag, mate?' Zeth's voice was still light, but Jay noticed Aeroplanes had not yet released his shirt.

'A cigarette?' He began to fumble in his pocket, clumsy with the need to get away, and pulled out a packet of Player's. 'Sure. Have one.'

Zeth took two and passed the packet to Sideburns, then to Aeroplanes.

'Hey, keep the packet,' said Jay, beginning to feel light-headed.

'Matches?' He pulled the box from his jeans and held it out.

'Keep them, too.'

Aeroplanes winked as he lit up, a somehow greasy, appraising look. The other two drew a little closer.

'Astha got any spice, anall?' asked Zeth pleasantly. Aeroplanes began to finger nimbly through Jay's pockets.

It was already too late to struggle. A minute earlier and he might have had the advantage of surprise, might have been able to duck between them towards the jetty and up onto the railway. Now it was too late. They had scented fear. Eager hands searched Jay's pockets with greedy, delicate fingers. Chewing gum, a couple of wrapped sweets, coins, all the contents of his pockets rolled into their cupped hands.

'Hey, get off there! Those things are mine!'

But his voice was trembling. He tried to tell himself that it didn't matter, that he could let them have the stuff – most of it was worthless, anyway – but that didn't stop the bleak, hateful feeling of helplessness, of shame.

Then Zeth picked up the radio.

'Nice,' he commented.

For a moment Jay had forgotten all about it; lying in the long grass under the shade of the trees it was almost invisible. A trick of the light, maybe, a freak reflection on the chrome, or just plain bad luck, but Zeth saw it, bent and picked it up.

'That's mine,' said Jay, almost inaudibly, his mouth filled with needles. Zeth looked at him and grinned.

'Mine,' Jay whispered.

'Course it is, mate,' said Zeth amicably and held it out.

Their eyes met above the radio. Jay put out his hand, almost pleadingly. Zeth withdrew the radio, just a little, then drop-kicked it with incredible speed and accuracy over their heads in a wide, gleaming arc into the air. For a second it gleamed there, like a miniature spaceship, then it crashed on the stone lip of the jetty and smattered into a hundred plastic and chrome fragments.

'*And it's a goo-aal!*' shrieked Sideburns, beginning to dance and caper amongst the wreckage. Aeroplanes chuckled sweatily. But Zeth just looked at Jay with the same curious expression, one hand resting on the butt of his air rifle, his eyes cool and oddly sympathetic, as if to say, What now, mate? What now? What now?

Jay could feel his eyes getting hotter and hotter, as if the tears gathering there were made of molten lead, and he struggled to stop them from spilling over onto his cheeks. He glanced at the pieces of the radio twinkling on the stones and tried to tell himself it didn't matter. It was just

an old radio, nothing worth getting beaten up for, but the
rage inside him wouldn't listen. He took a step towards the
lock, then turned back, without even thinking, and swung
as hard as he could towards Zeth's patient, amused face.
Aeroplanes and Sideburns were on Jay at once, punching
and kicking, but not before he had launched a good solid
kick into the pit of Zeth's stomach, which connected as his
first awkward punch had not. Zeth gave a wheezing scream
and curled up on the ground. Aeroplanes tried to grab Jay
again, but he was slippery with sweat and managed to
duck under the other boy's arm. Skidding on the remains of
his broken radio he made for the path, dodged Sideburns,
slid down the banking and across the bridle path towards
the railway bridge. Someone was shouting after him, but
distance and the thick local dialect made the words indis-
tinguishable, though the threat was clear. When he reached
the top of the banking, Jay kissed his middle finger at the
three distant figures, dug his bike out of the undergrowth
where he had hidden it, and in a minute was riding back
towards Monckton. His nose was bleeding and his hands
were torn from his dive through the bushes, but he was
singing inside with triumph. Even his dismay over the loss
of the radio was temporarily forgotten. Perhaps it was that
wild, almost magical feeling that drew him to Joe's house
that day. He told himself later that it was simply chance,
that there was nothing in his mind at all but the desire to
ride into the wind, but he thought later that it might have
been some kind of crazy predestination which pulled him
there, a kind of call. He felt it, too, a wordless voice of
exceptional clarity and tone, and for a moment he saw the
street sign – POG HILL LANE – light up briefly in the glow of
the reddening sun, as if somehow *marked* for his attention,
so that instead of cycling past the narrow mouth of the
street, as he had done so many times before, he stopped and
wheeled his bike slowly back to stare over the brick wall,
where an old man was cutting jackapples to make wine.

7

London, March 1999

THE AGENT MUST HAVE SCENTED HIS EAGERNESS. THERE WAS already a bid on the house, he said. A little below the asking price. The contracts had already been drawn up. But if Jay was interested there were other properties available. The information, true or false, made Jay reckless. It had to be this house, he insisted. This house. Now. In cash, if they liked.

A discreet phone call. Then another. Rapid French into the mouthpiece. Someone brought coffee and Italian pastries from across the road as they waited. Jay suggested another price, somewhat higher than the existing offer. He heard the voice on the other end of the line rise by half an octave. He toasted them in *café-latte*. It was so easy, buying a house. A few hours' wait, a little paperwork and it was his. He reread the short paragraph under the picture, trying to translate the words into stone and mortar. Château Foudouin. It looked unreal, a postcard from the past. He tried to imagine standing outside the door, touching the pink stone, looking over the vineyard towards the lake. Joe's dream, he told himself dimly, their dream fulfilled at last. It had to be fate. It had to be.

And now he was fourteen again, gloating over his picture, touching it, folding and unfolding the thin paper. He wanted to show other people. He wanted to be there *now*, to take possession, even though the paperwork was only half completed. His bank, his accountant, his solicitors could deal with the formalities. The signing of the papers was merely an afterthought. The essentials were already in motion.

A few phone calls and it could all be arranged. A flight to Paris. A train to Marseilles. By tomorrow he could be there.

8

Pog Hill, July 1975

JOE'S HOUSE WAS A DARK, CROOKED TERRACE, LIKE MANY OF the houses which lined the railway. The front gave directly on to the street, with only a low wall and a window box between the front door and the pavement. The back was all crowded little yards hung with washing, a shanty town of homemade rabbit hutches, hen houses and pigeon lofts. This side looked over the railway, a steep banking sheared away to form a cutting through which the trains passed. The road went over a bridge at that point, and from the back of Joe's garden you could see the red light of the railway signal, like a beacon in the distance. You could see Nether Edge, too, and the dim grey flanks of the slag heap beyond the fields. Staggering unevenly down the steep little lane, those few houses overlooked the whole of Jay's territory. Someone was singing in a nearby garden, an old lady by the sound of it, in a sweetly quavering voice. Somebody else was hammering wood, a comforting, primitive sound.

'D'you want a drink?' Joe nodded easily in the direction of the house. 'You look as if you wouldn't turn one down.'

Jay glanced towards the house, suddenly aware of his torn jeans and the dried blood on his nose and upper lip. His mouth was dry.

'OK.'

It was cool inside the house. Jay followed the old man through to the kitchen, a large bare room with clean wooden floorboards and a large pine table, scarred with the marks of many knives. There were no curtains at the window, but the entire window ledge was filled with leggy green plants, which formed a lush screen for the sunlight. The plants had a pleasant, earthy smell which filled the room.

'These are me toms,' remarked Joe, opening the larder, and Jay saw that there were indeed tomatoes growing amongst the warm leaves – small yellow ones, large misshapen red ones, or striped orange and green ones, like croaker marbles. There were more plants in pots on the floor, lining the walls and growing against the doorpost. To the side of the room a number of wooden crates contained fruit and vegetables, all arranged individually to avoid bruising.

'Nice plants,' he said, not really meaning it.

Joe shot him a satirical look.

'You've got to talk to em if you want em to grow. And tickle em,' he added, indicating a long cane propped up against the bare wall. There was a rabbit's tail tied to its extremity. 'This is me ticklin stick, see? Very ticklish, toms.'

Jay looked at him blankly.

'Looks like you ran into some trouble back there,' said Joe, opening a door at the far side of the room to reveal a big larder. 'Bin in a fight, or summat.'

Guardedly Jay told him. When he got to the part where Zeth broke the radio he felt his voice jump into a higher register, sounding childish and close to tears. He stopped, flushing furiously.

Joe didn't seem to notice. He reached into the larder, picking out a bottle of dark-red liquid and a couple of glasses.

'You get some of this down yer,' said Joe, pouring some out. It smelt fruity but unfamiliar, yeasty, like beer, but with a deceptive sweetness. Jay looked at it with suspicion.

'Is it wine?' he asked doubtfully.

41

Joe nodded.

'Blackbry,' he said, drinking his with obvious relish.

'I don't think I'm supposed to—' began Jay, but Joe pushed the glass at him with an impatient gesture.

'Try it, lad,' he urged. 'Put some art in yer.'

He tried it.

Joe clapped him on the back until he stopped coughing, carefully removing the precious glass from the boy's hand before he spilled it.

'It's *disgusting*!' managed Jay between coughing jags.

It certainly tasted like no wine he had ever tasted before. He was no stranger to wine – his parents often gave him wine with meals, and he had developed quite a fondness for some of the sweeter German whites, but this was a completely new experience. It tasted like earth and swamp water and fruit gone sour with age. Tannin furred his tongue. His throat burned. His eyes watered.

Joe looked rather hurt. Then he laughed.

'Bit strong for yer, is it?'

Jay nodded, still coughing.

'Aye, I shoulda known,' said Joe cheerily, turning back to the pantry. 'Takes a bit o gettin used to, I reckon. But it's got *art*,' he added fondly, replacing the bottle with care on the shelf. 'And that's what matters.'

He turned round, this time with a bottle of Ben Shaw's Yellow Lemonade in one hand.

'Reckon this'll do yer better for now,' he said, pouring a glassful. 'And as for the other stuff, you'll grow into it soon enough.'

He returned the wine bottle to the larder, hesitated, turned.

'I think I might be able to give you somethin for that other problem, if you'd like, though,' he said. 'Come with me.'

Jay was not sure what he expected the old man to give him. Kung-fu lessons, perhaps, or a bazooka left over from some war, grenades, a Zulu spear from his travels, a special invincible drop kick learned from a master in Tibet, guaranteed never to fail. Instead Joe led him to the side of the house, where a small red flannel bag dangled from a nail protruding from the stone. He unhooked the bag, sniffed briefly at the contents and handed it over.

'Take it,' he urged. 'It'll last a while yet. I'll make some fresh for us later.' Jay stared at him.

'What is it?' he said at last.

'Just carry it with you,' said Joe. 'In yer pocket, if you like, or on a bitta string. You'll see. It'll help.'

'What's in it?' He was staring now, as if the old man were crazy. His suspicions, allayed for a moment, flared anew.

'Oh, this an that. Sandalwood. Lavender. Bit o High John the Conqueror. Trick I learned off of a lady in Haiti, years back. Works every time.'

That was it, decided Jay. The old boy was definitely crazy. Harmless – he hoped – but crazy. He glanced uneasily at the blind expanse of garden at his back and wondered if he could make it to the wall in time if the old man turned violent. Joe just smiled.

'Try it,' he urged. 'Just carry it in yer pocket. Happen you'll even forget it's there.'

Jay decided to humour him.

'OK. What's it supposed to do, then?'

Joe smiled again.

'Praps nothin,' he said.

'Well, how will I know if it's worked?' insisted Jay.

'You'll know,' said Joe easily. 'Next time you go down Nether Edge.'

'There's no way I'm going down there again,' said Jay sharply. 'Not with those boys—'

'You goin to leave yer treasure chest for em to find, then?'

He had a point. Jay had almost forgotten about the treasure box, still hidden in its secret place beneath the loose stone. His sudden dismay almost overshadowed the certainty that he had never mentioned the treasure box to Joe.

'Used to go down there when I were a lad,' said the old man blandly. 'There were a loose stone at the corner of the lock. Still there, is it?'

Jay stared at him.

'How did you know?' he whispered.

'Know what?' asked Joe, with exaggerated innocence. 'What's tha mean? I'm only a miner's lad. I don't know owt.'

Jay didn't go back to the canal that day. He was too confused by everything, his mind racing with fights and broken radios and Haitian witchcraft and Joe's bright, laughing eyes. Instead, he took his bike and rode slowly past the railway bridge three or four times, heart pounding, trying to find the courage to climb the banking. Eventually he rode home, depressed and dissatisfied, all his triumph evaporated. He imagined Zeth and his friends going through his treasures, rocking with dirty laughter, scattering comics and books, stuffing sweets and chocolate bars into their mouths, pocketing the money. Worse still, there were his notebooks in there, the stories and poems he'd written. Finally he rode home, jaw aching with rage, watched *Saturday Night at the Movies* and went to bed to a late, unsatisfying sleep, through which he ran ceaselessly from an unseen enemy while Joe's laughter rang in his ears.

The next day he decided to stay at home. The red flannel bag sat on his bedside table like a mute challenge. Jay ignored it and tried to read, but all his best comics were still in the treasure box. The absence of the radio filled the air with a hostile silence. Outside the sun shone and there was just enough breeze to stop the air from scorching. It was going to be the most beautiful day of the summer.

He arrived at the railway bridge in a kind of daze. He hadn't meant to go there; even as he pedalled towards town something inside him knew he was going to turn round, take a different route, leave the canal to Zeth and his gang – their territory now. Perhaps he would go to Joe's house – he hadn't asked him to come back, but he hadn't asked him to keep away, either, as if Jay's presence was a matter of indifference to him – or maybe drop by at the newsagent's and buy some smokes. Either way, he certainly wasn't going to go back to the canal. As he hid his bike in the familiar stand of willowherb, as he climbed the banking, he repeated it to himself. Only an idiot would risk that again. Joe's red flannel bag was in his jeans pocket. He could feel it, a soft ball no bigger than a rolled-up hanky. He wondered how a bag full of herbs was supposed to help him. He had opened it the previous night, laying the contents out on his bedside table. A few pieces of stick, some brownish powder and some bits of green-grey aromatic stuff filled the bag. A part of him had expected shrunken heads. It was a joke, Jay told himself fiercely. Just an old man having his fun. And yet the stubborn part of him, which wanted desperately to believe, just wouldn't leave the thing alone. What if there was magic in the bag, after all? Jay imagined himself holding out the charm, incanting a magical spell in a ringing voice, Zeth and his mates cowering . . . The bag pressed comfortingly against his hip like a steadying hand. With a lurch of the heart, he began to make his way down the banking towards the canal. He probably wouldn't meet anyone, anyway.

Wrong again. He crept along the bridle path, keeping to the shade of the trees, his sneakers silent against the baked yellow earth. He was shaking with adrenalin, ready to run at the slightest sound. A bird flapped noisily out of its reed bed as he passed, and he froze, certain that an alarm had been given for miles around. Nothing. Jay was almost at the lock now, he could see the place in the banking where the treasure box was hidden. Pieces of broken plastic still littered the stones. He knelt down, removed the piece of turf which concealed the stone and began to work it out.

He'd been imagining them for so long that for a second he was sure the sounds were in his head. But now he could see their dim shapes coming over from the ash-pit side of the canal, shielded by bushes. There was no time to run. Half a minute at most before they broke cover. The bridle path was wide open from here, too far from the railway bridge to be sure. In seconds he would be an open target.

He realized there was only one place to hide. The canal

itself. It was mostly dry, except in patches, choked with reeds and litter and a hundred years' worth of silt. The little jetty stood about four feet above it, and he might be hidden, at least for a while. Of course, as soon as they stepped out onto the jetty, or joined the path, or bent down to examine something on the surface of the greasy water . . .

But there was no time to think of that now. Jay slid down from his kneeling position into the canal, pushing the treasure box back into place as he did so. For a moment he felt his feet slide into the mud without resistance, then he touched bottom, ankle-deep in the slime. It slid into his sneakers and oozed between his toes. Ignoring it, he crouched low, reeds tickling his face, determined to present as small a target as possible. Instinctively he looked for weapons: stones, cans, things to throw. If they saw him, surprise would be his only advantage.

He'd forgotten about Joe's charm in his jeans pocket. It got pulled out somehow as he crouched in the mud, and he picked it up automatically, feeling suddenly scornful at himself. How on earth could he have believed that a bag of leaves and sticks could protect him? Why had he wanted to believe it?

They were close now; ten feet away, he guessed. He could hear the sounds of their boots. Someone threw a bottle or a jar hard against the stones; it exploded, and he flinched as glass showered his head and shoulders. The decision to hide beneath their feet seemed ridiculous now; suicidal. All they had to do was look down and he was at their mercy. He should have run, he told himself bitterly, run when he had the chance. The footsteps came closer. Nine feet. Eight. Seven. Jay flattened his cheek against the wall's dank stones, trying to be the wall. Joe's charm was moist with sweat. Six feet. Five feet. Four.

Voices – Sideburns' and Aeroplanes' – sounding agonizingly close.

'Tha dun't reckon he'll be back, then?'

'Will he heckers, like. He's a fuckin' dead man if he does.'

That's me, thought Jay dreamily. They're talking about me.

Three feet. Two feet.

Zeth's voice, almost indifferent in its cool menace: 'I can wait.'

Two feet. One. A shadow fell over him, pinning him to the ground. Jay felt his hackles rising. They were looking down, looking over the canal, and he didn't dare raise his head, though the need to know was like a terrible itch, like nettle-rash of the mind. He could *feel* their eyes on the nape of his neck, hear the sound of Zeth's smoker's-corner breathing. In a moment he wouldn't be able to bear it. He'd have to look up, *have* to look—

A stone plapped into a greasy puddle not two feet away. Jay could see it from the corner of his eye. Another stone. *Plap.*

They had to be teasing him, he thought desperately. They had seen him and they were prolonging the moment, stifling mean laughter, silently picking up stones and missiles to throw. Or maybe Zeth had lifted his air rifle, his eyes pensive . . .

But none of that happened. Just as he was about to look up, Jay heard the sound of their boots moving away. Another stone hit the mud and skidded towards him, making him flinch. Then their voices, already receding lazily towards the ash pit, someone saying something about looking for bottles for target practice.

He waited, oddly reluctant to move. It was a ruse, he said to himself, a trick to make him break cover, there was no way they could have missed him. But the voices continued to recede, beyond the jetty, growing fainter as they took the overgrown path back towards the ash pit. The distant crack of the rifle. Laughter from behind the trees. It was impossible. They *had* to have seen him. But somehow . . .

Carefully Jay pulled out the treasure box. The charm was black with the sweat from his hands. It worked, he told himself in astonishment. It was impossible, but it worked.

9

London, March 1999

'EVEN THE DULLEST AND COLDEST OF CHARACTERS', HE TOLD HIS
evening students, 'may be humanized by giving him someone to love. A child, a lover, even, at a pinch, a dog.' Unless
you're writing sci-fi, he thought, with a sudden grin, in
which case you just give them yellow eyes.

He perched on his desk, next to his bulging duffel bag,
resisting the urge to touch it, to open it. The students looked
at him with awed expressions. Some took notes. 'Even' –
writing laboriously, straining so as not to miss a single
word – 'even . . . at pinch . . . dog'.

He taught them on Kerry's insistence, vaguely disliking
their ambition, their slavish obedience to the rules. There
were fifteen of them, dressed almost uniformly in black;
earnest young men and intense young women, with
cropped haircuts and eyebrow rings and clipped, public-
school vowels. One of the women – so like Kerry as she was
five years ago that they might have been sisters – was
reading aloud a short story she had written, an exercise in
characterization about a black single mother in a flat in
Sheffield. Jay touched the Escape brochure in his pocket
and tried to listen, but the girl's voice was no more than a
drone, a slightly unpleasant, waspish buzz of interference.

From time to time he nodded, as if he were interested. He still felt slightly drunk.

Since last night the world seemed to have shifted slightly, moving closer into focus. As if something he had been staring at for years without seeing it had suddenly come clear.

The girl's voice droned on. She scowled as she read and kicked one foot complusively against the table leg. Jay stifled a yawn. She was so intense, he told himself. Intense and rather disgusting in her self-absorption, like an adolescent looking for blackheads. She used the word 'fuck' in every sentence, probably an attempt at authenticity. He felt the urge to laugh. She pronounced it 'fark'.

He knew he wasn't drunk. He had finished the bottle hours ago – even then he had barely felt dizzy. After that day's business he had decided not to attend the tutorial, but went after all, suddenly appalled at the thought of going back to the house, to face the silent disapproval of Kerry's things. Killing time, he told himself silently. Killing time. Joe's wine really should have worn off, but still he felt oddly exhilarated. As if the normal running of things had been suspended for a day, like an unexpected holiday. Perhaps it came of thinking so much about Joe. The memories kept coming, too many to keep track, as if the bottle contained not wine, but *time*, uncoiling smokily, like a genie from the sour dregs, making him different, making him . . . what? Crazy? Sane? He could not concentrate. The oldies station, permanently tuned to summers past, jangled aimlessly at the back of his mind. He might be thirteen again, head filled with visions and fantasies. Thirteen and in school, with the smells of summer coming through the window and Pog Hill Lane just around the corner and the thick tick of the clock counting time to the end of term.

But he was the teacher now, he realized. The teacher going crazy with impatience for the end of school. The pupils wanted desperately to be there, drinking in every meaningless word. He was, after all, Jay Mackintosh, the man who wrote *Three Summers with Jackapple Joe*. The writer who never wrote. A teacher with nothing to teach.

The thought made him laugh aloud.

It must be something in the air, he thought. A whiff of happy gas, a scent of the outlands. The droning girl stopped reading – or maybe she had finished – and stared at him in hurt accusation. She looked so like Kerry that he couldn't help laughing again.

'I bought a house today,' he said suddenly.

They stared at him without reaction. One young man in a Byron shirt wrote it down: 'Bought . . . house today'.

Jay pulled out the brochure from his pocket and looked at it again. It was crumpled and grimy from so much handling, but at the sight of the picture his heart leaped.

'Not a house exactly,' he corrected himself. 'A *chatto*.' He laughed again. 'That's what Joe used to call it. His *chatto* in Bordo.'

He opened the brochure and read it aloud. The students listened obediently. Byron Shirt made notes.

Château Foudouin, Lot-et-Garonne. Lansquenet-sous-Tannes. This authentic eighteenth-century château in the heart of France's most popular wine-growing region includes vineyard, orchard, lake and extensive informal grounds, plus garage block, working distillery, five bedrooms, reception and living room, original oak-roof beaming. Suitable for conversion.

'Of course, it was a bit more than five thousand quid. Prices have gone up since nineteen seventy-five.' For a moment Jay wondered how many of those students were even born in 1975. They stared at him in silence, trying to understand.

'Excuse me, Dr Mackintosh.' It was the girl, still standing, now looking slightly belligerent. 'Can you explain what this has to do with my assignment?' Jay laughed again. Suddenly everything seemed amusing to him, unreal. He felt capable of doing anything, saying anything. Normality had been suspended. He told himself that this was what drunkenness was supposed to feel like. For all these years he had been doing it wrong.

'Of course.' He smiled at her. 'This' – holding up the leaflet so that everyone could see it – 'This is the most original and evocative piece of creative writing I've seen from anyone since the beginning of the term.'

Silence. Even Byron Shirt forgot his notes to gape at him. Jay beamed at the class, looking for a reaction. All were carefully expressionless.

'Why are you here?' he demanded suddenly. 'What are you expecting to get from these lessons?'

He tried not to laugh at their appalled faces, at their polite blankness. He felt younger than any of them, a delinquent pupil addressing a roomful of stuffy, pedantic teachers.

'You're young. You're imaginative. Why the hell are you all writing about black single mothers and Glaswegian dope addicts and gratuitously using the word "fark"?'

'Well, sir, you set the assignment.' He had not won over the belligerent girl. She glared at him, clutching the despised assignment in her thin hand.

'Stuff the assignment!' he shouted merrily. 'You don't write because someone sets assignments! You write because you need to write, or because you hope someone will listen, or because writing will mend something broken inside you, or bring something back to life—' To emphasize his words he slapped at the heavy duffel bag standing on his desk, and it gave out the unmistakable sound of bottles clinking together. Some of the students looked at each other. Jay turned back to the class, feeling almost delirious.

'Where's the magic, that's what I want to know?' he asked. 'Where are the magic carpets and Haitian voodoo and lone gunslingers and naked ladies tied to railway lines? Where are the Indian trackers and the four-armed goddesses and the pirates and the giant apes? *Where are the fucking space aliens?'*

There was a long silence. The students stared. The girl clutched her assignment so hard that the pages crumpled in her fist. Her face was white.

'You're pissed, aren't you?' Her voice was trembling with rage and disgust. 'That's why you're doing this to me. You've got to be pissed.'

Jay laughed again.

'To paraphrase someone or other – Churchill it might have been – I may be pissed, but you'll still be ugly in the morning.'

'Fuck you!' she flung at him, pronouncing it properly this time, and stalked towards the door. 'Fuck you and your tutorial! I'm going to see the head of faculty about this!'

For a second there was silence in her wake. Then the whisperings began. The room was awash with them. For a moment Jay was not sure whether these were real sounds or in his own head. The duffel bag clinked and clattered, rattled and rolled. The sound, imaginary or not, was overwhelming.

Then Byron Shirt stood up and began to clap.

A couple of the other students looked at him cautiously, then joined in. Several others joined them. Soon half the class was standing up, and most were clapping. They were still clapping as Jay picked up his duffel bag and turned towards the door, opened it, and left, closing it very gently behind him. The applause began to tail off, a number of voices murmuring confusion. From inside the duffel bag came the sound of bottles clinking together. Beside me, their work done, the Specials whispered their secrets.

10

Pog Hill, July 1975

HE WENT TO SEE JOE MANY MORE TIMES AFTER THAT, THOUGH HE
never really got to like his wine. Joe showed no surprise
when he arrived, but simply went to fetch the lemonade
bottle, as if he had been expecting him. Nor did he ask
about the charm. Jay asked him about it a few times, with
the scepticism of one who secretly longs to be convinced,
but the old man was evasive.

'Magic,' he said, winking to prove it was a joke. 'Learned
it off of a lady in Puerto Cruz.'

'I thought you said Haiti,' interrupted Jay.

Joe shrugged. 'Same difference,' he said blandly.
'Worked, didn't it?'

Jay had to admit that it worked. But it was just herbs,
wasn't it? Herbs and bits of stick tied into a piece of cloth.
And yet it had made him . . .

Joe grinned.

'Nah, lad. Not *invisible*.' He pushed the bill of his cap up
from his eyes.

'What then?'

Joe looked at him. 'Some plants have properties, don't
they?' he said.

Jay nodded.

'Aspirin. Digitalis. Quinine. What woulda been called magic in the old days.'

'Medicines.'

'If you like. But a few hundred years ago there were no difference between magic and medicine. People just knew things. Believed things. Like chewin cloves to cure toothache, or pennyroyal for a sore throat, or rowan twigs to keep away evil spirits.' He glanced at the boy, as if to check for any sign of mockery. 'Properties,' he repeated. 'You can learn a lot if you travel enough, an you keep an open mind.'

Jay was never certain later whether Joe was a true believer or whether his casual acceptance of magic was part of an elaborate plan to baffle him. Certainly the old man liked a joke. Jay's total ignorance of anything to do with gardening amused him, and for weeks he had the boy believing that a harmless stand of lemongrass was really a spaghetti tree — showing him the pale soft shoots of 'spaghetti' between the papery leaves — or that giant hogweeds could pull out their roots and walk, like triffids, or that you really could catch mice with valerian. Jay was gullible, and Joe delighted in finding new ways to catch him out. But in some things he was genuine. Maybe he had finally come to believe in his own fiction, after years of persuading others. His life was dominated by small rituals and superstitions, many taken from the battered copy of *Culpeper's Herbal* he kept by his bedside. He tickled tomatoes to make them grow. He played the radio constantly, claiming that the plants grew stronger with music. They preferred Radio 1 — he claimed leeks grew up to two inches bigger after *Ed Stewart's Junior Choice* — and Joe would be there, singing along to 'Disco Queen' or 'Stand By Your Man' as he worked, his old-crooner's voice rising solemnly above the redcurrant bushes as he picked and pruned. He always planted when there was a new moon and picked when the moon was full. He had a lunar chart in his greenhouse, each day marked in a dozen different inks: brown for potatoes, yellow for parsnips, orange for carrots.

Watering, too, was done to an astrological schedule, as was the pruning and positioning of trees. And the funny thing was that the garden thrived on this eccentric treatment, growing strong, luxuriant rows of cabbages and turnips, carrots which were sweet and succulent and mysteriously free of slugs, trees whose branches fairly touched the ground under the weight of apples, pears, plums, cherries. Brightly coloured Oriental-looking signs Sellotaped to tree branches supposedly kept the birds from eating the fruit. Astrological symbols, painstakingly set into the gravel path and constructed from pieces of broken pottery and coloured glass, lined the garden beds. With Joe, Chinese medicine rubbed shoulders companionably with English folklore, chemistry with mysticism. For all Jay knew he may have believed it. Certainly, Jay believed him. At thirteen anything is possible. Everyday magic, that was what Joe called it. Layman's alchemy. No fuss, no fireworks. Just a mixture of herbs and roots, gathered under favourable planetary conditions. A muttered incantation, a sketched air symbol learned from gypsies on his travels. Perhaps Jay would not have accepted anything less prosaic. But in spite of his beliefs – maybe even because of them – there was some-thing deeply restful about Joe, an inner calm which en-circled him and which filled the boy with curiosity and a kind of envy. He seemed so tranquil, alone in his little house, surrounded by plants, and yet he had a remarkable sense of wonder and a gleeful fascination with the world. He was almost without education, having left school at twelve to go down the mines, but he was an endless source of information, anecdotes and folklore. As the summer passed, Jay found himself going to see Joe more and more often. He never asked questions, but allowed Jay to talk to him as he worked in his garden or his unofficial allotment on the railway bank, occasionally nodding to show that he'd heard, that he was listening. They snacked on slabs of fruit cake and thick bacon and egg sandwiches – no Trimble loaves for Joe – and drank mugs of strong, sweet tea. From time to time Jay brought cigarettes and sweets or magazines, and Joe accepted these gifts without especial gratitude and without surprise, as he did the boy's presence. As his shyness abated Jay even read him some of his stories, to which he listened in solemn and, he thought, appreciative silence. When Jay didn't want to talk he would tell the boy about himself, about his work in the mines and how he went to France during the war and was stationed in Dieppe for six months before a grenade blew two fingers off his hand – wiggling the reduced limb like an agile starfish – then how, being unfit for service, it was the mines again for six years before he took off for America on a freighter.

'Cause you don't get to see much of the world from underground, lad, and I allus wanted to see what else there was. Have you done much travellin?'

Jay told him he had been to Florida twice with his parents, to the south of France, to Tenerife and the Algarve for holidays. Joe dismissed these with a sniff.

'I mean proper *travellin*, lad. Not all that tourist-brochure rubbish, but the real thing. The Pont-Neuf in the early morning, when there's no-one up but the tramps coming out from under the bridges and out of the Metro, and the sun shinin on the water. New York. Central Park in spring. Rome. Ascension Island. Crossin the Italian alps by donkey. The vegetable caique from Crete. Himalayas on foot. Eatin rice off leaves in the Temple of Ganesh. Caught in a squall off the coast of New Guinea. Spring in Moscow and a whole winter of dogshit comin out under the meltin snow.' His eyes were gleaming. 'I've seen all of those things, lad,' he said softly. 'And more besides. I promised messell I'd see *everything*.'

Jay believed him. He had his maps on the walls, carefully annotated in his crabby handwriting and marked with coloured pins to show the places he had been. He told stories of brothels in Tokyo and shrines in Thailand, birds of paradise and banyan trees and standing stones at the end of the world. In the big converted spice cupboard next

56

to his bed there were millions of seeds, painstakingly wrapped in squares of newspaper and labelled in his small careful script: *tuberosa rubra maritima, tuberosa panax odarata*, thousands and thousands of potatoes in their small compartments and, with them, carrots, squash, tomatoes, artichokes, leeks – over 300 species of onion alone – sages, thymes, sweet bergamots and a bewildering treasure store of medicinal herbs and vegetables collected on his travels, every one named and packaged and ready for planting. Some of these plants were already extinct in the wild, Joe said, their properties forgotten by everyone but a handful of experts. Of the millions of varieties of fruit and vegetables once grown, only a few dozen were still commonly used.

'It's your intensive farming does it,' he would say, leaning on his spade for long enough to take a mouthful of tea from his mug. 'Too much specialization kills off variety. Sides, people don't want variety. They want everythin to look the same. Round red tomatoes, and never mind there's a long yeller un that'd taste a mile better if they gave it a try. Red uns look better on shelves.' He waved an arm vaguely over the allotment, indicating the neat rows of vegetables rising up the railway embankment, the home-made cold frames in the derelict signal box, the fruit trees pegged out against the wall. 'There's things growin here that you wouldn't find anywhere else in the whole of England,' he said in a low voice, 'and there's seeds in that chest of mine that you might not find anywhere else in the whole world.' Jay listened to him in awe. He'd never been interested in plants before. He could hardly tell the difference between a Granny Smith and a Red Delicious. He knew potatoes, of course, but Joe's talk of blue jackapples and pink fir apples was beyond any experience of his. The thought that there were secrets, that arcane, forgotten things might be growing right there on the railway embankment with only an old man as their custodian fired Jay with an enthusiasm he had never imagined. Part of it was Joe, of course. His stories. His memories. The energy of the man himself. He began to see in Joe something he had never seen in anyone else. A vocation. A sense of purpose.

'Why did you come back, Joe?' he asked him one day. 'After all that travelling, why come back here?'

Joe peered out gravely from under the bill of his miner's cap.

'It's part of me plan, lad,' he said. 'I'll not be here for ever. Some day I'll be off again. Some day soon.'

'Where?'

'I'll show you.'

He reached into his workshirt and pulled out a battered leather wallet. Opening it, he unfolded a photograph clipped from a colour magazine, taking great care not to tear the whitened creases. It was a picture of a house.

'What's that?' Jay squinted at the picture. It looked ordinary enough, a big house built of faded pinkish stone, a long strip of land in front, with some kind of vegetation growing in ordered rows. Joe smoothed out the paper.

'That's me *chatto*, lad,' he said. 'In Bordo, it is, in France. Me *chatto* with the vineyard and me hundred-year-old orchard with peaches and almonds and apples and pears.' His eyes gleamed. 'When I've got me brass together I'll buy it – five grand would do it – and I'll make the best bloody wine in the south. Chatto Cox, 1975. How's that sound?'

Jay watched him doubtfully.

'Sun shines all year round down in Bordo,' said Joe cheerily. 'Oranges in January. Peaches like cricket balls. Olives. Kiwi fruit. Almonds. Melons. And space. Miles and miles of orchards and vineyards, land cheap as dirt. Soil like fruit cake. Pretty girls treadin out the grapes with their bare feet. Paradise.'

'Five thousand pounds is a lot of money,' said Jay doubtfully. Joe tapped the side of his nose with his forefinger.

'I'll get there,' he said mysteriously. 'You want somethin badly enough, you allus get there in the end.'

'But you don't even speak French.'

Joe's only response was a stream of sudden, incomprehensible gibberish, like no language Jay had ever heard before.

'Joe, I do French at school,' he told him. 'That's not anything like—'

Joe looked at him indulgently.

'It's dialect, lad,' he said. 'Learned it off of a band of gypsies in Marseilles. Believe me, I'll fit right in there.' He folded the picture carefully away again and replaced it in his wallet. Jay gaped at him in awe, utterly convinced.

'You'll see what I mean one day, lad,' he said. 'Jus you wait.'

'Can I come with you?' Jay asked. 'Will you take me with you?' Joe considered it seriously, head to one side.

'I might, lad, if you want to come. I might anall.'

'Promise?'

'All right.' He grinned. 'It's a promise. Cox and Mackintosh, best bloody winemakers in Bordo. That do yer?'

They toasted his dreams in warm Blackberry '73.

11

London, Spring 1999

BY THE TIME JAY ARRIVED AT SPY'S IT WAS TEN O'CLOCK AND THE party was well under way. Another of Kerry's literary launches, he thought ruefully. Bored journalists and cheap champagne and eager young things dancing attendance on blasé older things like himself. Kerry never tired of these occasions, dropping names like confetti – Germaine and Will and Ewan – flitting from one prestigious guest to the other with the zeal of a high priestess. Jay had only just realized how much he hated it.

Stopping at the house only long enough to pick up a few things, he saw the red light on the answerphone blinking furiously, but did not play the message. The bottles in his duffel bag were absolutely still. Now *he* was the one in ferment, jittering and rocking, exhilarated one moment, close to tears the next, rummaging through his possessions like a thief, afraid that if he stopped still for even a second he would lose his momentum and collapse listlessly back into his old life again. He turned on the radio and it was the oldies station again, playing Rod Stewart and 'Sailing', one of Joe's favourites – *allus reminds me of them times I were on me travels, lad* – and he listened as he stuffed clothes into the bag on top of the silent bottles. Amazing how little he could not bear to leave behind. His typewriter. The unfinished manuscript of *Stout Cortez*. Some favourite books. The radio itself. And, of course, Joe's Specials. Another impulse, he told himself. The wine was valueless, almost undrinkable. And yet he could not shake the feeling that there was something in those bottles he needed. Something he could not do without.

Spy's was like so many other London clubs. The names change, the décor changes, but the places stay the same: sleek and loud and soulless. By midnight most of the guests would have abandoned any pretentions to intellectualism that they might have had, instead settling down to the serious business of getting drunk, making advances to each other, or insulting their rivals. Getting out of the taxi with his duffel bag slung across his shoulder and his single case in his hand, Jay realized that he had forgotten his invitation. After some altercation with the doorman, however, he managed to get a message to Kerry, who emerged a few minutes later wearing her Ghost dress and steeliest smile.

'It's all right,' she flung at the doorman. 'He's just useless, that's all.' Her green eyes flicked at Jay, taking in the jeans, the raincoat, the duffel bag.

'I see you didn't wear the Armani,' she said.

The euphoria was finally gone, leaving only a kind of dim hangover in its wake, but Jay was surprised to find his resolve unchanged. Touching the duffel bag seemed to help somehow, and he did so, as if to test its reality. Under the canvas the bottles clinked quietly together.

'I've bought a house,' said Jay, holding out the crumpled brochure. 'Look. It's Joe's château, Kerry. I bought it this morning. I recognized it.' Beneath that flat green stare he felt absurdly childish. Why had he expected her to understand? He barely understood his impulse himself. 'It's called Château Foudouin,' he said. She looked at him.

'You bought a house.'

He nodded.

'Just like that, you bought it?' she asked in disbelief. 'You bought it today?'

He nodded again. There were so many things he wanted to say. It was destiny, he would have told her, it was the magic he had searched for twenty years to recapture. He wanted to explain about the brochure and the square of sunlight and how the picture had leaped out at him from the page. He wanted to explain about the sudden certainty of it, the feeling that it was the house which chose him, and not the other way around.

'You can't have bought a house.' Kerry was still struggling with the idea. 'God, Jay, you dither for hours over buying a *shirt*.'

'This was different. It was like . . .' He struggled to articulate what it had been like. It was an uncanny sensation, that overriding feeling of must-have. He hadn't felt this way since his teens. The knowledge that life could not be complete without this one infinitely desirable, magical, totemic object – a pair of X-ray spectacles, a set of Hell's Angels transfers, a cinema ticket, the latest band's latest single – the certainty that possession of it would change everything, its presence in the pocket to be checked, tested, retested. It wasn't an adult feeling. It was more primitive, more visceral than that. With a jolt of surprise, he realized he had not really wanted anything for twenty years.

'It was like . . . being back at Pog Hill again,' he said, knowing she wouldn't understand. 'It was as if the last twenty years hadn't happened.'

Kerry looked blank.

'I can't believe you impulse-bought a house,' she said. 'A car, yes. A motorbike, OK. It's the kind of thing you would do, come to think of it. Big toys to play with. But a *house*?' She shook her head, mystified. 'What are you going to do with it?'

'Live in it,' said Jay simply. 'Work in it.'

'But it's in France somewhere.' Irritation sharpened her voice. 'Jay, I can't afford to spend weeks in France. I'm due to start the new series next month. I've got too many commitments. I mean, is it even close to an airport?' She broke off, her eyes moving again to the duffel bag, taking in, as if for the first time, the suitcase, the travelling clothes. There was a crease between her arched brows.

'Look, Kerry—'

Kerry lifted a hand imperiously.

'Go home,' she said. 'We can't discuss this here. Go home, Jay, relax, and we'll talk it all through when I get back. OK?' She sounded cautious now, as if she were addressing an excitable maniac.

Jay shook his head. 'I'm not going back,' he said. 'I need to get away for a while. I wanted to say goodbye.'

Even now Kerry showed no surprise. Irritation, yes. Almost anger. But she remained untroubled, secure in her convictions.

'You're pissed again, Jay,' she said. 'You haven't thought any of this through. You come to me with this crazy idea about a second home, and when I'm not *instantly* taken by it—'

'It isn't going to be a second home.'

The tone of his voice surprised both of them. For a moment he sounded almost harsh.

'And what the fuck is that supposed to mean?' Her voice was low and dangerous.

'It means you're not listening to me. I don't think you've ever actually *listened* to me.' He paused. 'You're always telling me to grow up, to think for myself, to let go. But you're happy to keep me a permanent lodger in your house, to keep me dependent on you for everything. I don't have anything of my own. Contacts, friends – they're all yours, not mine. You even choose my clothes. I've got money, Kerry, I've got my books, I'm not exactly starving in a garret any more.'

Kerry sounded amused, almost indulgent.

'So *this* is what it's all about? A little declaration of independence?' She fluttered a kiss against his cheek. 'OK. I understand you don't want to go to the party, and I'm sorry I didn't realize that this morning, OK?' She put her hand on his shoulder and smiled. The patented Kerry O'Neill smile.

'Please. Listen. Just this once.'

Was this what Joe had felt, he wondered. So much easier to leave without a word, to escape the recriminations, the tears, the disbelief. To escape the guilt. But somehow he just couldn't do that to Kerry. She didn't love him any more, he knew that. If she ever had. All the same, he couldn't do it. Perhaps because he knew how it felt.

'Try to understand. This place —' His gesture included the club, the neon-lit street, the low sky, the whole of London, heaving, dark and menacing below it. 'I don't belong here any more. I can't think straight when I'm here. I spend all my time waiting for something to happen, some kind of sign—'

'Oh, for Christ's sake, grow up!' She was suddenly furious, her voice rising like an angry bird's. 'Is this your excuse? Some kind of idiotic *angst*? If you spent less time mooning on about that old bastard Joe Cox and looked *around* you for a change, if only you took *charge* instead of talking about signs and omens—'

'But I am,' he interrupted her. 'I am taking charge. I'm doing what you've always told me to do.'

'Not by running away to France!' The note in her voice was almost panic now. 'Not just like that! You owe me. You wouldn't have lasted two minutes without me. I've introduced you to people, used my contacts for you. You were nothing but a one-book wonder, a has-been, a fucking *fake*—'

Jay looked at her dispassionately for a moment. Strange, he thought remotely, how quickly gamine could shift to plain meanness. Her red mouth was thin, vicious. Her eyes were crescents. Anger, familiar and liberating, wrapped around him like a cloak, and he laughed.

'Can the bullshit,' he told her. 'It always was a mutual convenience. You liked to drop my name at parties, didn't you? I was an accessory. It did you good to be seen with me. It's just like people who read poetry on the tube. People saw you with me and assumed you were a real intellectual, instead of a media wannabe without a single original thought in her head.'

She stared at him, astonished and enraged. Her eyes were wide.

'*What?*'

'Goodbye.' He turned to go.

'Jay!' She snatched at him as he turned, slapping smartly against the duffel bag with the flat of her hand. Inside, the bottles whispered and snickered.

'How dare you turn your back on me?' she hissed. 'You were happy enough to use my contacts when it suited you. How dare you turn round and tell me you're leaving, without even giving me a proper explanation? If it's personal space you want, then say that. Go to your French château, if that's what you want, go wallow in atmosphere, if that's going to help.'

She looked at him suddenly. 'Is that it? Is it another book?' She sounded hungry now, her anger sharpening into excitement. 'If that's what it is you have to tell me, Jay. You owe me that. After all this time . . .'

Jay looked at her. It would be so easy to say yes, he told himself. To give her something she would understand, maybe forgive.

'I don't know,' he said at last. 'I don't think so.' A taxi went by then and Jay flagged it down, throwing his luggage onto the back seat and jumping in with it. Kerry gave a cry of frustration and slapped the window of the taxi as if it were his face.

'Go on then! Run away! Hide! You're just like him, you know: a quitter! That's all you know how to do! Jay! *Jay!*'

As the taxi pulled smoothly away from the kerb Jay grinned and settled back against his duffel bag. Its contents made small contented clicking sounds all the way to the airport.

12

Pog Hill, Summer 1975

SUMMER STEERED ITS COURSE AND JAY CAME MORE OFTEN TO Pog Hill Lane. Joe seemed pleased to see him when he came by, but never commented when he did not, and the boy spent days lurking by the canal or by the railway, watching over his uncertain territory, ever on the lookout for Zeth and his two friends. His hideout at the lock was no longer secure, so he moved the treasure box from its place in the bank and cast about for a safer place. At last he found one in the derelict car on the dumping ground, taping it to the underside of the rotten fuel tank. Jay liked that old car. He spent hours lounging in its one remaining seat, smelling the musty scent of ancient leather, hidden from sight by the rampant greenery. Once or twice he heard the voices of Zeth and his mates close by, but crouching in the low belly of the car – Joe's charm held tightly in his hand – he was safe from any but the closest investigation. He watched and listened, intoxicated with the delight of spying on his enemies. At such times he believed in the charm implicitly.

He realized, as summer drew inevitably to its close, that he had grown fond of Kirby Monckton. In spite of his resistance he had found something here that he never had elsewhere. July and August sailed by like cool white schooners. He went to Pog Hill Lane almost every day. Sometimes he and Joe were alone, but too often there were visitors, neighbours, friends, though Joe seemed to have no family. Jay was sometimes jealous of their time together, resentful of time given to other people, but Joe always welcomed everyone, giving out boxes of fruit from his allotment, bunches of carrots, sacks of potatoes, a bottle of blackberry wine to one, a recipe for tooth powder to another. He dealt in philtres, teas, sachets. People came openly for fruit and vegetables but stayed in secret, talking to Joe in low voices, sometimes leaving with a little packet of tissue paper or a scrap of flannel tucked into hands and pockets. He never asked for payment. Sometimes people gave him things in exchange: a loaf or two, a home-made pie, cigarettes. Jay wondered where he got his money, and where the £5,000 to pay for his dream château would come from. But when he mentioned such things the old man just laughed.

As September loomed closer, every day seemed to gain a special, poignant significance, a mythical quality. Jay walked the canal side in a haze of nostalgia. He took notes of the things Joe said to him in their long conversations over the redcurrant bushes and replayed them in his mind as he lay in bed. He cycled for hours over deserted, now-familiar roads and breathed the sooty warm air. He climbed Upper Kirby Hill and looked out over the purple-black expanse of the Pennines and wished he could stay for ever.

Joe himself seemed untouched. He remained the same as ever, picking his fruit and laying it out in crates, making jam from windfalls, pointing out wild herbs and picking them when the moon was full, collecting bilberries from the moors and blackberries from the railway banking, preparing chutney from his tomatoes, piccalilli from his cauliflowers, lavender bags for sleeplessness, wintergreen for rapid healing, hot peppers and rosemary in oil and pickled onions for the winter. And, of course, there was the wine. Throughout all that summer Jay smelt wine brewing, fermenting, ageing. All kinds of wine: beetroot, peapod, raspberry, elderflower, rosehip, jackapple, plum, parsnip, ginger, blackberry. The house was a distillery, with pans of fruit boiling on the stove, demijohns of wine waiting on the kitchen floor to be decanted into bottles, muslins for straining the fruit drying on the washing line, sieves, buckets, bottles, funnels, laid out in neat rows ready for use.

He kept the still in his cellar. It was a big copper piece, like a giant kettle, old but burnished and cared for. He used it to make his 'spirits', the raw, eyewatering clear alcohol he used to preserve the summer fruit which sat in gleaming rows on shelves in the cellar. Potato vodka, he called it, jackapple juice. Seventy per cent proof. In it he placed equal quantities of fruit and sugar to make his liqueurs. Cherries, plums, redcurrants, bilberries. The fruit stained the liquor purple and red and black in the dim cellar light. Each jar carefully labelled and dated. More than one man could ever hope to eat. Not that Joe minded; in any case, he gave away much of what he made. Apart from his wine and a few licks of strawberry jam with his morning toast, Jay never saw him touch any of those extravagant preserves and spirits. Jay supposed the old man must have sold some of these wares during the winter, though he never saw him do it. Most of the time he just gave things away.

Jay went back to school in September. The Moorlands School was as he remembered it, smelling of dust and disinfectant and polish and the bland, inescapable scent of ancient cooking. His parents' divorce went through smoothly enough, after many tearful phone calls from his mother and postal orders from the Bread Baron. Surprisingly, he felt nothing. During the summer his rage had sloughed away into indifference. Anger seemed childish to him somehow. He wrote to Joe every month or so, though the old man never wrote back as regularly. He was not much of a writer, he said, and contented himself with a card at Christmas and a couple of lines near the end of term. His silence did not trouble Jay. It was enough to know that he was there.

In the summer Jay went back to Kirby Monckton. Part of this was on his own insistence, but he could tell his parents were secretly relieved. His mother was filming in Ireland at the time, and the Bread Baron was spending the summer on his yacht, in the company, rumour had it, of a young fashion model called Candide.

Jay escaped to Pog Hill Lane without a second glance.

13

Paris, March 1999

JAY SPENT THE NIGHT AT THE AIRPORT. HE EVEN SLEPT A LITTLE on one of Charles de Gaulle's contoured orange chairs, though he was still too jumpy to relax. His energy seemed inexhaustible, a ball of electricity punching against his ribs. His senses felt eerily enhanced. Smells – cleaning fluid, sweat, cigarette smoke, perfume, early morning coffee – rolled at him in waves. At five o'clock he abandoned the idea of sleep and went to the cafeteria, where he bought an espresso, a couple of croissants and a sugar fix of Poulain chocolate. The first Corail to Marseilles was at six ten. From there, a slower train would take him to Agen, where he could get a taxi to . . . where was it? The map attached to the brochure was only a sketchy diagram, but he hoped to find clearer directions when he reached Agen. Besides, there was something pleasing about this journey, this blurring of speed to a place which was nothing yet but a cross on a map. As if by drinking Joe's wine he could suddenly *become* Joe, marking his passage by scratching signs on a map, changing his identity to suit his whim. And at the same time he felt lighter, freed of the hurt and anger he had carried for so long, such useless ballast, for so many years.

Travel far enough, Joe used to say, *and all rules are suspended*.

Now Jay began to understand what he meant. Truth, loyalty, identity. The things which bind us to the places and faces of home no longer applied. He could be anyone. Going anywhere. At airports, railway stations, bus stations, anything is possible. No-one asks questions. People reach a state of near-invisibility. He was just another passenger here, one of thousands. No-one would recognize him. No-one had even heard of him.

He managed to sleep for a few hours on the train, and dreamed – a dream of astonishing vividness – of himself running along the canal bank at Nether Edge, trying vainly to catch up with a departing coal train. With exceptional clarity he could see the somehow prehistoric metal of the train's undercarriage. He could smell coal dust and old grease from the trucks' axles. And on the last truck he could see Joe, sitting on top of the coal in his orange miner's overalls and a British Railways engineer's cap, waving goodbye with a bottle of home-brewed wine in one hand and a map of the world in the other, calling in a voice made tinny by distance words Jay could not quite hear.

He awoke, needing a drink, twenty miles from Marseilles, with the countryside a long bright blur at the window. He went to the minibar for a vodka and tonic and drank it slowly, then lit a cigarette. It still felt like a forbidden pleasure – guilt laced with exhilaration, like playing truant from school.

He pulled the brochure out of his pocket once more. Decidedly crumpled now, the cheap paper beginning to tear at the folds. For a moment he almost expected to feel differently, to find that the sense of must-have was gone. But it was still there. In the duffel bag at his side the Specials lolled and gurgled with the train's movement, and inside the sediment of past summers stirred like crimson slurry.

He felt as if the train would never reach Marseilles.

14

Pog Hill, Summer 1976

HE WAS WAITING ON THE ALLOTMENT. THE RADIO WAS PLAYING, tied with a piece of string to the branch of a tree, and Jay could hear him singing along – Thin Lizzy and 'The Boys Are Back In Town' – in his extravagant music-hall voice. He had his back turned, leaning over a patch of loganberries with secateurs in one hand, and he greeted Jay without turning round, casually, as if he had never been away. Jay's first thought was that he'd aged; the hair beneath the greasy cap was thinner, and he could see the sharp, vulnerable ridge of his spine through his old T-shirt, but when the old man turned round he could see it was the same Joe, jay-blue eyes above a smile more suited to a fourteen-year-old than a man of sixty-five. He was wearing one of his red flannel sachets around his neck. Looking more carefully around the allotment Jay saw that a similar charm adorned every tree, every bush, even the corners of the greenhouse and the home-made cold frame. Small seedlings protected under jars and bisected lemonade bottles each bore a twist of red thread or a sign crayoned in the same colour. It might have been another of Joe's elaborate jokes, like the earwig traps or the sherbert plant or sending him to the garden centre for a long weight, but this time there was a dogged, sombre look to the old man's amusement, like that of a man under siege. Jay asked him about the charms, expecting the usual joke or wink, but Joe's expression remained serious.

'Protection, lad,' he said quietly. 'Protection.'

It took the boy a long time to realize quite how serious he was.

Summer wound on like a dusty road. Jay called by Pog Hill Lane almost every day, and when he felt in need of solitude he went over to Nether Edge and the canal. Nothing much had changed. New glories on the dump: abandoned fridges, ragbags, a clock with a cracked casing, a cardboard box of tattered paperback books. The railway, too, delivered riches: papers, magazines, broken records, crockery, cans, returnable glass. Every morning he combed the rails, picking up what looked interesting or valuable, and he shared his finds with Joe back at the house. With Joe, nothing was wasted. Old newspapers went into the compost. Pieces of carpet kept the weeds down in the vegetable patch. Plastic bags covered the branches of his fruit trees and protected them from the birds. He demonstrated how to make *cloches* for young seedlings from the round end of a plastic lemonade bottle, and potato-planters from discarded car tyres. They spent a whole afternoon dragging an abandoned box freezer up the railway banking to make a cold frame. Scrap metal and old clothes were piled into cardboard boxes and sold to the rag-and-bone man. Empty paint tins and plastic buckets were converted into plant pots. In return, he taught Jay more about the garden. Slowly the boy learned to tell lavender from rosemary from hyssop from sage. He learned to taste soil – a pinch between the finger and thumb slipped under the tongue, like a man testing fine tobacco – to determine its acidity. He learned how to calm a headache with crushed lavender, or a stomach ache with peppermint. He learned to make skullcap tea and camomile to aid sleep. He learned to plant marigolds in the potato patch to discourage parasites, and to pick nettles from the top to make ale, and to fork the sign against the evil eye if ever a magpie flew past. There were times, of course, when the old man couldn't resist a little joke. Like giving him daffodil bulbs to fry instead of onions, or planting ripe strawberries in the border to see if they'd grow. But most of the time he was serious, or so Jay thought, finding real pleasure in his new role as a teacher. Perhaps he knew it was coming to an end, even then, though Jay never suspected it, but it was that year that he was happiest, sitting in the allotment with the radio playing, or sorting through boxes of junk, or holding the vegetable-cutter for Joe as they selected fruit for the next batch of wine. They discussed the merits of 'Good Vibrations' (Jay's choice) versus 'Brand New Combine Harvester' (Joe's). He felt safe, *protected*, as if all this were a little pocket of eternity which could never be lost, never fail. But something was changing. Perhaps it was in Joe: a new restlessness, the wary look he had, the diminishing number of visitors – sometimes only one or two in a whole week – or the new, eerie quiet in Pog Hill Lane. No more hammering, no singing in the yards, less washing hanging out to dry on clothes lines, rabbit hutches and pigeon lofts abandoned and derelict.

Often Joe would walk to the outer edge of his allotment and look over the railway in silence. There were fewer trains, too, a couple of passenger trains a day on the fast line, the rest shunters and coal trucks ambling slowly north to the yard. The rails, so shiny and bright last year, were beginning to show rust.

'Looks like they're plannin to close the line,' Joe remarked on one of these occasions. 'Goin to knock down Kirby Central next month.' Kirby Central was the main signal box down by the station. 'Pog Hill, anall, if I'm not mistaken.'

'But that's your greenhouse,' protested Jay. Since he had known Joe, the old man had used the derelict signal box fifty yards from his back garden as an unofficial green-house, and it was filled with delicate plants, tomatoes, two peach trees, a couple of vines branching out into the eaves, escaping onto the white roof in a spill of broad, bright leaves.

Joe shrugged.

'They usually knock em flat first off,' he remarked. 'I've bin lucky so far.' His eyes moved to the red charm bags nailed to the back wall and he reached out to pinch one between finger and thumb.

'Thing is, we've bin careful,' he continued. 'Not drawn attention to usselves. But if they shut that line, there'll be men taking up the track all down Pog Hill and towards Nether Edge. They might be here for months. And this here, it's private property. Belongs to British Railways. You an me, lad, we're trespassers.'

Jay followed his gaze across the railway cutting, taking in, as if for the first time, the breadth of the allotment, the neat straight rows of vegetables, the cold frames, the hundreds of plastic planters, dozens of fruit trees, thick stands of raspberries, blackcurrants, rhubarb. Funny, he'd never thought of it as trespassing before.

'Oh. D'you think they'd want to take it back?'

Joe didn't look at him. Of course they would take it back. He could see that in the old man's profile, in the calculating look on his face – how long to replant? How long to rebuild? Not because they wanted it, but because it was theirs to take, their territory, wasteland or not, theirs. Jay had a sudden, vivid memory of Zeth and his mates as Zeth booted the radio into the air. There would be the same expressions on their faces as they pulled up the railway, broke up the greenhouse, tore up plants and bushes, bulldozed through the sweet drifts of lavender and the half-ripened pears, unearthed potatoes and carrots and parsnips and all the arcane exotica of a lifetime's collection. Jay felt a sudden brimming rage for the old man, and his fists clenched painfully against the bricks.

'They can't do that!' he said fiercely.

Joe shrugged. Of course they could. Now Jay understood

the significance of the charm bags hanging on every surface, every protruding nail, every tree, everything he wanted to save. It couldn't make him invisible, but it might . . . might what? Keep the bulldozers away? Impossible.

Joe said nothing. His eyes were bright and serene. For a second he looked like the old gunslinger in a hundred Westerns, strapping on his guns for a final showdown. For a second everything — *anything* — seemed possible. Whatever might have happened later, he believed in it then.

15

Marseilles, March 1999

THE TRAIN REACHED MARSEILLES AROUND NOON. IT WAS WARM but cloudy, and Jay carried his coat over his arm as he moved through the aimless crowds. He bought a couple of sandwiches at a stand by the platform, but was still too nervous, too energized to eat. The train to Agen was almost an hour late, and slow; almost as long as the journey from Paris. Energy drained away into exhaustion. He slept uncomfortably as they nudged from one small station to another, feeling hot and thirsty and slightly hungover. He kept needing to take out the leaflet again, just to be sure he wasn't imagining it all. He tried to get the radio to work, but all he could get was white noise.

It was late afternoon when he finally reached Agen. He was beginning to feel more alert again, more aware of his surroundings. He could see fields and farms from the carriage, orchards and ploughed chocolate-coloured earth. Everything looked very green. Many of the trees were already in flower, unusually early for March, he thought, though his only experience of gardening was with Joe, a thousand miles further north. He took a taxi to the estate agent's — the address was on the leaflet — hoping to get permission to view the house, but the place was already shut. Damn!

In the excitement of his escape Jay had never considered what he would do if this happened. Find a hotel in Agen? Not without seeing his house. *His house.* The thought lifted the hairs on his forearms. Tomorrow was Sunday. Chances were that the agency would be closed again. He would have to wait until Monday morning. He stood, hesitating in front of the locked door as the taxi driver behind him grew impatient. How far exactly was Lansquenet-sous-Tannes? Surely there would be something, even something basic like a Campanile or an Ibis or, failing that, a *chambre d'hôte* where he could stay? It was half-past five. He would have time to see the house, even if it was only from the outside, before the light failed.

The urge was too strong. Turning back to the bored taxi driver with unaccustomed decisiveness Jay showed him the map.

'*Vous pouvez m'y conduire tout de suite?*'

The man considered for a moment, with the air of slow reflection typical of that part of the country. Jay pulled out a clip of banknotes from the pocket of his jeans and showed them to him. The driver shrugged incuriously and jerked his head towards the cab again. Jay noticed he didn't offer to help with the luggage.

The drive took half an hour. Jay dozed again in the leather-and-tobacco scented rear of the cab, whilst the driver smoked Gauloises and grunted to himself in satisfaction as he blared without indicating through files of motorway traffic, then sped down narrow small lanes, honking his horn imperiously at corners, occasionally sending flurries of chickens squawking into the air. Jay was beginning to feel hungry and in need of a drink. He had assumed he would find a place to eat when they reached Lansquenet. But now, looking at the dirt lane down which the taxi jolted and revved, he was beginning to have serious doubts.

He tapped the driver on the shoulder.

'*C'est encore loin?*'

The driver shrugged, pointing ahead, and slowed the car to a rumbling halt.

'*Là.*'

Sure enough, there it was, just behind a little copse of trees. The red slanting light of a modest sunset lit the tiled roof and the whitewashed walls with almost eerie brightness. Jay could see the gleam of water somewhere to the side, and the orchard – green in the photograph – was now a froth of pale blossoms. It was beautiful. He paid the driver too much of his remaining French money and pulled his case out onto the road.

'*Attendez-moi ici. Je reviens tout de suite.*'

The driver made a vague gesture, which he took to be agreement, and, leaving him to wait by the deserted roadside, Jay began to walk quickly towards the trees. As he reached the copse he found he could see more clearly down towards the house and across the vineyard. The photograph in the brochure was deceptive, showing little of the scale of the property. Being a city boy Jay had no idea of the acreage, but it looked huge, bordered on one side by road and river, and on the other by a long hedge, which reached beyond the back of the house on to more fields. On the far side of the river he could see another farmhouse, small and low-roofed, and beyond that the village – a church spire, a road winding up from the river, houses. The path to the house led past the vineyard – already green and leggy with growth among drifts of weeds – and past an abandoned vegetable plot, where last year's asparagus, artichokes and cabbages reared hairy heads above the dandelions.

It took about ten minutes to reach the house. As he came closer Jay noticed that, like the vineyard and the vegetable plot, it was in need of some repair. The pinkish paint was peeling away in places, revealing cracked grey plaster beneath. Tiles from the roof had fallen and smashed onto the overgrown path. The ground-floor windows were shuttered or boarded up, and some of the upstairs glass was broken, showing toothy gaps in the pale facing. The front door was nailed shut. The whole impression was of a building which had been derelict for years. And yet the vegetable plot showed signs of recent, or fairly recent, attention. Jay walked around the building once, noting the extent of the damage, and told himself that most of it looked superficial, the work of neglect and the elements. Inside might be different. He found a place where a broken shutter had come away from the plaster, leaving a gap large enough to look through, and put his face to the hole. It was dark inside, and he could hear a distant sound of water dripping.

Suddenly something moved inside the building. Rats, he thought at first. Then it moved again, softly, stealthily, scraping across the floor with a sound like metal-capped boots on cellar concrete. Definitely not rats, then.

He called out – absurdly, in English – 'Hey!' The sound stopped.

Squinting through the gap in the shutter Jay thought he could see something move, a dim shadow just in his line of vision, something which might almost have been a figure in a big coat with a cap pulled down over the eyes.

'Joe? *Joe?*'

It was crazy. Of course it wasn't Joe. It was just that he'd been thinking of him so much in the past few days that he had begun to imagine him everywhere. It was natural, he supposed. When he looked again the figure – if there ever was a figure – had gone. The house was silent. Jay knew a fleeting moment of disappointment, of something almost like grief, which he dared not analyse too closely in case it should reveal itself to be something even crazier, a conviction, perhaps, that Joe could have actually *been* there, waiting. Old Joe, with his cap and miner's boots and his baggy overcoat against the cold, waiting in the deserted house, living off the land. Jay's mind crept remorselessly to the recently abandoned vegetable plot – there must have been *someone* to plant those seeds – with a mad kind of logic. Someone had been there.

He looked at his watch and was startled to see that he had been at the house for almost twenty minutes. He had asked the taxi driver to wait at the roadside, and he didn't want to spend the night in Lansquenet. From what he had seen of the place it was unlikely that he would be able to find a decent place to stay, and he was beginning to feel very hungry. He broke into a run as he passed the orchard, goosegrass clinging to the laces of his boots as he passed, and he was sweating when at last he rounded the curve out of the copse and back onto the track.

There was no sign of the taxi.

Jay swore. His case and duffel bag were lined up incongruously by the roadside. The driver, tired of waiting for the crazy Englishman, had gone.

Like it or not, he was staying.

16

Pog Hill, Summer 1976

KIRBY CENTRAL WENT IN LATE AUGUST. JAY WAS THERE WHEN they closed it, hiding in a tall clump of seedy willowherb, and when they had gone – taking with them the levers, light signals and anything which might otherwise be stolen – he crept up the steps and peered in through the window. Train registers and route diagrams had been left in the box, though the lever frame gaped emptily, and it looked strangely inhabited, as if the signalman had just stepped out and might return at any moment. Jay reckoned there was plenty of usable glass left, if Joe and he came to fetch it.

'Don't bother, lad,' Joe said when he reported this. 'I'll already have me hands full this autumn.'

Jay needed no explanation for his words. Since the beginning of August Joe had become more and more concerned about the fate of his allotment. He rarely spoke about it openly, but he would sometimes stop working and gaze at his trees, as if measuring the time they had left. Sometimes he lingered to touch the smooth bark of an apple or a plum tree and spoke – to Jay, to himself – in a low voice. He always referred to them by name, as if they were people.

'Mirabelle. Doin well, int she? That's a French plum, a yeller gage, a goodun for jam or wine or just for eatin. She likes it here on the bank, it's nicely drained and sunny.' He paused. 'Too late to move t'old girl, though,' he said regretfully. 'She'd never survive. Yer sink yer roots deep, thinkin yer goin to stay for ever, and this is what happens. The buggers.'

It was the closest he had come in weeks to mentioning the allotment problem.

'Tryin to knock down Pog Hill Lane now, anall.' Joe's voice was louder now, and Jay realized that this was the first time he had ever seen him close to anger. 'Pog Hill Lane, that's bin standin for a hundred year-a-more, that were built when there were still a pit down Nether Edge, and navvies workin down at canal side.'

Jay stared at him.

'Knock down Pog Hill Lane?' he asked. 'You mean the *houses*?' Joe nodded.

'Got a letter int post tother day,' he told him shortly. 'Buggers reckon we're not safe any more. Goin to condemn em all. All t'row.' His face was grim in its amusement. 'Condemned. After all this time. Thirty-nine years I've bin here, since Nether Edge and Upper Kirby shut down. Bought me own pit house offat council anall. Didn't trust em, even then—' He broke off, holding up his reduced left hand in a mocking three-fingered salute. 'How much more do they want, eh? I left me fingers down that pit. I near as buggery left me *life*. You'd think that'd be worth somethin. You'd think they'd *remember* summat like that!'

Jay gaped at him. This was a Joe he had never seen before. Awe, and a kind of fear, kept him silent. Then Joe stopped as abruptly as he had begun, bending solicitously over a newly grafted branch to examine the healing joint.

'I thought it was during the war,' said Jay at last.

'What?'

Gaudy red cotton joined the new graft to the branch. On it Joe had smeared some kind of resin, which gave out a pungent sappy scent. He nodded to himself, as if satisfied with the tree's progress.

'You told me you'd lost your fingers in Dieppe,' insisted Jay. 'During the war.'

'Aye. Well.' Joe was unembarrassed. 'It were a kind of war down there any road. Lost em when I were sixteen – crushed between two trucks back in 1931. Wouldn't take me in the Army after that, so I signed up as a Bevan boy. We had three cave-ins that year. Seven men trapped underground when a tunnel collapsed. Not even grown men, some of em – boys my age and younger; you could go underground at fourteen on a man's wage. Worked double shifts for a week tryin to get em out. We could hear em behind the cave-in, yellin and cryin, but every time we tried to get to em another bit of the tunnel came down on us. We were workin in darkness because of the gas, knee-deep in slurry. We were soaked an half suffocated, an we all knew the roof could fall in again any minute, but we never stopped tryin. Not till at last the bosses came and closed down the shaft altogether.' He looked at Jay with unexpected vehemence, his eyes dark with ancient rage. 'So don't go tellin me I never went to war, lad,' he snapped. 'I know as much about war – what war *means* – as any o them lads in France.'

Jay stared at him, unsure of what to say. Joe looked off into the middle distance, hearing the cries and pleading of young men long dead from the quiet scar of Nether Edge. Jay shivered.

'So what will you do now?'

Joe looked at him closely, as if checking for any sign of condemnation. Then he relaxed and gave his old rueful smile, at the same time digging in his pocket to produce a grubby packet of Jelly Babies. He chose one for himself, then held out the packet to Jay.

'I'll do what I've allus done, lad,' he declared. 'I'll bloody well fight for what's mine. I'll not let em get away with it. Pog Hill's mine, an I'll not be moved onto some poxy estate by them or anyone.' He bit off the head of his Jelly Baby with relish and chose another from the packet.

'But what can you do?' protested Jay. 'There'll be eviction orders. They'll cut off your gas and electricity. Can't you—'

Joe looked at him.

'There's allus *somethin* you can do, lad,' he said softly. 'I reckon maybe it's time to find out what really works. Time to bring out sandbags and batten down hatches. Time to fatten up t'black cockerel, like they do in Haiti.' He winked hugely, as if to share a mysterious joke.

Jay glanced around at the allotment. He looked at the charms nailed to the wall and tied onto the tree branches, the signs laid out in broken glass on the ground and chalked onto flower pots and he felt a sudden, terrible hopelessness. It all looked so fragile, so touchingly doomed. He saw the houses then, those blackened, mean little terraces, with their crooked pointing and outside toilets and windows sheeted over with plastic. Washing hanging on a single line five or six houses down. A couple of kids playing in the gutter in front. And Joe – sweet old crazy Joe, with his dreams and his travels and his *chatto* and his millions of seeds and his cellar full of bottles – preparing himself for a war he could never hope to win, armed only with everyday magic and a few quarts of home-brewed wine.

'Don't take on, lad,' urged Joe. 'We'll be reight, you'll see. There's more than one trick up me sleeve, as them buggers from council'll find out.'

But his words sounded hollow. For all his talk it was really just bravado. There was nothing he could do. Of course Jay pretended, for his sake, to believe him. He gathered herbs on the railway embankment. He sewed dried leaves into red sachets. He repeated strange words and made ritual gestures in imitation of his. They had to *seal the perimeter*, as Joe called it, twice a day. This involved walking around the property – up the railway embankment and round the allotment, past Pog Hill box, which Joe counted as his, then into Pog Hill Lane and through the ginnel which linked Joe's house to his neighbour's, past the front door and back over the wall to the other side – carrying a red candle and burning bay leaves steeped in scented oil while they solemnly incanted a string of incomprehensible phrases, which Joe claimed were Latin. From what Joe said, this ritual was supposed to shield the house and its grounds from unwanted influences, deliver protection and affirm his ownership of the territory, and as the holidays came to an end it increased daily in length and complexity, growing from a three-minute dash around the garden to a solemn procession lasting fifteen minutes or more. In other circumstances Jay might have enjoyed these daily ceremonies, but whereas last year there had been an element of mockery in everything Joe said, now the old man had less time for jokes. Jay guessed that behind this screen of unconcern his anxiety was growing. He spoke increasingly about his travels, recounted past adventures and planned future expeditions, announced his immediate decision to leave Pog Hill Lane for his *château* in France, then in the same breath swore he'd never leave his old home unless they carried him out feet first. He worked frantically in the garden. Autumn came early that year and there was fruit to be harvested; jams, wine, preserves, pickles to be made; potatoes and turnips to be dug and stored, as well as the increasing demands of Joe's magical barrier, which now took thirty minutes to complete and involved much gesticulating and scattering of powders, as well as preparation of scented oils and herbal mixtures. There was a haunted look to Joe now, a *stretched* look to his features, a glittery brightness in his eyes, which came of sleeplessness – or drink. For he was drinking far more now than he had ever done, not just wine or nettle beer but spirits, too, the potato vodka from the pot-still in the cellar, last year's liqueurs from his downstairs store. Jay wondered whether, at this pace, Joe would survive the winter at all.

'I'll be reight,' Joe told him when he voiced his concern. 'It just needs a bit more work, that's all. Come winter I'll be reight again, I promise.' He stood up, hands in the small of his back, and stretched. 'That's better.' He grinned then, and for a moment he was almost the old Joe, eyes brimming with laughter under his greasy pit cap. 'I've looked after mesself for a few years before you came along, lad. It'd take a sight more than a few council monkeys to get the better of me.' And he immediately launched into a long, absurd story from his travelling days about a man trying to sell cheap trinkets to a tribe of Amazonian Indians.

'And the chief of the tribe – Chief Mungawomba, his name were – handed back the stuff and said – I'd been teachin him English in me free time – "Tha can keep thi beads, mate, but I'd be really grateful if tha could fix me toaster." '

They both laughed, and for a time the unease was forgotten, or at least dismissed. Jay wanted to believe Pog Hill was safe. On some days he looked at the arcane jumble of the allotment and the back garden and he almost did believe it. Joe seemed so sure, so permanent. Surely he would be there for ever.

17

Lansquenet, March 1999

HE STOOD BESIDE THE ROADSIDE FOR A MOMENT, DISMAYED AND disoriented. By then it was almost dark; the sky had reached that luminous shade of deep blue which just precedes full night, and the horizon beyond the house was striated with pale lemon and green and pink. The beauty of it — *his* property, he told himself again, with that breathless, unreal feeling inside — left him feeling a little shaken. In spite of his predicament he could not shrug off a sensation of excitement, as if this, too, were somehow meant to happen.

No-one — *no-one*, he told himself — knew where he was.

The wine bottles rattled against each other as he picked up the duffel bag from the side of the road. A scent — of summer, of wild spinach or shale dust and stagnant water — rose briefly from the damp ground. Something fluttering from the branch of a flowering hawthorn tree caught his eye and he picked at it automatically, bringing it closer towards him.

It was a piece of red flannel.

In the bag the bottles began to rattle and froth. Their voices rose in a whispering, crackling, sighing, chuckling of hidden consonants and secret vowels. Jay felt a sudden breeze tug at his clothing, a murmur of something, a throbbing deep in the soft air, like a heart. 'Home is where the heart is.' One of Joe's favourite sayings. 'Where the art is.'

Jay looked back at the road. It was not really so late. Not too late, in any case, to find somewhere to stay the night and to buy a meal. The village – a few lights now, winking over the river, the distant sound of music from across the fields – must be less than half an hour's walk away. He could leave his case here, safely hidden in the roadside bushes, and take only his bag. For some reason – inside the bottles joltered and chuckled – he felt reluctant to leave the duffel bag. But the house drew him. Ridiculous, he told himself. He had already seen that the house was un-inhabitable, at least for the moment. *Looked uninhabitable*, he amended, recalling Pog Hill Lane, the derelict gardens and boarded-up windows and the secret, gleeful life behind. What if, maybe, just behind the door . . .

Funny how his mind kept returning to that thought. There was no logic in it and yet it was slyly persuasive. That abandoned vegetable patch, the scrap of red flannel, that feeling, that certainty, that there really was someone *inside* the house.

Inside the duffel bag the carnival had begun again. Catcalls, laughter, distant fanfare. It sounded like coming home. Even I could feel it – I, grown in vineyards far from here, in Burgundy, where the air is brighter and the earth richer, kinder. It was the sound of home fires and doors opening and the smell of bread baking and clean sheets and warm, friendly unwashed bodies. Jay felt it, too, but assumed it came from the house; almost without thinking he took another step towards the darkened building. It would not hurt to have another look, he told himself. Just to be sure.

18

Pog Hill, Summer 1977

SEPTEMBER CAME. JAY WENT BACK TO SCHOOL WITH A SENSE OF finality, a feeling that something at Pog Hill had changed. If it had, then Joe's short, infrequent letters gave no sign. There was a card at Christmas – two lines, carefully inscribed with the round printing of the barely literate – then another at Easter. The terms crawled to an end as usual. Jay's fifteenth birthday came and went – a cricket bat from his father and Candide, theatre tickets from his mother. After that came exams; dorm parties; secrets told and promises broken; a couple of hot-weather fights; a school play, *A Midsummer Night's Dream*, with all the parts played by boys, as in Shakespeare's time. Jay played Puck, much to the chagrin of the Bread Baron, but all the time he was thinking of Joe and Pog Hill, and as the end of the summer term approached, he grew jumpy and irritable and impatient. This year his mother had decided to join him in Kirby Monckton for a few weeks, ostensibly to spend more time with her son, but in reality to escape the media attention following her most recent amorous break-up. Jay wasn't looking forward to being the focus of her sudden maternal interest, and said so clearly enough to provoke an outburst of outraged histrionics. He was in disgrace before the holidays had even started.

They arrived in late June, by taxi, in the rain. Jay's mother was doing her *Mater Dolorosa* act, and he was trying to listen to the radio as she passed between long, soulful silences and girlish exclamations on seeing forgotten landmarks.

'Jay, darling, look! That little church – isn't it just the *sweetest*?' He put it down to her being in so many sitcoms, but maybe she had always talked like that. Jay turned the radio up a fraction. The Eagles were playing 'Hotel California'. She gave him one of her pained looks and thinned her mouth. Jay ignored her.

The rain came down non-stop for the first week of the holiday. Jay stayed in the house and watched it and listened to the radio, trying to tell himself it couldn't last for ever. The sky was white and portentous. Looking up into the clouds, the falling raindrops looked like soot. His grandparents fussed over both of them, treating his mother like the little girl she had been, cooking all her favourite meals. For five days they lived on apple pie, ice cream, fried fish and scollops. On the sixth day Jay took his bike down to Pog Hill, in spite of the weather, but Joe's door was locked and there was no answer to his knocking. Jay left his bike by the back wall and climbed over into the garden, hoping to look in through the windows.

The windows were boarded up.

Panic washed over him. He hammered on one of the sealed windows with his fist.

'Hey, Joe? Joe?'

There was no answer. He hammered again, calling Joe's name. A piece of red flannel, bleached by the elements, was nailed to the window frame, but it looked old, finished, last year's magic. Behind the house a screen of tall weeds – hemlock and wormwood and rosebay willowherb – hid the abandoned allotment.

Jay sat down on the wall, regardless of the rain which glued his T-shirt to his skin and dripped from his hair into his eyes. He felt completely numb. How could Joe have gone, he asked himself stupidly. Why hadn't he said something? Written a note, even? How could Joe have gone without him?

'Don't take on, lad,' called a voice behind him. 'It's not as bad as it looks.'

Jay whipped round so fast he almost fell off the wall. Joe was standing some twenty feet behind him, almost hidden from sight behind the tall weeds. He was wearing a yellow sou'wester on top of his pit cap. He had a spade in one hand.

'Joe?'

The old man grinned.

'Aye. What d'you think, then?'

Jay was beyond words.

'It's me permanent solution,' explained Joe, looking pleased. 'They've cut off me lectrics, but I've wired mesself up to bypass the meter, so I can still use em. I've bin diggin a well round back so I can do waterin. Come over and tell me what you think.'

As always, Joe behaved as if no time had passed, as if Jay had never been away. He parted the weeds which separated them and motioned the boy to follow him through. Beyond, the allotment was as ordered as it had always been, with lemonade bottles sheltering small plants, old windows arranged to make cold frames, and tyres stacked up for potato-planters. From a distance the whole thing might just have been the accumulated detritus of years, but come a little closer and everything was there, just as before. On the railway banking, fruit trees – some shielded with sheets of plastic – dripped rain. It was the best camouflage job Jay had ever seen.

'It's amazing,' he said at last. 'I really thought you'd gone.'

Joe looked pleased.

'You're not the only one that thinks that, lad,' he said mysteriously. 'Look down there.'

Jay looked down into the cutting. The signal box which had been Joe's greenhouse was still standing, though in a state of dereliction; vines grew out of the punctured roof and tumbled down the peeling sides. The lines had been taken up and the sleepers dug out – all but the fifty-yard stretch between the box and Joe's house, as if overlooked by some accident. Between the rust-red tracks weeds were sprouting.

'Come next year no-one'll even remember there were a railway down Pog Hill. Praps people'll let us alone then.'

Jay nodded slowly, still speechless with amazement and relief.

'Perhaps they will.'

19

Lansquenet, March 1999

THE AIR SMELT OF NIGHTFALL, BITTER-SMOKY, LIKE LAPSANG TEA, mild enough to sleep outside. The vineyard on the left was filled with noises: birds, frogs, insects. Jay could still see the path at his feet, faintly silvered with the last of the sunset, but the sun had left the face of the house and it was lightless, almost forbidding. He began to wonder whether he should have postponed his visit till the morning.

The thought of the long walk to the village dissuaded him. He was wearing boots, which had seemed like a good enough idea when he left London, but which now, after so many hours of travelling, had grown tight and uncomfortable. If he could only get into the house – from what he'd seen of security that wouldn't be difficult – he could sleep there and make his way to the village in daylight.

It wasn't as if he were trespassing, really. After all, the house was nearly his. He reached the vegetable patch. Something on the side of the house – a shutter, perhaps – was flapping rhythmically against the plaster, making a nagging, mournful sound. On the far side of the building shadows moved under the trees, creating the illusion of a man standing there, a bent figure in cap and overcoat. Something whipped across his path with a snapping noise

– a prickly artichoke stem, still topped with last year's flower, now desiccated almost to nothing. Beyond it, the overgrown remnants of the vegetable patch swayed briskly in the freshening wind. Halfway across the abandoned garden something fluttered, as if snagged on a stiff piece of briar. A scrap of cloth. From where Jay was standing he could see nothing more, but he knew immediately what it was. Flannel. Red. Dropping his bag by the side of the path he strode into the drift of weeds which had been the vegetable garden, pushing aside the long stems as he passed. It was a sign. It had to be.

Just as he stepped forward to take hold of the piece of flannel something crunched briefly under his left foot and gave way with an angry clatter of metal, punching through the soft leather of his boot and into his ankle. Jay's feet gave way, tipping him backwards into the greenery, and the pain, bad enough at first, bloomed sickeningly. Swearing, he grabbed at the object in the dim light, and his fingers encountered something jagged and metallic attached to his foot.

A trap, he thought, bewildered. Some sort of trap.

It hurt to think straight, and for precious seconds Jay yanked mindlessly at the object as it bit deeper through his boot. His fingers felt slick on the metal, and he realized he was bleeding. He began to panic.

With an effort he forced himself to stop moving. If it was a trap, then it would have to be forced open. Paranoid to imagine someone had set it deliberately. It must have been someone trying to catch rabbits, perhaps, or foxes, or something.

For a moment anger dulled the pain. The irresponsibility, the criminal carelessness of placing animal traps so close to someone's house – to *his* house. Jay fumbled with the trap. It felt ancient, primitive. It was a clam-shell design, fixed into the ground by a metal peg. There was a catch at the side. Jay cursed and struggled with the mechanism, feeling the teeth of the trap crunching deeper into his ankle with every move he made. Finally he managed the catch, but it took several tries to push open the metal jaws, and when he finally got it clear he pulled himself back, awkwardly, and tried to assess the damage. His foot had already swollen tight against the leather, so that the boot would be difficult or impossible to remove in the normal way.

Trying not to think about the types of bacteria which might even now be working their way into him, he pushed himself upright and managed to hop clumsily back to the path, where he sat down on the stones to try to remove his boot.

It took him nearly ten minutes. By the time he had finished he was sweating. It was too dark to see very much, but even so he could tell it would be some time before he dared to try walking.

20

Pog Hill, Summer 1977

JOE'S NEW DEFENCES WERE NOT THE ONLY CHANGE AT POG HILL that year. Nether Edge had visitors. Jay still went to the Edge every couple of days, attracted by its promise of gentle dereliction, of things left to rot in peace. Even at the peak of that summer he never abandoned his favourite haunts; he still visited the canal side and the ash pit and the dump, partly to look for useful things for Joe and partly because the place still fascinated him. It must have attracted the gypsies, too, because one day there they were, a shabby foursome of caravans, squared together like pioneers' wagons against the enemy. The caravans were grey and rusting, axles sagging under the weight of accumulated baggage, doors hanging by a string, windows whitening with age. The people were equally disappointing. Six adults and as many children, clad in jeans or overalls or cheap bright market-stall nylons, they gave off an air of distant grubbiness, a visual extension of the smells which floated from their camp, the permanent odour of frying grease and dirty laundry and petrol and garbage.

Jay had never seen gypsies before. This drab, prosaic group was not what his reading had prepared him to expect. He had imagined horse-drawn wagons with outlandishly decorated sides, dark-haired dangerous girls with daggers in their belts, blind crones with the gift of far seeing. Certainly Joe's experiences with gypsies seemed to confirm this, and as Jay watched the caravans from his vantage point above the lock he felt annoyed at their intrusion. These seemed to be ordinary people, and until Joe confirmed their exotic lineage Jay was inclined to think they were nothing but tourists, campers from the south walking the moors.

'No, lad,' Joe said as he pointed out the distant camp, a pale string of smoke rising from a tin chimney into the sky of Nether Edge. 'They're not trippers. They're gypsies all right. Mebbe not proper Romanies, but gyppos, you might call em. Travellers. Like I was once.' He squinted curiously through cigarette smoke at the camp. 'Reckon they'll stay the winter,' he said. 'Move on when spring comes. No-one'll bother em downt Edge. No-one ever goes there any more.'

Not strictly true, of course. Jay considered Nether Edge his territory, and for a few days he watched the gypsies with all the resentment he had felt against Zeth and his gang that first year. He rarely saw much movement from the caravans, though sometimes there was washing strung out on nearby trees. A dog tethered to the nearest of the vehicles yapped shrilly and intermittently. Once or twice he saw a woman carry water in large canisters to her vehicle. The water came from a kind of spigot, set into the square of concrete by the dirt track. There was a similar dispenser on the other side of the camp.

'Set it up years back,' explained Joe. 'Gypsy camp, with water an lectricity laid on. There's a pay meter down there that they use, an a septic tank. Even rubbish gets collected once a week. You'd think more people'd use it, but they don't. Funny folk, gypsies.'

The last time Joe remembered gypsies on the waste ground was about ten years previously.

'Romanies, they were,' he said. 'You don't get many proper Romanies nowadays. Used to buy their fruit and

98

veg from me. There wasn't many that'd sell to em in them days. Said they were no better than beggars.' He grinned. 'Well, I'm not sayin everythin they did was dead-straight honest, but you've got to get by when you're on the road. They worked a way to beat the meter. It took fifty pences, see? Well, they used water and lectricity all summer, but when they'd gone and council came round to empty the meter, all there was at bottom was a pool of water. They never did find out how they'd done it. Lock hadn't been touched. Nothin seemed to have bin interfered with at all.'

Jay looked at Joe with interest.

'So how did they do it?' he enquired curiously.

Joe grinned again and tapped the side of his nose.

'*Alchemy*,' he whispered, to Jay's annoyance, and would say no more on the subject.

Joe's tales had renewed his interest in the gypsies. Jay watched the camp for several days after that, but saw no evidence of secret goings-on. Eventually he abandoned his lookout post at the lock to hunt more interesting game, searching for comics and magazines from the dump, combing the railway for its everyday leavings. He worked out a good way of getting free coal for Joe's kitchen stove. There were two coal trains a day, rumbling slowly along the line from Kirby Main. Twenty-four trucks on each, with a man sitting on the last one to make sure no-one tried to climb onto the wagons. There had been accidents in the past, Joe said; kids who'd dared each other to jump onto the trains.

'They might look slow,' he said darkly, 'but every one of them trucks is a forty-tonner. Never try to get up on one, lad.'

Jay never did. Instead he found a better way, and Joe's stove lived on it all through that summer into autumn, when they finally closed down the line altogether.

Every day, twice a day, just before the arrival of the train, Jay would line up a row of old tin cans on the side of the railway bridge. He arranged them in pyramids, like coconuts at a shy, for maximum appeal. The bored workman on the last truck could never resist the challenge they presented. Every time the train passed by he would lob chunks of coal at the cans, trying to knock them off the bridge, and Jay could always count on at least half-a-dozen good-sized pieces of coal each time. He stored these in an empty three-gallon paint tin, hidden in the bushes, and every few days, when this was full, he delivered the coal to Joe's house. It was on one of these occasions, when he was fooling about by the railway bridge, that he heard the sound of gunfire from Nether Edge and froze, the coalbox dropping from his hand.

Zeth was back.

21

Lansquenet, March 1999

JAY PULLED A HANDKERCHIEF OUT OF HIS DUFFEL BAG AND USED it to staunch the blood, beginning to feel cold now and wishing he'd brought his Burberry. He also took out one of the sandwiches he had bought at the station earlier that day and forced himself to eat. It tasted foul, but the sickness receded a little and he thought he felt a little warmer. It was almost night. A sliver of moon was rising, just enough to cast shadows, and in spite of the pain in his foot he looked around curiously. He glanced at his watch, almost expecting to see the luminous dial of the Seiko he got for Christmas when he was fourteen, the one Zeth broke during that last, most dreadful week of August. But the Rolex was not luminous. *Trop* tacky, *mon cher*. Kerry always went for class.

In the shadows at the corner of the building something moved. He called out, 'Hey!' hoisting himself up onto his good leg and limping towards the house. 'Hey! Please! Wait! Is anyone there?'

Something smacked against the side of the building with the same flat sound he heard before. A shutter, perhaps. He thought he saw it outlined against the purple-black sky, flapping loosely in the breeze. He shivered. No-one there after all. If only he could get into the house, out of the cold.

The window was about three feet from the ground. There was a deep ledge inside, half blocked with debris, but he found that he could clear enough space to push through. The air smelt of paint. He moved carefully, feeling for broken glass, swinging his leg over the ledge and into the room, pulling the duffel bag in behind him. His eyes had become accustomed to the dark and he could see that the room was mostly clear, except for a table and a chair in the centre and a pile of something – sacks, maybe – in one corner. Using the chair for support, Jay moved over to the pile and found a sleeping bag and a pillow rolled snugly against the wall, along with a cardboard box which contained paint tins and a bundle of wax candles.

Candles? What the hell . . . ?

He reached into his jeans pocket for a lighter. It was only a cheap Bic, and almost out of fuel, but he managed to strike a flame. The candles were dry. The wick spluttered, then flared. The room was mellowly illumined.

'That's something, I suppose.'

He could sleep here. The room was sheltered. There were blankets and bedclothes and the remains of that lunch-time's sandwiches. For a moment the pain in his foot was forgotten, and he grinned at the thought that this was home. It deserved a celebration.

Rummaging through the duffel bag, he pulled out one of Joe's bottles, and cut open the seal and the green cord with the tip of his penknife. The clear scent of elderflower filled the air. He drank a little, tasting that familiar, cloying flavour, like fruit left to rot in the dark. Definitely a vintage year, he told himself, and despite everything he began to laugh shakily. He drank a little more. In spite of the taste the wine was warming, musky; he sat down on the rolled-up bedding, took another mouthful and began to feel a little better.

He reached into his bag again and took out the radio. He

turned it on, half expecting the white noise he had heard on the train all the way from Marseilles, but surprisingly the signal was clear. Not the oldies station, of course, but some kind of local French radio, a low warble of music, something he didn't recognize. Jay laughed again, feeling suddenly light-headed.

Inside the duffel bag the four remaining Specials began their chorus again, a ferment of yahoos and catcalls and war cries, redoubling in frenzy until the pitch was wild, feverish, a vulgar champagne of sounds and impressions and voices and memories, all shaken into a delirious cocktail of triumph. It pulled me along, dragging me with it, so that, for a moment, I was no longer myself – Fleurie, a respectable vintage with just a hint of blackcurrant – but a cauldron of spices, frothing and seething and going to the head in a wild flush of heat. Something was getting ready to happen. I knew it. Then, suddenly, silence.

Jay looked around curiously. For a moment he shivered, as if a sudden breeze had touched him, a breeze from other places. The paint on the wall was fresh, he noticed; beside the box containing paint cans was a tray of paintbrushes, washed and neatly aligned. The brushes were not yet dry. The breeze was sharper now, smelling of smoke and the circus, hot sugar and apples and midsummer's eve. The radio crackled softly.

'Well, lad,' said a voice from the shadows. 'You took yer time.' Jay turned round so fast that he almost overbalanced.

'Steady on,' said Joe kindly.

'Joe?'

He had not changed. He was wearing his old cap, a Thin Lizzy T-shirt, his work trousers and pit boots. In one hand he held two wineglasses. In front of him, on the table, stood the bottle of Elderflower '76.

'I allus said you'd get used to it one day,' he remarked with satisfaction. 'Elderflower champagne. Gotta bittova kick, though, annit?'

'Joe?'

A flare of joy went through him, so strong that it made the bottles shake. It all made sense now, he thought deliriously; it was all coming together. The signs, the memories – all for this – all finally making sense.

Then the realization slammed him back, like awakening from a dream in which everything seems on the brink of being explained, but falls away into fragments with the light.

Of course it wasn't possible. Joe must be over eighty years old by now. That is, if he was alive at all. Joe left, he told himself fiercely, like a thief in the night, leaving nothing behind but questions.

Jay looked at the old man in the candlelight, his bright eyes and the laugh-wrinkles beneath them, and for the first time he noticed that everything about him was somehow *gilded* – even the toes of his pit boots – with an eerie glow, like nostalgia.

'You're not real, are you?' he said.

Joe shrugged.

'What's real?' he asked carelessly. 'No such thing, lad.'

'Real, as in the sense of really *here*.'

Joe watched him patiently, like a teacher with a slow pupil. Jay's voice rose almost angrily.

'Real, as in corporeally present. As in *not* a figment of my deluded wine-soaked imagination, or an early symptom of blood-poisoning or an out-of-body experience while the real me sits in a white room somewhere wearing one of those coats with no arms.'

Joe looked at him mildly.

'So, you grew up to be a writer, then,' he remarked. 'Allus said you were a clever lad. Write any gooduns, did yer? Make any brass?'

'Plenty of brass, but only one good one. Too long ago. Shit, I can't believe I'm actually sitting here talking to myself.'

'Only one, eh?'

Jay shivered again. The cold night wind sliced thinly

through the half-open shutter, bringing with it that feverish draught of other places.

'I must really be sick,' said Jay softly to himself. 'Toxic shock, or something, from that sodding trap. I'm delirious.'

Joe shook his head. 'Tha'll be reight, lad.' Joe always used to slip into dialect when he was being satirical. 'It were only a bit of a fox trap. Old feller used to live here kept hens. Foxes were allus in an out at night. He even used to mark where traps were with a bit o rag.' Jay looked at the piece of flannel in his hand.

'I thought . . .'

'I *know* what yer thought.' Joe's eyes were bright with amusement. 'You were allus same, jumpin in half cocked before you knew what were goin on. Allus askin questions. Allus needin to know summat an nowt.' He held out one of the wineglasses, now filled with the yellow elderflower wine. 'Get this down thi,' he suggested kindly. 'Do yer good. I'd tell yer to go out back an get yersen some bishop's leaves, but planets are all wrong for pickin.'

Jay looked at him. For a hallucination, he seemed very real. There was garden dirt under his fingernails and in the cracks in his palms.

'I'm sick,' whispered Jay softly. 'You left that summer. Never even said goodbye. You're not here now. I know that.'

Joe shook his head. 'Aye,' he said kindly. 'We'll talk about that another time, when you're feelin more yerself.'

'When I'm feeling more myself, you won't be there.'

Joe laughed and lit a cigarette. The scent was pungent in the cold air. Jay noticed, with no surprise, that it came from an old packet of Player's Number 6.

'Want one?' asked Joe, handing him the packet.

For a moment the cigarette felt almost real in Jay's hand. He took a drag, but the smoke smelt of the canal and bonfires burning. He flicked the butt against the concrete floor and watched the sparks fly. He felt slightly dizzy.

'Why don't you lie down for a while?' suggested Joe.

'There's a sleeping bag and some blankets – pretty clean anall. You look all-out knackered.'

Jay looked doubtfully at the pile of blankets. He felt exhausted. His head ached and his foot hurt and he was beyond confusion. He knew he should be worried. But for the moment he seemed to have lost the ability to question. He lay down painfully on the makeshift bed and pulled the sleeping bag over himself. It was warm, clean, comforting. He wondered fleetingly whether this might be a hallucination brought on by hypothermia, some sick adult version of *The Little Match Girl*, and laughed softly to himself. The Jackapple Man. Pretty funny, hey? They'd find him in the morning with a red rag in one hand and an empty bottle of wine in the other, frozen and smiling.

'Tha's not goin to *dee*,' said Joe in amused tones.

'Old writers never do,' muttered Jay. 'They just lose their marbles.' He laughed again, rather wildly. The candle guttered and went out, though Jay's mind still insisted he saw the old man *blow* it out. Without it the room was very dark. A single bar of moonlight touched the stone floor. Outside the window a bird loosed a brief, heart-rending warble of music. In the distance, something – cat, owl – screamed. He lay in the dark, listening for a while. The night was full of noises. Then came a sound from outside the window, like footsteps, and he froze.

'Joe?'

But the old man was gone – if he had ever been there. The sound came again, softly, furtively. It must be an animal, Jay told himself. A dog, maybe, or a fox. He got up and moved towards the shuttered window.

A figure was standing behind the shutter.

'*Jesus!*' He took a step backward and his injured ankle gave way, almost spilling him onto the floor. The figure was tall, its bulk exaggerated by the heavy overcoat and cap. He had a brief glimpse of blurry features beneath the cap's peak, of hair spilling out over the collar, of angry eyes in a pale face. A flash of almost recognition. Then the moment passed and the woman looking at him from outside the shutter was a complete stranger.

'What the hell are you doing here?' He spoke English automatically, not expecting her to understand. After that night's events he wasn't even certain she was real at all. 'And who are you, anyway?'

The woman looked at him. The old shotgun in her hand was not quite pointing at him, but by a tiny movement could be made to do so.

'You are trespassing.' Her English was strongly accented but good. 'This house is not abandoned. It is private property.'

'I know. I—' This woman must be some kind of caretaker, Jay told himself. Perhaps she was paid to ensure no damage was done to the building. Her presence explained the mysterious sounds, the candles, the sleeping bag, the smell of fresh paint. The rest – the unexpected appearance of Joe, for instance – had been his imagination. He smiled at the woman in relief.

'I'm sorry I shouted at you. I didn't understand. I'm Jay Mackintosh. The agency may have mentioned me.'

She looked at him blankly. Her eyes flicked momentarily behind him, taking in the typewriter, the bottles, the luggage.

'Agency?'

'Yes. I'm the man who bought the house. Over the phone. The day before yesterday.' He gave a short, nervous laugh. 'On an impulse. The first I've ever had. I couldn't wait for the paperwork. I wanted to see it straight away.' He laughed again, but there was no returning smile in her eyes.

'You say you *bought* the house?'

He nodded. 'I wanted to come over and see it. I couldn't get the keys. Somehow I managed to get stranded here. I hurt my ankle—'

'That is impossible.' Her voice was flat. 'I would have been told if there had been another buyer.'

'I don't think they were expecting me so soon. Look, it's

perfectly simple really. I'm sorry if I startled you. I'm actually very glad you're looking after the building.'

The woman looked at him oddly but said nothing.

'I can see they've been doing the place up a little. I noticed the paint pots. Did you do it yourself?'

She nodded, her eyes lightless. Behind her the sky was hazy, troubled. Jay found her silence disconcerting. Clearly his story hadn't convinced her.

'Do you . . . I mean, is there a lot of that kind of work hereabouts? Caretaking, I mean. Renovating old properties.'

She shrugged. The gesture might mean anything. Jay had no idea what it was supposed to convey.

'Jay Mackintosh.' He smiled again. 'I'm a writer.'

That look again. Her eyes flicked over him in contempt or curiosity.

'Marise d'Api. I work the vineyard across the fields.'

'Pleased to meet you.' Either shaking hands wasn't a local custom, or her refusal was a deliberate insult.

Not a caretaker, then, Jay told himself. He should have known it at once. That arrogance in her face, that harshness, proved it. This was a woman who tended her own farm, her vines. She was as stony as her land.

'I suppose we'll be neighbours.'

Again, no answer. Her face was a blind. No way to tell whether, beneath it, lay amusement, anger or simple indifference. She turned away. For a second her face, turning towards the moonlight, was silvered with light, and he saw that she was young – no older than twenty-eight or -nine – her features sharp and elfin beneath the big hat. Then she was gone, curiously graceful in spite of her bulky overclothes, her boots kicking a swathe through the damp weeds.

'Hey! Wait!' Too late Jay realized that this woman could help him. She would have food, hot water, antiseptic, perhaps, for his injured ankle. 'Wait a minute! Madame d'Api! Perhaps you could help me!'

If she heard him she did not reply. For a moment he thought he saw her, outlined briefly against the sky. The sound in the undergrowth might have been that of her passage, or something else altogether.

When he realized she was not coming back Jay returned to his makeshift bed in the corner of the room and lit a candle. The almost-empty bottle of Joe's wine was standing by the bedside, though Jay was certain he had left it on the table. He must have moved it himself, he thought, during his fugue. It was understandable. He'd had a shock. By the light of the candle he peeled away his sock to examine the damage to his ankle. It was an ugly slash, the flesh around it bruised and swelling. Bishop's leaves, the old man had said, and in spite of himself Jay smiled. Bishop's leaves – the Yorkshire name for water betony – had been a common ingredient for Joe's protection sachets.

But for now the only available antiseptic was the wine. Jay tilted the bottle and poured a thin stream of yellow liquid onto the gash. It stung for a minute, releasing its scent of summer and spice, and though he knew it was absurd, such was the power of that scent that Jay felt a little better.

The radio gave a sudden crackle of music and fell silent.

A breeze of other places – a scent of apples, a lullaby of passing trains and distant machinery and the radio playing. Funny how his mind kept going back to that song, that winter song, 'Bohemian Rhapsody'.

Jay slept, a piece of red flannel still curled tightly in his palm.

But the wine – raspberry red, blackberry blue, rosehip yellow, damson black – stayed awake. Talking.

22

Nether Edge, Summer 1977

ZETH HADN'T CHANGED. JAY WOULD HAVE RECOGNIZED HIM
instantly, even without the rifle crooked into his arm,
though in a year he seemed to have grown much taller, his
long hair tied back now in a thin pigtail. He was wearing
a denim jacket, with GRATEFUL DEAD written across the
back in biro, and engineer's boots. From his hiding place
above the canal Jay could not tell if he was alone or not.
As he watched, Zeth raised his rifle and took aim at
something just beyond the towpath. Some ducks which
had been sitting by the water sprayed upwards, their
wings going like clapperboards. Zeth yelled and fired
again. The ducks went crazy. Jay stayed where he was.
If Zeth wanted to shoot ducks, he thought, that was his
business. He wasn't going to interfere. But as he watched
he began to have his doubts. Zeth seemed to be firing not
at the canal, but somewhere beyond. Past the trees and
towards the river, though the terrain there was far too
open for birds. Rabbits, maybe, thought Jay, though with
the noise he was making, surely any animal would have
already fled. He narrowed his eyes against the lowering
sun, trying to make out what Zeth was doing. The bigger
boy fired again, twice, and reloaded. Jay realized he was

standing in almost exactly the same place he himself usually hid to watch . . .

The gypsies.

Zeth must have been firing at the washing line strung between the nearest two caravans, for one end already trailed limply into the grass, like a bird's broken wing, flapping half-heartedly in the wind. The dog, tethered in its usual place, set up a strident barking. Jay thought he caught sight of something moving at the window of one of the caravans, a curtain pulled aside briefly and a face, pale, blurry, eyes wide in anger or dismay before the curtain was yanked back in place. There was no further movement from the caravans, and Zeth laughed again and began to reload. Now Jay could hear what he was shouting.

'Gypp-o-oh! Gypp-o-oh!'

Well, Jay told himself, there was nothing he could do. Even Zeth wouldn't be crazy enough to actually hurt anyone. Firing at a washing line, that was his style. Trying to frighten people. Making a fair job of it, too, he imagined. He thought of himself that first summer, crouching under the lock, and felt heat creep into his face.

Dammit, there was nothing he could do.

The gypsies were safe enough in their caravan. They'd wait it out until Zeth got tired or ran out of ammunition. He had to go home sometime. Besides, it was only an air rifle. You couldn't do any *real* damage with an air rifle. Not really. Even if you hit a person.

I mean, what was he supposed to *do*, anyway?

Jay turned to go and let out a yelp of surprise. There was a girl crouching in the bushes not five feet behind him. He had been so absorbed watching Zeth that he hadn't heard her approach. She looked about twelve. Under a bramble of red curls her face was small and blotchy, as if her freckles had been stretched out of shape in an attempt to save on skin. She was wearing jeans and a white T-shirt so large that the sleeves flapped around her thin arms. In one hand she was carrying a grubby red bandanna, which looked to be filled with stones.

The girl was on her feet as quickly and silently as an Apache. Jay barely had time to react to her presence before she sent a stone whizzing through the air with incredible speed and accuracy to strike against his kneecap with an audible, agonizing crack. He gave another yell and fell over, clutching at his knee. The girl looked at him, a second stone ready in her hand.

'Hey,' protested Jay.

'Sorry,' said the girl, without putting down the stone.

Jay rolled up the leg of his jeans to inspect the injured knee. A bruise was already rising. He glared at the girl, who returned his gaze with a flat, unrepentant look.

'You shouldn't have turned round like that,' said the girl. 'You took me by surprise.'

'Took *you* . . . !' Jay struggled for speech.

The girl shrugged. 'I thought you was with him,' she said, jerking her small chin fiercely in the direction of the lock. 'Using our caravan and poor old Toffee as target practice.' Jay rolled back his trouser leg.

'*Him!* He's no friend of mine,' he said indignantly. 'He's crazy.'

'Oh. OK.'

The girl returned the stone to the bandanna. Another two rifle shots sounded, followed by Zeth's ululating war cry, '*Gypp-o-oh!*' The girl peered down warily through the bushes, then lifted a branch and prepared to slide underneath and down the banking.

'Hey, wait a minute.'

'What?'

The girl barely glanced back. In the shadow of the bush her eyes were golden, like an owl's.

'What are you doing?'

'What do you think?'

'But I told you already.' Jay's anger at her unprovoked attack had been replaced by alarm. 'He's crazy. You don't want to have anything to do with him. He'll get tired soon enough. He'll leave you alone when that happens.'

The girl stared at him with undisguised contempt. 'Spect that's what *you'd* do?' she demanded.

'Well . . . yes.'

She made a sound which might have been amusement or scorn, and passed effortlessly under the branch, steadying herself with her free hand as she slid down the banking, braking with her heels when she reached the scree. Jay could see where she was heading. Fifty yards down the slope there was a cutaway, which opened out right over the lock. Red shale and loose stones smattered the banking where the hill had been opened. A screen of thin bushes provided cover. A tricky place to reach – if approached fast or carelessly you could ride the scree right off the edge onto the stones below – but it would provide her with a good place to launch her attack. If that was what she was planning. It was hard to believe that she was. Jay peered down the banking again and caught sight of her, much further down now, barely visible in the undergrowth except for her hair. Let her do it if she wanted, he told himself. It wasn't as if he hadn't warned her.

None of this really had anything to do with him.

It was none of his business.

Sighing, he picked up the coalbox with its three-day load and began to scramble down the rocky path behind the girl.

He took the other path to the ash pit, shielded from view most of the way by bushes. In any case, he thought, Zeth wasn't looking. He was too busy shooting and yelling. Easy enough, then, to get across the open expanse of the ash pit and under the concealed lip beyond. It wasn't as good a hiding place as the girl's, but it would have to do, and with two of them against one even Zeth might have to concede defeat. If it *was* two against one. Jay tried not to think about any friends Zeth might have in the area, maybe just within shouting distance.

He put down the can of coal chunks and settled himself close to the edge of the ash pit. Zeth sounded very close now; Jay could hear his breathing and the snicking sound

113

of his rifle as he broke it to reload. Glancing swiftly over the edge of the ash pit he could see him, too, the back of his head and a slice of profile, his neck glaring with acne, his flag of greasy hair. Above the lock there was no sign of the girl, and he wondered, in sudden anxiety, whether she had gone. Then he saw a flicker of something red above the cutting and a stone zipped out of the bushes, hitting Zeth on the arm. Jay knew a moment's amazement at the accuracy of the girl's aim before Zeth swung round with a roar of pain and surprise. Another stone hit him in the solar plexus, and as he whipped round towards the cutting Jay threw two chunks of coal at his back. One hit, the other missed, but Jay felt a hot rush of exhilaration as he ducked down again.

'*Kill you, you fucker!*' Zeth's voice sounded both very close and horrifyingly adult, a teenage troll in disguise. Then the girl fired again, hitting him on the ankle, missing once, then scoring a direct hit on the side of his head, making a sound like a pool cue potting the ball.

'*You leave us alone, then!*' yelled the girl from her eyrie above the lock. '*Bloody well leave us alone, you bastard!*'

Now Zeth had seen her. Jay saw him move a little closer to the cutting, his rifle in his hand. He could see what Zeth was doing. He would try to move *under* the overhang and out of sight, reload, then jump out firing. He'd be firing blind, but all the same. Jay looked over the edge of the ash pit and took aim. He hit Zeth between the shoulder blades as hard as he could.

'Get lost!' he shouted deliriously, firing another coal chunk over the lip of the pit. 'Go pick on someone else!'

But it had been a mistake to show himself so openly. Jay saw Zeth's eyes widen in recognition.

'Well, well, well.' Zeth had changed after all. He'd broadened out, his shoulders fulfilling the promise of his height. He looked fully adult to Jay now, fully grown and ferocious. He smiled and began to move closer to the ash pit, rifle levelled. He kept under the overhang now, so that the girl could not target him. He was grinning. Jay threw another two pieces of coal, but his aim was off target and Zeth kept on coming.

'Get away!'

'Or what?' Zeth was close enough to see clearly into the ash pit now, with one eye on the overhang which shielded him. His grin looked like a bone sickle. He levelled his rifle with a quizzical, almost a gentle smile. 'Or *what*, eh? Or *what*?' Desperately Jay lobbed the remaining chunks of coal at him, but his aim was gone. They bounced off the bigger boy's shoulders like bullets off a tank. Jay looked into the barrel of Zeth's rifle. It was only an air rifle, his mind repeated, only an air rifle, only a poxy pellet gun. It's not as if it were a Colt or a Luger or anything, and anyway, he wouldn't dare shoot.

Zeth's finger tightened on the trigger. There was a click. At this range the gun didn't look poxy at all. It looked deadly.

Suddenly there was a sound from behind him and a flurry of small rocks slid from the cutaway, scattering down onto his head and shoulders. Zeth must have stepped out of the shelter of the overhang, Jay realized, into The Girl's sights again. Funny, that leap into proper-noun status. He moved back towards the edge of the pit, never taking his eyes off Zeth. His assumption that it was The Girl throwing stones from her bandanna had to be wrong: these were not isolated flung stones, but dozens – make that hundreds – of pebbles, shards, gravel chunks, small rocks and the occasional larger one falling down the banking in a cloud of ochre dust. Something had dislodged a part of the overhang and scree was shooting off the edge in a gathering rockslide. Above the scar he could see something moving – an oversized T-shirt, no longer very white, topped by a carroty tangle of hair. She was on her hands and knees on the banking, rabbit-kicking at the scree for all she was worth, dislodging chunks of rock and soil and dust, which fragmented onto the stones below, pelting Zeth

115

with earth and stones and acrid orange powder. Behind the sound of falling rubble Jay could just hear her thin, fierce voice screaming triumphantly, '*Eat shit, you bastard!*'

Zeth was taken completely off-balance by the attack. Dropping his rifle, his first instinct was to take shelter under the cutaway, but although the overhang protected him from thrown missiles it did nothing against the rock-fall, and he stumbled, choking, right into the thick of the falling scree. He swore, holding his arms protectively above his head, as chunks of rock suddenly came down on top of him. One piece the size of a housebrick caught him on the bony part of his elbow, and at that Zeth abruptly lost all interest in the fight. Coughing, choking and blinded by dust, clasping his injured arm to his stomach, he stumbled out from under the overhang. There came a triumphant war cry from above, followed by another avalanche of small rocks, but the battle was already won. Zeth flung a single murderous glance over his shoulder and fled. He ran up the side path until he reached the top, and only then did he stop to howl his defiance.

'Thar fuckin *dead*, atha listenin?' His voice rolled off the stones at the canal side. 'If I ever see thee again, tha fuckin *dead!*'

The Girl gave a mocking yell from the trees.

Zeth fled.

23

Lansquenet, March 1999

JAY AWOKE TO A SPILL OF SUNSHINE ON HIS FACE. THERE WAS A strange yellowish quality to the light, something strained and winey, unlike dawn's clear pallor, but he was amazed when, looking at his watch, he realized he had slept more than fourteen hours. He recalled being feverish, even delusional, that night, and he anxiously inspected his injured foot for signs of infection, but none were apparent. The swelling had subsided as he slept, and though there was some gaudy bruising, as well as an ugly cut, on his ankle, there seemed to be less damage than he remembered. The long sleep must have done him good.

He managed to replace his boot. With it on his foot was sore, but not as much as he had feared. After eating his remaining sandwich – very stale now, but he was ravenous – he picked up his things and made his way slowly back towards the road. He left his bag and case in the bushes and began the long walk into the village. It took almost an hour, with many rest stops, to reach the main street, and he had plenty of time to look at the scenery. Lansquenet is a tiny place; a single main street and a few side roads, a square with a few shops – a chemist's, a baker's, a butcher's, a florist's – a church between two rows of linden trees, then a long road down to the river, a café and some derelict houses staggering along the ragged banks towards the fields. He came up from the river, having found a place to cross where the water ran shallow over some stones, and so he came to the café first. A bright red-and-white awning shielded a small window, and a couple of metal tables were set out on the pavement. A sign above the door read Café des Marauds.

Jay went in and ordered a *blonde*. The *propriétaire* behind the bar looked at him curiously, and he realized how he must look to her: unwashed and unshaven, wearing a grubby T-shirt and smelling of cheap wine. He gave her a smile, but she stared back at him doubtfully.

'My name is Jay Mackintosh,' he explained to her. 'I'm English.'

'Ah, English.' The woman smiled and nodded, as if that explained everything. Her face was round and pink and shiny, like a doll's. Jay took a long drink of his beer.

'Joséphine,' said the *propriétaire*. 'Are you . . . a tourist?' She sounded as if the prospect amused her.

He shook his head. 'Not exactly. I had a few problems getting here last night. I . . . got lost. I had to sleep rough.' He explained briefly.

Joséphine looked at him with wary sympathy. Clearly she couldn't imagine getting lost in such a small, familiar place as Lansquenet.

'Do you have rooms? For the night?'

She shook her head.

'Is there a hotel, then? Or a *chambre d'hôte*?'

Again that look of amusement. Jay began to understand that tourists were not in plentiful supply. Oh well. It would have to be Agen.

'Could I use your telephone, then? For a taxi?'

'Taxi?' She laughed aloud at that. 'A taxi, on a Sunday night?' Jay pointed out that it was barely six o'clock, but Joséphine shook her head and laughed again. All the taxis would be on their way home, she explained. No-one would come this far for a pick-up. Village boys often made hoax calls, she explained with a smile. Taxis, takeaway pizzas . . . They thought it was funny.

'Oh.' There was the house, of course. His house. He had already slept there one night, and with the sleeping bag and the candles he could surely manage another. He could buy food from the café. He would be able to collect wood and light a fire in the grate. There were clothes in his suitcase. In the morning he would change and go to Agen to sign the papers and collect the keys.

'There was a woman, back there where I slept. Madame d'Api. I think she thought I was trespassing.'

Joséphine gave him a quick look.

'I suppose she did. But if the house is yours now—'

'I thought she was the caretaker. She was standing guard.' Jay grinned. 'To tell the truth, she wasn't very friendly.'

Joséphine shook her head.

'No. I don't suppose she was.'

'Do you know her?'

'Not really.'

Mention of Marise d'Api seemed to have made Joséphine wary. The doubtful look was back on her face, and she was rubbing at a spot on the countertop with a preoccupied air.

'At least I know she's real now,' remarked Jay cheerfully. 'At midnight last night I thought I'd seen a ghost. I suppose she comes out in the daytime?'

Joséphine nodded silently, still rubbing the countertop. Jay was puzzled at her reticence, but was too hungry to pursue the matter.

The bar menu was not extensive, but the *plat du jour* – a generous omelette with salad and fried potatoes – was good. He bought a packet of Gauloises and a spare lighter, then Joséphine gave him a cheese baguette wrapped in waxed paper to take back with him, along with three bottles of beer and a bag of apples. He left while it was still light, carrying his purchases in a plastic carrier, and made good time.

He brought the rest of his luggage from its hiding place by the roadside into the house. He was feeling tired by now, and his abused ankle was beginning to protest, but he dragged the case to the house before he allowed himself to rest. The sun was gone now, the sky still pale but beginning to darken, and he gathered some wood from the pile at the back of the house and stacked it in the gaping fireplace. The wood looked freshly cut and had been stored beneath a tarpaper cover to keep it from the rain. Another mystery. He supposed Marise might have cut the wood, but could not see why she might have done so. Certainly she hardly seemed the neighbourly type. He found the empty bottle of elderflower wine in a bin at the back of the house. He didn't remember putting it there, but in the state he'd been in last night he couldn't be expected to recall everything. He hadn't been thinking rationally, he told himself. The hallucination of Joe, so real he had almost believed it at the time, was proof enough of his state of mind. The single cigarette butt he discovered in the room where he'd spent the night looked old. It might have been there for ten years. He shredded it and threw it to the wind and closed the shutters from the inside.

He lit some candles, then made a fire in the grate, using old newspapers he had found in a box upstairs and the wood from the back of the house. Several times the paper flared furiously, then went out, but finally the split logs caught. Jay fed the fire carefully, with a slight feeling of surprise at the pleasure it gave him. There was something primitive in this simple act, something which reminded him of the Westerns he'd liked so much as a boy.

He opened his case and put his typewriter on the table next to the bottles of wine, pleased with the effect. He almost felt he might be able to write something tonight, something new. No science fiction tonight. Jonathan Winesap was on vacation. Tonight he would see what Jay Mackintosh could do.

He sat at the typewriter. It was a clumsy thing, springactioned, hard on the fingers. He'd kept it out of affectation at first, though it was years since he had used it regularly. Now the keys felt good beneath his hands and he typed a few lines experimentally across the ribbon.

It sounded good, too. But without paper . . .

The unfinished manuscript of *Stout Cortez* was in an envelope at the bottom of his case. He took it out, and reversed the first page as he slipped it into the slot. The machine in front of him felt like a car, a tank, a rocket. Around him the room buzzed and fizzled like dark champagne. Beneath his fingers the typewriter keys jumped and snapped. He lost track of time. Of everything.

24

Pog Hill, Summer 1977

THE GIRL'S NAME WAS GILLY. JAY SAW HER QUITE OFTEN AFTER that, down at Nether Edge, and they sometimes played together by the canal, collecting rubbish and treasures and picking wild spinach or dandelions for the family pot. They weren't really gypsies, Gilly told him scornfully, but *travellers*, people who couldn't stay in one place for long and who despised the capitalist property market. Her mother, Maggie, had lived in a tepee in Wales until Gilly was born, then had decided it was time for a more stable environment for the child. Hence the trailer, an old fish van, renovated and refurbished to accommodate two people and a dog.

Gilly had no father. Maggie didn't like men, she explained, because they were the instigators of the Judaeo-Christian patriarchal society, hell-bent on the subjugation of women. This kind of talk always made Jay a little nervous, and he was always careful to be especially polite to Maggie in case she ever decided he was the enemy, but although she sometimes sighed over his gender, in the same way that one might over a handicapped infant, she never held it against him.

Gilly got on with Joe immediately. Jay introduced them the week after the rock fight, and knew a tiny stab of jealousy at their rapport. Joe knew many of the region's itinerants, and had already begun to trade with Maggie, swapping vegetables and preserves for the afghans she knitted from thrift-shop bargains, with which Joe used to cover his tender perennials – this said with a chuckle which made Maggie squawk with laughter – on cold nights. She knew a great deal about plants, and both she and Gilly accepted Joe's talismans and perimeter-protection rituals with perfect serenity, as if such things were quite natural to them. As Joe worked in the allotment, Jay and Gilly would help him with his other tasks and he would talk to them or sing along to the radio as they collected seeds in jars or sewed charms into red flannel bags or fetched old pallets from the railway bank in which to store that season's ripening fruit. It was as if Gilly's presence had mellowed Joe somehow. There was something different in the way he spoke to her, something which excluded Jay, not unkindly, but palpably nevertheless. Perhaps because she, too, was a traveller. Perhaps simply because she was a girl.

Not that Gilly conformed in any way to Jay's expectations. She was fiercely independent, always taking the lead, in spite of his seniority, physically reckless, cheerily foul-mouthed to a degree which secretly shocked his conservative upbringing, filled with bizarre beliefs and ideologies culled from her mother's diverse store. Space aliens, feminist politics, alternative religions, pendulum power, numerology, environmental issues, all had their place in Maggie's philosophy, and Gilly, in her turn, accepted them all. From her Jay learned about the ozone layer and bread-cakes mysteriously shaped like Jesus, or what she called the New Killer Threat, or shamanism, or saving the whales. In turn she was the ideal audience for his stories. They spent days together, sometimes helping Joe, but often simply loafing around by the canal, talking or exploring.

They saw Zeth once more after the rock fight, some distance away by the dump, and were careful to avoid him. Surprisingly enough, Gilly wasn't in the least afraid of him, but Jay was. He hadn't forgotten what Zeth had shouted the day they routed him from the lock, and he would have been perfectly happy never to set eyes on him again. Obviously, he was never going to be that lucky.

25

Lansquenet, March 1999

IT WAS EARLY THE FOLLOWING MORNING WHEN HE GOT INTO AGEN. He learned from Joséphine that there were only two buses a day, and after a quick coffee and a couple of croissants at the Café des Marauds he left, eager to collect his paperwork from the agency. It took longer than Jay had expected. Legal completion had taken place the previous day, but electricity and gas had not yet been restored, and the agency was reluctant to hand over keys without all the documentation from England. Plus, the woman at the agency told him, there were additional complications. His offer on the farm had taken place at a time when another offer was under consideration – had, in fact, been accepted by the owner, although nothing had yet been made official. Jay's offer – superior to this earlier one by about £5,000 – had effectively scratched this previous arrangement, but the person to whom the farm had been promised had called earlier that morning, making trouble, making threats.

'You see, Monsieur Mackintosh,' said the agent apologetically. 'These small communities – a promise of land – they don't understand that a casual word cannot be said to be legally binding.' Jay nodded sympathetically. 'Besides,' continued the agent, 'the vendor, who lives in Toulouse, is a young man with a family to support. He inherited the farm from his great-uncle. He had no real contact with the old man for some time, and has no responsibility for what he might have promised before his death.'

Jay understood. He left them to it and went shopping for supplies. Then he waited in the café across the road while papers were faxed from London. Frantic phone calls were exchanged. Bank. Solicitor. Agent. Bank.

'And you're sure this person – this previous offer – has no legal right to the property?' he asked as, at last, the agent handed over the keys.

She shook her head.

'No, monsieur. The arrangement with Madame d'Api may be of long-standing, but she has absolutely no legal right. In fact we have only her word that the old man accepted her offer in the first place.'

'D'Api?'

'Yes, a Madame Marise d'Api. A neighbour of yours, in fact, with property adjacent to your own. A local business-woman, by all accounts.'

That explained a lot: her hostility, her surprise at being told that he'd bought the house, even the fresh paint on the ground floor. She had assumed the house would be hers. She had done what he himself had done: moved in a little early, before completion. No wonder she looked so angry! Jay resolved to see her as soon as he could, to explain. To reimburse her, if necessary, for the work she had done on the house. After all, if they were going to be neighbours . . .

It was nearing late afternoon by the time the business was finished. Jay was tired. Hasty negotiations meant that the gas supply had been restored to the house, though he would have to wait another five days for electricity. The agency woman suggested a hotel while the house was made habitable, but he refused. The romance of his derelict, lonely farmhouse was too much to resist. Besides, there was the question of the new manuscript, the twenty pages written that night on the reverse of *Stout Cortez*. To leave it for the sterile comfort of a hotel room might kill the idea before it had even begun. Even now, as he taxied back to Lansquenet with a cabful of purchases and his head ringing with fatigue, he could feel the drag of those written pages, the urge to continue, to feel the keys of the old typewriter beneath his fingers and to follow the story where it led.

When he got back the sleeping bag had gone. The candles, too, and the box of painting things. Nothing else had been touched. He guessed that Marise must have called by in his absence to remove all remaining traces of her illicit occupancy. It was too late to call at her house by then, but Jay promised himself he would do so the next day. There was no point in being on bad terms with his only close neighbour. He kindled a fire in the grate and lit the oil lamp – one of the day's purchases – and placed it on the table. He had bought a sleeping bag of his own, and some pillows, as well as a folding camp bed, and with these he managed to make a comfortable enough sleeping area in the inglenook. As it was still light, he ventured as far as the kitchen. There was a gas stove there, old but functional, and a fireplace. Above it a blackened cast-iron pot hung, furry with cobwebs. An ancient enamelled range covered half the space from wall to wall, but the oven was choked with leavings – coal, half-burnt wood and generations of dead insects. Jay decided to wait until he could clean it out properly. The fire was another matter, though. It lit fairly easily, and he managed to heat enough water for a wash and a cup of coffee, which he took with him on his tour of the house. This, he found, was even larger than his earlier search had revealed. Living rooms, dining room, still rooms, pantries, cupboards as large as storerooms, storerooms like caverns. Three cellars, though the darkness down there was too thick for him to risk the broken steps, stairs leading up into bedrooms, lofts, granaries. There was furniture there, too, much of it spoiled by rain and neglect, but some of it usable. A long table of some age-blackened wood, scarred and warped by many years of use; a dresser of the same rough make; chairs; a footstool.

Polished and restored, he told himself, they would be beautiful, exactly the type of furniture Kerry sighed over in elegant Kensington antiques shops. Other things had been stored in boxes in corners all over the house – tableware in an attic, tools and gardening equipment at the back of a woodshed, a whole case of linen, miraculously unspoiled, under a box of broken crockery. He pulled out stiff, starched sheets, yellowed at the creases, each one embroidered with an elaborate medallion, in which the initials D. F. twined above a garland of roses – some woman's trousseau from a hundred, two hundred, years back. There were other treasures too: sandalwood boxes of handkerchiefs; copper saucepans dulled with verdigris, an old radio from before the war, he guessed, its casing cracked to reveal valves as big as doorknobs. Best of all was a huge old spice chest of rough black oak, some of its drawers still labelled in faded brown ink – *Cannelle, Poivre Rouge, Lavande, Menthe Verte* – the long-empty compartments still fragrant with the scents of those spices, some dusted with a residue which coloured his fingertips with cinnamon, ginger, paprika and turmeric. It was a lovely thing, fascinating. It deserved better than this empty, half-derelict house. Jay promised himself that when he could he would have it brought downstairs and cleaned.

Joe would have loved it.

Night fell: reluctantly Jay abandoned his exploration of the house. Before retiring to his camp bed he inspected his ankle again, surprised and pleased at the speed of his recovery. He barely needed the arnica cream he had bought from the chemist's. The room was warm, the fire's embers casting hot reflections onto the whitewashed walls. It was still early – no later than eight – but his fatigue had begun to catch up with him, and he lay on his camp bed, watching the fire and thinking over the next day's plans. Behind the closed shutters he could hear the wind in the orchard, but there was nothing sinister about the sound tonight. Instead it sounded eerily familiar – the wind, the sound of distant water, the night creatures calling and bickering, and, beyond that, the church clock carrying distantly across the marshes. A sudden surge of nostalgia came over him – for Gilly, for Joe, for Nether Edge and that last day on the railway below Pog Hill Lane, for all the things he never wrote about in *Jackapple Joe* because they were too mired in disillusion to put into words.

He gave a sleepy, sour croak of laughter. *Jackapple Joe* never even came close to what really happened. It was a fabrication, a dream of what things should have been like, a naïve re-enactment of those magical, terrible summers. It gave a meaning to what had remained meaningless. In his book, Joe was the bluff, friendly old man who steered him towards adulthood. Jay was the generic apple-pie boy, rosily, artfully ingenuous. His childhood was gilded, his adolescence charmed. Forgotten, all those times when the old man bored him, troubled him, filled him with rage. Forgotten, the times Jay was sure he was crazy. His disappearance, his betrayal, his lies; papered over, tempered with nostalgia. No wonder everyone loved that book. It was the very triumph of deceit, of whimsy over reality, the childhood we all secretly *believe* we had, but which none of us ever did. *Jackapple Joe* was the book Joe himself might have written. The worst kind of lie – half true, but lying in what really matters. Lying in the heart.

'Tha should ave gone back, tha knows,' said Joe matter-of-factly. He was sitting on the table next to the typewriter, a mug of tea in one hand. He'd swapped the Thin Lizzy T-shirt for one from Pink Floyd's *Animals* tour. 'She waited for you, and you never came. She deserved better than that, lad. Even at fifteen, you should have known that.'

Jay stared at him. He looked very real. He touched his forehead with the back of his hand, but the skin was cool.

'Joe.'

He knew what it was, of course. All that thinking about Joe, his subconscious desire to find him there, his re-enactment of Joe's greatest fantasy.

'You never did find out where they went, did you?'

'No, I never did.' It was ridiculous, talking to a fantasy, but there was something oddly comforting in it, too. Joe seemed to listen, head cocked slightly to one side, the mug held loosely between his fingers.

'You were the one left me. After everything you promised. You left me. You never even said goodbye.' Even though it was a dream, Jay could feel anger crackling in his voice. 'You're one to tell me I should have gone back.'

Joe shrugged, unruffled. 'People move on,' he said calmly. 'People go to find themselves, or lose themselves, whatever. Pick your own clee-shay. Anyroad, isn't that what you're doing now? Runnin away?'

'I don't know what I'm doing now,' said Jay.

'That Kerry, anall.' Joe continued, as if he hadn't heard. 'She were another. You just never know when you've hit lucky.' He grinned. 'Did you know she wears green contact lenses?'

'What?'

'Contact lenses. Her eyes are really blue. All this time and you never knew.'

'This is ridiculous,' Jay muttered. 'Anyway, you're not even here.'

'Here? Here?' Joe turned towards him, pushing his cap back from his face in the characteristic gesture Jay remembered. He was grinning, the way he always did when he was about to say something outrageous. 'Who's to say where here is, anyroad? Who's to say *you're* here?'

Jay closed his eyes. The old man's after-image danced briefly on his retina like a moth at a window.

'I always hated it when you talked like that,' said Jay.

'Like what?'

'All that Grasshopper mystical stuff.'

Joe chuckled.

'Philosophy of the Orient, lad. Learned it off of monks in Tibet, that time when I were on the road.'

'You were never on the road,' Jay said. 'Nowhere further than the M1, anyhow.'

He fell asleep to the sound of Joe's laughter.

26

Pog Hill, Summer 1977

JOE WAS IN SPLENDID FORM FOR THE FIRST PART OF THAT SUMMER.
He seemed more youthful than Jay had ever seen him, filled
with ideas and projects. He worked on his allotment most
days, though with more caution than of old, and they took
their tea breaks in the kitchen, surrounded by tomato plants.
Gilly came over every couple of days, and they would go down
into the railway cutting and collect treasures in the usual way,
which they would then bring up the banking to Joe's house.

They had moved away from Monckton Town in May,
Gilly explained, when a group of local kids had begun
causing trouble at their previous camp.

'Bastards,' she said casually, dragging on the cigarette
they were sharing and passing it back to Jay. 'First it was
name-calling. Big fucking deal. Then they kept banging on
the doors at night, *then* it was stones at the windows, *then*
fireworks under the van. Then they poisoned our old dog,
and Maggie said enough was enough.'

Gilly had started at the local comprehensive that year.
She got on with most people, she said, but with these kids it
was different. She was casual enough about the problem,
but Jay guessed it must have got pretty bad for Maggie to
move the trailer so far away.

'The worst of them – the ringleader – is a girl called Glenda,' she told him. 'She's in the year above me at school. I fought her a couple of times. No-one else dares do anything to her because of her brother.'

Jay looked at her.

'You know him,' said Gilly, taking another drag on the cigarette. 'That big bastard with the tattoos.'

'Zeth.'

'Aye. At least *he's* left school now. I don't see him much, except down by the Edge sometimes, shooting birds.' She gave a shrug. 'I don't go there often,' she added with a touch of defensiveness. 'Not really often, anyway. I don't like to.'

Nether Edge was theirs now, Jay gathered. A gang of six or seven, aged twelve to fifteen and led by Zeth's sister. At weekends they would go into the town and dare each other to shoplift small items from the newsagent's – usually sweets and cigarettes – then down to the Edge to hang out or let off fireworks. Passers-by tended to avoid them, fearing abuse or harassment. Even the usual dog-walkers avoided the place now.

The news left Jay feeling strangely bereft. After the rock fight he had remained wary of the Edge, always carrying Joe's talisman in his pocket, always on the lookout for trouble. He avoided the canal, the ash pit and the lock, which seemed too risky now. He wasn't going to run into Zeth if he could help it. But Gilly wasn't afraid. Not of Zeth, or of Glenda. Her caution was for him, not for herself.

Jay felt a surge of indignation.

'Well, *I'm* not going to stay away,' he said hotly. 'I'm not afraid of a bunch of little girls. Are you?'

'Of course not!' Her denial confirmed his suspicions. Jay felt a sudden impulse to prove to her that he could hold his own as well as she could – ever since the rock fight in the ash pit he had felt that, when it came to natural aggression, she had him at a disadvantage.

'We could go tomorrow,' he suggested. 'Go to the ash pit and dig up some bottles.'

Gilly grinned. In the sunlight her hair glowed almost as brightly as the end of the cigarette. There was a pink stripe of sunburn over her nose. Jay felt a wave of some emotion he could not recognize wash over him, so strong that he felt slightly sick. As if something had shifted inside him, tuning into a frequency hitherto unknown and unguessed at. He felt a sudden, incomprehensible urge to touch her hair. Gilly looked at him derisively.

'You sure you're up for it?' she asked. 'You're not *chicken*, are you, Jay?' She pumped her arms and squawked, '*Bwrakka-bwraaak!* Not even a teeny-tiny bit?' The feeling, that moment of mysterious revelation, had passed. Gilly flicked her cigarette butt into the bushes, still grinning. Jay grabbed at her and mussed her hair to hide his confusion, until she screamed and kicked him in the shin. Normality — at least what passed for normal between them — was resumed.

That night he slept badly, lying awake in the dark thinking of Gilly's hair — that wonderful, gaudy shade between maple leaf and carrot — and the red shale of the scree above the ash pit, and Zeth's voice whispering *I can wait* and *You're dead* in his ears, until at last he had to get up and take out Joe's old red flannel talisman from its usual place in his satchel. He gripped it — worn and shiny with three years of handling — in the palm of his hand, and immediately felt better.

Scared? Of course he wasn't.

He had magic on his side.

27

Lansquenet, March 1999

I'VE BECOME FOND OF JAY. WE HAVE MATURED TOGETHER, HE and I, and in many ways we are very similar. We are complex in ways which are not immediately apparent to the casual observer. The uneducated palate finds in us a brashness, a garrulousness which belies the deeper feelings. Forgive me if I become pretentious with age, but that is what solitude does to wine, and travel and rough handling have not improved me. Some things are not meant to be bottled for too long.

With Jay, of course, it was something else. With Jay it was anger.

He did not remember a time when he was not angry at someone. His parents. His school. Himself. And most of all, there was Joe. Joe, who vanished that day without warning or reason, leaving only a packet of seeds, like something out of a mad fairy tale. A bad vintage, that anger. Bad for the spirit, mine and his. The Specials sensed it, too. On the table, the four remaining bottles waited in subdued, ominous silence, their bellies filled with dark fire.

When he awoke in the morning Joe was still there. Sitting at the table with his mug of tea, elbows propped on the wood, his cap at an angle, his little half-moon reading glasses perched on the end of his nose. Dusty sunlight came through a knot-hole in the shutters and gilded one shoulder into almost-invisibility. He was made of the same airy fabric which filled his bottles; I could see right through him where the light hit him full-on, though he looked solid enough to Jay, sitting bolt upright from one dream into another.

'Morning,' said the old man.

'I see what this is,' whispered Jay hoarsely. 'I'm going crazy.'

Joe grinned.

'You allus were a bit daft,' he said. 'Fancy throwin them seeds out over the railway. You were supposed to keep em. *Use* em. If you ad of done, like you were meant to, then none of this would ever ave appened.'

'What do you mean?'

Joe ignored the question.

'You know, there's still a good old crop of *tuberosa rosifea* growin under that railway bridge. Probly the only place in the world with such a good crop. You ought to go and see it some time. Make yerself some wine.'

'What do you mean, *use them*? They were only seeds.'

'Only seeds?' Joe shook his head in exasperation. 'Only seeds, after everything I taught you? Them jackapples were *Specials*, I told you. I even wrote it on the packet.'

'I didn't see anything special about them,' Jay told him, pulling on his jeans.

'You never? I tell you, lad, I put a couple of them *rosifeas* in every single bottle of wine I ever made. Every bottle I ever made, since I brought em back from South America. Took me five years just to get the soil right. I tell you—'

'Don't bother.' Jay's voice was harsh. 'You never went to South America. I'd be surprised if you ever even made it out of South Yorkshire.'

Joe laughed and brought out a packet of Player's from his coat pocket.

'Mebbe not, lad,' he admitted, lighting one. 'But I saw it all the same. Saw all of them places I told you about.'

'Course you did.'

Joe shook his head sorrowfully.

'*Astral* travel, lad. Astral bloody travel, how the bloody else d'you think I'd be able to do it if I was underground half me bloody life?'

He sounded almost angry. Jay eyed the cigarette in his hand with longing. It smelt like burning paper and Bonfire Night.

'I don't believe in astral travel.'

'Then how'd you bloody think I got *here*?'

Bonfire Night, licorice, frying grease, smoke and Abba singing 'The Name of the Game' at Number One all that month. Himself sitting in the empty dorm smoking – not out of pleasure but just because it was against the rules. Not a letter. Not a card. Not even a forwarding address.

'You're *not* here. I don't want to have this conversation.'

Joe shrugged.

'You allus were a stubborn beggar. Allus askin for explanations. Never happy just to take things as they were. Allus wantin' to know how it worked.'

Silence. Jay began to lace his boots.

'Remember them Romanies that beat the meter at Nether Edge that time?'

Jay looked up for a moment. 'Yes, I remember.'

'D'you ever figure out how they did it?'

Jay shook his head slowly.

'Alchemy, you said.'

Joe grinned.

'*Layman's* alchemy.' He lit a Player's, looking smug. 'Made emselves some moulds shaped like fifty pences, see? Made em out of ice. Lad fromt council thought them fifties had melted into thin air.' He laughed hugely.

'He were right anall, wan't he?'

28

Nether Edge, Summer 1977

JAY WALKED TO THE EDGE, JOE'S TALISMAN TUCKED SNUGLY INTO his pocket. The sun was veiled, as it was for most of that summer, but the sky was hot and pale, bleeding the air of oxygen and the countryside of colour. Fields, trees, flowers all looked to be varying shades of grainy grey, like the screen on Maggie's black-and-white portable. Above Nether Edge a small bright blur hung in the sky like a beacon. A warning, perhaps.

Gilly was wearing cut-off jeans and a striped T-shirt. Her hair was tied back with a piece of red ribbon. She was eating a sherbert fountain, and her tongue was black with the licorice.

'I wasn't sure you'd make it,' she said.

Jay thought of the talisman in his pocket and shrugged. They were safe, he told himself. Safe. Protected. Unseen. It had worked dozens of times before.

'Why shouldn't I?'

Gilly shrugged.

'They've got some kind of a den over there,' she said, jerking her head towards the canal. 'A tree house, I think, where they keep their stuff. I've seen them going there a couple of times. I dare you to go in.'

'I don't do dares,' said Jay.

Gilly gave him a satirical look.

'They won't be there,' she urged. 'This time in the morning they're still in town, or nicking stuff from the market. It's only a poxy den, Jay. Dare you.'

Her eyes gleamed slyly, that cat's-eye marble green reflecting the colourless sky. She finished the sherbert fountain and lobbed the packet into the canal, keeping the licorice stub in her mouth, like a cigar butt.

'Unlesh you're *yeller*,' she said, doing a passable Lee Marvin.

'OK.'

They found the den close to the lock. It wasn't a tree house, but a small shack built from assorted dump-rubbish: corrugated cardboard, sheets of tarpaper and fibreglass. It had windows of plastic sheeting and a door taken from somebody's old shed. It looked deserted.

'Go on, then,' said Gilly. 'I'll keep watch.'

Jay hesitated for a moment. Gilly grinned brashly; her face looked stretched into one giant freckle. He felt suddenly dizzy at the sight of her.

'Ah, get on with it, will you?' she urged.

Touching the talisman in his pocket, Jay walked resolutely towards the den. It was bigger than it had looked from the path and, despite its eccentric construction, it was solid. The door was padlocked, a heavy industrial lock which might have come from someone's coal cellar.

'Try the window,' said Gilly from behind him. Jay whipped round.

'I thought you were keeping watch!'

Gilly shrugged.

'Ah, there's nobody here,' she said. 'Go on, try the window.'

The window was just big enough to crawl through. Gilly pulled back the plastic sheeting and Jay squeezed inside. It was dark, and there was a smell of sour earth and cigarette smoke. A pile of blankets lay on the floor above a couple of crates. A box of clippings. A dog-eared poster cut from a girls' magazine was stapled to one wall. Gilly put her head through the window.

'Find anything good?' she enquired pertly.

Jay shook his head. He was beginning to feel uncomfortable in there, imagining himself trapped in the den as Zeth and his friends rounded the corner.

'Look in the crates,' suggested Gilly. 'That's where they keep their stuff. Magazines and cigarettes, stuff they've lifted.'

Jay pushed over one of the crates. Assorted rubbish spilled out across the floor. Make-up, empty lemonade bottles, comics. A battered transistor radio, sweets in a glass jar. A paper bag filled with fireworks, bangers and jumping-jacks and Black Cats in their waxy casings. Two dozen Bic lighters. Four unopened packets of Player's.

'Take something,' said Gilly. 'Take something. It's all nicked anyway.' Jay picked up a shoebox of clippings. Rather half-heartedly he scattered them across the earth floor of the den. Then he did the same with the magazines.

'Take the cigs,' urged Gilly. 'And the lighters. We'll give them to Joe.' Jay looked at her uneasily, but the thought of her contempt was more than he could take. He pocketed cigarettes and lighters, then, at Gilly's insistence, the sweets and the fireworks. Fired by her enthusiasm he tore down the poster from the wall, stamped the records, stomped the jars. Remembering how Zeth had smashed his radio, he took the transistor as well, telling himself they owed it to him. He spilled cosmetics, crunched lipsticks underfoot, threw a tin of face powder against the wall. Gilly watched, laughing wildly.

'I wish we could see their faces,' she gasped. 'If only we could!'

'Well, we can't,' Jay reminded her, climbing quickly out of the den. 'Come on, before they get back.' He took her hand and began to pull her after him up the path to the ash pit, their stomachs suddenly filled with butterflies at the

139

thought of what they'd done. The sensation was not altogether unpleasant, and suddenly they were both laughing like drunks, clinging to each other as they stumbled up the path.

'If only I could see Glenda's *face*,' spluttered Gilly. 'Next time we'll have to bring a camera or something, so we can have a permanent record.'

'Next time?' The thought killed the laughter.

'Well, of course.' She spoke as if it were the most natural thing in the world. 'We've won the first skirmish. We can't just leave it now.'

He supposed he should have told her, This is where it ends, Gilly. It's too dangerous. But it was the danger which attracted her, and he was too intoxicated by her admiration to plead caution. That look in her eyes.

'What are you staring at me for?' she demanded belligerently.

'I'm not staring at you.'

'Yes, you *are*.'

Jay grinned. 'I'm staring at the *great – big – earwig* that just landed in your hair from that bush,' he told her.

'*Bastard!*' screamed Gilly, shaking her head.

'Wait a minute! It's just *there*,' he said, slyly knuckle-rubbing the top of her head.

Gilly kicked him hard on the ankle. Again normality was restored.

For a while.

29

Lansquenet, March 1999

THE NEXT THING JAY DID IN LANSQUENET WAS TO FIND A builder's yard. The house needed extensive repairs, and although he could probably manage some of the work himself, most of it would have to be done by professionals. Jay was lucky to find them to hand. He imagined it would cost a great deal more to have them come over from Agen. The yard was large and sprawling. Wood had been stacked in towers at the back. Window frames and doors propped up the walls. The main warehouse was a converted farm, low-roofed, with a sign above the door which read, CLAIRMONT – MEUNUISERIE-PANNEAUX-CONSTRUCTION.

Unfinished furniture, fencing, concrete blocks, tiles and slates were piled messily by the door. The builder's name was Georges Clairmont. He was a short, squat man, with a mournful moustache and a white shirt, greyed with perspiration. He spoke with the thick accent of the region, but slowly, reflectively, and this gave Jay time to understand his words. Somehow everyone here knew about him already. He supposed Joséphine had spread word. Clairmont's labourers – four men in paint-spattered overalls and caps turned down against the sun – watched with wary curiosity as Jay passed. He caught the word *Anglishe* in a rapid mutter of patois. Work – money – was limited in the village. Everyone wanted a share in Château Foudouin's renovation. Clairmont flapped his hand in annoyance as four pairs of eyes followed them into the woodyard.

'Back to work, *héh*, back to *work!*'

Jay caught the eye of one of the labourers – a man with red hair tied back with a bandanna – and grinned. The redhead grinned back, one hand across his face to hide his expression from Clairmont. Jay followed the manager into the building.

The room was large and cool, like a hangar. A small table near the door served as a desk, with papers, files and a telephone-fax machine. Next to the telephone was a bottle of wine and two small glasses. Clairmont poured out two shots and handed one to Jay.

'Thanks.'

The wine was red-black and rich. It was good, and he said so.

'It should be,' said Clairmont. 'It was made on your land. The old proprietor, Foudouin, was well known here once. A good winemaker. Good grapes. Good land.' He sipped his wine appreciatively.

'I suppose you'll have to send someone out to see the house,' Jay told him.

Clairmont shrugged. 'I know the house. Went to see it again last month. Even drew up some estimates.'

He saw Jay's surprise and grinned.

'She's been working on it since December,' he said. 'Painting this, plastering that. She was so sure of her agreement with the old man.'

'Marise d'Api?'

'Who else, *héh*? But he'd already made a deal with his nephew. A steady income – a hundred thousand francs a year until his death – in exchange for the house and the farm. He was too old to work. Too stubborn to leave the place. No-one else wanted it but her. There's no money in farming nowadays, and as for the house itself, *héh!*' Clair-

142

mont shrugged expressively. 'But with her it's different. She's stubborn. Been eyeing the land for years. Waiting. Fencing it off bit by bit. Serve her right, *héh!*' Clairmont gave his short, percussive laugh. 'She'd never give me any work, she said. Rather get a builder in from town than owe money to someone from the village. Do it herself, more likely.' He rubbed his fingers together in a speaking gesture. 'Close with her savings,' he explained shortly, finishing the rest of his wine. 'Close with *everything*.'

'I expect I'll have to offer her some kind of compensation,' said Jay.

'Why?' Clairmont looked amused.

'Well, if she's spent money—'

Clairmont gave a raucous laugh.

'Money! More likely to have been robbing the place. Look at your fences, your hedges. Look how they've been moved. A dozen metres here, half a dozen there. Nibbling at the land like a greedy rat. She was at it for years when she thought the old man wasn't watching. Then, when he died . . .' Clairmont shrugged expressively. '*Héh!* She's poison, Monsieur Mackintosh, a viper. I knew her poor husband and, though he never complained, I couldn't help hearing things.'

That shrug again, philosophical and businesslike.

'Give her nothing, Monsieur Mackintosh. Come to my house this evening and meet my wife. Have dinner. We can discuss your plans for the Foudouin place. It will make a wonderful holiday home, *monsieur*. With investment anything is possible. The garden can be replanted and landscaped. The orchard restored. A swimming pool, maybe. Paving, like the villas in Juan les Pins. Fountains.' His eyes gleamed at the thought.

Cautiously Jay replied, 'Well, I hadn't really thought beyond immediate repairs.'

'No no, but there will be time, *héh?*' He slapped Jay's arm companionably.

'My house is off the main square. Rue des Francs

Bourgeois. Number four. My wife is longing to meet our new celebrity. It would make her very happy to meet you.' His grin, part humble, part acquisitive, was oddly infectious.

'Take dinner with us. Try my wife's *gésiers farcis*. Caro knows everything there is to know in the village. Get to know Lansquenet.'

JAY EXPECTED A SIMPLE MEAL. POT LUCK WITH THE BUILDER AND HIS wife, who would be small and drab, in an apron and headscarf, or sweet-faced and rosy, like Joséphine at the café, with bright bird's eyes. They would perhaps be shy at first, speaking little, the wife pouring soup into earthen-ware bowls, blushing with pleasure at his compliments. There would be home-made terrines and red wine and olives and pimentoes in their spiced oils. Later they would tell their neighbours that the new Englishman was *un mec sympathique, pas du tout prétentieux*, and he would be quickly accepted as a member of the community.

The reality was quite different.

The door was opened by a plump, elegant lady, twin-setted and stillettoed in powder-blue, who exclaimed as she saw him. Her husband, looking more mournful than ever in a dark suit and tie, waved to him over his wife's shoulder. From inside Jay could hear music and voices, and glimpse an interior of such relentless chintziness that he blinked. In his black jeans and T-shirt, under a simple black jacket, he felt uncomfortably underdressed.

There were three other guests as well as Jay. Caroline Clairmont introduced them as she distributed drinks — 'our friends Toinette and Lucien Merle, and Jessica Mornay, who owns a fashion shop in Agen,' — simultaneously pressing one cheek against Jay's and a champagne cocktail into his free hand.

'We've been *so* looking forward to meeting you, Monsieur Mackintosh, or may I call you Jay?'

He began to nod, but was swept away into an armchair.

'And, of course, you *must* call me Caro. It's so wonderful

to have someone new in the village – someone with *culture*
– I do think culture is so *important*, don't you?'

'Oh yes,' breathed Jessica Mornay, clutching at his arm
with red nails too long to be anything but false. 'I mean,
Lansquenet is wonderfully unspoilt, but sometimes an
educated person simply longs for something *more*. You
must tell us about yourself. You're a writer, Georges tells
us?'

Jay disengaged his arm and resigned himself to the
inevitable. He answered innumerable questions. Was he
married? No? But there was someone, surely? Jessica
flashed her teeth and drew closer. To distract her he
feigned interest in banalities. The Merles, small and dapper
in matching cashmere, were from the north. He was a wine-
buyer, working for a firm of German importers. Toinette
was in some kind of local journalism. Jessica was a pillar of
the village drama group – 'her Antigone was *exquisite*' –
and did Jay write for the theatre?

He outlined *Jackapple Joe*, which everyone had heard of
but no-one had read, and provoked excited squeals from
Caro when he revealed that he had begun a new book.
Caro's cooking, like her house, was ornate; he did justice to
the *soufflé au champagne* and the *vol-au-vents*, the *gésiers
farcis* and the *boeuf en croûte* – secretly regretting the
home-made terrine and olives of his fantasy. He gently
discouraged the ever more eager advances of Jessica Mornay. He was moderately witty, anecdotal. He accepted many
undeserved compliments on his *français superbe*. After
dinner he developed a headache, which he attempted,
without success, to dull with alcohol. He found it difficult
to concentrate on the ever-increasing rapidity of their
French. Whole segments of conversation passed by like
clouds. Fortunately his hostess was garrulous – and self-
centred – enough to take his silence for rapt attention.

By the time the meal was over it was almost midnight.
Over coffee and *petits fours* the headache subsided and Jay
was able to grasp the thread of the conversation once more.

Clairmont, his tie pulled away from the collar, his face mottled and sweaty: 'Well, all I can say is it's high time *something* happened to put Lansquenet on the map, *héh*? We've got as much going for us as Le Pinot down the road, if we could only get everybody organized.'

Caro nodded agreement. Jay could understand her French better than her husband's, whose accent had thickened as his wineglass emptied. She was sitting opposite him on the arm of a chair, legs crossed and cigarette in hand.

'I'm sure that now Jay has joined our little community' – she bared her teeth through the smoke – 'things will begin to progress. The *tone* changes. People begin to develop. God knows I've worked hard enough – for the church, for the theatre group, for the literary society. I'm sure Jay would agree to address our little writers' group one day soon?'

He bared his own teeth non-committally.

'Of *course* you would!' Caro beamed as if Jay had answered aloud. 'You're exactly what a village like Lansquenet needs most: a breath of fresh air. You wouldn't want people to think we were keeping you all to *ourselves*, would you?' She laughed, and Jessica exclaimed hungrily. The Merles nudged each other in glee. Jay had the strangest feeling that the lavish dinner had been peripheral, that in spite of the champagne cocktails and iced Sauternes and *foie gras* he was the real main course.

'But why Lansquenet?' It was Jessica, leaning forwards, her long blue eyes half shut against a sheet of cigarette smoke. 'Surely you would have been happier in a bigger place. Agen, maybe, or further south towards Toulouse?'

Jay shook his head. 'I'm tired of cities,' he said. 'I bought this place on impulse.'

'Ah,' exclaimed Caro rapturously. 'Artistic temperament!'

'Because I wanted somewhere quiet, away from the city.'

Clairmont shook his head. '*Héh*, it's quiet enough,' he said. 'Too quiet for us. Property prices rock-bottom, while in Le Pinot, only forty kilometres away—'

His wife explained rapidly that Le Pinot was a village on the Garonne, much beloved by foreign tourists.

'Georges does a lot of work there, don't you, Georges? He put in a swimming pool for that lovely English couple, and he helped renovate that old house by the church. If only we could generate the same kind of interest in *our* village.'

Tourists. Swimming pools. Gift shops. Burger bars. Jay's lack of enthusiasm must have shown in his face, because Caro nudged him archly.

'I can see that our Monsieur Mackintosh is a romantic, Jessica! He loves the quaint little roads and the vineyards and the lonely farmhouses. So very English!' Jay smiled and nodded and agreed that his eccentricity was *tout à fait anglais.*

'But a community like ours, *héh*, it needs to grow.' Clairmont was drunk and earnest. 'We need *investment.* Money. There's no money left in farming. Our farmers make barely enough to keep alive as it is. The work is all in the cities. The young move away. Only the old people and the riff-raff stay. The itinerants, the *pieds-noirs.* That's what people don't want to understand. We have to progress or die, *héh*. Progress or die.'

Caro nodded. 'But there are too many people here who can't see the way ahead,' she frowned. 'They refuse to sell their land for development, even when it's clear they can't win. When the plans were suggested to build the new Intermarché up the road they protested for so long that the Intermarché went to Le Pinot instead. Le Pinot was just like Lansquenet twenty years ago. Now look at it.'

Le Pinot was the local success story. A village of 300 souls put itself on the map thanks to an enterprising couple from Paris who bought and refurbished a number of old properties to sell as holiday homes. Thanks to a strong pound, and several excellent contacts in London, these were sold or rented to wealthy English tourists, and little by little a tradition was established. The villagers soon saw the potential in this. Business expanded to serve the new tourist trade. Several new cafés opened, soon followed by a couple of bed and breakfasts. Then came a scattering of speciality shops selling luxury goods to the summer trade, a restaurant with a Michelin star, and a small but luxurious hotel with a gym and a swimming pool. Local history was dredged for items of interest, and the wholly unremarkable church was revealed, by a combination of folklore and wishful thinking, to be a site of historical significance. A television adaptation of *Clochemerle* was filmed there, and after that there was no end to the new developments. An Intermarché within easy distance. A riding club. A whole row of holiday chalets along the river. And now, as if that wasn't enough, there were plans for an Aquadome and health spa only five kilometres away, which would bring trade all the way from Agen and beyond.

Caro seemed to take Le Pinot's success as a personal insult.

'It could just as easily have been Lansquenet,' she complained, taking a *petit four*. 'Our village is at least as good as theirs. Our church is genuine fourteenth century. We have the ruins of a Roman aqueduct down in Les Marauds. It could have been us. Instead, the only visitors we get are the summer farmhands and the gypsies down the river.' She bit petulantly at her *petit four*.

Jessica nodded. 'It's the people here,' she told me. 'They don't have any ambition. They think they can live exactly as their grandfathers did.'

Le Pinot, Jay understood, had been so successful that the production of its local vintage, after which the village was named, had ceased altogether.

'Your neighbour is one of those people.' Caro's mouth thinned beneath the pink lipstick. 'Works half the land between here and Les Marauds, and still barely makes enough from winemaking to keep body and soul together. Lives holed up all year round in that old house of hers, with never a word to anyone. And that poor child holed up with her . . .'

148

Toinette and Jessica nodded, and Clairmont poured more coffee.

'Child?' Nothing in Jay's brief glimpse of Marise d'Api had led him to imagine her as a mother.

'Yes, a girl. No-one ever sees her. She doesn't go to school. We never see them in church. We tried to suggest that they might,' Caro made a face, 'but the torrent of abuse from the mother was quite disgusting.'

The other women made sounds of agreement. Jessica moved a little closer, and Jay could smell perfume – he thought it was Poison – from her bobbed blond hair.

'She'd be better off with the grandmother,' said Toinette emphatically. 'At least she'd get the affection she needs. Mireille was absolutely devoted to Tony.' Tony, explained Caro, was Marise's husband.

'But she'd never let her have the child,' said Jessica. 'I think she only keeps her because she knows it galls Mireille. And, of course, we're too far out for anyone to take much notice of what an old woman says.'

'It was *supposed* to have been an accident,' continued Caro darkly. 'I mean, they *had* to say that, didn't they? Even Mireille played along, because of the funeral. Said his gun exploded when a cartridge got stuck in the chamber. But everyone knows that woman drove him to it. Did everything but pull the trigger. I'd believe anything of her. Anything at all.'

The conversation was beginning to make Jay feel uncomfortable. His headache had returned. This was not what he'd expected of Lansquenet, he told himself, this genteel spite, this gleeful hint of cruelty behind the prettiness. He hadn't come to Lansquenet to hear about this. His book – if there was ever going to be a book – didn't need this. The ease with which he'd written the twenty pages on the reverse of *Stout Cortez* proved it. He wanted apple-faced women picking herbs in their gardens. He wanted a French idyll, a *Cider With Rosette*, a lighthearted antidote to Joe.

And yet there was something curiously pervasive about

149

the story itself, about the three women's faces drawn close in identical expressions of vulpine enjoyment, eyes squinched down, mouths lipsticked wide over white, well-tended teeth. It was an old story – not even an original story – and yet it drew him. The feeling – that sense of being yanked forwards by an invisible hand in his gut – was not entirely unpleasant.

'Go on,' he said.

'She was always at him.' Jessica took over the narrative. 'Even when they were first married. He was such an easy-going, sweet man. A big man, but I'll swear he was frightened of her. He let her get away with anything. And when the baby was born she just got worse. Never a smile. Never made friends with anyone. And the rows with Mireille! I'm sure you could hear them right across the village.'

'That's what drove him to it in the end: the rows.'

'Poor Tony.'

'She found him in the barn – what was left of him. His head half blown away by the shot. She put the baby in the crib and rode off to the village on her moped, cool as you like, to fetch help. And at the funeral, when everyone was mourning' – Caro shook her head – 'cold as ice. Not a word or a tear. Wouldn't pay for anything more than the plainest, cheapest funeral. And when Mireille offered to pay for something better – Lord! The fight that caused!'

Mireille, Jay understood, was Marise's mother-in-law. Almost six years later, Mireille, who was seventy-one and suffered from chronic arthritis, had never spoken to her granddaughter, or even seen her except from a distance.

Marise reverted to her maiden name after her husband's death. She apparently hated everyone in the village so much that she employed only itinerant labour – and that on the condition that they ate and slept at the farm for the duration of their employment. Inevitably, there were rumours.

'I don't suppose you'll see much of her, anyway,' finished

150

Toinette. 'She doesn't talk to anyone. She even rides over to La Percherie to buy her weekly shopping. I imagine she'll leave you well alone.'

Jay walked home, despite offers from Jessica and Caro to drive him back. It was almost two, and the night was fresh and quiet. His head felt peculiarly light, and although there was no moon there was a skyful of stars. As he skirted the main square and moved downhill towards Les Marauds he became aware, with some surprise, of how dark it really was. The last street lamp stood in front of the Café des Marauds, and at the bottom of the hill, the river, the marshes, the little derelict houses teetering haphazardly into the water dipped into shadow so deep that it was almost blindness. But by the time he reached the river his eyes had adapted to the night. He crossed in the shallows, listening to the *hisssh* of the water against the banks. He found the path across the fields and followed it to the road, where a long avenue of trees stood black against the purple sky. He could hear sounds all around him: night creatures, a distant owl, mostly the sounds of wind and foliage, from which vision distracts us.

The cool air had cleared his head of smoke and alcohol and he felt alert and awake, able to walk all night. As he walked, he found himself going over the last part of the evening's conversation with increasing persistence. There was something about that story, ugly as it was, which attracted him. It was primitive. Visceral. The woman living alone with her secrets; the man dead in the barn; the dark triangle of mother, grandmother, daughter . . . And all around this sweet, harsh land, these vines, orchards, rivers, these whitewashed houses, widows in black headscarves, men in overalls and drooping, nicotine-stained moustaches.

The smell of thyme was pungent in the air. It grew wild by the roadside. Thyme improves the memory, Joe used to say. He used to make a syrup out of it, keeping it in a bottle in the pantry. Two tablespoonsful every morning before breakfast. The clear greenish liquid smelt exactly like the

151

night air over Lansquenet, crisp and earthy and nostalgic, like a summer day's weeding in the herb garden, with the radio on.

Suddenly Jay wanted to be home. His fingers itched. He wanted to feel the typewriter keys under them, to hear the clack-clacking of the old machine in the starry silence. More than anything he wanted to catch that story.

HE FOUND JOE WAITING FOR HIM, STRETCHED OUT ON THE CAMP bed, hands laced behind his head. He had left his boots by the foot of the bed, but he was wearing his old pit-helmet, cocked at a jaunty angle on his head. A yellow sticker on the front read, 'People will always need coal.'

Jay felt no surprise at seeing him. His anger had gone, and instead he felt a kind of comfort, almost as if he was expecting to see him – the ghostly apparition becoming familiar as he began to anticipate it, becoming . . .

Everyday magic.

He sat down at the typewriter. The story had him in its hold now and he typed rapidly, his fingers jabbing at the keys. He typed solidly for more than two hours, feeding sheet after sheet of *Stout Cortez* into the machine, translating it, reversing it with his own layman's alchemy. Words pranced across the page almost too fast for him to keep pace. From time to time he paused, vaguely conscious of Joe's presence on the bed beside him, though the old man said nothing while he worked. At one point he smelt smoke. Joe had lit a cigarette. At about five in the morning he made coffee in the kitchen, and when he returned to his typewriter he noticed, with a curious feeling of disappointment, that the old man had gone.

30

Nether Edge, Summer 1977

THEY WENT TO THE EDGE MORE OFTEN AFTER THAT. THEY KEPT out of sight most of the time, visiting when they were fairly certain no-one would be there. There were a couple of clashes with Glenda and her mates – once at the dump, over ownership of an old deep-freeze (Glenda won that encounter) and once at the river crossing (one-up to Gilly and Jay). Nothing serious ensued. Name-calling, a few flung stones, threats and gibes. Gilly and Jay knew Nether Edge better than the others, in spite of their out-of-town status. They knew the best hiding places, the short cuts. And they had imagination. Glenda and her mates had little but spite and swagger to sustain them. Gilly liked to lay traps. A bent sapling with a taut wire across the base, designed to fly in the face of anyone who tripped it. A paint tin of dirty canal water balanced, precarious, on the door of their den. The den itself was raided again and again, until it was finally abandoned, then Jay found the new den – in the dump, between a rusty hulk and an old fridge door – and raided that. They left their signature everywhere. On disused ovens in the dump. On trees. On the walls and doors of a series of dens. Gilly made a slingshot and practised shooting at discarded tins and jam jars. She was a natural.

She never missed. She could break a jar at fifty feet without even trying. Of course there were a few narrow escapes. Once they almost cornered Jay near the place where he hid his bike, close to the railway bridge. It was getting dark and Gilly had already gone home, but he'd found a stash of last year's coal – maybe as much as a couple of sacksful – in a patch of weeds, and he wanted to shift it before anyone else came across it by accident. He was too busy bagging coal chunks for Joe to notice the four girls coming out from the other side of the railway, and Glenda was almost on him before he knew it.

Glenda was Jay's age, but big for a girl. Zeth's narrow features were overlaid with a meatiness which squeezed her eyes into crescents and her mouth into a pouty bud. Her slabby cheeks were already raddled with acne. It was the first time he had seen her so close, and her resemblance to her brother was almost paralysing. Her friends eyed him warily, fanning out behind Glenda, as if to cut off his escape. The bike was ten feet away, hidden in the long grass. Jay began to edge towards it.

'Iz on iz own today,' remarked one of the other girls, a skinny blonde with a cigarette butt clamped between her teeth. 'Wheer's tha girlfriend?'

Jay moved closer to the bike. Glenda moved with him, skidding down the shingle of the banking towards the road. Pieces of gravel shot out from under her sneakers. She was wearing a cut-off T-shirt and her arms were red with sunburn. With those big, fishwife's arms she looked troublingly adult, as if she had been born that way. Jay feigned indifference. He would have liked to say something clever, something biting, but the words which would have come so easily in a story refused to co-operate. Instead, he scrambled down the bank to where he had hidden his bike and pulled it out of the long grass onto the road.

Glenda gave a crow of rage and began to slide towards him, paddling the shingle with large, spatulate hands. Dust flew.

'I'll fuckin ave thee, tha bastard,' she said, sounding alarmingly like her brother, but she was too busy watching Jay to control her slide, and she overshot the banking with comical suddenness, tipping into the dry ditch at the bottom, where a stand of nettles was just coming into flower. Glenda screamed with rage and chagrin. Jay grinned and straddled his bike. In the ditch, Glenda thrashed and struggled, her face in the nettles.

He rode off while Glenda's three friends were hauling her out, but as he reached the top of the street he stopped and turned. He could see Glenda, half out of the ditch now. Her face was a dark blur of fury. He gave a small, insolent wave.

'I'll ave thee!' Her voice reached him thinly across the space which separated them. 'Mi fuckin brother'll ave thee anall!'

Jay waved again and did a wheelie as he turned down the lane and out of sight. He was laughing-gas dizzy, his jaw aching with laughter, his ribs tight. The talisman tied to the loop of his jeans fluttered from his hip like a banner. He whoop-whooped all the way down the hill to the village, and his voice whipped past his face, stolen by the wind. He was exhilarated. He felt invulnerable.

But August was drawing to an end. September loomed like a nemesis. A single week to go before his downfall.

31

Lansquenet, March 1999

DURING THE WEEK THAT FOLLOWED JAY WROTE EVERY NIGHT. On Friday the electricity was finally restored, but by then he'd become accustomed to working by the light of the oil lamp. It was friendlier somehow, more atmospheric. The pages of his manuscript formed a tight wedge on the table top. He had almost a hundred now. On Monday Clairmont arrived with four workmen to make a start on the repairs to the house. They began with the roof, which was missing a great number of tiles. The plumbing, too, needed attention. In Agen he managed to find a car-hire company and rented a five-year-old green Citroën to carry his purchases and speed up his visits to Lansquenet. He also bought three reams of typing paper and some typewriter ribbons. He worked after dark, when Clairmont and his men had gone home, and the stack of typed pages mounted steadily.

He did not reread the new pages. Fear, perhaps, that the block which had afflicted him for so many years might still be waiting. But somehow he didn't think so. Part of it was this place. Its air. The feeling of familiarity in spite of the fact that he was a stranger here. Its closeness to the past. As if Pog Hill Lane had been rebuilt here amongst the orchards and vines.

On fine mornings he walked into Lansquenet to buy bread. His ankle had healed quickly and completely, leaving only the faintest of scars, and he began to enjoy the walk and to recognize some of the faces he saw along the way. Joséphine told him their names, and sometimes more. As the owner of the village's only café, she was in an excellent position to know everything that happened. The dry-looking old man in the blue beret was Narcisse, a market gardener who supplied the local grocer and the florist. In spite of his reserve, there was wry, hidden humour in his face. Jay knew from Joséphine that he was a friend of the gypsies who came downriver every summer, trading with them and offering them seasonal work in his fields. For years he and a succession of local *curés* battled over his tolerance of the gypsies, but Narcisse was stubborn, and the gypsies stayed. The redhaired man from Clairmont's yard was Michel Roux, from Marseilles, a traveller from the river, who stopped for a fortnight five years ago and never left. The woman with the red scarf was Denise Poitou, the baker's wife. The wan-looking fat woman in black, her eyes shaded from the sun by a wide-brimmed hat, was Mireille Faizande, Marise's mother-in-law. Jay tried to catch her eye as she passed the café *terrasse*, but she did not seem to see him.

There were stories behind all of these faces. Joséphine, leaning over the counter with her cup of coffee in one hand, appeared more than willing to tell them. Her early shyness of him had vanished, and she greeted him with pleasure. Sometimes, when there were not too many customers, they talked. Jay knew very few of the people she mentioned. But this did not seem to discourage Joséphine.

'Do you mean I never told you about old Albert? Or his daughter?' She sounded amazed at his ignorance. 'They used to live next door to the bakery. Well, what used to be the bakery, before it became the *chocolaterie*. Opposite the florist's.' At first Jay simply allowed her to talk. He paid little attention, letting names, anecdotes, descriptions wash past him as he sipped his coffee and watched the people go by.

'Didn't I ever tell you about Arnauld and the truffle pig? Or the time Armande dressed up as the Immaculate Conception and laid in wait for him in the churchyard? Listen . . .'

There were many stories of her best friend, Vianne, who left some years ago, and of people long dead, whose names meant nothing to him. But Joséphine was persistent. Perhaps she, too, was lonely. The morning *habitués* of the café were a silent lot for the most part, many of them old men. Perhaps she welcomed a younger audience. Little by little the ongoing soap opera of Lansquenet-sous-Tannes drew him in.

Jay was aware he was still an oddity here. Some people stared at him in frank curiosity. Some smiled. Most were reserved, politely dour, a nod in greeting and a sidelong glance as he walked past. Most days he called at the Café des Marauds for a *blonde* or a *café-cassis* on the way back from Poitou's. The walled *terrasse* was small, no more than a wide piece of pavement on the narrow road, but it was a good place to sit and watch as the village came to life. Just off the main square, it was a vantage point from which everything was visible: the long hill leading down towards the marshes; the screen of trees above the Rue des Francs Bourgeois; the church tower whose carillon rang out across the fields at seven every morning; the square, pink schoolhouse at the road's fork. At the bottom of the hill the Tannes was hazed and dimly gleaming, the fields beyond barely visible. The early sunlight was very bright, almost crude in comparison, cutting out the white fronts of the houses against their brown shadow. On the river a boat was moored, close to the huddle of derelict houses which overhung the river on their precarious wooden stilts. From the boat's chimney he could see a scrawl of smoke and smell frying fish.

Between seven and eight o'clock several people, mostly

women, passed by carrying loaves or paper bags of croissants from Poitou's bakery. At eight the bells rang for Mass. Jay always recognized the churchgoers. There was a look of solemn reluctance to their good spring coats, their polished shoes, their hats and berets, which defined them. Caro Clairmont was always there with her husband; he awkward in his tight shoes, she elegant in a series of silk scarves. She always greeted Jay as she passed, with an extravagant wave and a cry of, 'How's the book?' Her husband nodded briefly and hurried by, hunched, humble. While Mass was in progress, a number of old men parked themselves with tired defiance on the *terrasse* of the Café des Marauds to drink *café-crème* and play chess, or talk among themselves. Jay recognized Narcisse, the market gardener, always in the same place by the door. There was a tattered seed catalogue in his coat pocket, which he read in silence, a cup of coffee at his elbow. On Sundays Joséphine bought *pains au chocolat* and the old man always took two, his big brown hands oddly delicate as he lifted the pastry to his mouth. He rarely spoke, contenting himself with a brief nod in the direction of the other customers before settling in his usual place. At eight thirty the schoolchildren began to pass, incongruous in their anoraks and fleeces, a procession of logos against purple, scarlet, yellow, turquoise, lime-green. They looked at Jay with open curiosity. Some of them laughed and called out in cheery derision, '*Rosbif! Rosbif!*' as they dashed by. There were about twenty children of primary-school age in Lansquenet, divided into two classes; the older ones had to take the school bus into Agen, its windows snubbed with curious noses and thick with finger-graffiti.

During the day Clairmont had been overseeing the repairs to the house. Already the ground floor looked better and the roof was almost completed, though Jay could tell Georges was disappointed at his lack of ambition. Clairmont dreamed of conservatories and indoor swimming pools, jacuzzis and piazzas and landscaped lawns, though he was philosophical enough when Jay told him that he had no ambition to live in a St Tropez villa.

'*Bof, ce que vous aimez, à ce que je comprends, c'est le rustique,*' he told Jay with a shrug. Already there was a speculative look in his eyes. Jay understood that if he didn't take a hard line with the man he would almost certainly be deluged with unwanted objects – broken crockery, milking stools, bad reproduction furniture, walking sticks, cracked tiles, chopping boards and ancient farming utensils; all the unloved and abandoned detritus of loft and cellar, granted reprieve from the bonfire by the call of *le rustique* – which he would then be expected to buy. He should have withered him on the spot. But there was something rather touching about the man, something both humble and absurdly hopeful in the ratty black eyes gleaming above the drooping moustache, which made it impossible.

Sighing, Jay resigned himself to the inevitable.

On Thursday he caught sight of Marise for the first time since their initial, brief meeting. He was coming home after his morning walk, a loaf tucked under his arm. At the point at which his field backed onto hers there was a blackthorn hedge, along which a path ran parallel to the boundary. The hedge was young, three or four years at the most, the new March growth barely sufficient to form a screen. Behind it he could see the broken line where the old hedge had been, an uneven row of stumps and tussocks imperfectly hidden by a new furrow. Mentally Jay calculated the distance. Clairmont had been right. She had moved the boundary by about fifty feet. Probably when the old man first fell ill. He looked more closely through the hedge, faintly curious. The contrast between her side and his was striking. On the Foudouin side the vines were sprawling and untrimmed, their new growth barely showing, except for a few hard brown buds on the ends of the tendrils. Hers had been cut back hard, twelve inches from the ground, in readiness for the summer. There were no weeds on Marise's side of the hedge; the furrows neat and clean-edged, a path running along each row wide enough to allow easy passage for the tractor. On Jay's side the rows had run into each other, the uncut vines clinging lasciviously to one another across the paths. Gleeful spikes of ragwort, mint and arnica poked through the tangle. Looking back towards Marise's land, he found that he could just see the gable-end of her farm at the edge of the field, screened from full view by a stand of poplars. There were fruit trees there, too – the white of apple blossom against bare branches – and what might be a vegetable garden. A woodpile, a tractor, something else which could only be the barn.

She must have heard the shot from the house. She had put the baby in the crib. Gone out. Taken her time. The image was so vivid that Jay could almost see her doing it: pulling on her boots over thick socks, the oversized jacket around her shoulders – it was winter – the frosty soil crunching under her feet. Her face was impassive, as it had been when they met that first morning. The image haunted him. In this guise Marise had already walked more than once across the pages of his new book; he felt as if he knew her, and yet they had barely spoken. But there was something in her which drew him, an irresistible air of secrecy. He wasn't sure why she made him think of Joe. That coat, perhaps, or the man's cap jammed too far over her eyes, that confusing half-familiar silhouette just glimpsed behind an angle of brick. Certainly there was no resemblance to Joe in her features. Joe could never have had that bleak, empty face. Half turning to go, Jay caught sight of something – a figure moving quickly along the other side of the hedge a few hundred yards from where he was standing. Shielded by the thin screen of bushes, he saw her before she caught sight of him. It was a warm morning and she had shed her bulky outer clothes in favour of jeans and a striped fisherman's jumper. The change of clothing made her boyishly slender. Her red hair had been cut off inexpertly at jaw level – Jay guessed she'd probably done it herself. In that unguarded moment her face was vivid, eager. For a moment Jay barely recognized her.

Then her eyes flicked towards him, and it was as if a blind had been slammed down, so fast that he was left wondering if he had only imagined her before.

'*Madame*—'

For a second she halted, looked at him with a blankness which was almost insolent. Her eyes were green, a curiously light verdigris colour. In his book he'd coloured them black. Jay smiled and reached out his hand over the hedge in greeting.

'Madame d'Api. I'm sorry if I startled you. I'm—'

But before he could say anything else she had gone, turning sharply into the rows of vines without a backward glance, moving smoothly and quickly down the path towards the farmhouse.

'Madame d'Api!' he called after her. 'Madame!'

She must have heard, and yet she ignored his call. He watched her for a few minutes more as she moved further and further away, then, shrugging, turned towards the house. He told himself that his disappointment was absurd. There was no reason why she should want to talk to him. He was allowing his imagination too much freedom. In the bland light of day she was nothing like the slate-eyed heroine of his story. He resolved not to think of her again.

When Jay got home, Clairmont was waiting for him with a truckload of junk. He winked as Jay turned into the drive, pushing his blue beret back from his eyes.

'*Holà*, Monsieur Jay,' he called from the cab of his truck. 'I've found you some things for your new house!'

Jay sighed. His instincts had been right. Every few weeks he would be badgered to take off Clairmont's hands a quantity of overpriced *brocante* masquerading as country chic. From what he could see of the truck's contents – broken chairs, sweeping brushes, half-stripped doors, a really hideous papier-mâché dragon head left over from some carnival or other – his suspicions hardly began to cover the dreadful reality.

'Well, I don't know,' he began.

Clairmont grinned.

'You'll see. You'll love this,' he announced, jumping down from his cab. As he did, Jay saw he was carrying a bottle of wine. 'Something to put you in the mood, *héh*? Then we can talk business.'

There was no escaping the man's persistence. Jay wanted a bath and silence. Instead there would be an hour's haggling in the kitchen, wine he didn't want to drink, then the problem of how to dispose of Clairmont's *objets d'art* without hurting his feelings. He resigned himself.

'To business,' said Clairmont, pouring two glasses of wine. 'Mine and yours.' He grinned. 'I'm going into antiques, *héh*? There's good money in antiques in Le Pinot and Montauban. Buy cheap now, clean up when the tourists come.'

Jay tried the wine, which was good.

'You could build twenty holiday chalets on that vineyard of yours,' continued Clairmont cheerily. 'Or a hotel. How'd you like the idea of your own hotel, *héh*?'

Jay shook his head.

'I like it the way it is,' he said.

Clairmont sighed.

'You and *La Païenne* d'Api,' he sighed. 'Got no vision, either of you. That land's worth a fortune in the right hands. Crazy, to keep it as it is when just a few chalets could—'

Jay struggled with the word and his accent.

'*La Païenne*? The godless woman?' he translated hesitantly.

Clairmont jerked his head in the direction of the other farm.

'Marise as was. We used to call her *La Parisienne*. But the other suits her better, *héh*? Never goes to church. Never had the baby christened. Never talks. Never smiles. Hangs on to that land out of sheer stubborn spite, when anyone else . . .' He shrugged. '*Bof*. It's none of my business, *héh*? But I'd keep the doors locked if I were you, Monsieur Jay. She's

163

crazy. She's had her eye on that land for years. She'd do you an injury if she could.'

Jay frowned, remembering the fox traps around the house.

'Nearly broke Mireille's nose once,' continued Clairmont. 'Just because she went near the little girl. Never came into the village again after that. Goes into La Percherie on her motorbike. Seen her going into Agen, too.'

'Who looks after the daughter?' enquired Jay.

Clairmont shrugged.

'No-one. I expect she just leaves her.'

'I'm surprised the social services haven't—'

'*Bof*. In Lansquenet? They'd have to come all the way over from Agen or Montauban, maybe even Toulouse. Who'd bother? Mireille tried. More than once. But she's clever. Put them off the scent. Mireille would have adopted the child if she'd been allowed. She's got the money. The family would have stood by her. But at her age, and with a deaf child on top of that, I suppose they thought—'

Jay stared at him. 'A deaf child?'

Clairmont looked surprised.

'Oh yes. Didn't you know? Ever since she was tiny. *She's* supposed to know how to look after her.' He shook his head. 'That's what keeps her here, *héh*? That's why she can't go back to Paris.'

'Why?' asked Jay curiously.

'Money,' said Clairmont shortly, draining his glass.

'But the farm must be worth something.'

'Oh, it is,' said Clairmont. 'But she doesn't own it. Why do you think she was so anxious to get the Foudouin place? It's on a lease. She'll be out the day it expires – unless she can get it renewed. And there isn't much chance of that after what's happened.'

'Why? Who owns the lease?'

Clairmont drained his glass and licked his lips with satisfaction.

'Pierre-Emile Foudouin. The man who sold you your house. Mireille's great-nephew.'

They went out onto the drive then, to inspect Clairmont's offerings. They were as bad as he had feared. But Jay's mind was on other things. He offered Clairmont 500 francs for the whole truckload: the builder's eyes widened briefly, but he was quickly persuaded. Winking slyly: 'An eye for a good bargain, héh?'

The note disappeared into his rusty palm like a card trick.

'And don't worry, héh. I can find you plenty more!'

He drove off, his exhaust blatting out pink dust from the drive. Jay was left to sort out the wreckage.

Even then Joe's training held good: Jay still found it hard to throw away what might conceivably be useful. Even as he determined to use the entire truckload for firewood he found himself looking speculatively over this and that. A glass-panelled door, cracked down the middle, might make a reasonable cold frame. The jars, each turned upside down on a small seedling, would give good protection from late frost. Little by little the oddments Clairmont had brought began to spread themselves around the garden and the field. He even found a place for the carnival head. He carried it carefully to the boundary between his and Marise's vineyard and set it on top of a fence post, facing towards her farm. Through the dragon's open mouth a long crêpe tongue lolled redly, and its yellow eyes gleamed. Sympathetic magic, Joe would have called it, like putting gargoyles onto a church roof. Jay wondered what *La Païenne* would make of it.

32

Pog Hill, Summer 1977

JAY'S MEMORIES OF THAT LATE SUMMER WERE BLURRY IN A WAY
the previous ones were not. Several factors were to blame
– the pale and troubling sky, for one thing, which made him
squint and gave him headaches. Joe seemed a little distant,
and Gilly's presence meant they did not have the long
discussions they'd had the year before. And Gilly herself
. . . it seemed that as July turned into August Gilly was
always at the back of his mind. Jay found himself dwelling
upon her more and more. His pleasure at her company was
coloured by insecurity, jealousy and other feelings he found
it difficult to identify. He was in a state of perpetual
confusion. He was often close to anger, without knowing
why. He argued constantly with his mother, who seemed to
get more deeply under his skin that summer than ever
before – *everything* got under his skin that year – he felt
raw, as if every nerve were constantly exposed. He bought
the Sex Pistols' 'Pretty Vacant' and played it in his room at
full volume, to the horror of his grandparents. He dreamed
of piercing his ears. Gilly and he went to the Edge and
warred with Glenda's gang and filled bags with useful
rubbish and took them over to Joe's. Sometimes they helped
Joe in the allotment, and occasionally he would talk to them

about his travels and his time in Africa with the Masai, or his journeys through the Andes. But to Jay it seemed perfunctory, an afterthought, as if Joe's mind were already on something else. The perimeter ritual, too, seemed abbreviated, a minute or two at most, with a stick of incense and a sachet of sprinkler. It did not occur to him to question it then, but afterwards he realized. Joe knew. Even then he had already made the decision.

One day he took Jay into his back room and showed him the seed chest again. It had been over a year since he had last done so, pointing out the thousands of seeds packaged and wrapped and labelled for planting, and in the semi-darkness – the windows were still boarded up – the chest looked dusty, abandoned, the paper packages crisp with age, the labels faded.

'It dun't look like owt, does it?' said Joe, drawing his finger through the dust on the top of the chest.

Jay shook his head. The room smelt airless and damp, like a place where tomatoes have been grown. Joe grinned a little sadly.

'Never believe it, lad. Every one of them seeds is a goodun. You could plant em right now an they'd go up champion. Like rockets. Every one of em.' He put his hand on the boy's shoulder. 'Just you remember, it's not what things look like that matters. It's what's *inside*. The *art* of it.'

But Jay wasn't really listening. He never really listened that summer – too preoccupied by his own thoughts, too sure that what he had would be there for ever. He took this wistful little aside of Joe's as just another adult homily; nodding vaguely, feeling hot and bored and choked in the airless dark, wanting to get away.

Later it occurred to him that perhaps Joe had been saying goodbye.

33

Lansquenet, March 1999

JOE WAS WAITING WHEN HE REACHED THE HOUSE, LOOKING critically out of the window at the abandoned vegetable plot.

'You want to do something with that, lad,' he told Jay as he opened the door. 'Else it'll be no good this summer. You want to get it dug over and weeded while you've still got time. And them apple trees, anall. You want to check em for mistletoe. Bloody kill em if you let it.'

During the past week Jay had almost become used to the old man's sudden appearances. He had even begun, in a strange way, to look forward to them, telling himself they were harmless, finding ingenious post-Jungian reasons to explain their persistence. The old Jay – the Jay of '75 – would have relished this. But that Jay believed in everything. He *wanted* to believe. Astral projection, space aliens, spells, rituals, magic. Strange phenomena were *that* Jay's daily business. That Jay believed – trusted. *This* Jay knew better.

And still he continued to see the old man, regardless of belief. A part of it was loneliness, he told himself. Another was the book – that stranger growing from the manuscript of *Stout Cortez*. The process of writing is a little like madness, a kind of possession not altogether benign. Back in the days of *Jackapple Joe* he talked to himself all the time, striding back and forth in his little Soho bedsit, with a glass in one hand, talking, arguing fiercely with himself, with Joe, with Gilly, with Zeth and Glenda, almost expecting to see them there as he looked up from the typewriter, his eyes grainy with exhaustion, his head pounding, the radio playing full blast. For a whole summer he was a little insane. But this book would be different. Easier, in a way. The characters were all around him. They marched effortlessly across the pages: Clairmont the builder, Joséphine the café owner, Michel from Marseilles, with the red hair and the easy smile. Caro in a Hermès headscarf. Marise. Joe. Marise. There was no real plot. Instead there were a multitude of anecdotes, loosely knitted together – some remembered from Joe and relocated to Lansquenet, some recalled by Joséphine over the counter of the Café des Marauds, some put together from scraps. He liked to think he had caught something of the air, of the light of the place. Perhaps some of Joséphine's bright, untrained narrative style. Her gossip was never tainted by malice. Her anecdotes were always warm, often amusing. He began to look forward to his visits, enough to feel a dim sense of disappointment on the days Joséphine was too busy to talk. He found himself going to the café every day, even when he had no other excuse to be in the village. He made mental notes.

When he had been in the village for a little under three weeks, he went into Agen and sent the first 150 pages of the untitled manuscript to Nick Horneli, his agent in London. Nick handled Jonathan Winesap, as well as the royalties for *Jackapple Joe*. Jay had always liked him, a wryly humorous man who was in the habit of sending little cuttings from newspapers and magazines in the hope of generating new inspiration. He sent no contact address, but a poste-restante address in Agen, and waited for a reply.

To his disappointment, he found that Joséphine would not speak to him about Marise. In the same way, there were people she rarely mentioned: the Clairmonts, Mireille Faizande, the Merles. Herself. Whenever he tried to encourage her to talk about these people, she would find work to do in the kitchen. He felt more and more strongly that there were things – secret things – she was reluctant to discuss.

'What about my neighbour? Does she ever come to the café?'

Joséphine picked up a cloth and began to polish the gleaming surface of the bar.

'I don't see her. I don't know her very well.'

'I've heard she doesn't get on with people from the village.'

A shrug. '*Bof.*'

'Caro Clairmont seems to know a lot about her.'

Again the shrug.

'Caro makes it her business to know everything.'

'I'm curious.'

Flatly: 'I'm sorry. I have to go.'

'I'm sure you must have heard something—'

She faced him for a second, her cheeks flushing. Her arms were folded tightly against her body, the thumbs digging into her ribs in a defensive gesture.

'Monsieur Jay. Some people like to pry into other people's business. God knows, there was enough gossip about me once. Some people think they can judge.' He was taken aback by her sudden fierceness. Suddenly she was someone else, her face tight and narrow. It occurred to him that she might be afraid.

LATER THAT NIGHT, BACK AT THE HOUSE, HE WENT OVER THEIR conversation. Joe was sitting in his usual spot on the bed, hands laced behind his neck. The radio was playing light music. The typewriter keys felt cold and dead under his fingertips. The bright thread of his narrative had finally run out.

'It's no good.' He sighed and poured coffee into his halfempty cup. 'I'm not getting anywhere.'

Joe watched him lazily, his cap over his eyes.

'I can't write this book. I'm blocked. It doesn't make sense. It isn't going anywhere.'

The story, so clear in his mind a few nights before, had receded into almost nothing. His head was swimming with wakefulness.

'You should get to know her,' advised Joe. 'Forget listening to other people's talk and make up your own mind. That or kick it into touch altogether.'

Jay made an impatient gesture.

'How can I do that? She obviously doesn't want to have anything to do with me. Or anyone else, for that matter.'

Joe shrugged.

'Please yourself. You never did learn how to put yourself out much, did yer?'

'That isn't true! I tried—'

'You could live next door to each other for ten years and neither of you'd make the first move.'

'This is different.'

'I reckon.'

Joe got up and wandered to the radio. He fiddled with the dial for a moment before finding a clear signal. Somehow Joe had the knack of locating the oldies station wherever he happened to be. Rod Stewart was singing 'Tonight's the Night'.

'You could try, though.'

'Maybe I don't want to try.'

'Happen you don't.'

Joe's voice was growing fainter, his outline fading, so that Jay could see the newly whitewashed wall behind him. At the same time the radio crackled harshly, the signal breaking up. A burr of white noise replaced the music.

'Joe?'

The old man's voice was almost too faint to hear.

'I'll sithee, then.'

It's what he always used to say as a sign of disapproval, or when signalling the end of a discussion.

'Joe?'

But Joe had already gone.

34

Pog Hill, Summer 1977

IT REALLY STARTED WITH ELVIS. MID-AUGUST, THAT WAS, AND Jay's mother grieved with a vehemence which was almost genuine. Perhaps because they were the same age, he and she. Jay felt it, too, even though he'd never been an especial fan. That overcast sense of doom, the feeling that things were coming apart at the centre, unravelling like a ball of string. There was death in the air that August, a dark edge to the sky, an unidentifiable taste. There were more wasps that summer than he ever remembered before – long, curly, brown wasps which seemed to scent the end coming and turned spiteful early. Jay was stung twelve times – once in the mouth as he swigged a bottle of Coke, lucky not to be taken to Casualty – and together Gilly and he burned seven nests. Gilly and Jay started a crusade against the wasps that summer. On hot, moist afternoons, when the insects were sleepy and more docile, the two of them went wasp-ing. They would find the nests, stuff the hole with shredded newspaper and firelighters and flame the whole thing. As the fire took and smoke poured into the nest the wasps would come flying out, some buzzing and burning like German aircraft in old black-and-white war movies, dar-kening the air and sighing, an eerie, chill sound, as they spread, bewildered and enraged, over the war zone. Gilly and Jay lay quiet in a hollow near by, far enough away from the danger spot, but as close as they dared, watching. Needless to say, this tactic was Gilly's idea. She would squat, eyes wide and bright, as close as she could. No wasp ever stung her. She seemed as immune to them as a honey badger to bees, and as naturally lethal. Jay was secretly terrified, crouching in the hollows with his head down and pounding with black exhilaration, but the fear was addictive and they sought it time and again, clinging to each other and laughing in terror and excitement. Once, urged by Gilly, Jay put two Black Cat bangers into a nest under a dry-stone wall and lit the fuses. The nest blew apart, but smokelessly, scattering stunned and angry wasps everywhere. One managed to get into the T-shirt he was wearing and stung him again and again. It felt like being shot, and Jay screamed and rolled on the ground. But the wasp was indestructible, twitching and stinging even as he crushed it beneath his frantic body. They killed it at last by tearing off the shirt and dousing it in lighter fluid. Later Jay counted nine separate stings. Autumn loomed close, smelling of fire.

35

Lansquenet, April 1999

HE SAW HER AGAIN THE NEXT DAY. AS APRIL RIPENED TOWARDS
May the vines had grown taller, and Jay occasionally
saw her at work amongst the plants, dusting with fungi-
cides, inspecting the shoots, the soil. She would not speak
to him. She seemed enclosed in a capsule of isolation,
profile turned towards the earth. He saw her in a succession of overalls, bulky jumpers, men's shirts, jeans, boots,
her bright hair pulled back severely under her beret.
Difficult to make out her shape beneath them. Even her
hands were cartoonish in overlarge gloves. Jay tried to talk
to her several times with no success. Once he called at her
farm, but there was no answer to his knock, though he was
sure he could hear someone behind the door.

'I'd have nothing to do with her,' said Caro Clairmont
when he mentioned the incident. 'She never talks to anyone
in the village. She knows what we all think of her.'

They were on the *terrasse* of the Café des Marauds. Caro
had taken to joining him there after church while her
husband collected cakes from Poitou's. In spite of her
exaggerated friendliness, there was something unpleasant
about Caro which Jay could not quite analyse. Perhaps her
willingness to speak ill of others. When Caro was there

Joséphine kept her distance and Narcisse scrutinized his seed catalogue with studied indifference. But she remained one of the few people from the village who seemed happy to answer questions. And she knew all the gossip.

'You should talk to Mireille,' she advised, sugaring her coffee extravagantly. 'One of my dearest friends. Another generation, of course. The things she's had to bear from that woman. You can't imagine.' She blotted her lipstick carefully on a napkin before taking the first sip. 'I'll have to introduce you one day,' she said.

As it happened, no introduction was necessary. Mireille Faizande sought him out herself a few days later, taking him completely by surprise. It was warm. Jay had begun work on his vegetable garden some days earlier, and now that the major repairs to the house were completed, he was spending a few hours a day in the garden. He hoped somehow that physical exertion might give him the insight he needed to finish his book. The radio was hanging from a nail sticking out of the side of the house, and the oldies station was playing. He had brought out a couple of bottles of beer from the kitchen, which he had left in a bucket of water to cool. Stripped to the waist, with an old straw hat he had found in the house to keep the sun from his eyes, he hadn't anticipated visitors.

He was hacking at a stubborn root when he noticed her standing there. She must have been waiting for him to look up.

'Oh, I'm sorry.' Jay straightened up, surprised. 'I didn't see you.'

She was a large shapeless woman, who should have looked motherly but did not. Huge breasts rolling, hips like boulders, she looked curiously *solid*, the comfortable wadding of fat petrified into something harder than flesh. Beneath the brim of her straw hat her mouth turned downwards, as if in perpetual grief.

'It's a long way out,' she said. 'I'd forgotten how long.' Her local accent was very pronounced, and for a moment Jay barely understood what she was saying. Behind him the radio was playing 'Here Comes the Sun', and he could see Joe's shadow just behind her, the light gleaming off the bald patch at his crown.

'Madame Faizande—'

'Let's not be formal, please. Call me Mireille. I'm not disturbing you, *héh*?'

'No. Of course not. I was just about to call it a day, anyhow.'

'Oh.' Her eyes flicked briefly over the half-finished vegetable patch. 'I didn't realize you were a gardener.'

Jay laughed.

'I'm not. Just an enthusiastic amateur.'

'You're not planning on maintaining the vineyard, *héh*?' Her voice was sharp. He shook his head.

'I'm afraid that's probably beyond me.'

'Selling it, then?'

'I don't think so.'

Mireille nodded.

'*Héh*, I thought you might have come to some agreement,' she said. 'With her.' The words were almost toneless. Against the dark fabric of her skirt her arthritic hands twisted and moved.

'With your daughter-in-law?'

Mireille nodded.

'She's always had her eye on this land,' she said. 'It's higher above the marshes than her place. It's better drained. It never floods in winter or dries up in summer. It's good land.'

Jay looked at her uncertainly.

'I know there was a . . . misunderstanding,' he said carefully. 'I know Marise expected . . . perhaps if she spoke to me we could arrange—'

'I will top any price she offers you for the land,' said Mireille abruptly. 'It's bad enough that she has my son's farm, *héh*, without having my father's land, too. My father's farm,' she repeated in a louder voice, 'which should have been my son's, where he should have raised his children. If it hadn't been for her.'

Jay switched the radio off and reached for his shirt.

'I'm sorry,' he said. 'I didn't realize there was a family connection.'

Mireille's eyes went almost tenderly to the façade of the house.

'Don't apologize,' she said. 'It looks better now than it has in years. New paintwork, new windows, new shutters. After my mother died my father let it all go to ruin. Everything but the land. The wine. And when my poor Tony—' She broke off abruptly, her hands twisting. 'She wouldn't live in the family house, *héh*, no. Madame wanted her own house, down by the river. Tony converted one of the barns for her. Madame wanted her flower garden, her patio, her sewing room. Every time it seemed as if the house was finished, Madame would think of something else. As if she was stalling for time. And then, at last, he brought her home.'

Mireille's face twisted. 'Home to me.'

'She's not from Lansquenet?' That would explain the physical differences. The light eyes, small features, exotic colouring and her accented but accurate English.

'She is from Paris.' Mireille's tone conveyed all her mistrust and resentment of the capital. 'Tony met her there on holiday. He was nineteen.' She must not have been more than a few years older, thought Jay. Twenty-three, maybe twenty-four. Why had she married him? This farmer's boy from the country? Mireille must have read the question in his face.

'He looked older than that, Monsieur Jay. And he was handsome, *héh oui*. Too much for his own good. An only son. He could have had the farm, the land, everything. His father never refused him a thing. Any girl from the village would have thought herself lucky. But my Tony wanted better. *Deserved* better.' She broke off with a shake of the head.

'Enough, *héh*. I didn't come here to talk about Tony. I wanted to know if you were planning to sell the land.'

'I'm not,' he told her. 'I like owning the land, even if I don't have any serious plans for the vineyard. For a start, I enjoy the privacy.'

Mireille seemed satisfied.

'You would tell me if you changed your mind, *héh*?'

'Of course. Look, you must be hot.' Now that she was here Jay didn't want her to go without knowing more about Tony and Marise. 'I have some wine in the cellar. Perhaps you'd like to take a glass with me?'

Mireille looked at him for a moment and nodded.

'Perhaps a small glass,' she said. 'If only to be back in my father's house again.'

'I hope you'll approve,' said Jay, leading her through the doorway.

THERE WAS NOTHING OF WHICH TO DISAPPROVE. JAY HAD LEFT the house much as it was, substituting modern plumbing for the ancient waterworks, but keeping the porcelain sinks, the woodstove, the pine cupboards, the scarred old kitchen table as they were. He liked the feeling of age in these things, the way each mark and scar told a story. He liked the worn-shiny flagstones on the floor, which he swept but did not attempt to cover with rugs, and though he oiled and cleaned the wood, he made no attempt to sand away the damage of years.

Mireille looked at everything with a critical eye.

'Well?' asked Jay, smiling.

'*Héh*,' replied Mireille. 'It could have been worse. I expected plastic cupboards and a dishwasher.'

'I'll get the wine.'

The cellar was dark. The new electrics had not yet been fitted, and the only lighting was a dim bulb on the end of a bitten flex. Jay reached for a bottle from the short rack by the stairs.

There were only five bottles left in the rack. In his haste

to offer hospitality he had forgotten this; a bottle of sweet Sauternes was the last, finished the previous night as he typed far into the early hours. But his mind was on other things. He was thinking about Marise and Tony, and of how he could ask Mireille for the conclusion of her tale. His fingers tightened around my neck for a moment, then moved on. He must have forgotten about the Specials. He was certain there was another bottle of Sauternes in there somewhere, maybe an extra he had overlooked. Beside me the Specials moved imperceptibly, shifting, snugging, rubbing up against each other like sleeping cats, purring. The bottle next to me – its label read 'Rosehip '74' – began to rattle. A rich golden scent of hot sugar and syrup reached his nostrils. Inside the bottle I could hear soft laughter. Jay could not hear it, of course. All the same his hand stopped on the bottle's neck. I could hear it beneath his fingers, whispering, cajoling, shifting its shape and turning its label slyly downwards as it released that secret scent. Sauternes, it whispered seductively, lovely yellow Sauternes from the other side of the river. Wine to loosen an old woman's tongue, wine to cool a dry throat, wine mellow *aaaaall* the way down. Jay picked up the bottle with a small sound of satisfaction.

'I *knew* I had one left.'

The label was smeared, and in the dimness he did not try to read it. He carried it up the stairs and into the kitchen, opened, poured. A tiny chuckle emerged from the bottle's throat as the wine filled the glass.

36

'MY FATHER USED TO MAKE THE BEST WINE IN THE REGION,' SAID
Mireille. 'When he died his brother Emile took over the
land. After that it should have been Tony's.'

'I know. I'm sorry.'

She shrugged.

'At least when he died it passed back to the male line,'
she said. 'I would have hated to think it went to her, *héh*?'

Jay smiled, embarrassed. There seemed to be something
in her which went far beyond grief. Her eyes were flaming
with it. Her face was stone. He tried to imagine what it must
be like to lose an only son.

'I'm surprised she stayed,' he told her. 'Afterwards.'

Mireille gave a short laugh.

'Of course she stayed,' she said harshly. 'You don't know
her, *héh*? Stayed out of sheer spite and stubbornness. Knew
it was only a matter of time till my uncle died, then she'd
have the estate to herself, just as she'd always wanted. But
he knew what he was doing, *héh*. Kept her hanging on, the
old dog. Made her think she could have it cheap.' She
laughed again.

'But why should she want it? Why not leave the farm and
move back to Paris?'

Mireille shrugged.

'Who knows, *héh*? Maybe to spite me.' She sipped
curiously at her wine.

'What is this?'

'Sauternes. Oh. Damn!'

Jay couldn't understand how he had mistaken it. The smudgy handwritten label. The yellow cord tied round the neck. Rosehip, '74.

'Oh damn. I'm sorry. I must have picked up the wrong bottle.'

He tried his own glass. The taste was incredibly sweet, the texture syrupy and flecked with particles of sediment. He turned to Mireille in dismay.

'I'll open another. I do apologize. I never meant to give you this. I don't know how I could have mistaken the bottles—'

'It's quite all right.' Mireille held on to her glass. 'I like it. It reminds me of something. I'm not sure what. A medicine Tony had as a child, perhaps.' She drank again, and he caught the honeyed scent of the wine from her glass.

'Please, *madame*. I really—'

Firmly: 'I *like* it.'

Behind her, through the window, he could still see Joe under the apple trees, the sun bright on his orange overalls. Joe waved as he saw him watching and gave him the thumbs up. Jay corked the bottle of rosehip wine again and took another mouthful from his glass, reluctant somehow to throw it away. It still tasted terrible, but the scent was pungent and wonderful – waxy red berries bursting with seeds, splitting their sides with juice into the pan by the bucketful and Joe in his kitchen with the radio playing full volume – 'Kung Fu Fighting' at Number One all that month – pausing occasionally to demonstrate some specious *atemi* learned on his travels through the Orient, and the October sunlight dazzling through the cracked panes . . .

It seemed to have a similar effect on Mireille, though her palate was clearly more receptive to the wine's peculiar flavour. She took the drink in small, curious sips, each time pausing to savour the taste.

Dreamily: '*Héh*, it tastes like . . . rosewater. No, roses. Red roses.'

So he was not the only one to experience the special effect of Joe's home-brewed wine. Jay watched the old woman closely as she finished the glass, anxiously scanning her expression for possible ill effects. There were none. On the contrary, her face seemed to lose some of its habitual fixed look, and she smiled.

'*Héh*, fancy that. Roses. I had my own rose garden once, you know. Down there by the apple orchard. Don't know what happened to it. Everything went to ruin when my father died. Red roses, they were, with a scent, *héh*! I left when I married Hugues, but I used to go there and pick my roses every Sunday while they were in bloom. Then Hugues and my father died in the same year – but that was the year my Tony was born. A terrible year. But for my dear Tony. The best summer for roses I ever remember. The house was filled with them. Right to the eaves. *Héh*, but this is strong wine. Makes me feel quite dizzy.'

Jay looked at her, concerned.

'I'll drive you home. You mustn't walk back all that way. Not in this sun.' Mireille shook her head.

'I want to walk. I'm not so old that I'm afraid of a few kilometres of road. Besides' – she jerked her head in the direction of the other farm – 'I like to see my son's house across the river. If I'm lucky I might catch sight of his daughter. From a distance.'

Of course. Jay had almost forgotten there was a child. Certainly he had never seen her, either in the fields or on the way to school.

'My little Rosa. Seven years old. Haven't been close to her since my son died. Not once.' Her mouth was beginning to regain its customary sour tuck. Against her skirt her big misshapen hands moved furiously. '*She* knows what that's done to me. She knows. I'd have done anything for my son's child. I could have bought back the farm, *héh*, I could have given them money – God knows I've no-one else to give it to.' She struggled to stand up, using her hands on the table top to hoist her bulk upwards.

'But she knows that for that she'd have to let me see the child,' continued Mireille. 'I'd find out what's happening. If they knew how she treated my Rosa; if I could only prove what she's doing—'

'Please.' Jay steadied her with a hand under her elbow. 'Don't upset yourself. I'm sure Marise looks after Rosa as well as she can.'

Mireille snapped him a contemptuous look. 'What do you know about it, *héh*? Were you there? Were you perhaps hiding behind the barn door when my son died?' Her voice was brittle. Her arm felt like hot brick beneath his fingers.

'I'm sorry. I was only—'

Mireille shook her head effortfully. 'No, it is I who should apologize. The sun and the strong wine, *héh*? It makes my tongue run wild. And when I think of her my blood boils — *héh*!' She smiled suddenly, and Jay caught an unexpected glimpse of the charm and intelligence beneath the rough exterior. 'Forget what I said, Monsieur Jay. And let me invite you next time. Anyone can point you to my house.'

Her tone allowed no refusal.

'I'd be pleased to. You can't imagine how happy I am to find someone who can bear my dreadful French.'

Mireille looked at him closely for a second, then smiled. 'You may be a foreigner, but you have the heart of a Frenchman. My father's house is in good hands.'

Jay watched her go, picking her way stiffly along the overgrown path towards the boundary, until she finally vanished behind the screen of trees at the end of the orchard. He wondered whether her roses still grew there.

He poured his glass of wine back into the bottle and stoppered it once more. He washed the glasses and put away the gardening tools in the shed. It was only then that he realized. After days of inactivity, struggling to put together the fugitive pieces of his unfinished novel, he could see it again, bright as ever, like a lost coin shining in the dust.

He ran for the typewriter.

*   *   *

'I RECKON YOU COULD START EM AGAIN IF YOU WANTED,' SAID JOE,
eyeing the tangled rose hedge. 'It's been a while since they
were cut back, and some of em have run to wild, but you
could do it, with a bit of work.'

Joe always pretended indifference to flowers. He preferred fruit trees, herbs and vegetables, things to be picked
and harvested, stored, dried, pickled, bottled, pulped, made
into wine. But there were always flowers in his garden all
the same. Planted as if on an afterthought: dahlias, poppies,
lavender, hollyhocks. Roses twined amongst the tomatoes.
Sweet peas amongst the beanpoles. Part of it was camouflage, of course. Part of it a lure for bees. But the truth was
that Joe liked flowers and was reluctant even to pull weeds.

Jay would not have seen the rose garden if he had not
known where to look. The wall against which the roses had
once been trained had been partly knocked down, leaving
an irregular section of brick about fifteen feet long. Greenery had shot up it, almost reaching the top, creating a dense
thicket in which he hardly recognized the roses. With the
secateurs he clipped a few briars free and revealed a single
large red rose almost touching the ground.

'Old rose,' remarked Joe, peering closer. 'Best kind for
cookin. You should try makin some rose-petal jam. Champion.'

Jay made with the secateurs again, pulling the clinging
tendrils away from the bush. He could see more rosebuds
now, tight and green away from the sun. The scent from the
open flower was light and earthy.

He had been writing half the night. Mireille had brought
enough of the story for ten pages, and it fitted easily with
the rest, as if it needed only this to carry on. Without this
central tale his book was no more than a collection of
anecdotes, but with Marise's story to bind them together it
might become a rich, absorbing novel. If only he knew
where it was leading.

In London he used to go to the gym to think. Here he made
for the garden. Garden work clears the mind. He remem-

bered those summers at Pog Hill Lane, cutting and pruning under Joe's careful supervision, mixing resin for graftings, preparing herbs for the sachets with Joe's big old mortar. It felt right to do that here, too – red ribbons on the fruit trees to frighten the birds, sachets of pungent herbs for parasites.

'They'll need feeding, anall,' remarked Joe, leaning over the roses. 'You want to get some of that rosehip wine onto the roots. Do em no end of good. Then you'll want summat for them aphids.'

Sure enough the plants were infested, the stems sticky with insect life. Jay grinned at the persistence of Joe's guiding presence.

'Perhaps I'll just use a chemical spray this year,' he suggested.

'You bloody won't, though,' exclaimed Joe. 'Buggerin everything up with chemicals. That's not what you came here for, is it?'

'So what did I come here for?'

Joe made a disgusted sound.

'Tha knows nowt,' he said.

'Enough not to be caught out again,' Jay told him. 'You and your magic bags. Your talismans. Your travels in the Orient. You really had me going, didn't you? You must have been splitting yourself laughing all the time.'

Joe looked at him sternly over his half-moon glasses.

'I never laughed,' he said. 'An if you'd had any sense to look further than the end o' yer nose—'

'Really?' Jay was getting annoyed now, tugging at the loose brambles around the rose bed with unnecessary violence. 'Then what did you leave for? Without even saying goodbye? Why did I have to come back to Pog Hill and find the house empty?'

'Oh, back to that again, are we?'

Joe settled against the apple tree and lit a Player's. The radio lying in the long grass began to play 'I Feel Love', that August's Number One.

'Cut that out,' Jay told him crossly.

Joe shrugged. The radio whined briefly and went off. 'If only you'd planted them *rosifeas*, like I meant you to,' said Joe.

'I needed a bit more than a few poxy seeds,' retorted Jay.

'You allus was hard work.' Joe flipped his cigarette butt neatly over the hedge. 'I couldn't tell you I was going because I didn't know messell. I needed to get on the move again, breathe a bit of sea air, see a bit of road. And besides, I thought I'd left you provided for. I telled yer, if only you'd planted them seeds. If only you'd had some *faith*.'

Jay had had enough. He turned to face him. For a hallucination Joe was very real, even down to the grime under his fingernails. For some reason that enraged him all the more.

'I never asked you to come!' He was shouting. He felt fifteen again, alone in Joe's cellar, with broken bottles and jars all around. 'I never asked for your help! I never wanted you here! Why *are* you here, anyway? Why don't you just leave me alone!'

Joe waited patiently for him to finish. 'Ave you done?' he said when Jay fell silent. 'Ave you bloody done?'

Jay began to cut away at the rose bushes again, not looking at him. 'Get lost, Joe,' he said, almost inaudibly.

'I bloody might, anall,' said Joe. 'Think I've not got better things to be doing? Better places to travel to? Think I've got allt time int bloody world, do yer?' His accent was thickening, as it always did on the rare occasions Jay saw him annoyed. Jay turned his back.

'*Reight*.' There was a heavy finality in the word, which made him want to turn back, but he did not. 'Please thyssen. I'll sithee.'

Jay forced himself to work at the bushes for several minutes. He could hear nothing behind him but the singing of birds and the shlush of the freshening wind across the fields. Joe had gone. And this time, Jay wasn't sure whether he ever would see him again.

37

GOING INTO AGEN THE NEXT MORNING, JAY FOUND A NOTE FROM his agent. In it Nick sounded plaintive and excited, the words underscored heavily to emphasize their importance. '<u>Get in touch with me. It's urgent.</u>' Jay phoned him from Joséphine's café. There was no phone at the farm, and he had no plans to install one. Nick sounded very faint, like a distant radio station. In the foreground Jay could hear café sounds, the chinking of glasses, the shuffle of draughts pieces, laughter, raised voices.

'Jay! Jay, I'm so glad to hear you. It's going crazy here. The new book's great. I've sent it to half a dozen publishers already. It's—'

'It isn't finished,' Jay pointed out.

'That doesn't matter. It's going to be terrific. Obviously the foreign climate is doing you good. Now what I urgently need is a—'

'Wait.' Jay was beginning to feel disorientated. 'I'm not ready.'

Nick must have heard something in his voice, because he slowed down then. 'Hey, take it easy. No-one's going to pressure you. No-one even knows where you are.'

'That's fine by me,' Jay told him. 'I need some more time on my own. I'm happy here, pottering around the garden, thinking about my book.'

He could hear Nick's mind clicking over the possibilities. 'OK. If that's what you want, I'll keep people away. I'll slow things down. What do I tell Kerry? She's been on the phone to me every other day, demanding to know what—'

'You *definitely* don't tell Kerry,' Jay told him urgently. 'She's the last person I want over here.'

'Oho,' said Nick.

'What do you mean?'

'Been doing a bit of *cherchez la femme*, have you?' He sounded amused. 'Checking out the talent?'

'No.'

'You sure?'

'Positive.'

It was true, he thought. He had hardly thought about Marise in weeks. Besides, the woman who first strode out across the pages of his book was a far cry from the recluse across the fields. It was her story he was interested in.

At Nick's insistence, he gave him Joséphine's number in case he needed to pass on an urgent message. Again, Nick asked when he would be able to see the rest of the manuscript. Jay couldn't tell him. He didn't even want to think about it. He already felt uncomfortable that Nick had shown it unfinished without his permission, even though he was only doing his job. He put down the phone to find that Joséphine had already brought over a fresh pot of coffee to his table. Roux and Poitou were sitting there with Popotte, the postwoman. Jay knew a moment's complete disorientation. London had never seemed so far away before.

He came home as usual, across the fields. It had rained during the night and the path was slippery, the hedges dripping. He skirted the road and followed the river to the border of Marise's land, enjoying the silence and the rain-heavy trees. There was no sign of Marise in the vineyard. Jay could see a small blur of smoke above the chimney of the other farm, but that was the only movement. Even the birds were silent. He was planning to cross the river at its narrowest, shallowest point, where Marise's land joined his. On either side there was a swell of banking topped by trees; a screen of fruit trees on her side and a messy tangle of hawthorn and elder on his. He noticed, as he passed, that the red ribbons he had tied to the branches had gone – blown away by the wind again, most likely. He would have to find a better way of securing them. The river flattened and shallowed out at that point, and when it rained the water spread out, making islands of the clumps of reeds and digging the red soil of the riverbank to make extravagant shapes, which the sun baked hard as clay. There were stepping stones at this crossing place, worn shiny by the river and the passage of many feet, though only he passed here now. At least, so he thought.

But when he reached the crossing place there was a girl squatting precariously by the riverbank, poking a stick at the silent water. At her side a small brown goat stared placidly. The movement he made alerted the child, and she stiffened. Eyes as bright and curious as the goat's fixed on him.

For a moment they stared at each other, she frozen to the spot, eyes wide; Jay transfixed with an overwhelming sense of *déjà vu*.

It was Gilly.

She was wearing an orange pullover and green trousers rolled up to her knees. Her discarded shoes lay a short distance away in the grass. To her side lay a red rucksack, its mouth gaping. The necklace of knotted red ribbons around her neck solved the mystery of what had been happening to Jay's talismans.

Looking at her more closely he could see now that she wasn't Gilly after all. The curly hair was more chestnut than red, and she was young, surely no more than eight or nine, but all the same, the resemblance was more than striking. She had the same vivid, freckled face, wide mouth, suspicious green eyes. She had the same way of looking, the same knee cocked out at an angle. Not Gilly, no, but so like her that it caught at the heart. Jay understood that this must be Rosa.

She fixed him with a long unsmiling stare, then grabbed for her shoes and fled. The goat shied nervously and danced across towards Jay, stopping briefly to chew at the straps of the abandoned rucksack. The girl moved as quickly as the goat, using her hands to pull herself up the slippery banking towards the fence.

'Wait!' Jay called after her. She ignored him. Quick as a weasel she was up the banking, only turning then to poke out her tongue at him in mute challenge.

'Wait!' Jay held out his hands to show her he meant no harm. 'It's all right. Don't run away.'

The girl stared at him, whether in curiosity or hostility he couldn't tell, her head slightly to one side, as if in concentration. There was no way of knowing whether she had understood.

'Hello, Rosa,' said Jay.

The child just stared.

'I'm Jay. I live over there.' He pointed to the farm, just visible behind the trees.

She was not looking directly at him, he noticed, but at something slightly to the left and down from where he was standing. Her posture was tense, ready to pounce. Jay felt in his pocket for something to give her – a sweet, perhaps, or a biscuit – but all he could find was his lighter. It was a Bic, made of cheap coloured plastic, and it shone in the sun.

'You can have this, if you like,' he suggested, holding it out across the water. The child did not react. Maybe she couldn't lip-read, he told himself.

On his side of the riverbank the goat bleated and butted gently against his legs. Rosa glanced at him, then at the goat, with a mixture of scorn and anxiety. He noticed her eyes kept moving back to the discarded rucksack, abandoned by the side of the river. He bent down and picked it up. The goat transferred its interest from Jay's legs to the sleeve of his shirt with unnerving rapidity. He held out the rucksack.

'Is this yours?'

On the far bank the girl took a step forwards.

'It's all right.' Jay spoke slowly, in case she couldn't lip-read, and smiled. 'Look. I'll bring it over.' He made for the stepping stones, holding the heavy rucksack in his arms. The goat watched him with a cynical expression. Hampered as he was with the rucksack his approach was clumsy. He looked up to smile at the girl, lost his footing on a rain-slippery stone, skidded and almost fell. The goat, which was following him curiously across the stones, nudged past unexpectedly, and Jay took a blind step forwards, and landed squarely in the swollen river.

Rosa and the goat watched in silence. Both seemed to be grinning.

'Damn.' Jay tried wading back to the bank. There was more current than he had expected, and he moved drunkenly across the river stones, his boots skidding in the mud. The rucksack seemed to be the only dry thing on his person.

Rosa grinned again.

The expression transformed her. It was a curiously sunny, sudden grin, her teeth very white in her dappled face. She laughed almost soundlessly, stamping her bare feet on the grass in a pantomime of mirth. Then she was off again, picking up her shoes and clambering up the incline towards the orchard. The goat followed her, nibbling affectionately at a dangling shoelace. As they reached the top, Rosa turned and waved, though whether this was a gesture of defiance or affection Jay could not tell.

When she had gone he realized he still had her rucksack. On opening it he found inside a number of items only a child could treasure: a jar of snails, some pieces of wood, river stones, string and a number of the red talismans, carefully tied together with their ribbons to form a bright garland. Jay replaced all the treasures inside the bag, then he hung the rucksack up on a gatepost close to the hedge, in the same place he had hung the dragon's head a fortnight earlier. He was sure Rosa would find it.

*   *   *

'I HAVEN'T SEEN HER FOR MONTHS,' SAID JOSÉPHINE LATER IN THE café. 'Marise doesn't send her to school any more. It's a pity. A little girl like that needs friends.' Jay nodded.

'She used to go to the village playgroup,' remembered Joséphine. 'She must have been three, maybe a little younger. She could still talk a little then, but I don't think she could hear anything.'

'Oh?' Jay was curious. 'I thought she was born deaf.'

Joséphine shook her head. 'No. It was some kind of infection. It was the year Tony died. A bad winter. The river flooded again, and half of Marise's fields were underwater for three months. Plus there was that business with the police . . .'

Jay looked at her enquiringly.

'Oh yes. Ever since Tony died Mireille has been trying to pin the blame on Marise. There'd been some kind of a quarrel, she said. Tony would never have killed himself. She tried to make out there was another man, or something, that together they'd conspired to murder Tony.' She shook her head, frowning. 'Mireille was half out of her mind,' she said. 'I think she would have said anything. Of course, it never came to that. The police came round, asked some questions, went away. I think they had the measure of Mireille by then. But she spent the next three or four years writing letters, campaigning, petitioning. Someone came round once or twice, that's all. But nothing came of it. She's been spreading rumours that Marise keeps the child locked up in a back room, or something.'

'I don't think that's true.' The vivid, dappled child Jay had seen gave no impression of having ever been shut up in a back room.

Joséphine shrugged. 'No, I don't think so either,' she said. 'But by that time the damage was done. Gangs of people gathering at the gate of the farm and across the river. Dogooders, for the most part, harmless enough, but Marise wasn't to know that, holed up in her house, with torches burning outside and people letting off firecrackers and throwing stones at the shutters.' She shook her head. 'By the time things settled down it was too late,' she explained. 'She was already convinced everyone was against her. And then when Rosa disappeared . . .'

Joséphine poured a measure of cognac into her coffee. 'I suppose she thought we were all in it. You can't hide much in a village, and everybody knew that Mireille had Rosa staying with her. The child was three then, and we all thought they must have made it up between them somehow, and Rosa was there for a visit. Of course, Caro Clairmont knew otherwise, and so did a few others, Joline Drou, who was her best friend at the time, and Cussonnet the doctor. But the rest of us . . . well, no-one asked. People reckoned that after what had happened perhaps they ought to mind their own business. And no-one really knew Marise, of course.'

'She doesn't make it easy,' observed Jay.

'Rosa was missing for about three days. Mireille only tried taking her out of the house once. The first day. That didn't last long. You could hear her screaming right down to Les Marauds. Whatever else was wrong with her, she had a good pair of lungs. Nothing would make her be quiet, not sweets, or presents, or fussing, or shouting. They all tried – Caro, Joline, Toinette – but still the child wouldn't stop screaming. Finally Mireille got worried and called the doctor. They put their heads together and took her to a specialist in Agen. It just wasn't normal for a child that age to scream all the time. They thought she was disturbed, that perhaps she'd been mistreated in some way.' She frowned. 'Then Marise came to pick up Rosa from the playgroup, and found that the doctor and Mireille had taken her to Agen instead. I've never seen *anyone* so angry. She followed them on her moped, but all she could find out was that Mireille had taken Rosa to some kind of hospital. For tests, she said. I don't know what they were trying to prove.'

She shrugged again. 'If she'd been anyone else she could have counted on help from the village,' she said. 'But Marise

– never says a word unless she has to, never smiles – I suppose people just minded their own business. That's all it was really; there was no malice in it. She wanted to be left alone, and that's what people did. Not that anyone really knew where Mireille had taken Rosa – except maybe Caro Clairmont. Oh, we heard all kinds of stories. But that was afterwards. How Marise stamped into Cussonnet's surgery with a shotgun and marched him out to the car. To hear people talking you'd think half of Lansquenet saw that. It's always the same, *héh*! All I can say is, I wasn't there. And though Rosa was back at home before the end of that week, we never saw her in the village again – not in the school, or even at the firework display on the fourteenth of July, or the chocolate festival at Easter.' Joséphine drained her coffee abruptly and wiped her hands on her apron. 'So that was that,' she concluded with an air of finality. 'That was the last we saw of Marise and Rosa. I see them from time to time – perhaps once a month or so – on the road to Agen or walking to Narcisse's nursery, or in the field across the river. But that's all. She hasn't forgiven the village for what happened after Tony's death, or for taking sides, or for turning a blind eye when Rosa disappeared. You can't tell her it was nothing to do with you; she won't believe it.'

Jay nodded. It was understandable. 'It must be a lonely life for them,' he said. Thinking of Maggie and Gilly, of the way they always managed to make friends wherever they went, trading and fixing and doing odd jobs to make ends meet, always on the move, fielding insults and prejudice with the same cheery defiance. How different was this dour, suspicious woman from Joe's friends of Nether Edge. And yet the child looked so very like Gilly. He checked for the rucksack on his way back to the farm, but, as he expected, it had already been removed. Only the dragon's head remained, still lolling its long crêpe tongue, now embellished with a garland of fluttering red ribbons, which sat jauntily on the thick green mane. Coming closer, Jay noticed that the stump of a clay pipe had been carefully positioned between the dragon's teeth, from which a dandelion clock protruded. And as he passed, hiding a grin, he was almost sure he saw something move in the hedge next to him, a brief flash of orange under the new green, and heard the impudent bleating of a goat in the distance.

38

LATER, OVER HIS FAVOURITE *GRAND CRÈME* IN THE CAFÉ DES
Marauds, he was listening with half an ear to Joséphine
as she told him the story of the village's first chocolate
festival and the resistance with which it had been met
by the church. The coffee was good, sprinkled with
shavings of dark chocolate and with a cinnamon biscuit
by the side of the cup. Narcisse was sitting opposite
with his usual seed catalogue and a *café-cassis*. In the
afternoons the place was busier, but Jay noticed that
the clientele still consisted mainly of old men, playing
chess or cards and talking in their low rapid patois. In
the evening it would be full of workers back from the
fields and the farms. He wondered where the young
people went at night.

'Not many young people stay here,' Joséphine explained.
'There isn't the work, unless you want to go into farming.
And most of the farms have been divided so often between
all the family's sons that there isn't much of a livelihood left
for anyone.'

'Always the sons,' said Jay. 'Never the daughters.'

'There aren't many women who'd want to run a farm in
Lansquenet,' said Joséphine, shrugging. 'And some of the
growers and distributors don't like the idea of working for
a woman.'

Jay gave a short laugh.

Joséphine looked at him. 'You don't believe that?'

He shook his head. 'It's hard for me to understand,' he explained. 'In London—'

'This isn't London.' Joséphine seemed amused. 'People hold close to their traditions here. The church. The family. The land. That's why so many of the young people leave. They want what they read about in their magazines. They want the cities, cars, clubs, shops. But there are always some who stay. And some who come back.'

She poured another *café-crème* and smiled. 'There was a time when I would have given anything to get out of Lansquenet,' she said. 'Once I even set off. Packed my bags and left home.'

'What happened?'

'I stopped on the way for a cup of hot chocolate.' She laughed. 'And then I realized I couldn't leave. I'd never really wanted to in the first place.' She paused to pick up some empty glasses from a nearby table. 'When you've lived here long enough you'll understand. After a time, people find it hard to leave a place like Lansquenet. It isn't just a village. The houses aren't just places to live. Everything belongs to everybody. Everyone belongs to everyone else. Even a single person can make a difference.'

He nodded. It was what had first attracted him to Pog Hill Lane. The comings and goings. The conversations over the wall. The exchange of recipes, of baskets of fruit and bottles of wine. The constant presence of other people. While Joe was still there Pog Hill Lane stayed alive. Everything died with his departure. Suddenly he envied Joséphine her life, her friends, her view over Les Marauds. Her memories.

'What about me?' he wondered. 'Will I make a difference?'

'Of course.'

He hadn't realized he had spoken aloud.

'Everyone knows about you, Jay. Everyone asks me about you. It takes a little time for someone to be accepted here. People need to know if you're going to stay. They don't want to give themselves to someone who won't stay. And some of them are afraid.'

'Of what?'

'Change. It may seem ridiculous to you, but most of us like the village the way it is. We don't want to be like Montauban or Le Pinot. We don't want tourists passing through, buying up the houses at high prices and leaving the place dead in the winter. Tourists are like a plague of wasps. They get everywhere. They eat everything. They'd clean us out in a year. There'd be nothing of us left but guest houses and games arcades. Lansquenet – the *real* Lansquenet – would disappear.'

She shook her head. 'People are watching you, Jay. They see you so friendly with Caro and Georges Clairmont, and they think perhaps you and they . . .' She hesitated. 'Then they see Mireille Faizande going to visit you, and they think how perhaps you might be planning to buy the other farm, next year, when the lease expires.'

'Marise's farm? Why should I want to do that?' he asked, curious.

'Whoever owns it controls all the land down to the river. The fast road to Toulouse is only a few kilometres away. Easy enough to develop. To build. It's happened before, in other places.'

'Not here. Not me.' Jay looked at her evenly. 'I'm here to write, that's all. To finish my book. That's all I'm interested in.'

Joséphine nodded, satisfied. 'I know. But you were asking so many questions about her. I thought per-haps—'

'No!'

Narcisse shot him a curious glance from behind his seed catalogue.

Lowering his voice quickly: 'Look. I'm a writer. I'm interested in what goes on. I like stories. That's all.'

Joséphine poured another coffee and sprinkled hazelnut sugar on the froth.

'It's the truth,' insisted Jay. 'I'm not here to make any changes. I like the place the way it is.'

Joséphine looked at him for a moment, then nodded, seemingly satisfied. 'All right, Monsieur Jay,' she said, smiling. 'I'll tell them you're OK.'

They toasted her decision in hazelnut coffee.

39

SINCE THAT TIME AT THE STREAM JAY HAD SEEN ROSA ONLY from a distance. A few times he thought he had caught her watching from behind the hedge, and once he was sure he heard quiet footfalls from behind an angle of the house, and, of course, he had seen her leavings. The modifications to the dragon head, for instance. The little garlands of flowers and leaves and feathers left on gateposts and fences to replace the red ribbons she had stolen. Once or twice a drawing – a house, a garden, stick-children playing under improbably purple trees – tacked to a stump, the paper already curling and fading in the sunlight. There was no way of telling whether these things were offerings, toys or some way of taunting him. She was as elusive as her mother, but as curious as her goat, and their meeting must have convinced her that Jay was harmless. Once, he saw them together. Marise was working behind the hedge. For a time Jay was able to see her face. Again he realized how far this woman differed from the heroine of his book. He had time to notice the fine arch of her brows, the thin but graceful line of her mouth, the sharp angle of cheekbone, barely grazed with colour by the sun. Given the right circumstances she could be beautiful. Not round and pretty-plump like Popotte, or brown and sensual like the young girls of the village. No, hers was a grave, pale, northern beauty, small-featured beneath the blunt red hair. Something moved behind her. She sprang to her feet, whipping round as she did, and in that instant he had time to glimpse another change. She was quicker than a cat, turning defensively — not towards him, but away — though even her speed didn't hide that look . . . of what?

Fear?

It lasted less than a second. Rosa leaped at her, crowing, arms outstretched, face split in a wide, delighted grin. Another twist. Jay had imagined the child intimidated, perhaps hiding amongst the vines as he hid from Zeth in the old Nether Edge days, but that look held nothing but adoration. He watched as she climbed Marise like a tree, legs wrapped around her mother's waist, arms locked around her neck. For a moment Marise held her and he saw their profiles close together. Rosa's hands moved softly, close to her mother's face, signing in the language of the deaf. Marise snubbed Rosa's nose gently against hers. Her face was illuminated more sweetly than he could ever have imagined. Suddenly he felt ashamed at having believed, or half believed, Mireille's suggestion that Marise might be mistreating the child. Their love was something which coloured the air between them like sunlight. The interchange between them was completely, perfectly silent.

Marise put Rosa down and signed to her. Jay had never watched anyone signing before, and he was struck by the grace and animation of the movements, of the facial expressions. Rosa signed back, insistently. His feeling of intrusion increased. The gestures were too quick for him to guess at the subject of the conversation. They were in their circle of privacy. Their conversation was the most intimate thing Jay had ever witnessed.

Marise laughed silently, like her daughter. The expression illuminated her like sunlight through glass. Rosa rubbed her stomach as she laughed and stamped her feet. They held each other as they communicated, as if every part of the body were a part of their talk, as if, instead of losing a sense, they had gained something more.

Since then he thought about them both more often. It had gone far beyond his curiosity for her story and into something he could not define. Joséphine teased him about it. Narcisse refrained entirely from comment, but there was a knowing look in his eye when Jay talked about her. He did so too often. He could not stop himself. Mireille Faizande was the only person he knew who would talk about her interminably. Jay had been to see her several times, but could not bring himself to mention the intimate scene he witnessed between mother and daughter. When he tried to hint at a warmer relationship between them than she had portrayed, Mireille turned on him in scorn.

'What do you know about it?' she snapped. 'How can you possibly know what she's like?' Her eyes went to the fresh vase of roses by the table. There was a framed photograph beside it, showing a laughing boy sitting on a motorbike. Tony.

'She doesn't want her,' she said in a lower voice. 'Just as she didn't want my son.' Her eyes were hard. 'She took my son as she takes everything. To spoil. To play with. That's what my Rosa is to her now. Something to play with, to discard when she's had enough.' Her hands worked. 'It's her fault if the child's deaf,' she said. 'Tony was perfect. It couldn't have come from his side of the family. She's vicious. She spoils everything she touches.'

She glanced again at the photograph by the side of the vase.

'She'd been deceiving him all the time, you know. There was another man all along. A man from the hospital.'

Jay remembered someone saying something about a hospital. A nerve clinic in Paris.

'Was she ill?' he enquired.

Mireille made a scornful sound. 'Ill? That's what Tony said. Said she needed protecting. My Tony was a rock to her, young as he was. *Héh*, he was strong, clear. He imagined everyone was as clear and honest as he was.' She glanced again at the roses. 'You've been busy,' she commented without warmth. 'You've brought my poor rose bushes back from the dead.'

The phrase hung between them like smoke.

'I tried to feel sorry for her,' said Mireille. 'For Tony's sake. But even then it wasn't easy. She'd hide out in the house, wouldn't talk to anyone, not even to family. Then, for no reason, rages. Terrible rages, screaming and throwing things. Sometimes she'd hurt herself with knives, razors, anything which came to hand. We had to hide everything which could be dangerous.'

'How long were they married?'

She shrugged. 'Less than a year. He courted her for longer. He was twenty-one when he died.'

Her hands moved again, clenching and unclenching.

'I can't stop thinking about it,' she said finally. 'Thinking about both of them. He must have followed her from the hospital. Settled somewhere close, where they could meet. Héh, I can't stop thinking that during all that year when she was married to Tony, when she was carrying his baby, the bitch was laughing at him. Both of them laughing at my boy.' She glared at me. 'You think about that, héh, before you go talking about things you don't understand. You think about what that did to my boy.'

'I'm sorry. If you'd prefer not to talk about it—'

Mireille snorted. 'It's other people who'd prefer not to talk about it,' she said sourly. 'Prefer not to think about it, héh, prefer to think it's only crazy old Mireille talking. Mireille who's never been the same since her son killed himself. So much easier to mind your own business, to let her get on with her life, and never mind that she stole my son and ruined him just because she could, héh, the way she's stolen my Rosa.' Her voice cracked, whether with rage or grief he could not tell. Then her face smoothed again, became almost smug with satisfaction.

'But I'll show her,' she went on. 'Come next year, héh, when she needs a roof over her head. When the lease runs out. She'll have to come to me then if she wants to stay here, héh? And she does want to stay.' Her face was sly and glossy.

'Why should she?' It seemed that whomever he asked it

came back to this. 'Why should she want to stay here? She has no friends. There's no-one for her here. If she wants to get away from Lansquenet, how can anyone stop her?'

Mireille laughed. 'Let her want,' she said shortly. 'She needs me. She knows why.'

Mireille refused to explain her final statement, and when Jay visited her again he found her guarded and uncommunicative. He understood that one of them had overstepped the mark with the other, and he tried to be more cautious in future, wooing her with roses. She accepted the gifts cheerfully enough, but made no further move to confide in him. He had to be content with what information he had already gleaned.

What fascinated him most about Marise was the conflicting views of her in the village. Everyone had an opinion, though no-one, except Mireille, seemed any more informed than the others. To Caro Clairmont she was a miserly recluse. To Mireille, a faithless wife who had deliberately taken advantage of a young man's innocence. To Joséphine, a brave woman raising a child alone. To Narcisse, a shrewd businesswoman with a right to privacy. Roux, who had worked her *vendanges* every year when he was travelling on the river, remembered her as a quiet, polite woman who carried her baby in a sling on her back, even when she was working in the fields, who brought him a cooler of beer when it was hot, who paid cash.

'Some people are suspicious of us, *héh*,' he said with a grin. 'Travellers on the river, always on the move. They imagine all kinds of things. They lock up their valuables. They watch their daughters. Or they try too hard. They smile too often. They slap you on the back and call you *mon pote*. She wasn't like that. She always called me *monsieur*. She didn't say much. It was business between us, man to man.' He shrugged and drained his can of Stella.

Everyone he spoke to had their own image of her. Popotte remembered a morning just after the funeral, when Marise turned up outside Mireille's house with a suitcase and the baby in a carrier. Popotte was delivering letters and arrived at the house just as Marise was knocking at the door.

'Mireille opened it and fairly dragged Marise inside,' she recalled. 'The baby was asleep in the carrier, but the movement woke her and she started to scream. Mireille grabbed the letters from my hand and slammed the door behind them, but I could hear their voices, even through the door, and the baby screaming and screaming.' She shook her head. 'I think Marise was planning to leave that morning – she looked all ready and packed to go – but Mireille talked her out of it somehow. I know that after that she hardly came into the village at all. Perhaps she was afraid of what people were saying.'

The rumours began soon after. Everyone had a story. She had an uncanny ability to arouse curiosity, hostility, envy, rage.

Lucien Merle believed that her refusal to give up the uncultivated marshland by the river had blocked his plans for redevelopment.

'We could have made something of that land,' he repeated bitterly. 'There's no future in farming any more. The future's in tourism.' He took a long drink of his *diabolo-menthe* and shook his head. 'Look at Le Pinot. One man was all it took to begin the change. One man with vision.' He sighed. 'I bet that man's a millionnaire by now,' he said mournfully.

Jay tried to sift through what he had heard. In some ways he felt he had gained insights into the mystery of Marise d'Api, but in others he was as ignorant as he had been from the start. None of the reports quite tallied with what he had seen. Marise had too many faces, her substance slipping away like smoke whenever he thought he had captured it. And no-one had yet mentioned what he saw in her that day, that fierce look of love for her child. And that moment of fear, the look of a wild animal which will do anything, including kill, to protect itself and its young.

Fear? What could there be for her to fear in Lansquenet? He wished he knew.

40

Pog Hill, Summer 1977

IT WAS AUGUST WHEN EVERYTHING SOURED FOR GOOD. THE TIME of the wasps' nests, the den at Nether Edge, Elvis. Then the Bread Baron wrote to say that he and Candide were getting married, and for a while the papers were full of them both, snapped getting into a limo on the beachfront at Cannes, at a movie première, at a club in the Bahamas, on his yacht. Jay's mother gathered these articles with a collector's zeal and read and reread them, insatiably relishing Candide's hair, Candide's dresses. His grandparents took this badly, mothering his mother even more than before, and treating Jay with cool indifference, as if his father's genes were a time bomb inside him which might at any moment explode.

The grey weather grew hotter, mulchy and dull. There was often rain, but it was warm and unrefreshing. Joe worked cheerlessly in his allotment; the fruit was spoiled that year, rotting on the branches and green from lack of sunlight.

'Might as well not bother, lad,' he would mutter, fingering the blackened stem of a pear or apple. 'Might as well just bloody jack it in this year.'

Gilly's mother did well enough out of it, though; she'd somehow got hold of a whole truckload of those transparent bell-shaped umbrellas which were so popular then and was selling them at a mighty profit in the market. Gilly reckoned they could live until December on the takings. The thought merely accentuated Jay's sense of doom. It was only days to the end of August, and the return to school was barely a week away. Gilly would move on in the autumn – Maggie was talking about moving south to a commune she'd heard of near Abingdon, and there was no certainty she would ever come back. Jay felt prickly inside, fey one moment and the next blackly paranoid, saying the opposite of what he meant, reading mockery in everything that was said to him. He quarrelled repeatedly with Gilly about nothing. They made up, cautiously and incompletely, circling each other like wary animals, their intimacy broken. A sense of doom coloured everything.

On the last day of August he went to Joe's house alone, but the old man seemed distant, preoccupied. Although it was raining, he did not invite Jay in, but stood with him by the door in an oddly formal manner. Jay noticed that he had piled up a number of old crates by the back wall, and his gaze kept moving towards these, as if he were eager to get back to some job he had abandoned. Jay felt a sudden surge of anger. He deserved better than that, he thought. He thought Joe respected him. He ran down to Nether Edge with his cheeks flaring. He left his bike close to Joe's house – after the incident at the railway bridge that hiding place was no longer secure – and walked down the abandoned railway track from Pog Hill, cutting down into the Edge and towards the river. He wasn't expecting to see Gilly – they had made no plans to meet – and yet Jay was unsurprised when he caught sight of her by the riverbank, her hair scrawling down towards the water, a long stick in one hand. She was on her knees, poking the stick at something in the water, and he got quite close to her before she looked up.

Her face was pinkish and mottled, as if she'd been crying. Jay rejected the thought almost instantly. Gilly never cried.

'Oh, it's you,' she said indifferently.

Jay said nothing. He dug his hands into his pockets and tried a smile, which felt stupid on his face. Gilly didn't smile back.

'What's that?' He nodded at the thing in the water.

'Nothing.' She slung the stick into the current and it washed away. The water was scummy, brownish. Gilly's hair was starred with droplets, which clung to her curls like burrs.

'Bloody rain.'

Jay would have liked to say something then, something which might have made it all right between them. But the sky felt heavy over them, and the smell of smoke and doom was overwhelming, like an omen. Suddenly Jay was certain he would never see Gilly again.

'Shall we go and have a look at the dump?' he suggested. 'I thought I saw some good new stuff there on the way down. Magazines and stuff. You know.'

Gilly shrugged. 'Nah.'

'Good wasping weather.' It was a last, desperate ploy. He had never known Gilly to refuse an offer of wasping. Wasps are sleepy in wet weather, allowing easier, safer access to the nest. 'Do you want to come and look for nests? I've seen a place down by the bridge that might have a couple.'

Again, the shrug. Gilly shook her damp curls. 'I'm not that bothered.'

The silence was longer still this time, spinning out endlessly, unravelling.

'Maggie's moving on next week,' said Gilly at last. 'We're going to some bloody commune in Oxfordshire. She's got a job waiting for her there, she says.'

'Oh.'

He had expected it, of course. This was nothing new. So why then did his heart wrench when she said it? Her face was turned towards the water, studiously watching something on the brown surface. Jay's fists clenched in his

208

pockets. As they did he felt something brush against his hand. Joe's talisman. It felt greasy, smooth with much handling. He had become so accustomed to carrying it with him that he had forgotten it was even there. He squatted next to her. He could smell the river, a sour, metallic smell, like pennies soaked in ammonia.

'Are you coming back?' he asked.

'Nah.'

There must have been something interesting on the surface of the water. Her eyes refused to meet his.

'Don't think so. Maggie says I need to go to a proper school now. Don't need all this moving about.'

Again that flare of hateful, irrational rage. Jay looked at the water in loathing. Suddenly he wanted to hurt someone – Gilly, himself – and he stood up abruptly.

'*Shit.*' It was the worst word he knew. His mouth felt numb. His heart, too. He kicked viciously at the river's edge and a clod of earth and grass tore free and plunked into the water. Gilly didn't look at him.

He let his temper run freely then, kicking again at the banking so that earth and grass showered into the water. Some of it flew at Gilly, too, spattering her jeans and her embroidered shirt.

'Stop it, for crying out loud,' said Gilly flatly. 'Stop being so sodding childish.'

It was true, he thought, he *was* being childish, and to hear it from her enraged him. That she should accept their separation with such ease, such indifference. Something yawned blackly inside Jay's head, yawned and grimaced.

'Fuck it, then,' he said. 'I'm off.'

Feeling slightly dizzy he turned and walked off up the banking towards the canal towpath, sure she'd call him back. Ten paces. Twelve. He reached the towpath, not looking back, knowing she was watching. He passed the trees, where she couldn't see him, and turned, but Gilly was still sitting where she'd been before, not watching, not following, just looking down into the water, hair over her face and the crazy silver scrawl of the rain fanning down from the hot summer sky.

'Fuck it then,' Jay repeated fiercely, wanting her to hear. But she never turned, and at last it was he who turned away and began to walk, feeling angry and somehow deflated, towards the bridge.

He often wondered what might have happened if he had gone back, or if she had looked up just at that moment. What might have been saved or averted. Certainly the events at Pog Hill might have been very different. Perhaps he could even have said goodbye to Joe. As it was, though he did not know it at the time, he would not see either of them again.

41

Lansquenet, May 1999

HE HAD NOT SEEN JOE SINCE THE DAY AFTER MIREILLE'S VISIT.
At first Jay felt relieved by his absence, then as days passed
he grew uneasy. He tried to *will* the old man to appear, but
Joe remained stubbornly absent, as if his appearances were
not a matter of Jay's choosing. His leaving left a strangeness
behind, a bereavement. At any moment Jay expected him to
be there, in the garden, looking over the vegetable patch; in
the kitchen, lifting the lid of a pan to find out what was
cooking. He was aware of Joe's absence as he sat at his
typewriter, of the Joe-shaped hole in the centre of things, of
the fact that, try as he might, he could not seem to get the
radio to pick up the oldies station which Joe found with
such everyday ease. Worse, his new book had no life
without Joe. He no longer felt like writing. He wanted a
drink, but drunkenness merely accentuated his feeling of
loss.

He told himself that this was ridiculous. He could not
miss what was never there in the first place. But still he
could not shake off the feeling of something terribly lost,
terribly wrong.

If only you'd had some faith.

That was really the problem, wasn't it? Faith. The old Jay

would have had no hesitation. He believed everything. Somehow he knew he had to get back to the old Jay, to finish what they had left unfinished, Joe and he, in the summer of '77. If only he knew how. He would do anything, he promised himself. Anything at all.

Finally, he brought out the last of Joe's rosehip wine. The bottle was dusty from its time in the cellar, the cord at its neck straw-coloured with age. Its contents were silent, waiting. Feeling self-conscious, but at the same time oddly excited, Jay poured a glassful and raised it to his lips.

'I'm sorry, old man. Friends, OK?'

He waited for Joe to come.

He waited until dark.

In the cellar, laughter.

42

JOSÉPHINE MUST HAVE SPREAD THE WORD ABOUT HIM AT LAST. JAY found people becoming more friendly. Many of them greeted him as he passed, and Poitou in the bakery, who had spoken to him only with a shopkeeper's politeness before, now asked about his book and gave him advice on what to buy.

'The *pain aux noix* is good today, Monsieur Jay. Try it with goat's cheese and a few olives. Leave the olives and the cheese on a sunny window-ledge for an hour before you eat them to release the flavours.' He kissed his fingertips. '*That*'s something you won't find in London.'

Poitou had been a baker in Lansquenet for twenty-five years. He had rheumatism in his fingers, but claimed that handling the dough kept them supple. Jay promised to make him a grain pack which would help – another trick of Joe's. Strange, how easily it all came back. With Poitou's approval came more introductions – Guillaume the ex-schoolteacher, Darien who taught the infants' class, Rodolphe the minibus driver who took the children to school and brought them home every day, Nénette who was a nurse in the nearby old people's home, Briançon who kept bees at the other side of Les Marauds – as if they were merely waiting for the all-clear to indulge their curiosity. Now they were all questions. What did Jay do in London? Was he married? No, but surely someone, *héh*? No? Astonishment. Now suspicions had been allayed they were insatiably curious, broaching the most personal of topics with the same innocent interest. What was his last book? How much exactly did an English writer earn? Had he been on television? And America? Had he seen America? Sighs of rapture over the reply. This information would be eagerly disseminated across the village over cups of coffee and bottles of *blonde*, whispered in shops, passed from mouth to mouth and elaborated upon each time in the telling.

Gossip was currency in Lansquenet. More questions followed, robbed of offence by their ingenuousness. And I? Am I in your book? And I? And I? At first Jay hesitated. People don't always respond well to the idea that they have been observed, their features borrowed, their mannerisms copied. Some expect payment. Others are insulted by the portrayal. But here it was different. Suddenly everyone had a story to tell. You can put it in your book, they told him. Some even wrote them down – on scraps of notepaper, wrapping paper, once on the back of a packet of seeds. Many of these people, especially the older ones, rarely picked up a book themselves. Some, like Narcisse, had difficulty reading at all. But still the respect for books was immense. Joe was the same, his miner's background having taught him from an early age that reading was a waste of time, hiding his *National Geographics* under the bed, but secretly delighted by the stories Jay read to him, nodding his head as he listened, unsmiling. And though Jay never saw him read more than *Culpeper's Herbal* and the odd magazine, he would occasionally come out with a quote or a literary reference which could only have come from extensive, if secret, study. Joe liked poetry in the same way he liked flowers, hiding his affection almost shamefacedly beneath a semblance of disinterest. But his garden betrayed him. Pansies stared up from the edges of cold frames. Wild roses intertwined with runner beans. Lansquenet was like Joe in this. There was a thick vein of romance running through its practicality. Jay found that almost overnight he had become someone new to cherish, to shake heads over in bewilderment – the English writer, *dingue mais sympa, héh!* – someone who provoked laughter and awe in equal doses. Lansquenet's holy fool. For the moment he could do no wrong. There were no more cries of *Rosbif!* from the schoolchildren. And the presents. He was overwhelmed with presents. A jar of comb honey from Briançon, with an anecdote about his younger sister and how she once tried to prepare a rabbit – 'after over an hour in the kitchen she flung it out of the doorway shouting, "Take it back! I can't pluck the damn thing!" ' and a note: 'You can use it in your book.' A cake from Popotte, carried carefully in her postbag with the letters and balanced in her bicycle basket for the journey. An unexpected gift of seed potatoes from Narcisse, with mumbled instructions to plant them by the sunny side of the house. Any offer of payment would have caused offence. Jay tried to repay this stream of small kindnesses by buying drinks in the Café des Marauds, but found he still bought fewer rounds than anyone else.

'It's all right,' explained Joséphine when he mentioned this to her. 'It's how people are here. They need a little time to get used to you. Then . . .' She grinned. Jay was carrying a shopping bag filled with gifts which people left for him under Joséphine's bar – cakes, biscuits, bottles of wine, a cushion-cover from Denise Poitou, a terrine from Toinette Arnauld. She looked at the basket and her grin widened. 'I think we can say you've been accepted, don't you?'

There was one exception to this new-found welcome. Marise d'Api remained as remote as ever. It was three weeks since he had last tried to speak to her. He had seen her since, but only from a distance, twice in the tractor and once on foot, always at work in the field. Of the daughter, nothing. Jay told himself that his feeling of disappointment was absurd. From what he had heard Marise was hardly going to be affected by what happened in the village.

He wrote back to Nick with another fifty pages of the new manuscript. Since then progress had been slower. Part of this was to do with the garden. There was a great deal of work to be done there, and now that summer was in sight the weeds had begun to take over. Joe was right. He would need to sort it out while it was still possible. There were plenty of plants there worth saving, if he could only clear the mess. There was a square of herbs about twenty feet across, with the remains of a tiny thyme hedge around it. Three rows each of potatoes, turnips, globe artichokes, carrots and what might be celeriac. Jay seeded marigolds between the rows of potatoes to eliminate beetles, and lemon balm around the carrots for the slugs. But he needed to consider the winter's vegetables and the summer's salads. He went to Narcisse's nursery for seeds and seedlings: sprouting broccoli for September, rocket and frisée for July and August. In the cold frame he had made from Clairmont's doors he had already seeded some baby vegetables – Little Gem lettuces and fingerling carrots and parsnips – which might be ready in a month or so. Joe was right, the land here was good. The soil was a rich russet, at the same time moist and lighter than across the river. There were fewer stones, too. The ones he found he slung onto what would become his rockery. He had almost finished restoring the rose garden. Pinned into place against the old wall the roses had begun to swell and bud; a cascade of half-opened flowers dripping against the pinkish brick to release their winey scent. They were almost free of aphids now. Joe's old recipe – lavender, lemon balm and cloves stitched into red flannel sachets and tied onto the stems just above the soil – had worked its usual magic. Every Sunday or so he would pick a bunch of the most open blooms and take them to Mireille Faizande's house in the Place Saint-Antoine after the service.

Jay was not expected to attend Mass. *En tout cas, tous les Anglais sont païens.* The term was used with affection. Not so with *La Païenne* across the river. Even the old men on the café's *terrasse* viewed her with suspicion. Perhaps because she was a woman alone. When Jay asked outright, he found he was politely stonewalled. Mireille looked at the roses for a long time. Lifting them to her face, she breathed the scent. Her arthritic hands, oddly delicate in comparison with her bulky body, touched the petals gently.

'Thank you.' She gave a formal little nod. 'My lovely roses. I'll put them into water. Come in, and I'll make some tea.'

Her house was clean and airy, with the whitewashed walls and stone floors of the region, but its simplicity was deceptive. An Aubusson rug hung on one wall, and there was a grandfather clock in the corner of the living room which Kerry would have sold her soul for. Mireille saw him looking. 'That belonged to my grandmother,' she said. 'It used to be in my nursery when I was a child. I remember listening to the chimes when I lay awake in bed. It plays a different carillon for the hour, the half and the quarter. Tony loved it.' Her mouth tightened, and she turned away to arrange the roses in a bowl. 'Tony's daughter would have loved it.'

The tea was weak, like flower water. She served it in what must have been her best Limoges, with silver tongs for the sugar and lemon.

'I'm sure she would. If only her mother were a little less reclusive.'

Mireille looked at him. Derisively. 'Reclusive? *Héh!* She's antisocial, Monsieur Jay. Hates everyone. Her family more than anyone else.' She sipped her tea. 'I would have helped her if she'd let me. I wanted to bring them both to live with me. Give the child what she needs most. A proper home. A family. But she—' She put down the cup. Jay noticed that she never called Marise by name. 'She insists on maintaining the terms of the lease. She insists she will stay until next July, when it expires. Refuses to come to the village. Refuses to talk to me or to my nephew, who offers to help her. And afterwards, *héh?* She plans to buy the land from Pierre-Emile. Why? She wants to be independent, she says. She doesn't want to owe us anything.' Mireille's face was a clenched fist. '*Owe* us! She owes me everything. I gave her a home. I gave her *my son!* There's nothing left of him now but the child. And even there she's managed to take her from us. Only she can talk to her, with that sign language she uses. She'll never know about her father and how he died. She's even fixed that. Even if I could—'

The old woman broke off abruptly. 'Never mind, *héh!*' she said with an effort. 'She'll come round eventually. She'll have to come round. She can't hold out for ever. Not when I—' Again she broke off, her teeth snapping together with a small brittle sound.

'I don't see why she should be so hostile,' said Jay at last. 'The village is such a friendly place. Look how friendly everyone's been to me. If she gave people a chance I'm sure they'd welcome her. It can't be easy, living on her own. You'd think she'd be pleased to know people were concerned—'

'You don't understand.' Mireille's voice was contemptuous. 'She knows what sort of welcome she'd get if she ever showed her face here. That's why she stays away. Ever since he brought her here from Paris it's been the same. She never fitted in. Never even tried. Everyone knows what she did, *héh.* I've made sure of that.' Her black eyes narrowed in triumph.

'Everybody knows how she murdered my son.'

43

'WELL, SHE EXAGGERATES, YOU KNOW,' SAID CLAIRMONT peaceably. They were in the Café des Marauds, which was filling up rapidly with its after-work crowd, he in his oil-stained overalls and blue beret, a group of his workers, Roux amongst them, gathered around a table behind him. The comfortable reek of Gauloises and coffee filled the air. Someone behind them was discussing a recent football match. Joséphine was busy microwaving pizza slices.

'Héh, José, un croque, tu veux bien?'

On the counter stood a bowl of boiled eggs and a dish of salt. Clairmont took one and began to peel it carefully. 'I mean, everyone knows she didn't actually kill him. But there are plenty of other ways than pulling the trigger, héh?'

'Driven him to it, you mean?'

Clairmont nodded. 'He was an easy-going lad. Thought she was perfect. Did everything for her, even after they were married. Wouldn't hear a word spoken against her. Said she was highly strung and delicate. Well, maybe she was, héh?' He helped himself to salt from the dish. 'The way he was with her, you'd have thought she was glass. She'd just come out of one of those hospitals, he said. Something wrong with her nerves.' Clairmont laughed. 'Nerves, héh! Wasn't anything wrong with her nerves. But anyone dared say anything about her—' He shrugged. 'Killed himself trying to please her, poor Tony. Worked himself half to death for her, then shot himself when she tried to leave him.' He bit into his egg with melancholy gusto.

'Oh yes, she was going to leave,' he added, seeing Jay's surprise. 'Had her bags all packed and ready. Mireille saw them. There'd been some row,' he explained, finishing the egg and gesturing to Joséphine for a second *blonde*. 'There was always some kind of a row going on in that place. But this time it really looked as if she was going to go through with it. Mireille—'

'What is it?' Joséphine was carrying a tray of microwaved pizzas, and looked flushed and tired.

'Two Stellas, José.'

Joséphine handed him the bottles, which he opened using the bottle-opener fixed into the bar. She gave him a narrow look before moving on with the pizzas.

'Well anyway, that was that,' finished Clairmont, pouring the beers. 'They made out it was an accident, *héh*, as you would. But everyone knows that crazy wife of his was behind it.' He grinned. 'The funny thing was that she didn't get a penny from his will. She's at the mercy of the family. It was a seven-year lease – they can't do anything about that – but when it runs out, *héh!*' He shrugged expressively. 'Then she'll be gone, and good riddance to her.'

'Unless she buys the farm herself,' said Jay. 'Mireille said she might try.'

Clairmont's face darkened for a moment. 'I'd bid against her myself if I could afford it,' he declared, draining his glass. 'That's good building land. I could build a dozen holiday chalets on that old vineyard. Pierre-Emile's an idiot if he lets it go to her.' He shook his head. 'All we need is a bit of luck and land prices in Lansquenet could rocket. Look at Le Pinot. That land could make a fortune if you developed it properly. But you'd never see her doing that. Wouldn't even give up the marshland by the river when they were thinking about widening the road. Blocked the plan out of sheer meanness.' He shook his head.

'But things are on the up now, *héh*?' His good humour

was already restored, his grin oddly at variance with his mournful moustache. 'In a year, maybe two, we could make Le Pinot look like a Marseilles *bidonville*. Now that things are beginning to change.' Once again he gave his humble, eager grin. 'All it takes is one person to make a difference, Monsieur Jay. Isn't that right?'

He tapped the rim of his glass against Jay's and winked. '*Santé!*'

44

FUNNY, HOW EASILY IT ALL CAME BACK. FOUR WEEKS NOW since his last sighting of Joe and still he felt as if the old man might reappear at any moment. The red flannel sachets were in place in the vegetable garden and at the corners of the house. The trees at the land's boundary were similarly adorned, though the wind kept stripping them off. Marigolds, propagated in the home-made cold frame, were beginning to open their bright petals amongst Narcisse's seed potatoes. Poitou baked a special *couronne* loaf in thanks for his grain pack, which, he claimed, had given him more relief than any drug. Of course, Jay knew he would have said that anyway.

Now his garden had the best collection of herbs in the village. The lavender was still green, but already more pungent than Joe's had ever been, and there was thyme and cologne mint and lemon balm and rosemary and great drifts of basil. He gave a whole basket of these to Popotte when she came by with the mail, and another to Rodolphe. Joe often gave out little charms – goodwill charms, he called them – to visitors, and Jay began to do the same: tiny bunches of lavender or mint or pineapple sage, tied with ribbons of different colours – red for protection, white for luck, blue for healing. Funny how it all came back. People assumed this was another English custom, the general explanation for all his eccentricities. Some took to wearing these little posies pinned to their coats and jackets – though it was May it was still too cool for the locals to wear their summer clothing, though Jay had long since turned to shorts and T-shirts for everyday wear. Strangely enough Jay found the return to Joe's familiar customs rather comforting. When he was a boy Joe's perimeter rituals, his incense, sachets, pig-Latin incantations and sprinklings of herbs too often irritated him. He found them embarrassing, like someone singing too fervently in school assembly. To his adolescent self, much of Joe's everyday magic seemed rather *too* commonplace, too natural, like cookery or gardening, stripped of its mysteries. Serious though he was about his workings, there was a cheery practicality to all of it, which made Jay's romantic soul rebel. He would have preferred solemn invocations, black robes and midnight ritual. *That* he might have believed. Reared on comic books and trash fiction, that at least would have rung true. Now that it was too late, Jay found he had rediscovered the peace of working with the soil. Everyday magic, Joe used to call it. Layman's alchemy. Now he understood what the old man meant. But in spite of all this Joe stayed away. Jay prepared the land for his return like a well-raked seedbed. He planted and weeded according to the lunar cycle, as Joe would have done. He did everything right. He tried to have faith.

He told himself that Joe was never there at all, that it was in his imagination. But perversely, now Joe was gone he needed to believe it was otherwise. Joe was really there, a part of him insisted. Really there, and he had blown it with his anger and disbelief. If only he could make him come back, Jay promised himself, things would be different. There were so many things left unfinished. He felt a helpless rage at himself. He'd had a second chance, and stupidly he'd blown it. He worked in the garden every day until dusk. He was sure Joe would come. That he could make him come.

45

PERHAPS AS A RESULT OF DWELLING SO CONSTANTLY ON THE past, Jay found himself spending more and more time by the river, where the cutaway dropped sharply into the water. There he found a wasps' nest in the ground, under the hedge close by, and he watched it with relentless fascination, recalling that summer in 1977, and how he was stung, and Gilly's laughter at the den at Nether Edge. He lay on his stomach and watched the wasps shuttling in and out of the hole in the ground and imagined he could hear them moving just under the surface. Above them the sky was white and troubling. The remaining Specials were as silent, as troubling as the sky. Even their whispering was suspended.

It was as he lay beside the riverbank that Rosa found him. His eyes were open, but he did not seem to be looking at anything. The radio, swinging from a branch over-hanging the water, was playing Elvis Presley. At his side stood an opened bottle of wine. Its label, too far away for her to read it, said 'Raspberry '75'. There was a red cord knotted around the neck of the bottle, which caught her eye. As she watched, the Englishman reached for the bottle and drank from it. He made a face, as if the taste were unpleasant, but from across the river she caught the scent of what he was drinking – a sudden bright flare of ripe scarlet, wild berries gathered in secret. She studied him for a moment from the other side of the river. In spite of what *maman* told her, he looked harmless. And this was the man who tied the funny little red bags on the trees. She wondered why. At first her taking them was a defiant gesture, erasing him as much as possible from her place, but she had come to like them, their dangling shapes like small red fruit on the shaken branches. She no longer minded sharing her secret place with him. Rosa shifted her position to squat more comfortably in the long weeds on the far side of the river. She considered crossing, but the stepping stones had submerged in recent showers, and she was wary of jumping to the far bank. At her side the curious brown goat nuzzled restlessly at her sleeve. She pushed the goat away with a flapping motion of her hand. *Later, Clopette, later.* She wondered whether the Englishman knew about the wasps' nest. He was, after all, less than a metre from its opening.

Jay lifted the bottle again. It was over half empty, and already he felt dizzy, almost drunk. It was in part the sky which gave him this impression, the raindrops zigzagging down onto his upturned face like flakes of soot. The sky went on for ever.

From the bottle the scent intensified, became something which bubbled and seethed. It was a gleeful scent, a breath of high summer, of overripe fruit dripping freely from the branches, heated from below by the sun reflecting from the chalky stones of the railbed. This memory was not entirely pleasant. Perhaps because of the sky he also associated it with his last summer at Pog Hill, the disastrous confrontation with Zeth and the wasps' nests, Gilly watching in fascination and himself crouching close by. Gilly was always the one who enjoyed wasping. Without her he would never have ventured near a wasps' nest at all. The thought somehow disturbed him. This wine should have brought back 1975, he told himself aggrievedly. That's when it was made. A bright year, full of promise and discovery. 'Sailing' playing on the radio. That's what happened before, with the other bottles. But his time machine was two years out, bringing him here instead, sending Joe even further away. He poured the rest of the wine onto the ground and closed his eyes.

A red chuckle from the bottom of the bottle. Jay opened his eyes again, uneasy, certain that someone was watching him. The dregs were almost black in this dull daylight, black and syrupy, like treacle, and from where he was lying there almost seemed to be movement around the neck of the bottle, as if something were trying to escape. He sat up and looked a little closer. Inside the bottle, several wasps were gathered, attracted by the scent of sugar. Two crawled stickily on the neck. Another had flown right into the belly of the bottle to investigate the residue at the bottom. Jay shivered. Wasps sometimes hide in bottles and drinks cans. He knew from that summer. A sting inside the mouth is both painful and dangerous. The wasp crawled thickly against the glass. Its wings were clotted with syrup. He thought he could hear the insect inside the bottle, buzzing in a growing frenzy, but perhaps that was the wine itself calling, its hot bright scent distressing the air, rising like a column of red smoke, a signal, perhaps, or a warning.

Suddenly his closeness to the wasps' nest appalled him. He realized he could hear the insects beneath him under the soil's thin crust. He sat up, meaning to move away, but a recklessness seized him, and instead of retreating he moved a little closer.

If Gilly was here . . .

Nostalgia was upon him again before he could stop it. It dragged at him like a caught bramble. Perhaps it was the scent from the bottle, from the spilled wine on the ground making him feel this way, this trapped summer scent, intoxicating, overwhelming. The radio near by gave a quick crackle of static and began to play 'I Feel Love'. Jay shivered.

This was ridiculous, he told himself. He had nothing to prove. It was twenty years since he last fired a wasps' nest. It seemed a reckless, lethal thing to do now, the kind of

226

thing only a child would do, oblivious of the risks. Besides . . .

A voice – from the bottle, he thought, though it might still be the wine talking – cajoling, a little scornful. It sounded something like Gilly's voice, something like Joe's. It was impatient, amused beneath the irritation. *If Gilly was here you wouldn't be so chicken.*

Something moved in the long grass on the other side of the river. For a second he thought he saw her, a blur of russet which might be her hair, something else which might be a stripy T-shirt or pullover.

'Rosa?'

No response. She stared out at him from the long grass, her green eyes bright with curiosity. He could see her now he knew where to look. From a short distance away, he could hear the sound of a goat bleating.

Rosa seemed to look at him with encouragement, almost with expectation. Beneath him he could hear the wasps buzzing, a strangely yeasty sound, as if something below the earth were fermenting wildly. The sound, coupled with Rosa's expectant look, was too much for him. He felt a burst of exhilaration, something which stripped the years away and made him fourteen again, invulnerable.

'Watch this,' he said, and began to move closer to the nest.

Rosa watched him intently. He moved awkwardly, inching towards the hole in the bank. He moved with his head down, as if this would fool the wasps into thinking him invisible. A couple of wasps settled momentarily on his back. She watched as he pulled his handkerchief out of his pocket. There was a lighter in one hand, the same lighter he had offered Rosa that day by the stream. Carefully, he opened the lighter and doused the handkerchief in the fluid. Holding the object at arm's length, he moved closer to the nest. There was a larger hole under the banking, a hole which might once have housed rats. Around it, a complex of mud honeycomb. A moment's hesitation, choosing his spot, then he pushed the handkerchief right into the nest, leaving a tag-end of fabric dangling down like a fuse. As she watched, he looked at her and grinned.

Banzai.

He must have been drunk. That was the only explanation he could think of later, but it didn't feel like being drunk at the time. At the time it felt right. Good. Exciting. Amazing how quickly these things came back. He only had to flip the Bic once. The flame caught instantly, flaring with sudden, incredible fierceness. There must have been plenty of oxygen down the hole. Good. Briefly Jay wished he had brought some firecrackers. For a second or two there was no response from the wasps, then half a dozen came flying out like hot cinders. Jay felt a surge of euphoria and jumped to his feet, ready to run. That was the first mistake. Gilly always taught him to keep low, to find a hiding place from the start and to crouch low, under a root or behind a tree stump, as the enraged wasps came flying out. This time Jay was too busy watching Rosa. The wasps came out in a dreadful surge, and he ran for the bushes. Second mistake. Never run. The movement attracts them, excites them. The best thing is to lie flat on the ground, covering the face. But he panicked. He could smell burning lighter fluid and a vicious stink like burnt carpet. Something stung him on the arm and he slapped at it. Several wasps stung him then, maddeningly, through his T-shirt and on his hands and arms, zinging by his ears like bullets, darkening the air, and Jay lost what cool he had. He swore and slapped at his skin. Another wasp stung him just under the left eye, driving a brilliant lance of pain into his face, and he stepped out blindly, right over the edge of the cutaway and into the water. If the river had been shallower he might have broken his neck. As it was his fall saved him. He hit the water face-first, sank, screamed, swallowed river water, surfaced, sank again, made for the far banking and found himself a minute later several yards downriver, his T-shirt nubby with drowned wasps.

Under the nest, the fire he had lit was already out. Jay regurgitated river water. He coughed and swore shakily. Fourteen had never seemed so far away. From her distant island in time he thought he could hear Gilly laughing.

The water was shallow on that side of the river, and he waded out onto the bank and flopped on all fours into the grass. His arms and hands were already swelling from the dozens of stings, and one eye was puffed shut like a boxer's. He felt like a week-old corpse.

Gradually he became aware of Rosa watching from her vantage point upstream. She had wisely moved back to avoid the angry wasps, but he could see her, perched on the top rung of the gatepost beside the dragon's head. She looked curious but unconcerned. Beside her the goat cropped grass.

'Never again,' gasped Jay. 'God, never again.'

He was just beginning to consider the idea of getting up when he heard footfalls in the vineyard beyond the fence. He looked up, just in time to see Marise d'Api as she arrived breathlessly at the gate and swept Rosa into her arms. It took her a few moments to register his presence, for she and Rosa had begun a rapid interchange of signing. Jay tried to get up, slipped, smiled and made a vague gesture with one hand, as if by following the rules of country etiquette he might somehow make her overlook everything else. He felt suddenly very conscious of his swollen eye, wet clothes, muddy jeans.

'I had an accident,' he explained.

Marise's eyes went to the wasps' nest in the banking. The remains of Jay's charred handkerchief still protruded from the hole, and he could smell lighter fluid across the water. Some accident.

'How many times were you stung?' For the first time he thought he heard amusement in her voice.

Jay looked briefly at his arms and hands.

'I don't know. I . . . didn't know they'd come out so fast.'

He could see her looking at the discarded wine bottle, drawing conclusions.

'Are you allergic?'

'I don't think so.' Jay tried to stand up again, slipped and fell on the wet grass. He felt sick and dizzy. Dead wasps clung to his clothes. Marise looked both dismayed and almost ready to laugh.

'Come with me,' she said at last. 'I have a stings kit in the house. Sometimes there can be a delayed reaction.'

Carefully Jay pulled himself up the banking towards the hedge. Rosa trotted behind, closely followed by the goat. Halfway to the house Jay felt the child's small cold hand slip into his and, looking down, he saw that she was smiling.

The house was larger than it seemed from the road, a converted barn with low gables and high, narrow windows. Halfway up the front wall, a door stared out in midair from the loft where bales of hay were once kept. An old tractor was parked by one of the outbuildings. There was a neat kitchen garden by the side of the house, a small orchard – twenty well-kept apple trees – at the back and a woodpile at the other side, with cords of carefully stacked wood for the winter. Two or three of the small brown goats wandered skittishly across the vineyard's small paths. Jay followed Marise along the rutted pathway between the rows of vines, and Marise put out a hand to steady him as they approached the gate, though he sensed this was less out of concern for him than for the vines, which his clumsy approach might have damaged.

'In here,' she told him shortly, indicating the kitchen door. 'Sit down. I'll get the kit.'

Her kitchen was bright and tidy, with a shelf of stone jugs above a porcelain sink, a long oak table, like the one at his own farm, and a giant black stove. Bunches of herbs hung from low beams above the chimney: rosemary, sage and pennyroyal. Rosa went to the pantry and fetched some lemonade, pouring a glassful and sitting at the table to drink it, watching Jay with curious eyes.

'*Tu as mal?*' she asked.

He looked at her. 'So you can talk,' he said.

Rosa smiled mischievously.

'Can I have some of that?' Jay gestured at the glass of lemonade, and she pushed it across the table towards him. So, he told himself, she can lipread as well as sign. He wondered whether Mireille knew. Somehow he didn't think so. Rosa's voice was childish but steady, without any of the usual fluctuations of tone of the deaf. The lemonade was home-made and good.

'Thank you.'

Marise flicked him a suspicious look as she came into the kitchen with the stings kit. She had a disposable syringe in one hand.

'It's adrenalin. I used to be a nurse.'

After a moment's hesitation Jay held out his arm and closed his eyes.

'There.'

He felt a small burning sensation in the crook of his elbow. There was a second's light-headedness, then nothing. Marise was looking at him in some amusement.

'You're very squeamish for a man who plays with wasps.'

'It wasn't quite like that,' said Jay, rubbing his arm.

'If you behave like that, you can expect to be stung. You got away lightly.'

He supposed that was true, but it didn't feel that way. His head was still pounding. His left eye was swollen tight and shiny. Marise went to the kitchen cupboard and brought out a shaker of white powder. She shook some into a cup, added a little water and stirred it with a spoon. Handing him the cup: 'Baking soda,' she advised. 'You should put some of this onto the stings.'

She did not offer to help. Jay followed her advice, feeling rather foolish. This wasn't how he'd envisaged their meeting at all. He said so.

Marise shrugged and turned back to the cupboard. Jay

watched as she poured pasta into a pan, added water and salt, placed the pan carefully on the hob.

'I have to make lunch for Rosa,' she explained. 'Take what time you need.' In spite of her words, Jay got the distinct impression she wanted him out of her kitchen as soon as possible. He struggled with the baking soda, trying to reach the stings on his back. The brown goat poked its head around the door and bleated.

'*Clopette, non! Pas dans la cuisine!*' Rosa jumped from her place and shooed the goat away. Marise shot her a look of fierce warning, and the child put her hand over her mouth, subdued. Jay looked at her, puzzled. Why should Marise not want her child to speak in front of him? She motioned towards the table, asking Rosa to set the plates out. Rosa took out three plates from the cupboard. Marise shook her head again. Reluctantly the child replaced one of the plates.

'Thanks for the first aid,' said Jay carefully.

Marise nodded, busy chopping tomatoes for the sauce. There was fresh basil in a window box on the ledge and she added a fistful.

'You have a lovely farm.'

'Oh?' He thought he detected an edge in her voice.

'Not that I was thinking of buying it,' added Jay quickly. 'I mean, it's just a nice farm. Pretty. Unspoilt.'

Marise turned and looked at him.

'What do you mean?' Her face was vivid with suspicion. 'What do you mean, buying it? Have you been talking to someone?'

'No!' he protested. 'I was just trying to make conversation. I swear—'

'Don't,' she said flatly. The fleeting warmth he had glimpsed in her was gone. 'Don't say it. I know you've been talking to Clairmont. I've seen his van parked outside your house. I'm sure he's been giving you all kinds of ideas.'

'Ideas?'

She laughed.

'Oh, I know about you, Monsieur Mackintosh. Sneaking

around, asking questions. First, you buy the old Château Foudouin, then you show a great curiosity about the land down to the river. What are you planning? Holiday chalets? A sports' complex, like Le Pinot? Something even more exciting?'

Jay shook his head.

'You've got it wrong. I'm a writer. I came here to finish my book. That's all.'

She looked at him cynically. Her eyes were lasers.

'I don't want to see Lansquenet turned into Le Pinot,' he insisted. 'I told Clairmont right from the start. If you've seen his van, it's just that he keeps delivering *brocante* to the farm; he's got it into his head that I'm interested in buying junk.'

Marise began to add chopped shallots to the pasta sauce, seemingly unconvinced, but Jay thought the curve of her spine relaxed, just a little.

'If I ask questions,' he said, 'it's just because I'm a writer; I'm curious. I was blocked for years, but when I came to Lansquenet—' He was hardly aware of what he was saying now, his eyes fixed on the hollow of her back beneath the man's shirt. 'The air's different here, somehow. I've been writing like crazy. I've left everything to be here—'

She turned then, a red onion in one hand, the knife in the other.

He persisted: 'I promise I'm not here to develop anything. For Christ's sake, I'm sitting in your kitchen soaked to the skin and covered in baking soda. Do I look like an entrepreneur?'

She considered this for a moment. 'Perhaps not,' she said at last.

'I bought the place on impulse. I didn't even know you were . . . I didn't think you . . . I don't usually have impulses,' he finished lamely.

'I find that hard to believe,' said Marise, smiling. 'For a man who deliberately puts his hand into a wasps' nest, I find it very hard.'

233

It was a small smile, maybe two on a scale of one to ten, but it was there anyway.

They talked after that. Jay told her about London and Kerry and *Jackapple Joe*. He talked about the rose garden and the vegetable patch beside the house. Of course he didn't mention Joe's mysterious presence and subsequent disappearance, or the six bottles, or the way she herself had infiltrated his new book. He didn't want her to think he was crazy.

She made lunch – pasta with beans – and invited him to join them. Then they drank coffee and Armagnac. She let him change his wet clothes for a pair of Tony's overalls while Rosa played outside with Clopette. Jay found it strange that she did not refer to Tony as her husband, but as 'Rosa's father', but the rapport between them was too new, too tenuous, for him to endanger it by asking questions. When – if – she wanted to discuss Tony, she would do it in her own time.

So far, she was giving little away. A fierce independence, tenderness for her daughter, pride in her work, in the house, the land. A way of smiling, grave-seeming, but with a kernel of sweetness. A way of listening in silence, an economy of movement which belied the quick mind, the occasional wry twist of humour beneath the practicality. Thinking back to his first glimpse of her, to his previous assumptions, to the way he had listened to, and half believed, the opinions of people like Caro Clairmont and Mireille Faizande he felt a rush of shame. The heroine of his novel – unpredictable, dangerous, possibly mad – bore no relation to this quiet, calm woman. He had let his imagination run far ahead of the truth. He drank his coffee, abashed, and resolved to pry no further into her affairs. Her life and his fiction had nothing in common.

It was only later, much later, that the unease resurfaced. Oh, Marise was charming. Clever, too, in the way she had led him to talk about himself whilst evading all mention of her own background. By the end of the afternoon she knew

234

everything about him. But even so there was something more. Something about Rosa. He considered Rosa. Mireille was convinced she was being ill-treated, but there were no signs of that. On the contrary, the love between mother and daughter was clear. Jay remembered the time he had seen them together by the hedge. That unspoken rapport. *Unspoken.* That was it. But Rosa *could* talk, spontaneously and with ease. The way she had shouted at the goat in the kitchen proved it, that quick, excited outburst. *Clopette, non! Pas dans la cuisine!* As if she talked to the goat habitually. And the way Marise looked at her, as if warning her to be quiet.

Why should she warn her? He went over the question again and again. Was it something Marise didn't want him to hear? And the child – hadn't she been sitting with her back to the door when the goat made its entrance?

So how could she have known it was there?

Nether Edge, Summer

AFTER HE LEFT GILLY, JAY SAT BY THE BRID
feeling angry and guilty and certain she w
him. When she didn't appear, he lay in the
while, relishing the bitter smells of earth a
looked into the sky until the falling drizzle m
He began to feel cold, so he got up and beg
way back to Pog Hill along the disused rai
every now and then to examine something by
tracks, more out of habit than real interest. I
in his brooding that he completely failed to he
four figures which emerged silently from the
back and fanned out behind him in pursuit.

By the time he saw them it was too late.
there, and two of her mates: the skinny blonde
her name was Karen – and a younger girl, Paul
Patty? – ten or eleven, maybe, with pierced ears
sulky mouth. They were already moving across
cut him off, Glenda to one side, Karen and P
other. Their faces shone with rain and eagernes
eyes met his across the track and they were glea
moment she looked almost pretty.

Worse still, Zeth was with her.

everything about him. But even so there was something more. Something about Rosa. He considered Rosa. Mireille was convinced she was being ill-treated, but there were no signs of that. On the contrary, the love between mother and daughter was clear. Jay remembered the time he had seen them together by the hedge. That unspoken rapport. *Unspoken*. That was it. But Rosa *could* talk, spontaneously and with ease. The way she had shouted at the goat in the kitchen proved it, that quick, excited outburst. *Clopette, non! Pas dans la cuisine!* As if she talked to the goat habitually. And the way Marise looked at her, as if warning her to be quiet.

Why should she warn her? He went over the question again and again. Was it something Marise didn't want him to hear? And the child – hadn't she been sitting with her back to the door when the goat made its entrance?

So how could she have known it was there?

46

Nether Edge, Summer 1977

AFTER HE LEFT GILLY, JAY SAT BY THE BRIDGE FOR A WHILE, feeling angry and guilty and certain she would come after him. When she didn't appear, he lay in the wet grass for a while, relishing the bitter smells of earth and weeds, and looked into the sky until the falling drizzle made him dizzy. He began to feel cold, so he got up and began to make his way back to Pog Hill along the disused railbed, stopping every now and then to examine something by the side of the tracks, more out of habit than real interest. He was so lost in his brooding that he completely failed to hear, or see, the four figures which emerged silently from the trees at his back and fanned out behind him in pursuit.

By the time he saw them it was too late. Glenda was there, and two of her mates: the skinny blonde – he thought her name was Karen – and a younger girl, Paula – or was it Patty? – ten or eleven, maybe, with pierced ears and a mean, sulky mouth. They were already moving across his path to cut him off, Glenda to one side, Karen and Paula to the other. Their faces shone with rain and eagerness. Glenda's eyes met his across the track and they were gleaming. For a moment she looked almost pretty.

Worse still, Zeth was with her.

For a second or two Jay froze. The girls were nothing special. He had outrun, outtalked and outbluffed them before, and there were only three of them. They were familiar, part of the Edge, like the open-cast mine or the scree above the canal lock; a natural hazard, like the wasps – something to be treated with caution but not fear.

Zeth was another matter.

He was wearing a Status Quo T-shirt with the sleeves rolled up. A pack of Winstons was tucked in one sleeve. His hair was long, flapping around his thin, clever face. His acne had cleared up, but there were deep marks on his cheeks where it had been – initiation scars, channels for crocodile tears. He was grinning.

'Astha been pickin on my sister?'

Jay was already running before he finished his sentence. It was the worst possible place to be cornered; high above the canal and its many hiding places, the straight, open railbed lay in front of him like a desert. The bushes on either side were too thick to squeeze through, too small to offer protection. A deep ditch and a screen of bushes hid him from even the closest houses. His sneakers skidded dangerously on the gravel. Glenda and her mates were in front of him, Zeth was a heartbeat behind. Jay took the best option, dodging the two girls and making straight for Glenda. She stepped out to intercept him, her meaty arms held out as if fielding a wide ball, but he pushed her with all his strength, shouldering her aside like an American foot-baller, and hurtled free down the abandoned tracks. Behind him he heard Glenda wail. Zeth's voice pursued him, ominously close: 'Tha little bastard!'

Jay didn't look round. There was a railway bridge and a cutting about a quarter of a mile from Pog Hill, with a path leading up onto the street. There would be other paths, too, leading to the cutaway and waste ground beyond. If he could only get there . . . The bridge wasn't far. He was younger than Zeth, and lighter. He could outrun him. If he could reach the bridge there would be places to hide.

He glanced over his shoulder. The gap between them had widened. Thirty or forty yards separated them. Glenda was back on her feet and running, but in spite of her size Jay wasn't worried about her. She looked out of breath already, her overlarge breasts bobbing ludicrously under her straining shirt. Zeth was jogging quite slowly next to her, but as Jay looked round he put on a sudden, terrifying burst of speed, his arms pumping, gravel spraying up fiercely around his ankles.

Jay was beginning to feel dizzy now, his breath a hot stone. He could see the bridge just around the curve of the line, and the row of poplars which marked the abandoned points. Five hundred yards would do it.

Joe's talisman was still in his pocket. He could feel it against his hip as he ran, and he felt dim relief that he'd brought it along. He could just as easily have forgotten it. He had been too busy that summer, too snarled up in himself to think very much about magic.

He just hoped it still worked.

He reached the bridge, with the gap between them widening, and cast about for somewhere to hide. Too risky to try the steep path up towards the road. Jay was winded by now, and there was maybe fifty feet of twisting dirt path before the road and safety. He clenched his fist over Joe's talisman and took the opposite direction, the one they wouldn't expect him to take, under the bridge and behind, towards Pog Hill. There was a swathe of willowherb gone to seed behind the rail arch, and he bobbed down in it, head pounding, heart tight with dark exaltation.

He was safe.

From his hideout he could hear voices. Zeth's sounded close, Glenda's more remote, thickened by distance, rebounding over the empty space between the bridge and the cutaway.

'Wheer the bleedinell izzy?'

Jay could hear him on the other side of the arch, imagined him checking the path, measuring distances. He made himself small under the waving white heads of the willow-herb.

Glenda's voice, breathy with running.

'Thaz lost 'im, tha beggar!'

' 'Ave not. He's here somewhere. He can't have gone far.'

Minutes passed. Jay clung to the talisman as they went over the area. Joe's talisman. It had worked before. He had not fully believed in it then, but he knew better now. He believed in magic. He truly believed in magic. He heard a sound as someone crunched over the accumulated litter in the space underneath the bridge. Footsteps crossed the gravel. But he was safe. He was invisible. He believed.

'Iz ere!'

It was the ten-year-old, Paula-or-Patty, standing waist-deep in the foamy weeds.

'Quick, Zeth, gettim! Gettim!'

Jay began to back off towards the bridge, clouds of white seeds puffing away with every move he made. The talisman dangled loosely from his fingers. Glenda and Karen rounded the curve of the arch, faces sweaty. There was a deep ditch just beyond the arch, ripe with late-summer nettles. No escape that way. Then Zeth came from under the bridge, took his arm, drew Jay towards him by the shoulders in a dreadfully matey, not-to-be-refused gesture of welcome, and smiled.

'Gotcha.'

The magic had finally run out.

Jay didn't like to think about what happened after that. It existed in a curious silence, like some dreams. First they pulled off his T-shirt and pushed him, kicking and screaming, into the ditch where the nettles bloomed. He tried to climb out, but Zeth kept pushing him back, the leaves raising welts which would itch and burn for days. Jay put his arms up to cover his face, thinking remotely, *How come this never happens to Clint*, before someone yanked him up by the hair and Zeth's voice said, very gently, 'Now it's my turn, yer bastard.'

In a story he would have fought back. He didn't. He would at least have shown defiance, some hint of desperado swagger. His heroes all did.

Jay was no hero.

He began to scream before he felt the first blow. Perhaps that was how he escaped a serious beating. It could have been worse, he thought as he assessed the damage later. A bloody nose, some bruises, both the knees of his jeans taken out from a skid across the railbed. The only thing broken was his watch. Later he came to understand that there had been something more, something more serious, more permanent than a watch, or even a bone broken that day. It was to do with faith, he thought dimly. Something inside had been broken and could not be mended.

As Joe might have said, the art was gone.

He told his mother he'd fallen off his bike. It was a plausible lie – plausible enough, anyway, to explain his shredded jeans and swollen nose. She didn't fuss as much as Jay had feared; it was late, and everyone was watching a rerun of *Blue Hawaii*, part of the Elvis post-mortem season.

Slowly he put his bike away. He made himself a sandwich and took a can of Coke from the fridge, then he went to his room and listened to the radio. Everything seemed speciously normal, as if Gilly, Zeth and Pog Hill were already a long time in the past. The Stranglers were playing 'Straighten Out'.

Jay and his mother left that weekend. He didn't say goodbye.

47

Lansquenet, May 1999

JAY WAS AT WORK IN THE GARDEN WHEN POPOTTE ARRIVED with her postbag. She was a little, round, pansy-faced woman in a scarlet jumper. She always left her ancient bicycle at the side of the road and brought any mail along the footpath.

'*Héh*, Monsieur Jay,' she sighed, handing over a packet of letters. 'If only you lived a little closer to the road! My *tournée* is always half an hour longer when there's something for you. I lose ten kilos every time I come over here. It can't go on! You must put up a postbox!'

Jay grinned. 'Come in and have one of Poitou's fresh *chaussons aux pommes*. I have some coffee on the stove. I was just going to have some myself.'

Popotte looked as severe as her merry face would allow. 'Are you trying to bribe me, *Rosbif*?'

'No, *madame*.' He grinned. 'Just lead you astray.'

She laughed. 'Maybe one. I need the calories.'

Jay opened the letters as she ate her pastry. An electricity bill; a questionnaire from the town hall in Agen; a small flat package, wrapped in brown paper, addressed to him in small, careful, almost-familiar script.

It was postmarked Kirby Monckton.

Jay's hands began to tremble.

'I hope they're not all bills,' said Popotte, finishing her pastry and taking another. 'Don't want to wear myself out bringing you unwanted post.'

Jay opened the packet with difficulty.

He had to pause twice for his hands to stop shaking. The wrapping paper was thick and stiffened with a sheet of card. There was no note inside. Instead there was a piece of yellow paper carefully folded over a small quantity of tiny black seeds. One word was inscribed in pencil on the paper.

'Specials.'

'Are you all right?' Popotte seemed concerned. He must have looked strange, the seeds in one hand, the paper in the other, gaping.

'Just some seeds I was expecting from England,' said Jay with an effort. 'I . . . I'd forgotten.'

His mind was dizzied with possibilities. He felt numbed, shut down by the enormity of that tiny packet of seeds. He took a mouthful of coffee, then laid the seeds out on the yellow paper and examined them.

'They don't look like much,' observed Popotte.

'No, they don't, do they?' There were maybe a hundred of them, barely enough to cover the palm of his hand.

'For God's sake, don't sneeze,' said Joe behind him, and Jay nearly dropped the lot. The old man was standing against the kitchen cupboard, as casually as if he had never left, wearing improbable madras shorts and a Springsteen 'Born to Run' T-shirt with his pit boots and cap. He looked absolutely real standing there, but Popotte's gaze never flickered, even though she seemed to be staring right at him. Joe grinned and lifted a finger to his lips.

'Take your time, lad,' he advised kindly. 'Think I'll go and have a look at the garden while I'm waiting.'

Jay watched helplessly as he sauntered out of the kitchen and into the garden, fighting back an almost uncontrollable urge to run after him. Popotte put down her coffee mug and looked at him curiously.

242

'Have you been making jam today, Monsieur Jay?'

He shook his head. Behind her, through the kitchen window, he could see Joe leaning over the makeshift cold frame.

'Oh.' Popotte still looked doubtful, sniffing the air. 'I thought I could smell something. Blackcurrants. Burning sugar.'

So she too could sense his presence. Pog Hill Lane had always had that scent of yeast and fruit and caramelized sugar, whether or not Joe was making wine. It was steeped in the carpets, the curtains, the wood. The scent followed him around, clinging to his clothes, even permeating the fug of cigarette smoke which so often surrounded him.

'I should really get back to work,' said Jay, trying to keep his voice level. 'I want to get these seeds into the ground as soon as I can.'

'Oh?' She peered at the seeds again. 'Something special, are they?'

'That's right,' he told her. 'Something special.'

48

Pog Hill, Autumn 1977

SEPTEMBER WAS NO BETTER. ELVIS WAS IN THE CHARTS AGAIN with 'Way Down'. Jay studied listlessly for next year's O levels. Normality seemed restored. But that sense of doom was still there, accentuated, if anything, by the humdrum continuation of things. He heard from neither Joe nor Gilly, which surprised him, even though it was unsurprising, given that he'd left Kirby Monckton without saying goodbye to either of them. His mother was snapped by *Sun* photographers on the arm of a twenty-four-year-old fitness instructor outside a Soho nightclub. Marc Bolan died in a car accident, then, only a few weeks later, Ronnie Van Zant and Steve Gaines of Lynyrd Skynyrd were wiped out in a plane crash. It seemed suddenly as if everything and everyone around him was dying, coming apart. No-one else seemed to notice. His friends smoked illicit cigarettes and sneaked off to the pictures after hours. Jay watched them with contempt. He'd practically stopped smoking. It seemed so pointless, almost childish. The gulf between himself and his classmates broadened. On some days he felt ten years older.

Bonfire night came. The others lit a bonfire and roasted potatoes in the quad. Jay stayed in the dorm and watched from a distance. The scent of the air was bitter, nostalgic.

Showers of sparks puffed up from the bonfire into the smoke and the mild sky. He could smell the hot scent of grease frying and the cigarette-paper reek of bangers. For the first time he realized how much he missed Joe.

In December he ran away.

He took his coat and his sleeping bag, his radio and some money, which he stuffed into his sports' bag. He forged his exeat and left school just after breakfast, to give himself plenty of time to get as far as possible. He hitched a lift from town to the motorway, then another down the M1 towards Sheffield. He knew exactly where he was going.

It took him two days to reach Kirby Monckton. He walked most of the way after leaving the motorway, cutting across fields onto the higher ground of the moor. He slept in a bus shelter until a police patrol car drew up, then lost his nerve and dared not stop again in case he was picked up. It was cold but not snowing, the sky sullen, and Jay put on all the spare clothing he had brought, without managing to feel any warmer. His feet were blistered, his boots clotted with mud, but throughout it all he clung to the memory of Pog Hill Lane, to the knowledge that Joe was waiting for him there. Joe's house, with its warm kitchen and the scent of hot jam and oven-dried apples and the radio playing on the window ledge above the tomato plants.

It was late afternoon when he arrived. He pulled himself up the last few feet to the back of Pog Hill Lane, slung his sports bag over Joe's wall and himself after it. The yard was deserted.

Beyond it the allotment looked bare, abandoned. Joe had certainly done a fine camouflage job on it. Even from the yard it looked as if no-one had lived there for months. Weeds had sprouted between the flagstones and died there in the cold, silvered with frost. The windows were nailed shut. The door was locked.

'Joe!' He knocked on the door. 'Joe? Open up, will you?'

Silence. The house looked blind, stolid beneath its winter sheen. Under Jay's fist the door handle rattled meaninglessly. From inside his voice returned to him, a dim echo in a hollow chamber.

'Joe!'

'It's empty, lad.'

The old woman was peering over the wall, black eyes curious beneath a yellow headscarf. Jay recognized her vaguely; she had been a frequent visitor that first summer, and she would sometimes make strawberry pies, which she brought to Joe in exchange for allotment produce.

'Mrs Simmonds?'

'Aye, that's right. You'll be wantin Mester Cox, will yer?'

Jay nodded.

'Well, iz gone. Thought he'd passed on, like, but our Janice sez he just upped an left one day. Upped an left,' she repeated. 'You'll not find im ere now.'

Jay stared at her. It wasn't possible. Joe hadn't gone. Joe had promised—

'They're knockin down Pog Hill Lane, you know,' said Mrs Simmonds conversationally. 'Goin to build some luxury flats. Could do with a bit of luxury after everythin we've bin through.'

Jay ignored her. 'I know you're in there, Joe! Come out! Bloody come out!'

'There's no call for that kind of language,' said Mrs Simmonds.

'Joe! Joe! Open up! *Joe!*'

'You watch it, lad, or I'm callin the police.'

Jay spread his hands placatingly. 'OK. OK. I'm sorry. I'm going. I'm sorry.'

He waited until she was gone. Then he crept back and made his way around the house, still certain Joe was in there somewhere, angry at him perhaps, waiting for him to give up and leave. After all, he had been taken in before. He searched the overgrown allotment, expecting to see him checking his trees or in his greenhouse at the signal box, but there was no sign of any recent presence but his own. It was only when he realized what had gone that the truth of it came home. Not a rune, not a ribbon, not a scrawled sign on a tree trunk or a stone. The red sachets had disappeared from the sides of the greenhouse, from the wall, from the branches of the trees. The careful arrangements of pebbles on the paths had been scattered to meaningless debris. The lunar charts tacked to the wall of the shed and the greenhouse, the arcane symbols Sellotaped to the trees – all the signs Joe had put up as part of his permanent solution were gone. The cold frames had been tumbled, leaving the plants inside to fend for themselves. The orchard was strewn with summer's windfalls, grey-brown and half melted into the hard ground now. Hundreds of them. Pears, apples, plums, cherries. That was when he really knew. Those windfalls.

Joe had gone.

The back door was imperfectly closed. Jay managed to lever it open and let himself into the empty house. It smelt foul, like fruit gone to rot in a cellar. In the kitchen, tomato plants had grown monstrously leggy in the dark, reaching out pale, fragile fingerlings towards the thin edge of light at the window before dying, stretched out and waterless, against the sink top. Apparently Joe had left everything just as it was: his kettle on the hob, his biscuit box – still with a few biscuits in it, stale but edible – his coat hanging up on the peg behind the door. The light in the cellar was out, but there was enough daylight from the kitchen to see the rows of bottles, jars and demijohns ranked neatly on the shelves there, gleaming like buried gems in the undersea light.

Jay searched the house. There was little enough to find; Joe's possessions had not been extensive, and as far as he could see the old man had taken practically nothing with him. His old kitbag was missing, his *Culpeper's Herbal* and his few clothes – his pit cap and boots among them. The seed chest was still there by his bed, but when Jay opened it he found its contents had been removed. The seeds, roots, packages, envelopes and neatly labelled twists of crinkly brown newspaper were gone. Inside the chest nothing but dust remained.

Wherever Joe had gone, he'd taken his seeds with him.

But where had he gone? His maps were still hanging in place on the walls, labelled and marked in Joe's small painstaking script, but there was no clue as to where he might be heading. There was no pattern to his many itineraries, the coloured lines joining at a dozen different points: Brazil, Nepal, Haiti, French Guyana. Jay searched under his bed, but found nothing but a cardboard box filled with old magazines. He pulled them out, curious. Joe had never been a great reader. Except for *Culpeper's Herbal* and the occasional paper, Jay rarely saw him read anything, and when he did it was with the frowning slowness of a man who had left school at fourteen, following the script with his finger. But these magazines were old, faded but kept tidily away in the box and covered with a piece of card so that the dust would not damage them. The dates on the covers were a revelation: 1947, 1949, 1951, 1964 . . . Old magazines, their covers coloured the same distinctive yellow and black. Old copies of *National Geographic*.

Jay sat on the ground for a few minutes, turning pages gone crispy with age. There was something comforting about those magazines, as if by simply touching them he could bring Joe closer. Here were the places Joe had seen, the people among whom Joe had lived – mementoes, perhaps, of his long years on the road.

Here was French Guyana, Egypt, Brazil, South Africa, New Guinea. The once-bright covers lay side by side on the dusty floor. Jay saw that he had marked some passages in pencil, annotated others. Haiti, South America, Turkey, Antarctica. These were his travels, this the itinerary of his wandering years. Each one dated, signed, coded in many colours.

Dated and signed.

A cold finger of suspicion traced its way down his back.

Slowly at first, then turning the pages with growing, dreadful certainty, he began to understand. The maps. The anecdotes. The back copies of *National Geographic*, dating right back to the war . . .

He stared at the magazines, trying to find another reason, something to explain. But there could only be one explanation.

There had never been any years on the road. Joe Cox was a miner and had always been a miner, from the day he left school to the moment he retired. When Nether Edge pit closed down he'd gone to his council pit house on Pog Hill Lane on his miner's pension – maybe with invalidity, too, because of his maimed left hand – and dreamed of travelling. All his experiences, his anecdotes, his adventures, his near-misses, his swashbucklings, his ladies in Haiti, his travelling gypsies – all taken from this pile of old magazines, all as fake as his magic, his layman's alchemy, his precious seeds, no doubt collected from growers or mail-order suppliers while he wove his dreams – his *lies* – alone.

Lies. All of it. Fakery and lies.

Sudden, overwhelming anger shot through him. It was beyond reason – it was all the hurt and confusion of the past few months; it was Gilly's abandonment and Joe's betrayal; it was his parents, himself, his school; it was Zeth; it was Glenda and her gang; it was the wasps; it was his rage at everything, coalesced for a moment into a single bolt of pain and fury. He flung the magazines across the floor, kicking and stamping on the pages. He tore off the covers, treading the pictures into the mingled dust and mud. He pulled down the maps from the walls. He tipped over the empty seed chest. He ran down into the cellar and smashed everything he could see – the bottles, the jars, the fruit and the spirits. His feet crunched on broken glass.

How could Joe have lied?

How could he?

He forgot that it had been he who had run away, he who had lost his faith. All he could think of was Joe's deception. Besides, he had come back, hadn't he? He had come back. But if there had been magic, it was long gone.

His back hurt – he must have strained it when he greyed out in the cellar – and he went back into the kitchen feeling leaden and useless. He had cut his hand on a piece of glass. He tried to rinse it in the sink, but the water had already been turned off. That was when he saw the envelope.

It had been propped up neatly against the draining board by the window, next to the dried-up bar of coal tar soap. His name was written across the top in small, shaky capitals. Too large to be simply a letter, it looked plump, like a small packet. Jay tore the envelope clumsily, thinking perhaps this was it, Joe hadn't forgotten him after all; this had to be some kind of explanation, a sign . . .

A talisman.

There was no letter in the envelope. He looked twice, but there wasn't even a slip of paper. Instead there was a small packet – he recognized it as one of Joe's seed packets from the chest, faintly labelled in red pencil. 'Specials'.

Jay tore open a corner. There were seeds inside, tiny blackfly seeds, a hundred or more, rolling between his clumsy fingers as he tried to understand. No note. No letter. No instructions. Just seeds.

What was he supposed to do with them? Anger lashed him again. Plant them in his garden? Grow a beanstalk to the Land of Make-Believe? He gave a furious croak of laughter. Just what exactly was he supposed to *do* with them?

The seeds rolled meaninglessly between his fingers. Tears of angry, desolate laughter squirted from his eyes.

Jay went outside and climbed up onto the back wall. He tore the packet open and let the seeds float down into the cutting, blackfly on the damp winter wind. He sent the shredded envelope fluttering after them. He felt sourly exultant.

Later he thought that maybe he shouldn't have done it, that maybe there was magic in those seeds after all, but it was too late. Whatever Joe had left for him to find, he hadn't found it.

49

Lansquenet, Summer 1999

JUNE CAME IN LIKE A SHIP, BLUE SAILS UNFURLED AND SWELLING.
A good time for writing – Jay's book lengthened by another
fifty pages – but even better for planting, picking out the
new seedlings and setting them in their raked beds, thin-
ning out potato plants and putting them in rows, or weeding, stripping garlands of goosegrass and ground elder
from the currant bushes, or picking strawberries and
raspberries from their green hollows to make jam. Joe
was especially pleased by this.

'There's nothin like pickin yer own fruit from yer own
garden,' he pointed out, teeth clamped around the stub of a
cigarette. The strawberries were abundant this year – three
rows fifty metres long, enough to sell if he had a mind to –
but Jay was uninterested in selling. Instead he gave them
away to his new friends, made jam, ate strawberries by the
pound, sometimes straight from the field, with the pink soil
still dusting the flesh. Joe's crow-scarers – flexible canes
decorated with foil streamers and the inevitable red talisman – were enough to discourage the bird population.

'You should make some wine, lad,' advised Joe. 'Never
made any strawberry mesself. Never grew enough of 'em to
bother. I'd like to see what it turns out like.' Jay found he

could accept Joe's presence without question now, though not because he had no questions to ask. It was simply that he could not bring himself to ask them. Better to remain as he was, to accept it as another everyday miracle. Too much investigation might open up more than he was willing to examine. Nor was his anger entirely gone. It remained a part of him, like a dormant seed, ready to sprout in the right conditions. But in the face of everything else it seemed less important now, something which belonged to another life. Too much ballast, Joe always said, slows you down. Besides, there was too much to do. June was a busy month. The vegetable patch needed attention: new potatoes to dig and store in pallets filled with dry earth, young leeks to peg out, endives to cover with black plastic shells to protect them from the sunlight. In the evenings, when the day cooled, he worked on his book as Joe watched from the corner of the room, lying on the bed with his boots against the wall, or smoking and watching the fields with bright, lazy eyes. Like the garden and the orchard, the book needed more work than ever at this stage. As the last hundred pages drew to a close, he began to slow, to falter. The ending was still as hazy in his mind as when he first started. He spent more and more of his time staring at the typewriter, or out of the window, or looking for patterns in the shadows against the whitewashed walls. He went over the typed pages with correcting fluid. He renumbered sheets, underlined titles. Anything to fool himself that he was still working. But Joe was not fooled.

'Tha's not written much tonight, lad,' he commented on one unproductive evening. His accent had broadened, as it did when he was at his most satirical. Jay shook his head.

'I'm doing all right.'

'Tha wants to get it finished,' continued Joe. 'Get it out of your system while you still can.'

Irritably: 'I can't do that.'

Joe shrugged.

'I mean it, Joe. I can't.'

'No such bloody word.' It was another of Joe's sayings. 'Does tha want to finish that bloody book or not? I'm not goin to be here for ever, tha knows.'

It was the first time Joe had hinted that he might not stay. Jay looked up sharply.

'What do you mean? You've only just come back.'

Again Joe gave his loose shrug. 'Well . . .' As if it were obvious. Some things did not need to be said. But Joe was more blunt. 'I wanted to get you started,' he said at last. 'See you in, if you like. But as for *stayin* . . .'

'You're going away.'

'Well, probably not just yet.'

Probably. The word was like a stone dropping into still water.

'Again.' The tone was more than accusing.

'Not just yet.'

'But soon.'

Joe shrugged. Finally: 'I don't know.'

Anger, that old friend. Like a recurring fever. He could feel it in him, a blush and prickle at the nape of his neck. Anger at himself, at this neediness never to be satisfied.

'Got to move on sometime, lad. Both of us have. You more than ever.'

Silence.

'I'll probly hang on for a while, though. Till autumn, at least.'

It occurred to Jay that he had never seen the old man in winter. As if he were a figment of the summer air.

'Why are you here, Joe, anyway? Are you a ghost? Is that it? Are you haunting me?'

Joe laughed. In the slice of moonlight needling from behind the shutters he did look ghostly, but there was nothing ghoulish in his grin.

'Tha allus did ask too many questions.' The thickening of his accent was a mockery of itself, a dig at nostalgia. Jay suddenly wondered how much of that, too, was a fake. 'I told yer first off, didn't I? *Astral* travel, lad. I travel in me sleep. Got it down to an art, anall. I can do anywhere. Egypt, Bangkok, the South Pole, dancin girls in Hawaii, northern lights. I've done em all. That's why I do so much bloody sleepin.' He laughed, and flicked the stub of his cigarette onto the concrete floor.

'If that's true, where are you now?' Jay's tone was suspicious, as it always was when he thought Joe was mocking him. 'I mean, where are you, really? The seed packet was marked Kirby Monckton. Are you . . .'

'Aye, well.' Joe lit another cigarette. Its scent was eerily strong in the small room. 'That dun't matter. Thing is, I'm here now.'

He would say no more. Beneath them, in the cellar, the remaining Specials rubbed together in longing and anticipation. They made barely any sound, but I could feel their activity, a fast and yeasty ferment, like trouble brewing. *Soon*, they seemed to whisper from their glassy cradles in the dark. Soon. Soon. *Soon*. They were never silent now. Beside me in the cellar they seemed more alive, more alert than ever before, their voices swelling to a cacophony of squeaks, grunts, laughter and shrieking which rocked the house to its foundations. Blackberry blue, damson black. Only these remained, but still the voices had grown louder. As if the spirit released from the other bottles were still active, lashing the remaining three to greater frenzies. The air sparkled with their energy. They had even penetrated the soil. Joe, too, was here all the time, rarely leaving, even when other people were present. Jay had to remind himself that others could not see Joe, though their reactions showed that they usually felt something in his presence. With Popotte it was a smell of cooking fruit. With Narcisse, a sound like a car backfiring. With Joséphine, something like a storm coming, which raised the hairs on her arms and made her prickle like a nervous cat. Jay had a great many visitors. Narcisse, delivering garden supplies, had become quite friendly. He looked at the newly restored vegetable garden with gruff approval.

'Not bad,' he said, thumbing a shoot of basil to release the scent. 'For an Englishman. You might make a farmer yet.'

Now that Joe's special seeds had been planted, Jay began work on the orchard. He needed ladders to climb high enough to strip the invasive mistletoe and nets to protect the young fruit from birds. There were maybe a hundred trees there, neglected in recent years but still good: pears, apples, peaches, cherries. Narcisse shrugged dismissively.

'There's not much of a living in fruit,' he said dourly. 'Everyone grows it, but there's too much and you end up feeding it to the pigs. But if you like preserves ∴ . .' He shook his head at the eccentricity. 'There's no harm in it, I suppose, *héh*?'

'I might try and make some wine,' admitted Jay, smiling. Narcisse looked puzzled. 'Wine from fruit?'

Jay pointed out that grapes were also a fruit, but Narcisse shook his head, bewildered.

'*Bof*, if you like. *C'est bien anglais, ça.*'

Humbly Jay admitted that it was indeed very English. Perhaps Narcisse would like to try some? He gave a sudden, malicious grin. The remaining Specials rubbed against each other in anticipation. The air was filled with their carnival glee.

Blackberry 1976. A good summer for blackberries, ripe and purple and swimming in crimson juice. The scent was penetrating. Jay wondered how Narcisse would respond to the taste.

The old man took a mouthful and rolled it on his tongue. For a moment he thought he heard music, a brash burst of pipes and drums from across the water. River gypsies, he thought vaguely, though it was a little early in the year for gypsies, who came mostly for the seasonal work in the autumn. With it came the smell of smoke, fried potatoes and *boudin* the way Marthe used to make it, though Marthe had been dead for ten years, and it must be thirty or more since she came with the gypsies that summer.

'Not bad.' His voice was a little hoarse as he put the

empty glass back onto the table. 'Tastes of . . .' He could hardly recall what it did taste of, but that scent remained with him, the scent of Marthe's cooking and the way the smoke used to cling to her hair and make the apples of her cheeks stand out red. Combing it out at night, loosening the brown curls from the tight bun in which she kept them, all the day's cooking smells would be trapped in the tendrils at the nape of her neck – olive bread and *boudin* and baking and woodsmoke. Freeing the smoke with his fingertips, her hair tumbling free into his hands.

'Tastes a little of smoke.'

Smoke. It must be the smoke which made his eyes water as they did, thought Narcisse dimly to himself. That or the alcohol. Whatever the Englishman put in his wine, it's . . .

'Strong.'

50

AS JULY VEERED INTO SIGHT THE WEATHER GREW HOTTER, THEN
scorching. Jay found himself feeling grateful that he had
only a few rows of vegetables and fruit to care for, for in
spite of the closeness of the river the earth had become dry
and cracked, its usual russet colour paling into pink and
then almost white under the sun's attack. Now he had to
water everything for two hours every day, choosing the cool
evenings and early mornings so the soil's moisture would
not be lost. He used equipment he found in Foudouin's
abandoned shed: large metal watering cans to carry the
water and, to bring it up from the river, a handpump which
he installed close to the dragon head at the boundary
between his land and Marise's vineyard.

'She'll be doing well enough from this weather,' confided
Narcisse over coffee in Les Marauds. 'That land of hers
never dries out, even in high summer. Oh, there was some
kind of drainage put in years ago, when I was a boy, pipes
and tiling, I think, but that was before old Foudouin even
thought of buying it. Now it's fallen into disrepair, though. I
doubt she's ever thought of restoring the drainage.' There
was no rancour in his voice. 'If she can't do it herself,' he
said bluntly, 'then she won't have it done at all. It's the way
she is, *héh!*'

Narcisse was suffering from July's intense heat. His
nursery garden was at its most delicate, with gladioli
and peonies and camellia just ready to be sold to the shops,

with baby vegetables at their most tender and fruit just forming on the branches of his trees. The sudden clap of heat would wither the flowers – each one needed a whole canful of water every day – burn the fruit from the branches, scorch the leaves.

'*Bof.*' He shrugged, philosophical. 'It's been looking that way all year. No rain to speak of since February. Maybe enough to wet the soil, *héh*, but not enough to go deep, where it matters. Business will be bad again.' He gestured towards the basket of vegetables beside him – a gift for Jay's table – and shook his head. 'Look at that,' he said. The tomatoes looked as large as cricket balls. 'I feel ashamed to sell them. I'm giving them away.' He drank his coffee mournfully. 'I might as well give it up now,' he said.

Of course, he meant no such thing. Narcisse, once so monosyllabic, had become quite garrulous in recent weeks. There was a kindly heart beneath his dour exterior, and a gruff warmth which made him liked by people who took the time to get to know him. He was the only person from the village with whom Marise did business, perhaps because they used the same workers. Once every three months he delivered supplies – fertilizer, insecticide powder for the vines, seeds for planting – to the farm.

'She keeps herself to herself,' was his only comment. 'More women should do the same.' Last year she installed a sprinkler at the far edge of her second field, using water from the nearby river. Narcisse helped her carry it and put it together, though she installed the thing herself, digging trenches across the field to the water, then burying the pipes deep. She grew maize there, and sunflowers every third year. These crops do not withstand dryness as vines do.

Narcisse offered to help her with the installation, but she refused.

'If it's worth doing, it's worth doing yourself,' she commented. The sprinkler was working all night by then – it was useless in the daytime, the water evaporating in midair before it even touched the crop. Jay could hear it from his open window, a dim whickering in the still air. In the moonlight the white spume from the pipes looked ghostly, magical. Her main crop was the grapes, Narcisse said. She grew the maize and sunflowers for cattle feed, the vegetables and fruit for her personal use and Rosa's. There were a few goats, for cheese and milk, and these roamed free around the farm, like pets. The vineyard was small, yielding only 8,000 bottles a year. It sounded a lot to Jay, and he said so. Narcisse smiled.

'Not enough,' he said shortly. 'Of course, it's good wine. Old Foudouin knew what he was doing when he put in those vines. You've noticed how the land tilts sharply down towards the marshes?'

Jay nodded.

'That's how she can grow those vines. Chenin grapes. She picks them very late, in October or November, sorts them, one by one, by hand on the vine. They're almost dried out by then, *héh*. But as the mist rises from the marshes every morning, it dampens the vine and encourages the *pourriture noble*, the rot which gives the grape its sweetness and flavour.' Narcisse looked thoughtful. 'She must have a hundred barrels of it by now, maturing in oak, in that cellar of hers. I saw them when I made last year's delivery. Eighteen months on, that wine's worth a hundred francs a bottle, maybe more. That's how she could afford to bid for your farm.'

'She must really want to stay here,' commented Jay. 'If she has money, I would have thought she'd have been only too pleased to leave. I've heard she doesn't get on well with people from the village.'

Narcisse looked at him. 'She minds her own business,' he said sharply. 'That's all.'

Then the talk turned once again to farming.

51

SUMMER WAS A DOOR SWINGING OPEN INTO A SECRET GARDEN. HIS book remained incomplete, but he rarely thought about it now. His interest in Marise had gone further than merely the need to collect material. Until the end of July the heat intensified, made worse by a brisk, hot wind which dried out the maize so that its husks rattled wildly in the fields. Narcisse shook his head glumly and said he'd seen it coming. Joséphine doubled her sales of drinks. Joe consulted tidal and lunar charts, and gave Jay specific instructions on when to water in order to achieve the best effect.

'It'll change soon enough, lad,' he said. 'You'll see.'

Not that there was a great deal to lose. A few rows of vegetables. Even with the drought the orchard would yield more fruit than Jay could possibly use. In the café, Lucien Merle shook his head in dark relish.

'You see what I mean,' he said. 'Even the farmers know it. There's no future in it any more. People like Narcisse carry on because they don't know anything else, but the new generation, héh! They know there's no money in it. Every year the crop sells for less. They're living from Government subsidies. All it takes is for one year to be bad, and then you're taking out loans from the Crédit Mutuel so you can plant next year. And the vines are no better.' He gave a short laugh. 'Too many small vineyards, too little money. There's no living to be made in a small farm any more. That's what people like Narcisse don't understand.' He lowered his voice and came closer. 'All that's going to change, though,' he said slyly.

'Oh?' Jay was getting a little bored with Lucien and his great plans for Lansquenet. His only topic of conversation nowadays seemed to be about Lansquenet and how it could be made more like Le Pinot. He and Georges Clairmont had put up signs on the main road and the Toulouse road near by, which were supposed to encourage the influx of tourists.

> Visitez *LANSQUENET-sous-Tannes!*
> *Visitez notre église historique*
> *Notre viaduc romain*
> *Goûtez nos spécialités*

Most people viewed this with indulgence. If it brought business, good. Mostly they were indifferent, as Georges and Lucien were known for hatching grandiose schemes which never came to anything. Caro Clairmont had tried several times to invite Jay to dinner, though so far he had managed to delay the inevitable. She hoped that he would address her literary group in Agen. The thought appalled him.

That day it rained for the first time in weeks. A fierce rain from a hot white sky, barely refreshing. Narcisse grumbled that, as usual, it had come too late and that it would never last long enough to wet the ground, but in spite of this, it endured late into the night, pouring out of the gutterings and onto the baked ground with lively plashing sounds.

The next morning was foggy. The heavy rain had stopped, to be replaced by a dull drizzle. Jay could see from the waterlogged state of the garden how heavy the downpour must have been, but even without sunlight to dry it out the standing water had already begun to dissipate, drawing the cracks in the earth together, sinking down deep.

'We needed that,' remarked Joe, bending down to examine some seedlings. 'Good job you got these jackapples covered, otherwise they'd have been washed away.' The Specials were in a cold frame, carefully snugged against the side of the house, and remained unharmed. Jay noticed they were a remarkably quick-growing plant; the ones he seeded first were twelve inches tall now, their heart-shaped leaves fanning out against the glass. He had about fifty seedlings ready to be bedded out, an excellent success rate for such a demanding species. Joe was fond of saying how it took him five years just to get the soil right.

'Aye.' Joe looked at the plants with satisfaction. 'Mebbe the soil's right just as it is.'

That morning, too, another letter from Nick arrived, with news of two more offers from publishers for Jay's incomplete novel. These were not final offers, he said, though already the sums involved seemed extravagant, almost ridiculous, to Jay. His life in London, Nick, the university, even the negotiations on the novel seemed abstract here, eclipsed by even the small damage caused by an unexpected rainstorm. He worked in the garden for the rest of the morning, thinking of nothing at all.

52

AUGUST WAS FREAKISHLY WET FOR LANSQUENET. RAIN EVERY other day, overcast the rest of the time, and with winds which lashed at crops and stripped their leaves. Joe shook his head at this and said he expected it. He was the only one. The rain was merciless, stripping away topsoil and washing tree roots bare. Jay went to the orchard in the rain and used pieces of carpet to wrap around the bases of his trees to protect them from water and rot. It was another old trick from Pog Hill Lane, and it worked well. But without adequate sunshine the fruit would fall unformed and unripened from the branches. Joe shrugged. There would be other years. Jay was not so sure. After the old man's return he had become preternaturally sensitive to the changes in Joe, marking every change of expression, going over every word. He noticed that Joe spoke less than he had before, that sometimes his outline was blurry, that the radio, tuned permanently to the oldies station since May, sometimes played white noise for minutes before finding a signal. As if Joe, too, were a signal, gradually fading into oblivion. Worse, he had the feeling that it was somehow his fault that it was happening, that Lansquenet was somehow taking over – eclipsing Joe. The rain and the falling temperature dampened the scents which were so characteristic of the old man's appearances, the scents of sugar and fruit and yeast and smoke. During the past few weeks these too had faded, so that for unbearable moments Jay felt absolutely alone, bereaved, a man sitting at a dying friend's bedside, listening for the next breath.

Since the wasp incident Marise no longer avoided him. They greeted each other over the fence or the hedge, and though she was rarely exuberant or forthcoming, Jay thought Marise had begun to like him a little. Sometimes they talked. September was a busy time for her, with the grapes fully formed and beginning to turn yellow, but the rain, which had not really given up since last month, was causing renewed problems. Narcisse blamed the disastrous summer on global warming. Others muttered vaguely about El Niño, the Toulouse chemical plants, the Japanese earthquake. Mireille Faizande curled her lip and talked about Last Times. Joséphine remembered the dreadful summer of '75, when the Tannes dried up and rabid foxes came running out of the marshes into the village. It did not rain every day, but even so the sun was barely present, a tarnished coin in the sky, giving little warmth.

'If it goes on like this there won't be any fruit for anyone this autumn,' said Narcisse dourly. Peaches and apricots and other soft-skinned fruit were already done for. The rain ate through the tender flesh and they dropped, rotten, to the ground, before they had even finished developing. Tomatoes failed to ripen. Apples and pears were hardly any better. Their waxy skin might protect them to some extent, but not enough. Vines were the worst.

At this stage the grapes needed sunlight, Joe said — especially for the later harvests, the Chenin grapes for the noble wines, which had to be sun-dried, like raisins. These grapes rely on the exceptional conditions of Lansquenet's marshland: the hot, long summers, the mists which the sun brings from across the river. This year, however, the *pourriture noble* had nothing noble about it. Rot, pure and simple, set in. Marise did what she could. She ordered plastic coverings from town, which she fixed into place over the rows of vines with the help of metal hoops. This saved the vines from the worst of the rain, but did nothing to protect the exposed roots. Any sunlight was hampered by the presence of the sheets, and the fruit sweated inside the plastic. The earth had long since been trodden into mud soup. Like Joe, she laid pieces of carpeting and cardboard between the rows to avoid further damage to the ground. But it was a futile gesture.

Jay's own garden fared a little better. Further from the marshland, raised above the water level, his land had natural drainage channels, which carried excess water down to the river. Even so the Tannes rose higher than ever, spilling out across the vineyard on Marise's side, and cutting dangerously close on Jay's, eroding the banking so sharply that great slices of earth had already fallen into the river. Rosa was under instructions not to approach the damaged banking.

The barley was a disaster. Fields all around Lansquenet had already been abandoned to the rain. In one of Briançon's fields a crop circle appeared, and the more gullible of Joséphine's drinkers began to speculate about space aliens, though Roux thought it more likely that Clairmont's mischievous young son and his girlfriend knew more than they were telling. Even the bees were less productive this year, Briançon reported, with fewer flowers and poor-grade honey. Belts would have to be tightened throughout the winter.

'It's hard enough getting the money from this year's crop to plant next spring,' explained Narcisse. 'When the crop's bad, you have to plant on credit. And with rented land becoming less and less viable, *héh!*' He poured Armagnac carefully into the hot dregs of his coffee and downed it in a single mouthful. 'There's not enough money in sunflowers or maize any more,' he admitted. 'Even flowers and nursery produce aren't making what they used to. We need something new.'

'Rice, maybe,' suggested Roux.

Clairmont was less downcast, in spite of poor business throughout the summer. Recently, he had been north with

Lucien Merle for a few days, returning full of enthusiasm for his Lansquenet project. It transpired that he and Lucien were planning to go into partnership on a new scheme to promote Lansquenet in the Agen region, though both of them seemed unusually secretive about the matter. Caro, too, was arch and self-satisfied, calling at the farm twice 'in passing', though it was miles out of her way, and staying for coffee. She was full of gossip, delighted with the way Jay had renovated the farm, intensely curious about the book and hinting that her influence with the regional literary societies would be certain to make it a success.

'You really should try to get yourself some French contacts,' she told him naïvely. 'Toinette Merle knows a lot of people in the media, you know. Perhaps she could arrange for you to give an interview to a local magazine?'

He explained, with an attempt not to smile, that one of the main reasons for escaping to Lansquenet had been to avoid his media contacts.

Caro simpered and said something about the artistic temperament.

'Still, you really should consider it,' she insisted. 'I'm sure the presence of a famous writer would give us all the boost we need.'

At the time Jay barely paid attention. He was close to completing the new book, for which he now had a contract with WorldWide, a large international publisher, and had set himself a deadline of October. He was also working on improving the old drainage channels on his land, with the aid of some concrete piping supplied by Georges. His roof, too, had developed a leak, and Roux had offered to help him mend it and repoint the brickwork. His days were too busy to give much time to Caro and her plans.

That was why the newspaper article took him completely by surprise. He would have missed it altogether if Popotte hadn't spotted it in an Agen paper and cut it out for him to read. Popotte was touchingly pleased by the whole thing, but it immediately made Jay uneasy. It was, after all, the first sign that his whereabouts were known. He could not remember the exact words. There was a great deal of nonsense about his brilliant early career. There was some crowing about the way he had fled London and rediscovered himself in Lansquenet. Much of it consisted of second-hand platitudes and vague speculation. Worse, there was a photograph, taken in the Café des Marauds on 14 July, showing Jay, Georges, Roux, Briançon and Joséphine sitting at the bar with bottles of *blonde* in their hands. In the picture Jay was wearing a black T-shirt and madras shorts, Georges was smoking a Gauloise. He did not remember who took the photograph. It could have been anyone. The caption read, 'Jay Mackintosh and friends at the Café des Marauds, Lansquenet-sous-Tannes.'

'Well, tha couldn't have kept it quiet for ever, lad,' observed Joe when Jay told him. 'It had to get out some time.'

He was at his typewriter in the living room, a bottle of wine at one elbow, a cup of coffee at the other. Joe was wearing a T-shirt which read 'Elvis is alive and well and living in Sheffield'. Jay noticed that now, more and more often, his outline seemed translucent at the edges, like an overdeveloped photograph.

'I don't see why,' he said. 'If I want to live here it's my business, isn't it?'

Joe shook his head.

'Aye. Mebbe. But you're not goin to carry on like this for ever, are you?' he said. 'There's papers to sort out. Permits. Practical things. Brass, anall. You'll be short of that soon.' It was true that four months of living in Lansquenet had cut heavily into his savings. The repairs to the house, furniture, tools, supplies for the garden, drainage pipes, the day-to-day expenses of food and clothing, plus, of course, the purchase of the farm itself, had eroded them beyond his expectations.

'There'll be money soon enough,' he replied. 'I'm signing the book contract any time now.' He mentioned the sum involved, expecting Joe to be awed into silence. Instead he shrugged.

'Aye. Well, I'd rather have a quid in me hand than a cheque int post,' he said dourly. 'I just wanted to see you sorted, that's all. Make sure you're all right.'

Before I go. He didn't have to say it. The words were as clear as if he'd spoken aloud.

53

STILL THE RAIN CONTINUED UNRELENTING. ODDLY, THE TEMPERA-
ture remained high and the wind was hot and unrefreshing.
At night there were often storms, with lightning dancing on
stilts across the horizon and ominous red lights in the sky. A
church in Montauban was hit by lightning and burnt down.
Since the incident with the wasps' nest Jay wisely kept away
from the river. In any case, it was dangerous, Marise told
him. The banks, sharply eroded by the current, had a habit of
slicing away into the slipstream. Easy to fall, to drown.
Accidents happen. She did not mention Tony in their conversations. When Jay touched on the subject she shied away.
Rosa, too, was only mentioned in passing. Jay began to think
that his suspicions that day were unfounded. He had been,
after all, feverish and in pain. A delusion induced by wasp
venom. Why should Marise deceive him? Why should Rosa?
In any case, Marise was preoccupied. The rain had ruined
the maize, working wet fingers of rot into the ripening ears.
The sunflowers were soft and heavy with water, their heads
bowed or broken. But the vines were the biggest disaster. On
13 September the Tannes finally broke its banks and flooded
the vineyard. The top end of the field suffered less because of
the sharp incline, but the lower end was a foot below water.
Other farmers suffered, too, but it was Marise, with her
marshy pastures, who was the worst affected. Standing
pools of rainwater surrounded the house. Two goats were
lost in the flood water from the Tannes. She had to bring the

remaining goats into the barn to avoid further damage to the ground, but the fodder was wet and unappetizing, the roof began to leak and the stores were suffering from damp.

She told no-one of her predicament. It was a habit with her, a matter of pride. Even Jay, who could see some of the damage, did not guess at the full extent. The house was in the hollow, below the vineyard. Water from the Tannes now stood around it like a lake. The kitchen was flooded. She used a broom to sweep the water from the flags. But it always returned. The cellar was knee-deep in water. The oak barrels had to be moved, one by one, to safety. The electricity generator, which was housed in one of the small outbuildings, short-circuited and failed. The rain continued unabated. Finally Marise contacted her builder in Agen. She ordered fifty thousand francs' worth of drainage pipes, and asked for them to be delivered as soon as possible. She planned to use the existing drainage channels to install a system of piping, which would channel the water away from the house and back towards the marshes, where it would drain away naturally into the Tannes. A bank of earth, like a dyke, would be raised to give some protection to the farmhouse. But it would be difficult. The builder was unable to spare any of his work-ers until November – there was a big project to finish in Le Pinot – and she refused to enlist Clairmont's help. Even if she asked, he would be unlikely to help her. And besides, she did not want him on her land. To call him in would be to admit defeat. She began the job herself, digging out chan-nels while she waited for the delivery of pipes. It was a slow business, like digging war trenches. She told herself that it was indeed a war, herself against the rain, the land, the people. The thought cheered her a little. It was romantic.

On 15 September Marise took another decision. Until now Rosa had slept with Clopette, in her little room under the eaves of the house. But now, with no electricity and hardly any dry firewood, she had little choice. The child must leave.

The last time the Tannes flooded, Rosa contracted the

infection which had left her deaf in both ears. She was three then, and there was no-one to whom Marise could send her. They had slept together in the room under the eaves for a whole winter, with the fire gouting black smoke and rain streaming down the panes. The child developed abscesses in both ears and screamed incessantly during the night. Nothing, not even penicillin, seemed to offer any relief. Never again, Marise told herself. This time Rosa must go away until the rain stopped, until the generator could be fixed, until the drainage could be put into place. This rain would not last for ever. Its end was already overdue. Even now, if the work could be completed, some of the crop might be salvaged.

There was no choice. Rosa must go away for a few days. But not to Mireille. Marise felt her heart tighten at the thought of Mireille. Who, then? No-one from the village. She did not trust any of them. Mireille spread the rumours, yes. But everyone listened. Well, maybe not everyone. Not Roux, or newcomers like him. Not Narcisse. She trusted both of them to some extent. But to leave Rosa with either of them would be impossible. People would find out. In the village, nothing could remain a secret for long.

She considered a *pension* in Agen, a place where Rosa might be left in safety for a while. But that, too, was dangerous. The child was very young to be left alone. People would ask questions. And besides, the thought of Rosa so far away was like a pain in her chest. She needed to be close.

Only the Englishman remained. The location was ideal: far enough from the village for privacy, but close enough to her own farm for her to see Rosa every day. He could make up a room for Rosa in one of the old bedrooms. Marise remembered a blue room under the south gable, which must have been Tony's, a child's bed shaped like a boat, a blue glass ball which was a lamp. It would only be for a few days, maybe a week or two. She would pay him. It was the only solution.

54

SHE ARRIVED UNANNOUNCED ONE EVENING. JAY HADN'T SPOKEN
to her for several days. In fact, he hadn't really gone out,
except to the village to buy bread. The café was mournful in
the rain, the *terrasse* reverting to a road as the tables and
chairs were taken in, rain dripping steadily from parasols
bleached colourless by the weather. In Les Marauds the
Tannes had begun to stink, hot foul waves rolling off
the marshes towards the village. Even the gypsies moved
on, taking their houseboats to calmer, sweeter waters.
Arnauld was talking about calling in a weatherworker
to solve the rain problem – there were still a few in this
part of the country – and the idea met with less scorn than
it would have a few weeks before. Narcisse scowled and
shook his head and repeated that he had never seen anything like it. Nothing in living memory even came close.

It was nearly ten o'clock. Marise was wearing a yellow
slicker. Rosa was standing behind her in her sky-blue mac
and red boots. Rain silvered their faces. Behind them the
sky was a dull orange, occasionally lit by the dim flare of
distant lightning. Wind shook the trees.

'What's wrong?' Their appearance surprised Jay so much
that at first he didn't even think to invite them in. 'Has
something happened?'

Marise shook her head.

'Come in, please. You must be freezing.' Jay cast an
automatic glance behind him. The room was tidy enough

to pass muster. Only a few empty coffee cups littered the table. He caught Marise looking curiously at his bed in the corner. Even after the roof had been fixed he'd never quite got round to moving it.

'I'll make you a drink,' he suggested. 'Here, take your coats off.' He hung their slickers in the kitchen to drip and put on some water to boil. 'Coffee? Chocolate? Wine?'

'Some chocolate for Rosa, thank you,' said Marise. 'Our electricity is down. The generator shorted.'

'Jesus.'

'It doesn't matter.' Her voice was calm and businesslike. 'I can fix it. We've had this kind of problem before. The marshland is very prone to flooding.' She looked at him. 'I have to ask you for help,' she said reluctantly.

Jay thought it was an odd way of putting it. *I have to ask you.*

'Of course,' he said. 'Anything.'

Marise sat down stiffly at the table. She was wearing jeans and a green jumper, which brought out the green in her eyes. She touched the typewriter keys tentatively. Jay saw that her nails were cut very short, and that there was dirt under them.

'You don't have to say yes,' she said. 'It's just an idea I had.'

'Go on.'

'Do you write with this?' She touched the typewriter again. 'Your books, I mean?'

Jay nodded. 'I always did have a retrogressive streak,' he admitted. 'Can't stand computers.'

She smiled. She looked tired, he noticed, her eyes strained and bruised-looking. For the first time, and with a feeling of surprise, he saw her as vulnerable.

'It's Rosa,' she said at last. 'I'm worried she might catch cold – fall ill – if she stays in the house. I wondered if you would perhaps find room for her in your farm for a few days. Only a few days,' she repeated. 'Until I can get the house back into shape. I'll pay you.' She pulled out a bundle of notes from the pocket of her jeans and pushed them across the table. 'She's a good girl. She wouldn't interfere with your work.'

'I don't want money,' said Jay.

'But I—'

'I'd be happy to take Rosa. You, too, if you like. I have plenty of room for both of you.' She looked at him with an air of bewilderment, as if in surprise that he had given in so easily.

'I can imagine the problems the flooding has caused,' he told her. 'You're very welcome to use the farm for as long as you like. If you want to bring some clothes—'

'No,' she said quickly. 'I have too many things to do at home. But Rosa . . .' She swallowed. 'I would be very grateful. If you would.'

Rosa was exploring the room. Jay could see her looking at the pile of typed sheets he had arranged in a box on the end of his bed.

'Is this English?' she enquired curiously. 'Is this your English book?' Jay nodded. 'See if you can find some biscuits in the kitchen,' he told her. 'The chocolate will be ready soon.' Rosa scampered off through the doorway.

'Can I bring Clopette with me when I come?' she called from the kitchen.

'I don't see why not,' said Jay mildly.

From the other room Rosa gave a crow of triumph. Marise looked at her hands. Her face was careful and expressionless. Outside the wind rattled the shutters.

'Perhaps you'd like that wine now,' Jay suggested.

55

AND THEN THERE WAS ONE. THE LAST OF JOE'S SPECIALS. NO more after that, not ever. As he reached for it in the rack he felt a sudden reluctance to open it, but it was already alive in his hand, black-corded Damson '76, releasing its scent as he touched it, effervescent. Joe made himself scarce, as he often did when Jay had company, but Jay could just see him, standing in the shadows beside the kitchen door, the light from the table lamp gleaming on his bald forehead. He was wearing a Grateful Dead T-shirt and holding his pit cap in his hand. His face was little more than a blur, but Jay knew he was smiling.

'I don't know if you'll like it,' said Jay, pouring the wine. 'It's a special kind of home-brew.' The purple scent was thick, almost cloying. To Jay it had an aftertaste which reminded him of the sherbert fountains Gilly had enjoyed so much. To Marise it was more like a jar of jam which has remained sealed for too long and has become sugar. The taste was tannic, penetrating. It warmed her.

'It's strange,' she said through numbed lips. 'But I think I like it.' She sipped again, feeling the heat crawl down her throat and into her body. A scent like distilled sunlight filled the room. To Jay it felt suddenly right that they should drink it together, this last of Joe's bottles. Strange, too, that the taste, though peculiar, should be oddly pleasant. Maybe at last, as Joe had predicted, he was getting used to it.

'I've found the biscuits,' announced Rosa, appearing at

the doorway with one in each hand. 'Can I go upstairs and look at my room?'

Jay nodded.

'You do that. I'll call you when the chocolate's ready.'

Marise looked at him. She knew she should feel wary, but instead there was a softness working through her, smoothing away all tension. She felt very young again, as if the scent of the strange wine had released something from her childhood. She remembered a party dress precisely the colour of the wine, a velvet party dress cut down from an old skirt of *Mémée*'s, a tune played on the piano, a night sky wide with stars. His eyes were exactly the same colour. She felt as if she had known him for years.

'Marise,' said Jay quietly. 'You know you can talk to me.'

It was as if she had been dragging something heavy behind her for the past seven years and had only just realized it. It was as simple as that. *You can talk to me.* Joe's bottle was a hive of secrets, uncoiling like busy vines in the still air, peopling the shadows.

'There's nothing wrong with Rosa's hearing, is there?' It was barely a question. She shook her head. She forced the words out like bullets.

'It was a bad winter. She developed ear infections. There was a complication. She was deaf for six months. I took her to see specialists. There was an operation – very expensive. I was told not to expect too much.' She drank a little more of Joe's wine. It was rough with sugar. There was a syrupy residue at the bottom of the glass which tasted like damson jelly. 'I paid for special lessons for her,' she continued. 'I learned sign language and continued to teach her myself. There was another operation – even more expensive. Within two years ninety per cent of her hearing was restored.'

Jay nodded. 'But why the pretence? Why not simply—'

'Mireille.' Strange that this wine, which should have made her garrulous, should instead have made her terse. 'She's already tried to take her from me. All she has left of Tony, she says. I knew that if she once managed to get hold of Rosa I'd never get her back. I wanted to stop her. It was the only way I could think of. If she couldn't talk to her, if she thought she was damaged in some way . . .' She swallowed. 'Mireille can't bear imperfection. Less than perfect doesn't interest her. That's why when Tony—' She stopped abruptly.

She should not trust him, Marise thought to herself. The wine was drawing more out of her than she was prepared to give. Wine talks, and talk is dangerous. The last man she had trusted was dead. Everything she touched – the vines, Tony, Patrice – died. Easy enough to believe that it was something she carried, passing it on to everyone with whom she came into contact. But the wine was strong. It rocked her gently in a cradle of scents and memories. It teased out her secrets.

Trust me. The voice from the bottle snickered and crooned. *Trust me.*

She poured another glassful and downed it recklessly.

'I'll tell you,' she said.

56

'I MET HIM WHEN I WAS TWENTY-ONE,' SHE BEGAN. 'HE WAS MUCH older than me. He was a day patient in the psychiatric ward in Nantes hospital, where I was a student nurse. His name was Patrice.'

He was tall and dark, like Jay. He spoke three languages. He told her he was a lecturer at the Université de Rennes. He was divorced. He was funny and wry and wore his depression with style. There was a ladder of cuts up his right wrist from an unsuccessful suicide attempt. He drank. He'd taken drugs. She'd thought he was cured.

Marise did not look up as she spoke of him, but instead watched her hands climb up and down the stem of the wineglass, as if playing a glass flute.

'At twenty-one you're so eager to find love that you see it in every stranger's face,' she said softly. 'And Patrice was a real stranger. I saw him several times outside the hospital. I slept with him once. That was enough.'

After that he changed almost instantly. As if a steel cage had come down over them, they were trapped together. He became possessive, not in the charming, slightly insecure way which had first attracted her, but in a cold, suspicious manner, which frightened her. He quarrelled with her constantly. He followed her to work and harangued her on the ward. He tried to make up for his rages with lavish presents, which frightened her even more. Finally, he broke into her flat one evening and tried to rape her at knifepoint.

'That was it,' she remembered. 'I'd had enough. I played along for a while, then made an excuse to go to the bathroom. He was full of plans. We were going to go away together to a place he knew in the country, where I'd be safe. That was what he said. Safe.' She shivered.

Marise locked herself in the bathroom and climbed out of the window onto the roof, using the fire escape to reach the street. But by the time the police arrived, Patrice was gone. She changed the locks on her doors and secured the windows.

'But it didn't stop there. He would park his car outside the flat and watch me all the time. He would have things delivered to my door. Presents. Threats. Flowers.' He was persistent. Over weeks his harassment escalated. A funeral wreath, delivered to her workplace. The locks forced and the entire flat redecorated in black while she was at work. A parcel of excrement, gift-wrapped in silver paper, on her birthday. Graffiti on her door. A mountain of unwanted mail-order items in her name: fetishwear, farm equipment, orthopaedic supplies, erotic literature. Little by little her courage was eroded. The police were powerless to help. Without proof of physical harm, they would have had little with which to charge him. They called on the address Patrice had given to the hospital, only to find it was that of a timber yard outside Nantes. No-one there had even heard of him.

'Finally I moved out,' she said. 'I left the flat and bought a ticket to Paris. I changed my name. I rented a little apartment in Rue de la Jonquière, and I found a job in a clinic in Marne-la-Vallée. I thought I was safe.'

It took him eight months to find her.

'He used my medical records,' explained Marise. 'He must have managed to talk someone at the hospital into giving them to him. He could be very persuasive. Very plausible.'

She moved again, changed her name again and dyed her hair. For six months she worked as a waitress in a bar in Avenue de Clichy before finding another nursing job. She tried to erase herself from all official documentation. She allowed her medical insurance to lapse and did not transfer her records. She cancelled her credit card and paid all her bills in cash. This time it took Patrice almost a year to find her new address.

He had changed in a year. He had shaved his head and wore army surplus clothes. His siege of her flat had all the precision of a military campaign. There were no more practical jokes, no unwanted pizzas or begging notes. Even the threats stopped. She saw him twice, sitting in a car beneath her window, but when two weeks passed and there was no further sign of him she began to believe she had been mistaken. A few days later she awoke to the smell of gas. He had bypassed the main supply somehow, and she could find no way to turn it off. She tried the door, but it was jammed shut, wedged from the outside. The windows, too, were nailed shut, though her flat was on the third floor. The phone was out. She managed to break a window and scream for help, but it had been too close. She fled to Marseilles. Began again. That was where she met Tony.

'He was nineteen,' she remembered. 'I was working on the psychiatric ward of Marseilles general hospital, and he was a patient. From what I understood he had been suffering from depression following his father's death.' She smiled wryly. 'I should have known better than to involve myself with another patient, but we were both vulnerable. He was so young. His attention flattered me, that was all. And I was good with him. I could make him laugh. That flattered me, too.'

By the time she had realized how he felt it was too late. He was infatuated with her.

'I told myself I could love him,' she said. 'He was funny and kind and easy to manipulate. After Patrice, I thought that was all I wanted. And he kept telling me about this farm, this place. It sounded so safe, so beautiful. Every day I would wake up and wonder if this was going to be the day

Patrice found me again. It would have been easy enough if he'd traced me to Marseilles. There were only so many hospitals and clinics he could check. Tony offered me a kind of protection from that. And he needed me. That already meant a lot.'

She allowed herself to be persuaded. At first Lansquenet seemed everything she had ever wanted. But soon there were clashes between Marise and Tony's mother, who refused to accept the truth about his illness.

'She wouldn't listen to me,' explained Marise. 'Tony was up and down all the time. He needed medication. If he didn't take it he got worse, locking himself up in the house for days at a time, not washing, just watching TV and drinking beer and eating. Oh, he looked all right to outsiders. That was part of the problem. I had to keep him in check all the time. I played the part of the nagging wife. I had to.'

Jay poured the last of the wine into her glass. Even the dregs were highly scented, and for a moment he thought he could distinguish all the rest of Joe's wines in that final glassful, raspberry and roses and elderflower and blackberry and damson and jackapple, all in one. No more Specials, he told himself with a tug of sadness. No more magic. Marise had stopped talking. Her maple-red hair obscured her face. Jay had the sudden feeling that he'd known her for years. Her presence at his table was as natural, as familiar as that of his old typewriter. He put his hand on hers. Her kiss would taste of roses. She looked up, and her eyes were as green as his orchard.

'*Maman!*'

Rosa's voice cut through the moment with shrill insistence.

'I've found a little room upstairs! There's a round window and a blue bed, shaped like a boat! It's a bit dusty, but I could clean it up, couldn't I, *Maman*? Couldn't I?'

Her hand moved away.

'Of course. If *monsieur* . . . if Jay . . .' She looked confused, awoken in the middle of a dream. She pushed the half-empty wineglass away from her.

'I should go,' she said quickly. 'It's getting late. I'll bring Rosa's things across. Thank you for—'

'It's all right.' Jay tried to put his hand on her arm, but she pulled away. 'You can both stay if you like. I have plenty of—'

'No.' Suddenly she was the old Marise again, the confidences at an end. 'I have to bring Rosa's sleeping things. It's time she was in bed.' She hugged Rosa briefly but fiercely. 'You be good,' she advised. 'And please' – this was to Jay – 'don't mention this in the village. Not to anyone.'

She unhooked her yellow slicker from the peg behind the kitchen door and pulled it on. Outside, the rain was still falling.

'Promise,' said Marise.

'Of course.'

She nodded, a curt, polite nod, as if concluding the business between them. Then she was gone into the rain.

Jay closed the door behind her and turned to Rosa.

'Well? Is the chocolate ready?' she asked.

He grinned. 'Let's see, shall we?'

He poured the drink into a wide-mouthed cup with flowers on the rim. Rosa curled up on his bed with the cup and watched curiously as he tidied away the cups and glasses and put the empty bottle aside.

'Who was he?' she asked at last. 'Is he English, too?'

'Who's that?' Jay called from the kitchen, running water into the sink.

'The old man,' said Rosa. 'The old man from upstairs.'

Jay turned off the tap and looked at her.

'You saw him? You talked to him?'

Rosa nodded.

'An old man with a funny hat on,' she said. 'He told me to tell you something.' She took a long drink of her chocolate, emerging from the cup with a frothy foam moustache. Jay felt suddenly shivery, almost afraid.

'What did he say?' he whispered.

Rosa frowned.

'He said to remember the Specials,' she said. 'That you'd know what to do.'

'Anything else?' Jay's mouth was dry, his head pounding.

'Yes.' She nodded energetically. 'He told me to say good-bye.'

57

Pog Hill Lane, February 1999

IT WAS TWENTY-TWO YEARS BEFORE JAY WENT BACK TO POG HILL. Part of it was anger, another part fear. He had never felt as if he belonged before. London certainly wasn't home. The places he'd lived all looked the same to him, with small variations in size and design. Flats. Bedsits. Even Kerry's Kensington house. Places in passing. But this year was different. Pick your own cliché, as Joe would have said. Perhaps it was simply that for the first time there were greater fears than going back to Pog Hill. Nearly fifteen years since *Jackapple Joe*. Since then, nothing. This went beyond writer's block. He felt as if he were stuck in time, forced to write and rewrite the fantasies of his adolescence. *Jackapple Joe* was the first – the only – adult book he had written. But instead of releasing him it had trapped him in childhood. In 1977 he had rejected magic. He had had enough, he told himself. Enough and enough and enough. He was on his own, and that was the way he wanted it. As if when he dropped Joe's seeds into the cutting at Pog Hill he was also letting go of everything he'd clung to during those past three years: the talismans, the red ribbons, Gilly, the dens, the wasps' nests, the treks along the railway lines and the fights at Nether Edge. Everything blowing away into the cutting with the litter and the ash of the railbed. Then *Jackapple Joe* put it to rest at last. Or so he had thought. But there must have been something left. Curiosity, perhaps. An itch at the back of his mind which refused to be scratched. Some remnant of belief.

Perhaps he'd mistaken the signs. After all, what evidence had he found? A few boxes of magazines? A map marked in coloured pencils? Perhaps he had jumped to a false conclusion. Perhaps Joe was telling the truth after all.

Perhaps Joe had come back.

It was something he hardly dared imagine. Joe back at Pog Hill? In spite of himself it brought his heart into his throat. He imagined the house as it was, overgrown perhaps, but with the allotment still well ordered behind the camouflage of Joe's permanent solution, the trees decorated with red ribbons, the kitchen warm with the scent of brewing wine . . . He waited several months before he made the move. Kerry was supportive, cloyingly so, imagining perhaps a renewed source of inspiration, a new book which would propel him back into the limelight. She wanted to come with him; was so persistent that he finally agreed.

It was a mistake. He knew it the moment they arrived. Rain the colour of soot scrawling from the clouds. Nether Edge reclaimed as a riverside building development; bulldozers and tractors crawling across the disused railbed and neat identical bungalows. Fields had become car showrooms, supermarkets, shopping centres. Even the newsagent's, where Jay had gone so many times to buy cigarettes and magazines for Joe, had become something else.

Kirby's remaining mines had been closed for years. The canal was being renovated, and with the help of millennium funding there were ongoing plans for the development of a visitors' centre, where tourists could go down a specially converted mine shaft or ride a barge on the newly cleaned canal.

Needless to say, Kerry thought it was charming.

But that wasn't the worst.

In spite of everything, he was expecting Pog Hill at least to have survived. The main road was still more or less unchanged, with its graceful if slightly blackened Edwardian houses and its avenue of lindens. The bridge, too, was as he remembered it, a new pedestrian crossing at one end, but the same line of poplars which marked the entrance to Pog Hill Lane, and Jay's heart played a funny little riff against his ribs as he pulled the car up to the yellow line and looked up the hill.

'Is that it?' Kerry was checking her reflection in the passenger-seat mirror. 'I don't see any sign or anything.'

Jay said nothing and got out of the car. Kerry followed him.

'So this is where it all began.' She sounded a little disappointed. 'Funny. I thought it would be more atmospheric, somehow.'

He ignored her and took a few steps forward up the hill.

They had changed the name of the lane. You won't find Pog Hill on any map now, or Nether Edge, or any of the places around which his life had revolved for those three long-ago summers. It's called Meadowbank View now, the houses knocked down to give way to a row of brick-built two-storey flats with little balconies and geraniums in plastic planters. A sign on the nearest building read, 'Meadowbank Quality Retirement Flats'. Jay went to stand where Joe's house would have been. There was nothing. A small tarmacked parking area – residents only – to the side. Behind the flats, where Joe's garden had once stood, was a bland square of lawn with a single small tree. Of Joe's orchard, of the herb garden, the rows of blackcurrants and raspberries and gooseberries, the vines, plums, pears, the carrots, parsnips, the Specials, nothing remained.

'Nothing.'

Kerry took his hand. 'Poor darling,' she whispered in his ear. 'You're not too *terribly* upset, are you?' She sounded almost pleased, as if the prospect appealed to her. Jay shook his head.

'Wait for me in the car, OK?'

Kerry frowned. 'But Jay—'

'Two minutes, OK?'

Just in time. He felt as if he might explode if he held it in any more. He ran to the back of the garden and looked over the wall down into the cutting. It was filled with rubbish. Sacks of household waste covered the ground: discarded fridges, car tyres, crates, pallets, tin cans, stacks of magazines tied together with twine. Jay felt a kind of laughter welling in his throat. Joe would have loved this. His dream come true. Rubbish sprawled down the steep hill, as if flung there by passers-by. A baby's pram. A shopping trolley. The frame of an ancient bicycle. Pog Hill cutting had been converted into a landfill site. With an effort, Jay pulled himself up so that he could straddle the wall. The hidden railbed looked a long way down from here, a sheer drop for most of the way into a scrub of bushes and a continent of litter. On the far side of the wall graffiti artists had been at work. A scree of broken glass sparkled in the sun. One unbroken bottle lay against a protruding stump, the light gleaming on its dusty base. A red cord, grubby with age, was knotted around its neck. He knew at once it was Joe's.

How it had escaped the demolition of Joe's house Jay couldn't imagine, still less how it could have remained intact since then. But it was one of Joe's bottles, all right. The coloured cord proved it, as did the label, still legible in the old man's painstaking handwriting: 'Specials'. As he made his way down towards the bridge he thought he saw more of Joe's belongings strewn down the banking. A broken clock. A spade. Some buckets and pots in which plants had once grown. It looked exactly as if someone had stood at the top of the hill and simply hurled the contents of Joe's house into the cutting below. Jay picked his way across the sad wreckage, trying to avoid broken glass. There were ancient copies of *National Geographic* and pieces of a kitchen chair. And finally, a little further down, he found the seed chest, its legs broken off, one door hanging. Sudden, white rage pumped through him. It was a complex feeling, directed as much at himself and his foolish expectations as at Joe for letting this happen, or at the person who had stood at the top of the hill and dumped an old man's life into the gap, as if it were just rubbish to be disposed of. Worse, there was fear, the dreadful knowledge that he should have come here sooner, that there had been something here for him to find, but that, as always, he had come too late.

He searched until Kerry came to find him, almost an hour later. He was filthy, muddied to the knees. In a cardboard box he carried six bottles, discovered in various places on the way down and miraculously unbroken.

Specials.

58

Lansquenet, Summer 1999

THAT WAS IT. JAY KNEW AT ONCE HE WAS GONE. THERE WAS A
finality in that goodbye which could not be ignored. As
if, with the last drop of his wine, the old man had vanished
completely. For several days he denied the certainty, telling
himself Joe would come back, that he hadn't left for good,
that he wouldn't have gone away a second time. But the
heart had gone. The house no longer smelt of his smoke.
The oldies station had stopped broadcasting, to be replaced
by a local radio on the same frequency, blasting out modern
hits. And there were no more glimpses of Joe just around
the corner of a cold frame, or behind the shed, or in the
orchard inspecting the trees. No-one sat and watched him
work at his typewriter, unless it was Rosa, who sometimes
crept downstairs and watched him from his bed. Wine was
just wine, with no special effects. This time he felt no anger.
Instead, there was a sense of inevitability. Once again, the
magic had run out.

A week passed. The rain began to taper off, leaving more
damage in its wake. Jay and Rosa stayed mostly indoors.
Rosa was easy to please. She occupied herself. She stayed
reading in her newly furnished room under the eaves or
played Scrabble on the floor or went for splashy walks

around the field with Clopette. Sometimes she listened to the radio or played with dough in the kitchen. Sometimes she baked small, hard, floury biscuits. Every evening Marise joined them and made dinner, staying just long enough to eat and check on Rosa before returning to work. The generator had been restored. The drainage ditches were taking time, but would be complete in a few more days. She had enlisted Roux and some other workers from Clairmont's yard to help her. Even so the vineyard remained half flooded.

Jay had few visitors. Popotte called by twice with the mail and once with a cake from Joséphine, but Rosa was round the back of the house and went unnoticed. Once Clairmont came by with another load of bric-à-brac, but did not stay. Now that the worst of the weather was past, most of the others had work of their own to do.

Rosa's presence filled the house. After Joe's departure this was more than welcome, for the house seemed oddly bereft, as if something familiar had been taken away. For a child of her age she was very silent, however, and sometimes Jay could almost believe that she belonged more to Joe's world than to his. She missed her mother. Except on one occasion, they had never been apart. She greeted Marise every evening with a fierce, wordless hug. Their meals together were cheerful and animated, but there was a reserve in Marise which Jay had not yet managed to penetrate. She rarely talked about herself. She did not mention Tony, or offer to finish the story she began on the day of the flood. Jay did not try to press her. It could wait.

A few days later Popotte brought a package from Nick, containing the contracts from Jay's new publisher and a number of newspaper clippings, dated from July to September. A brief note from Nick read, 'I thought you might be interested in this.'

Jay pulled out the clippings.

They all related to him in some way. He read them. Three

small news items from British papers speculating about his disappearance. A piece from *Publishers Weekly* outlining his return to the writing scene. A retrospective from *The Sunday Times* entitled WHATEVER HAPPENED TO JACKAPPLE JOE? with pictures of Kirby Monckton. Jay turned the page. There, staring out at him with an impudent smile, was a photograph of Joe.

WAS THIS THE ORIGINAL JACKAPPLE MAN? queried the headline.

He stared at the picture. In it, Joe was fifty, maybe fifty-five. Bareheaded, a cigarette at the corner of his mouth, his small half-moon glasses perched on the end of his nose. In his hands he was holding a large pot of chrysanthemums adorned with a rosette. The caption read, 'Local eccentric'.

'Mackintosh, with his usual reticence, has never chosen to reveal the identity of the original Joe,' continued the article, 'though sources suggest that this man may have been the inspiration for the nation's favourite gardener. Joseph Cox, born in Sheffield in 1912, worked first as head gardener at a stately home, then for thirty years at Nether Edge Coalworks in Kirby Monckton before ill-health forced him to retire. A well-known local eccentric, Mr Cox lived for many years in Pog Hill Lane, but was not available for interview at his residence, now the Meadowbank Retirement Home. Miss Julie Moynihan, a day nurse at the home, described him to our reporter. "He's really a lovely old gentleman, with such a wonderful store of anecdotes. I'm thrilled to think he might have been the original Joe."'

Jay barely looked at the rest of the article. Conflicting emotions raked through him. Amazement that he should have come so close to him and not known, not sensed his presence somehow. Most of all, an overwhelming sense of relief, of joy. The past could be redeemed after all. Joe was still living at Pog Hill. Everything could be remade.

He forced himself to read the rest of the article. There was nothing especially new. A summary of *Jackapple Joe*, with a picture of the original cover. A small photograph of the Bread Baron with Candide on his arm, taken two years before their divorce. The journalist's name at the bottom was K. Marsden and was slightly familiar. It took him several minutes to recognize Kerry's pre-television name.

Of course. Kerry. That made sense. She knew about Pog Hill Lane, and about Joe. And, of course, she knew a great deal about Jay. She had access to photographs, diaries, papers. Five years of listening to his ramblings and reminiscences. He knew a fleeting moment of anxiety. What exactly had he told her? What had he given away? He didn't suppose that after the way he'd walked out he had a right to expect any loyalty or discretion from her. He could only hope that she would stay professional and keep his private life private. He realized that he really didn't know Kerry well enough to know what she'd do.

But none of that seemed important then. What mattered was Joe. He could be on a plane to London within a few hours, he told himself giddily, then catch the express north. He could be there by that evening. He could see him again. He could even bring him back with him, if that's what the old man wanted. He could show him Château Foudouin. A strip of newsprint, barely the size of a book of stamps, fluttered free of the rest and came to land on the floor. Jay picked it up and turned it over. It was too small to be an article. He must have missed it among the other cuttings.

A note in biro at the top of the paper read, 'Kirby Monckton Post'.

Obituaries – ctd.

Joseph Edwin COX, on 15 September 1999, quietly, after a long illness.

> 'The kiss of the sun for pardon,
> The song of the birds for mirth,
> One is nearer God's Heart in a garden
> Than anywhere else on earth.'

Jay looked at it for a long time. The paper slipped from between his fingers, but he could still see it, brightly illuminated in his mind's eye, in spite of the dullness of the day. His mind refused to process the information. Blanked. Refused. Jay stared at nothing, thought nothing.

59

THE NEXT FEW DAYS WERE A KIND OF VACUUM. HE SLEPT, ATE AND drank in a daze. The Joe-shaped hole in things had become something monstrous, blotting out the light. The book lay abandoned, close to completion, gathering dust in a box under his bed. Even though the rain had stopped he could not bear to look at the garden. The Specials grew leggy, unattended in their pots, awaiting transferral. What fruit had survived the weather fell unregarded to the ground. The weeds, which had grown hungrily throughout the wet weather, were beginning to take over. In a month there would be no sign of any of his work.

The kiss of the sun for pardon—

The worst of it was not knowing. To have been within reach of the mystery and to have lost it again, stupidly, without explanation. It all seemed so pointless. He imagined Joe watching from the wings, waiting to jump out. *Surpri-ise!* All a joke, after all. An elaborate deception, friends lined up behind the curtain with party-favours and streamers, Gilly and Maggie and Joe and everyone from Pog Hill Lane, masks drawn aside to reveal their real faces. Distress turning to laughter as the truth was revealed. But this was a party to which Jay had not been invited. No more Specials. All run dry – blackberry and elderflower, jackapple and rosehip. No more magic. Ever.

And yet I could still hear them. As if some part of their essence had evaporated into the air, become a part of this place, ingrained, like the scent of cigarettes and burning sugar, in the woodwork and plaster. Everything was buzzing with that vanished presence, buzzing and singing and laughing louder than ever before, stone and tile and polished wood, all whispering with agitation and excitement; never still, never silent. Only Jay did not hear it. He had gone beyond nostalgia, into a bleakness from which he felt nothing could drag him. He remembered all the times he hated Joe. All the times he raged against the old man's desertion; the things he said to himself, to others. The dreadful things. He thought of the years when he could have traced Joe but made no real effort to do so. He could have hired a detective. He could have paid someone to find him if he couldn't do it himself. Instead, he sat and waited for Joe to find him. All those wasted years, sacrificed to pride. And now it was too late.

There was a quote he could not quite remember, something about the past being an island surrounded by time. He had missed the last boat to the island, he told himself bitterly. Pog Hill was now relegated to the list of places irretrievably lost to him, worse than lost. With Joe gone, it was as if Pog Hill had never existed.

The kiss of the sun for pardon—

But what he had done was beyond that. Joe was there, he told himself. Joe was alive at Pog Hill throughout that summer. *Astral travel*, he'd said. *That's why I do so much bloody sleepin.* Joe had come to him after all. Joe had tried to make amends. And still Joe had died alone.

It was good for him that Rosa was still here. Marise's visits, too, lifted him temporarily. At least this way he had to stay sober during the daytime. Routines needed to be observed, even if they had become meaningless.

Marise half noticed a change in him, but there was already too much to think about at the farm for her to give him more than passing attention. The drainage work was almost completed, the vineyard free of standing water, the Tannes shrinking back to normality at last. She had to give up a proportion of her savings to pay for the work and the new supplies, but she felt heartened. If the harvest could be salvaged there was still hope for next year. If only she could raise enough money to buy the land – poor enough land for building, most of it too marshy to plant. She knew Pierre-Emile was uninterested in leasing the property: there was too little profit in such an arrangement. He had a family in Toulouse. No. He would sell. She knew he would. There was a good chance that the price would be low, she told herself. After all, this was not Le Pinot. Even now there was a good chance she would be able to raise the money. Twenty per cent was all she needed. She only hoped Mireille would not interfere. After all, the old woman had no interest in seeing her leave. Quite the opposite. But Marise needed to be in charge of the property. She would not be at the mercy of a lease arrangement. Mireille understood why. They needed each other, however much the old woman loathed the thought. Balanced on a bridge, each one holding one end of the rope. If one fell, they both fell.

Marise had no qualms about lying. She had, after all, done Mireille a favour. The lie protected them, like a weapon too terrible to be used in war. But time was running out for both of them. For herself, the lease's end. For Mireille, age and illness. The old woman wanted her off the farm because it made her vulnerable. Marise only wondered whether the old threat would hold fast. Perhaps it meant nothing to her now. The thought of losing Rosa had once kept them both silent. But now . . . She wondered what Rosa still meant to Mireille.

She wondered what each of them still had to lose.

60

JAY AWOKE TO BIRDSONG. HE COULD HEAR ROSA MOVING AROUND upstairs, straw-coloured sunlight was coming through the shutters. For a fleeting moment, he had a sensation of well-being. Then the recollection of Joe's death hit him, a bolt of grief he was unable to field, taking him by surprise. Every day he woke up expecting things to be different, but every morning it was the same.

He stumbled out of bed half-dressed and put some water on to boil. He splashed cold water on his face from the kitchen tap. He made coffee and drank it scalding. Upstairs he could hear Rosa running a bath. He put food and milk on the table for her breakfast. One bowl of *café au lait*, with three wrapped sugar lumps on the side. A slice of melon. Cereal. Rosa had a healthy appetite.

'Rosa! Breakfast!' His voice sounded hoarse. There were a number' of cigarette butts in a saucer on the table, though he could not recall having bought or smoked any. For a second he felt a stab of something which might have been hope. But none of the butts were Player's.

There was a knock at the door. Popotte, he thought dimly, probably bringing another bill, or an anxious letter from Nick demanding to know why Jay hadn't returned the contracts. He drank another mouthful of stale-tasting coffee and made for the door.

Someone was standing outside, immaculate in grey

slacks and cashmere cardigan, smart new crop, J. P. Tod's, Burberry and red Louis Vuitton document case.

'Kerry?'

For a second he saw himself through her eyes: barefoot, unshaven, harried. She gave him a brilliant smile.

'Poor Jay. You look absolutely *derelict*. Can I come in?'

Jay hesitated. It was too smooth. He'd always mistrusted Kerry's smoothness. It was too often the signal for warfare. 'Yeah. Sure. OK.'

'What a *wonderful* place.' Drifting past on a wave of Envy. 'I absolutely adore the spice chest. And the dresser.' She hovered elegantly, looking for an uncluttered place to sit. Jay pulled some dirty clothes off the back of a chair and nodded to her.

'Sorry it's such a mess,' he began. Too late he realized his apologetic tone gave her the advantage. She gave him the patented Kerry O'Neill smile and sat down, crossing her legs. She looked like a very beautiful Siamese cat. Jay had no idea what she was thinking. He never did. The smile might have been genuine. Who could know?

'How did you find me?' Again he tried to get the apology out of his voice. 'I didn't exactly go out of my way to advertise where I was staying.'

'What do you think? Nicky told me.' She smiled. 'Of course, I had to *persuade* him. You know everyone's been very worried about you? Running off like that. Keeping this new project to yourself.'

She looked at him archly and put her hand on his shoulder. He noticed her eyes had changed colour – blue instead of green. Joe was right about the contact lenses.

He shrugged, feeling graceless.

'Of course, I understand completely.' Her hand moved to his hair, smoothing it from his forehead. Jay remembered she'd always been at her most dangerous when she was being maternal. 'But you look positively *wasted*. What have you been doing to yourself? Too many late nights?'

Jay brushed away her hand.

'I read your article,' he said.

Kerry shrugged. 'Yes, I've been writing a few pieces for the literary supplements,' she said. 'I couldn't help thinking that *Forum!* was getting to be just that little bit too cliquey, don't you think? Too restrictive?'

'What's wrong? Didn't they offer you another series?' Kerry raised her eyebrows.

'Darling, you've learned sarcasm,' she said. 'I'm *so* pleased for you. But now Channel Five have come up with a wonderful idea.' She glanced at the cereal, coffee and fruit laid out on the table. 'May I? I'm absolutely *starving*.' Jay watched her pour a bowlful of *café au lait*, and her eyes flicked again to the cup in his hand. 'You've really gone native, haven't you? I mean. Coffee in bowls and Gauloises for breakfast. Were you expecting company, or am I not supposed to ask?'

'I'm looking after a neighbour's child,' Jay told her, trying not to sound defensive. 'Just for a few days until the floods go down.'

Kerry smiled. 'How lovely. I'm sure I can guess which child, too. After reading your manuscript—'

'You've read it?' So much for defensiveness. She would have had to be blind to miss the way his arm jerked, slopping hot coffee onto the floor. She smiled again.

'I glanced at it. That kind of naïve style is very refreshing. Very *now*. And there's such an amazing sense of place – I just had to see it all for myself. Then, when I saw how well it could tie in – your book, and my programme –' Jay shook his head. It was aching, and he couldn't help thinking that he'd missed something important.

'What do you mean?'

Kerry looked at him in mock impatience. 'Well, I was about to tell you. The Channel Five programme, of course,' she said. '*Pastures New*. It's going to be all about British people living abroad. One of those lifestyle-travelogue shows. And when Nicky mentioned this *wonderful* place – plus everything that's happening with your book – it just seemed like serendipity, or something.'

'Wait a minute.' Jay put down the coffee cup. 'You're not thinking of getting me involved in this scheme of yours, are you?'

'Why, of *course*,' replied Kerry impatiently. 'The place is ideal. I've already spoken to a few of the locals, and there's terrific interest. And *you're* ideal. I mean, just think of the publicity. When the new book comes out—'

Jay shook his head. 'No. I'm not interested,' he said. 'Look, Kerry, I know you're trying to help, but the last thing I want right now is publicity. I came here to be alone.'

'*Alone?*' said Kerry ironically. Jay saw that she was looking beyond him into the kitchen. He turned round. Rosa was standing behind the door in her red pyjamas, eyes bright with curiosity, hair corkscrewing in all directions.

'*Salut!*' said Rosa, grinning. '*C'est qui, cette dame? C'est une Anglaise?*'

Kerry's smile grew a little broader. 'You must be Rosa,' she said. 'I've heard so much about you. And do you know, sweetheart, I always imagined you'd be deaf?'

'Kerry.' Jay was looking edgy and uncomfortable. 'We can talk later. Right now it's really not a good time. OK?'

Kerry sipped her coffee lazily. 'You really don't have to stand on ceremony with me,' she said. 'What a lovely little girl. I'm sure she takes after her mother. I feel I know them both already, of course. So sweet of you to have based all the characters on real people. It's almost like a *roman-à-clef*. I'm sure that will come out marvellously in the programme.'

Jay looked at her. 'Kerry, I'm not going to do any programme.'

'I'm sure you'll change your mind when you've had the chance to have a think about it,' she said.

'I won't,' said Jay.

Kerry raised her eyebrows. 'Why ever not? It's just perfect. Plus it could relaunch your career.'

'And yours,' he said drily.

'Perhaps. Is that so bad? After all, after everything I've

300

done for you – the *work* I've put into you – perhaps you owe me a little something in return. Maybe when all this is settled I could write your biography, giving my insights into Jay Mackintosh. I could still do your career a great deal of good, you know, if you'd let me do it.'

'*Owe* you?' Once he might have felt angry at that. Even guilty. Now it was almost funny. 'You've used that on me too often, Kerry. It doesn't work any more. Emotional blackmail is no basis for a relationship. It never was.'

'Oh, please.' She controlled herself with an effort. 'What would you know about that? The only relationship *you've* ever cared about was with an old faker who took you for a ride and dumped you when it suited him. It was always Joe this, Joe that. Maybe now he's dead you'll grow up enough to appreciate that it's money, and not magic, that makes the world go round.'

Jay smiled. 'That's quite a little soundbite,' he said mildly. 'But as you pointed out, Joe's dead. This isn't about him any more. Maybe it was when I first came here. Maybe I was trying to recreate the past. Trying to be Joe somehow. But not now.'

She looked at him. 'You've changed,' she said.

'Perhaps.'

'At first I thought it was this place,' she continued. 'This pathetic little place with its single stop sign and its wooden houses on the river. It would have been just like you to fall in love with it. To make it another Pog Hill. But that isn't it, is it?'

He shook his head. 'Not entirely, no.'

'It's worse than that. And it's so *obvious*.' She gave a brittle laugh. 'It's exactly the kind of thing you would do. You've found your muse here, haven't you? Here among the ridiculous goats and scraggy little vineyards. How wonderfully gauche. How fucking like you.'

Jay looked at her. 'What do you mean?'

Kerry shrugged. She managed to look amused and vicious at the same time. 'I know you, Jay. You're the most selfish person I've ever met. You never put yourself out for anyone. So why are you looking after her child? Anyone can see it isn't just this *place* you've fallen in love with.' She gave an angry titter. 'I knew it would happen some time,' she declared. 'Someone would manage to light the fuse. At one point I even thought it was going to be me. God knows, I did enough for you. I *deserved* for it to be me. I mean, what has *she* done for you? Does she even know about your work? Does she even *care* about it?'

Jay poured himself a second coffee and lit a cigarette. 'No,' he said. 'I don't think she does. She cares about the land. The vines. Her daughter. Real things.' He smiled at the thought.

'You'll tire of that quickly enough,' predicted Kerry scornfully. 'You never were one for living in the real world. You've never had a problem yet that you couldn't run away from. Just wait till things get a bit *too* real for you. You'll be off like a shot.'

'Not this time.' His voice was level. 'Not this time.'

'We'll see,' she said coolly. 'Won't we? After we finish *Pastures New*.'

AS SOON AS KERRY HAD LEFT, JAY DROVE INTO LANSQUENET, leaving Rosa with strict instructions not to leave the house, and blew off some of his anger on the phone to Nick Horneli. Nick was less receptive than he'd hoped.

'I thought it would be a good bit of promotion for you,' he said blandly. 'It isn't often you get a second chance in the publishing business, Jay, and I have to say, I thought you'd be a bit more keen to make the most of this one.'

'Oh.' It wasn't what he'd expected to hear, and for a moment he was taken off-balance. He wondered what exactly Kerry had been saying.

'Plus, I don't like to rush you, but I'm still waiting for your signed contracts and the last part of the new manuscript. The publishers are getting edgy, wondering when you're going to finish. If I could only have a first draft—'

302

'No.' Jay could hear the strain in his voice. 'I'm not going to be pressured, Nick.'

Nick's tone was suddenly, terrifyingly indifferent. 'Remember you're an unknown quantity nowadays, Jay. A bit of a legend, sure. That's no bad thing. But you've got a reputation, too.'

'What reputation?'

'I don't think it's very constructive at this—'

'*What* fucking reputation?'

Nick's shrug was audible. 'OK. You're a risk, Jay. You're full of great ideas, but you haven't produced anything of real value in years. You're temperamental. You don't meet deadlines. You're always late to meetings. You're a bloody prima donna living on a reputation ten years out of date, who doesn't understand that in this business you can't afford to be precious about publicity.'

Jay tried to keep his voice level. 'What are you trying to say, Nick?'

Nick sighed. 'All I'm saying is be a little flexible,' he said. 'Publishing has moved on since *Jackapple Joe*. In those days it was OK for you to be eccentric. It was expected. Even a little cute. But nowadays you're just another product, Jay, and you can't afford to let anyone down. Least of all me.'

'So?'

'So I'm telling you that if you don't sign the contract and finish the manuscript within a reasonable time – say a month or so – then WorldWide will pull out and I'll have blown my credibility for nothing. I have other clients, Jay. I have to think about them, too.'

Heavily, Jay replied, 'I see.'

'Look, Jay. I'm on your side, you know.'

'I know.' Suddenly he wanted to get away. 'I've had a bad week, Nick. Too much has been happening. And when Kerry turned up on my doorstep—'

'She wants to help, Jay. She cares about you. We all do.'

'Sure. I know.' He made his voice gentle, though he was burning with rage. 'I'll be OK, Nick. You'll see.'

'Sure you will.'

He hung up with the definite feeling that he'd had the worst of that interchange. Something had shifted. As if with the removal of Joe's protective influence he had become suddenly vulnerable again. Jay clenched his fists.

'Monsieur Jay? Are you all right?'

It was Joséphine, her face pink with concern.

He nodded.

'You'll have some coffee? A slice of my cake?'

Jay knew he ought to be getting back to check on Rosa, but the temptation to stay awhile was too strong. Nick's words had left a nasty taste in his mouth, not least because they were true.

Joséphine was full of news.

'Georges and Caro Clairmont have been in touch with an English lady, someone from the television. She says she might want to make a film here, something about travel. Lucien Merle is full of it, too. He thinks it could be the making of Lansquenet.'

Jay nodded wearily. 'I know.'

'You know her?'

He nodded again. The cake was good, glazed apple on almond pastry. He concentrated on eating. Joséphine explained that Kerry had been talking to people for several days, making notes with her little tape recorder, taking snapshots. There was a photographer with her, too, an Englishman, *très comme il faut*. Jay read disapproval of Kerry in Joséphine's expression. No wonder. Kerry wasn't the kind of woman other women took to. She only made an effort with men. It seemed that both of them had been in the region for some time, staying with the Merles. He remembered Toinette Merle was in journalism. That explained the photograph and the article in the *Courrier d'Agen*.

'They're here because of me.'

He explained the situation, from his hasty departure from London to Kerry's arrival. Joséphine listened in silence.

'How long will they stay, do you think?'

Jay shrugged indifferently. 'As long as it takes.'

'Oh.' Pause. 'Georges Clairmont is already talking about buying up derelict properties in Les Marauds. He thinks land prices will go up when word gets out.'

'They probably will.'

She looked at him oddly. 'It is a good time to buy now, after the wet summer,' she continued. 'People need the money. There's been no harvest to speak of. They can't afford to keep unproductive land. Lucien Merle has already spread word in Agen.'

Jay couldn't shake the idea that her eyes were disapproving. 'It won't harm your business, though, will it?' he said, with an attempt at lightness. 'All those thirsty people hanging around the place.'

She shrugged. 'Not for long,' she said. 'Not here.'

Jay could see what she meant. Le Pinot had twenty cafés, restaurants, a McDonald's and a leisure centre. Local businesses had closed down to be replaced by more enterprising outfits from the cities. Locals had moved away, unable to change rapidly enough with the times. Farms had become unviable. Rents doubled, trebled. He wondered if Joséphine could handle the competition. On the whole, it was unlikely.

Did Joséphine blame him? Impossible to tell from her expression. Her face, usually so flushed and smiling, seemed closed now. Her hair fell lankly across her brow as she fussed with the empty cups.

He drove back to the farm with a feeling of unease which Joséphine's lukewarm goodbye did nothing to alleviate. He saw Narcisse on the road and waved at him, but he did not wave back.

IT WAS ALMOST AN HOUR LATER WHEN JAY GOT BACK TO Château Foudouin. He parked the car on the drive and went in search of Rosa, who, he supposed, must be getting hungry. The house was empty. Clopette was wandering

305

about at the edge of the vegetable patch. Rosa's raincoat and hat were hanging on the back of the kitchen door. He called her. There was no reply. Feeling slightly worried now, he went around the back of the house, then to Rosa's favourite spot by the river. Still nothing. What if she had fallen in the water? The Tannes was still dangerously swollen, its banks eroded to the point of near collapse. What if she had wandered into one of the old fox traps? Or fallen down the cellar steps?

He searched the house again, then the grounds. The orchard. The vineyard. The shed and the old barn. Nothing. Not even footprints. Finally he crossed Marise's field, hoping the child might have gone to see her mother. But Marise was putting the finishing touches to her newly dry and repainted kitchen, her hair bound up in a red scarf, paint on the knees of her jeans.

'Jay!' She seemed pleased to see him. 'Is everything all right? How's Rosa?'

He couldn't tell her.

'Rosa's fine. I wondered if you needed anything from the village.' Marise shook her head. She seemed not to have noticed his unease.

'No, I'm all right,' she said cheerfully. 'I've almost finished here. Rosa can come back in the morning.'

Jay nodded. 'Great. I mean . . .'

She flashed him one of her rare, warm smiles. 'I know,' she said. 'You've been very kind and patient. But I know you'll be pleased to have the house to yourself again.'

Jay grimaced. His head was beginning to hurt again. He swallowed. 'Look, I should be getting back,' he said awkwardly. 'Rosa . . .'

She nodded. 'I know,' she said. 'You've been very good with her. You can't imagine—' Jay couldn't bear her gratitude. He ran all the way back to the farm.

HE SPENT ANOTHER HOUR GOING OVER POSSIBLE HIDING PLACES. He knew he should never have left her. Rosa was a mischievous child, subject to all kinds of whims and fancies. She might even now be hiding from him, as she had often hidden during his first weeks on the farm. All this might easily be her idea of a joke. But as time passed and Rosa was nowhere to be found, he began to consider other options. It was all too easy, for example, to imagine her climbing the banks of the Tannes and sliding in, being taken downriver for a couple of kilometres to be washed up against a mudbank, or even as far as Les Marauds. Easy, too, to imagine her simply wandering off down the road to Lansquenet, perhaps being picked up by some stranger in a car.

Some stranger? But there were no strangers in Lansquenet. Everyone knew everyone else. Doors were left unlocked. Unless . . . Suddenly he remembered Patrice, Marise's stalker from her Paris days. Surely not – in seven years. But that would explain many things. Her reluctance to come into the village. Her refusal to leave the place which had become a safe haven for her. Her fierce protectiveness of Rosa. Could Patrice have somehow traced them to Lansquenet? Had he been watching the farm, waiting for an opportunity to make his move? Could he be one of the villagers themselves, keeping close, biding his time? The idea was ridiculous, pure comic-book fiction; the kind of thing he himself might have written, aged fourteen, on a lazy afternoon by the canal. All the same he felt his chest contract at the thought. He imagined Patrice looking a little like Zeth, grown taller and meaner with age, his tribal cheeks thinner, his eyes mad and clever. Zeth, with a real shotgun this time, waiting at the gate with that look of mean appraisal in his eyes. It was ridiculous but it seemed very possible then, a logical conclusion to the rest of that summer, to Joe's final disappearance, to the way events had slipped back relentlessly towards that last October and to Pog Hill Lane. No more ridiculous, in any case, than the rest of it.

He thought of taking the car, but rejected the idea. Rosa might be hiding in a bush or by the roadside, too easy to miss for even a slow driver. Instead he walked along the road towards Lansquenet, stopping occasionally to call her name. He looked in ditches and behind trees. He detoured to a welcoming duckpond, which might possibly have tempted an inquisitive child, then to a deserted barn. But there was no sign of her. Finally, on reaching the village, he tried his last realistic option. He made for Mireille's house.

The first thing he noticed on arrival was the car parked in front: a long grey Mercedes, with a smoked-glass windscreen and hire-car plates. A gangster's car, he thought, or that of a game-show host. Heart pounding in sudden realization, Jay made for the door. Without pausing to knock, he opened it, calling harshly, 'Rosa?'

She was sitting on the landing in her orange jumper and jeans, looking at an album of photographs. Her wellingtons were parked by the door. She looked up as Jay called her name, and grinned. Relief almost brought him to his knees.

'What did you think you were playing at? I've been looking everywhere for you. How did you get here?'

Rosa looked at him, unabashed. 'But your friend came to fetch me. Your English friend.'

'Where is she?' Jay could feel the relief washing away into black rage. 'Where the fuck is she?'

'Jay, darling.' Kerry was standing in the kitchen doorway, very much at home with a glass of wine in one hand. 'That's hardly the kind of language you want to be using in front of a child in your care.' She gave one of her winsome smiles. Behind her stood Mireille, monumental in her black housedress.

'I called to have another word with you, but you'd gone out,' explained Kerry sweetly. 'Rosa answered the door. She and I have been having a lovely talk, haven't we, Rosa?' This last utterance was in French, presumably to include Mireille, who stood wordlessly behind her. 'I have to say you've been frightfully secretive about everything, Jay darling. Poor Madame Faizande had absolutely no idea.'

Jay glanced at Mireille, who was watching, hands crossed over her enormous bosom.

'Kerry,' he began. She gave another of her hard, brilliant smiles.

'Charming reunion,' she remarked. 'You know, I'm beginning to understand what you see in this place. So many secrets. So many fascinating characters. Madame d'Api, for example. Madame Faizande has been telling me all about her. Not *quite* the way she comes across in your book, though.'

Jay looked upstairs at Rosa. 'Come here, Rosa,' he said quietly. 'Time to go home.'

'You're very popular here, by all accounts,' said Kerry. 'I imagine you'll be quite the local hero when *Pastures New* takes off. Give the place a boost.'

Jay ignored her. 'Rosa,' he said again. The child sighed theatrically and stood up.

'Are we really going to be on television?' queried Rosa smartly, stepping into her wellingtons. '*Maman* and you and everyone? We've got a television at home. I like *Cocoricoboy* and *Nos Amis Les Animaux*. But *Maman* doesn't let me watch *Cinéma de Minuit*.' She made a face. 'Too much kissing.'

Jay took her hand. 'No-one's going to be on television,' he told her.

'Oh.'

'I don't think you'll have the option,' remarked Kerry blandly. 'I have the makings of an excellent programme already, with or without you. The artist, his influences, you know the thing. Forget Peter Mayle. Before you know it people will be flocking here to Jay Mackintosh Country. You really ought to be grateful.'

'Please, Kerry.'

'Oh, for Christ's sake! Anyone would think I had a gun to your head. Anyone else would give their right arm for this kind of free publicity!'

'Not me.'

She laughed. 'I always did have to do all the work myself,' she remarked cheerily. 'Meetings, interviews. Getting you to the right kind of parties. Pulling strings. And now you're turning your nose up at a terrific opportunity – for what? Grow up, sweetheart. No-one finds *gauche* endearing any more.'

She sounded so like Nick that, for a moment, Jay had the dreadful conviction that they were in it together, that they'd planned it between them.

'I don't want people rushing here,' he said. 'I don't want tourists and burger bars and souvenir shops springing up in Lansquenet. You know what that kind of publicity does to a place.'

Kerry shrugged. 'Seems to me that's exactly what this place needs,' she said reasonably. 'It looks half dead.' She scrutinized her nails for a second, frowning. 'Anyway, it's hardly up to you to decide, is it? I don't see anyone turning business away.'

She was right, of course. That was the worst of it. The momentum sweeps everything away in front of it, welcome or not. He imagined Lansquenet, like Pog Hill, relegated to the growing ranks of things which only existed in the past.

'Not here. It's not going to happen here.'

Kerry's laughter followed him down the street.

61

MARISE ARRIVED AT SEVEN AS USUAL, CARRYING A BOTTLE OF wine and a closed wicker basket. She had washed her hair, and for the first time since he'd known her she was wearing a long red skirt with her black sweater. It made her look different, gypsylike, and there was a touch of colour on her lips. Her eyes were shining.

'I feel like celebrating,' she announced, putting the bottle on the table. 'I've brought some cheese and *foie gras* and nut bread. There's a cake, too, and some almond biscuits. And some candles.'

She brought out two brass candlesticks from the hamper and stood them on the table.

Then she fixed a pair of candles into the sockets.

'It looks nice, doesn't it?' she said. 'I can't remember when we last had dinner by candlelight.'

'Last year,' replied Rosa pertly. 'When the generator broke down.'

Marise laughed. 'That doesn't count.'

That evening she was more relaxed than Jay had ever seen her. She and Rosa laid the table with brightly painted plates and crystal wineglasses. Rosa picked flowers from the garden for a centrepiece. They had *foie gras* on nut bread with Marise's own wine, which tasted of honey and peaches and toasted almonds, then salad and warm goat's cheese, then coffee, cakes and *petits fours*. Throughout the little party Jay tried hard to concentrate his thoughts. Rosa,

311

under instructions not to mention their visit to Lansquenet, was cheery, insisting on her *canard* – a sugar lump dipped in wine – surreptitiously feeding Clopette scraps under the table, and then, when the goat was banished to the garden, through the half-open window. Marise was bright and talkative and lovely in the golden light. It should have been perfect.

He told himself he was waiting for the right time. Of course he knew there was no right time, simply a delaying tactic. He had to tell her before she found out for herself. Worse still, before Rosa let something slip.

But as the evening passed it became harder and harder to make the move. His conversation died. His head began to ache. Marise seemed not to notice. Instead she was full of details about the next phase of her drainage plan, the extension to the cellar, relief that there would still be a wine crop, though much reduced, optimism for next year. She was planning to buy out the land when the lease ran out, she said. There was money in the bank, plus fifty barrels of *cuvée spéciale* in her cellar, just waiting for the right market. Land was cheap in Lansquenet, especially poorly drained problem land like hers. After the bad summer prices might drop still more. And Pierre-Emile, who had inherited the estate, was no businessman. He would be happy to get what he could for the farm and the vineyard. The bank would make up the rest with a long-term loan.

The more she said, the worse Jay felt. Remembering what Joséphine had told him about land prices his heart sank. Tentatively he asked what might happen if, by chance, perhaps . . . Her face hardened a little. She shrugged.

'I would have to leave,' she said simply. 'Leave everything, go back to Paris or to Marseilles. Somewhere big. Let Mireille—' She bit off the rest of the sentence and made her expression resolutely cheerful. 'But that won't happen,' she said firmly. 'None of that will happen. I've always dreamed of a place like this,' she went on, her face softening. 'A farm, land of my own, trees, perhaps a little river. Somewhere private. Safe.' She smiled. 'Perhaps when I have the land to myself and there is no lease to hang over my head, things will be different,' she said unexpectedly. 'Perhaps I could begin again with Lansquenet. Find Rosa some friends her own age. Give people another chance.' She poured another glass of the sweet golden wine. 'Give myself another chance.'

Jay swallowed with difficulty. 'But what about Mireille? Wouldn't she cause problems for you?'

Marise shook her head. Her eyes were half closed, catlike, sleepy. 'Mireille won't live for ever,' she said. 'After that – I can handle Mireille,' she said at last. 'Just as long as I have the farm.'

For a while the conversation turned to other things. They drank coffee and Armagnac, and Rosa fed *petits fours* to the goat through the gap in the shutters. Then Marise sent Rosa to bed with only a token complaint – it was almost midnight and she had been up for much longer than she was used to. Jay could hardly believe that the child had not given him away during the course of the meal. In a way he regretted it. As Rosa vanished upstairs – with a biscuit in each hand and a promise of pancakes for breakfast – he turned on the radio, poured another glass of Armagnac and passed it to Marise.

'Mmm. Thanks.'

'Marise.'

She glanced at him lazily.

'Why does it have to be Lansquenet?' he asked. 'Couldn't you have moved somewhere else after Tony died? Avoided all this . . . this business with Mireille?'

She reached for the last *petit four*. 'It has to be here,' she said at last. 'It just has to be.'

'But why? Why not Montauban or Nérac or one of the villages near by? What is there in Lansquenet which you can't have anywhere else? Is it because Rosa grew up here? Is it . . . is it because of Tony?'

She laughed then, not unkindly, but on a note he couldn't quite identify. 'If you like.'

Jay's heart tightened suddenly. 'You don't talk about him much.'

'No. No, I don't.'

She looked into her drink in silence.

'I'm sorry. I shouldn't interfere. Forget I said it.'

Marise gave him an odd look, then stared back into her drink. Her long fingers moved nervously. 'It's all right. You've helped me. You've been kind. But it's complicated, you know? I wanted to tell you. I've wanted to for a long time.'

Jay tried to say that she was wrong, that he didn't want to know, that there was something else he desperately needed to tell her. But nothing came out.

'For a long time I had a problem with trust,' said Marise slowly. 'After Tony. After Patrice. I told myself I didn't need anyone else. That we would be safer on our own, Rosa and I. That no-one would believe the truth if I told it anyway.' She paused, tracing a complicated figure on the dark table top. 'Truth is like that,' she went on. 'The more you want to tell someone, the harder it gets. The more impossible it seems.'

Jay nodded. He understood that perfectly.

'But with you . . .' She smiled. 'Maybe it's because you're a foreigner. I feel I've known you for a long time. Trusted you. Why else should I have trusted you with Rosa?'

'Marise.' He swallowed again. 'There's something I really—'

'Shh.' She looked languid, flushed with the wine and the warmth of the room. 'I need to tell you. I need to explain. I tried before, but—' She shook her head. 'I thought it was so complicated,' she said softly. 'It's really very simple. Like all tragedies. Simple and stupid.' She took a breath. 'I was caught up in it all before I knew it. Then I realized it was too late. Pour me some more Armagnac, please.'

He did.

'I liked Tony. I didn't love him. But love doesn't sustain anything for long anyway. Money does. Security, the farm, the land. That was what I needed, I told myself. Escape from Patrice. Escape from the city, and from loneliness. I fooled myself it was OK, that I didn't need anything else.'

It had been all right for a time. But Mireille was becoming increasingly demanding, and Tony's behaviour more and more erratic. Marise tried to talk to Mireille about it, but without success. As far as Mireille was concerned there was nothing wrong with Tony.

'He's a strong, healthy boy,' she would repeat stubbornly. 'Stop trying to wrap him in cotton. You'll make him as neurotic as you are.'

From then on every peculiarity in Tony's behaviour was attributed to Marise: the rages, the bouts of depression, the fixations.

'Once it was mirrors,' she said. 'Every mirror in the house had to be covered up. He said it was because the reflection took all the light out of his head. He used to shave without a mirror. He was always cutting himself shaving. Once he shaved his eyebrows off, too. Said it was more hygienic.'

When he learned Marise was pregnant Tony entered a different phase. He became extremely protective. He would follow her everywhere she went, including to the bathroom. He waited on her constantly. Mireille saw this as evidence of his devotion. Marise felt stifled. Then the letters started coming.

'I knew it was Patrice straight away,' admitted Marise. 'It was his style. The usual abuse. But somehow here he didn't frighten me. We had guard dogs, guns, space. I thought Patrice knew it, too. Somehow he'd found out about my pregnancy. The letters were all about it. Get rid of the baby and I'll forgive you, that kind of thing. I ignored them.'

Then Tony found out.

'I told him everything,' she said wryly. 'I thought I owed it to him. Besides, I wanted him to understand that we were safe, that it was all in the past. Even the letters weren't coming as often. It was dying down.'

She sighed. 'I should have known better. From then on we lived a siege. Tony would go into town once a month for supplies, that was all. He stopped going to the café with his friends. That was no bad thing, I thought. At least he was sober. He hardly slept at night. He spent most of the time on guard. Of course, Mireille blamed me.'

Rosa was born at home. Mireille helped deliver her. She was disappointed Rosa wasn't a boy, but there would be plenty of time for that later. She expressed surprise that Rosa looked so small and delicate. She gave advice on feeding, changing and care. Often the advice came close to tyranny.

'Of course, he'd already told her everything,' Marise remembered. 'I should have expected it. He was incapable of hiding anything from her. In her mind I quickly became the villain of the story, a woman who led men on then expected her husband to protect her from the consequences.'

A fierce cold sprang up between the two women. Mireille was always at the house, but rarely addressed Marise directly. Whole evenings would pass, with Tony and Mireille talking animatedly of events and people of which Marise knew nothing. Tony never seemed to notice her silence. He was always cheery and animated, allowing his mother to fuss over him, as if he were still a boy instead of a married man with a newborn baby. Then, out of the blue, Patrice came to call.

'It was late summer,' Marise recalled. 'About eight in the evening. I'd just fed Rosa. I heard a car on the drive. I was upstairs and Tony went to the door. It was Patrice.' He had changed since the last time she had seen him. Now he was plaintive, almost humble. He did not demand to see Marise. Instead he told Tony how sorry he was about what had happened, that he had been ill, that only now had he been able to face up to that fact. Marise listened from upstairs.

He had brought money, he explained, 20,000 francs. Not enough to pay for the harm he had done, but perhaps enough to start a trust fund for the baby.

'He and Tony went out back together. They were gone a long time. When Tony returned it was dark, and he was alone. He told me it was over, that Patrice wouldn't trouble us again. He was more loving than he'd been for a long time. I began to think things were going to be OK.'

For a few weeks they were happy together. Marise looked after Rosa. Mireille kept her distance. Tony no longer stood guard at night. Then one day, as she went to pick some herbs by the side of the house, Marise found the barn door half open. Going to shut it, she found Patrice's car, ill-concealed behind some bales of straw.

'At first he denied it,' she said. 'Just like a boy. Refused to admit I'd seen it at all. Then he went into one of his rages. Called me a whore. Accused me of seeing Patrice behind his back. At last he admitted it. He'd taken Patrice into the barn that day and killed him with a spade.'

He showed no remorse. He'd had no choice. If anyone was at fault it was Marise herself. Grinning like a guilty schoolboy, he explained how he had brought the car into the barn and hidden it, then buried Patrice somewhere on the estate.

'Where?' asked Marise.

Tony grinned again and shook his head slyly. 'You'll never know,' he said.

After that Tony's behaviour worsened rapidly. He would spend hours alone with his mother, then would lock himself in his room with the television blaring. He would not even look at Rosa. Marise, recognizing the symptoms of schizophrenia, tried to persuade him to return to his medication, but he no longer trusted her. Mireille had seen to that. He killed himself soon afterwards, and Marise had felt nothing but a guilty kind of relief.

'I tried to leave after that,' she said in a flat voice. 'There was nothing left for me in Lansquenet but bad memories. I packed my bags. I even booked a train ticket to Paris for myself and Rosa. But Mireille stopped me. Tony had left her a letter, she said, telling her everything. Patrice was buried somewhere on the Foudouin estate, at our end or across the river. Only she knew where.'

'You'll have to stay here now, *héh*,' said Mireille in triumph. 'I won't let you take my Rosa away. Otherwise I'll tell the police you killed the man from Marseilles, that my son told me about it before he died, that he killed himself because he couldn't stand the burden of protecting you.'

'She was very persuasive,' said Marise, with a touch of bitterness. 'Made it clear that she was keeping quiet for Rosa's sake. Keeping it in the family.'

After that came the campaign to separate Marise from the rest of the village. It wasn't difficult; in the course of that year she had hardly spoken to anyone and had spent most of her time isolated on the farm. Mireille released all her hidden resentment. She spread rumours around the village, hinted at dark secrets. Tony had been popular in Lansquenet. Marise was only an outsider from the city. Soon the reprisals began.

'Oh, nothing too serious,' said Marise. 'Letting off fireworks under my windows. Letters. General harassment. I'd had worse with Patrice.'

But it soon became clear that Mireille's campaign was designed for more than simple spite.

'She wanted Rosa,' explained Marise. 'She thought that, if she could drive me out of Lansquenet, she might be able to keep Rosa for herself. I'd have to let her keep her, you see. Because of what she knew. And if I were arrested for murdering Patrice, she would have had Rosa anyway, as her only close relative.'

She shivered.

And so she'd kept them at bay. All of them. She holed herself up in her farm, deliberately isolating herself from everyone in Lansquenet. Isolating Rosa by using her temporary deafness to deceive Mireille. Patrice's car she dumped in the marshes, letting it sink deep under the reeds and standing water. Its presence incriminated her still further, she understood. But she needed it to be close. On her land. Where she knew where it was. Remained the body.

'At first I looked for it,' she told me. 'I searched the buildings. Under the floors. Methodically. But it was no use. All the land right down to the marshes belonged to the estate. I couldn't search every metre.'

Plus there was old Emile. It was always possible that Tony had gone as far as his place. In fact, Mireille had hinted at it already, in her sour, gleeful way, relishing her power and her hold. It was this which made Marise so eager to bid for the Foudouin farm. Jay tried to imagine what she must have felt, seeing him in the house, watching him dig up the beds, wandering round the orchard. Wondering every day whether maybe today—

Impulsively he took her hand. It was cold. He could feel a thin tremor through her fingertips, almost imperceptible. A wave of admiration for her dizzied him. For her courage.

'That was why you didn't want anyone working on your land,' he said. 'That was why you didn't give up the marshland for the new hypermarket. That's why you have to stay here.'

She nodded. 'I couldn't let anyone find what he'd hidden,' she said. 'So long after the event no-one would believe I had nothing to do with it. And I knew Mireille wouldn't back me up. She'd never admit that her precious Tony—' She took a deep breath.

'So now you know,' she said with an effort. 'Now some-one else knows.' She smelt of thyme and rain. Her hair was a fall of flowers. Jay imagined himself telling her what had happened today, seeing the light go out of her green eyes, seeing her face tighten, stony, forbidding.

Someone else might have told her then. Someone of equal courage, equal clarity. Instead he pulled her towards him, feeling her hair against his face, her lips against his, her eager softness in his arms and her breath against his cheek. Her kiss tasted exactly how he'd imagined it: raspberries and smoky roses. They made love there, on Jay's unmade bed, with the goat looking curiously through the half-closed shutters, and the sweet golden light kaleidoscoping across the dim blue walls.

For a while that seemed enough.

62

SOON. SOON. THEY WERE IN EVERYTHING NOW, THE SPECIALS – IN the air, the ground, the lovers; he lying on his bed, staring at the ceiling; she asleep, her face turned into the pillow like a child's, her bright hair a pennant against the linen. More potent than ever now, I could feel them, hear their eager voices urging, coaxing. *Soon*, they whispered. *It has to be soon. It has to be now.*

Jay looked at Marise asleep beside him. She looked trusting, secure. She murmured something quiet and word-less in her sleep. She smiled. Jay pulled the blanket closer around her and she buried her face in it with a long sigh.

Jay watched her and thought about the morning. There must be something he could do. He could not let her lose the farm. He could not abandon Lansquenet to developers. The film crew was arriving tomorrow. That gave him what? Six hours? Seven?

To do what? What could he do in seven hours? Or seventy, for that matter? What could *anyone* do?

Joe could do something.

The voice was almost familiar. Cynical, hearty, a little amused.

You know he could.

Sure. He almost spoke aloud. But Joe was dead. Grief surprised him again, as it always did when he thought of Joe. Joe was dead. No more magic. Like the Specials, it had finally run out for good.

321

Tha never did have much sense, lad.

This time it really was Joe's voice. For a second his heart leaped, but he realized that Joe's voice was in his mind, in his memory. Joe's presence – his real, independent presence – was gone. This was just a substitute. A game. A conceit, like whistling in the dark.

Remember the Specials, I told you. Don't you remember?

'Of course I do,' whispered Jay helplessly. 'But there are no Specials any more. They're all gone. I finished them. I *wasted* them on trivial stuff, like getting people to tell me things. Like getting Marise—'

Why don't you bloody listen? Joe's voice, if it was Joe's voice, was everywhere now – in the air, in the light from the dying embers, in the glow of her hair spread out across the pillow. *Where were you when I was teaching you all those times at Pog Hill? Didn't you learn anything?*

'Sure.' Jay shook his head, puzzled. 'But without Joe none of that stuff works any more. Like that last time at Pog Hill—'

From the walls, laughter. The air was rich with it. A phantom scent of apples and smoke seemed to rise from the coals. The night sparkled.

Put your hand often enough in a wasps' nest, said Joe's voice, *and you're going to get stung. Even magic won't stop that. Even magic doesn't go against nature. You've got to give magic a hand sometimes, lad. Give it summat to use. A chance to work for itself. You've got to create the right conditions for magic to work.*

'But I had the talisman. I believed—'

Never needed any talisman, replied the voice. *You could have helped yourself. You could have fought back, couldn't you? But no. All you did was run away. Call that faith? Sounds like plain daft to me. So don't come that faith bullshit with me.*

Jay thought about that for a moment.

You've already got all you need, continued the voice

cheerily. *It's inside you, lad. Allus has been. You don't need some old bloke's home-brew to do that work for you. You can do it all on your own.*

'But I can't—'

No such bloody word, lad, said the voice. *No such bloody word.*

Then the voices were gone, and suddenly his head was ringing, not with dizziness but with sudden clarity. He knew what he had to do.

Six hours, he told himself. He had no time to lose.

NO-ONE SAW HIM LEAVE THE HOUSE. NO-ONE WAS WATCHING. Even if they were no-one would question his presence, or find it odd. Nor was the deep basket of herbs which he carried in any way unusual. The broad-leaved plants which filled it might be a present for someone, a gift for a flagging garden. Even the fact that he was muttering something under his breath, something which sounded a little like Latin, would not surprise them. He was, after all, English, therefore a little crazy. *Un peu fada, Monsieur Jay.*

He found he remembered Joe's perimeter ritual very well indeed. There was no time to make incense, nor to prepare any new sachets, but he did not think that mattered now. Even he could sense the Specials around him, hear their whispering voices, their fairground laughter. He took the seedlings carefully from the cold frame, as many as he could carry, along with a trowel and a tiny fork. He planted them at intervals on the roadside. He planted several at the intersection with the Toulouse road, two more at the stop sign, two more on the road to Les Marauds. Fog, Lansquenet's special fog, which rolls off the marshes and into the vineyards, rose about him like a bright sail in the early sun. Jay Mackintosh hurried on his circuit, half running in his haste to make the deadline, planting Joe's *tuberosa rosifea* wherever there was a branch in the road, a gateway, a sign. He turned round roadsigns or covered them with greenery when he could not dig them out of the soil. He removed

Georges' and Lucien's welcome placard altogether. By the time he had finished there was not a single signpost for Lansquenet-sous-Tannes remaining. It took him almost four hours to complete the fourteen-mile circuit, looping around the village towards the Toulouse road, then back across Les Marauds. By the end he was exhausted. His head ached, his legs felt shaky as stilts. But he had finished. It was done.

As Joe hid Pog Hill Lane, he thought in triumph, he had hidden the village of Lansquenet-sous-Tannes.

Marise and Rosa had gone by the time he got back. The sky began to lighten. The mist cleared.

63

IT WAS ELEVEN O'CLOCK BEFORE KERRY ARRIVED. CRISP AND COOL in a white blouse and grey skirt, her document case in one hand. Jay was waiting for her.

'Good morning, Jay.'

'You're back.'

She looked over his shoulder into the room, noting the empty glasses and the wine bottles.

'We *should* have started earlier,' she said, 'but would you believe it? We got lost in the fog. Great blankets of white fog, just like the dry ice at a heavy-metal concert.' She laughed. 'Can you imagine? Half a day wasted already. And on our budget. I'm still waiting for the camera crew. Seems they took some kind of a wrong turning and ended up halfway back to Agen. These roads. It's a good thing I already knew the way.'

Jay looked at her. It hadn't worked, he thought bleakly. In spite of everything, in spite of his faith.

'So you're still going ahead with it?'

'Well, of course I'm going ahead,' replied Kerry impatiently. 'It's too good an opportunity to miss.' She examined her nails. 'You're a celebrity. When the book comes out I can show the world where you got your inspiration.' She smiled brightly. 'It's such a wonderful book,' she added. 'It's going to be a terrific success. If anything, it's even better than *Jackapple Joe*.'

Jay nodded. She was right, of course. Pog Hill and

Lansquenet; two sides of the same tarnished coin. Both sacrificed, each in its own way, to the writing career of Jay Mackintosh. After publication the place just wouldn't be the same. Inevitably, he would move on. Narcisse, Joséphine, Briançon, Guillaume, Arnauld, Roux, Poitou, Rosa – even Marise – all reduced to the status of words on a page, glib fictions to be passed over and forgotten, while in his absence, the developers moved in, planning and demolishing, rethinking and modernizing . . .

'I don't know why you're looking like that,' said Kerry. 'After all, you've got the WorldWide contract. That's a very generous sum you're looking at. More than generous. Or am I being vulgar?'

'Not at all.' A most peculiar feeling of calm, almost of drunkenness, was beginning to steal over him. His head felt as if it were filled with bubbles. The yeasty air seethed and hissed.

'They must want you very much,' remarked Kerry.

'Yes,' said Jay slowly. 'I think they do.'

Put your hand often enough in a wasps' nest, Joe had said, *and you're going to get stung. Even magic won't stop that. You've got to give magic a hand sometimes, lad. Give it summat to use . . . the right conditions.*

That was it, he thought dazedly. So simple. So . . . simple.

Jay laughed. All at once his head was full of light. He could smell smoke and swampy water and the sweet heady scent of ripe blackberries. The air was elderflower champagne. He knew Joe was with him, that Joe had never left. Not even in '77. Joe had never left. He could almost see him standing by the door in his old pit cap and boots, grinning in that way he had when he was especially pleased with something, and though Jay knew it was in his imagination, he knew it was real, too. Sometimes real and imaginary are the same thing after all.

Two paces took him to the bed where the manuscript and the WorldWide contracts were still lying in their box. He pulled it out. Kerry turned towards him curiously.

'What are you doing?'

Jay picked up the manuscript in his arms and began to laugh.

'Do you know what this is?' he asked her. 'It's the only copy I have of the book. And this' – holding out the signed contract for her to see – 'is the paperwork. Look. It's all completed. Ready to be sent off.'

'Jay, what are you doing?' Her voice was sharp.

Jay grinned and took a step towards the fireplace.

'You can't—' began Kerry.

Jay looked at her.

'No such bloody word,' he said.

And behind Kerry's sudden shriek he thought he could hear the sound of an old man's chuckle.

She shrieked because she suddenly knew what he was going to do. It was crazy, ridiculous, the kind of impulse to which he had never been prone, and yet there was also a strange light in his eyes which had never been there before. As if someone had lit a fuse. His face was illuminated. He took the contracts in his hands, crumpled them and pushed them into the back of the grate. Then he began to do the same with the pages of the typescript. The paper began to catch, first crisping, then turning brown, then leaping into gleeful flame. The air was whirling with black butterflies.

'What are you playing at?' Kerry's voice rose shrilly. 'Jay, what the fuck are you doing now?'

He grinned at her, breathless with laughter.

'What do you think? Wait a day or two, till you can get in touch with Nicky, and you'll be sure.'

'You're crazy,' said Kerry sharply. 'You're not going to make me believe you don't have copies of that typescript. Plus the contracts can be replaced—'

'Sure they can.' He was relaxed, smiling. 'But it isn't going to be replaced. None of it is. And what use to anyone is a writer who never writes? How long can you sustain public interest in that? What's it worth? What am *I* worth without it?'

Kerry looked at him. The man who left six months ago was unrecognizable. The old Jay was vague, sullen, directionless. This man was driven, illuminated. His eyes were shining. In spite of what he was throwing away – stupid, criminal, mad – he looked happy.

'You really are crazy,' she said in a strangled voice. 'Throwing everything away – and for what? Some gesture? It isn't you, Jay. I know you. You'll regret it.'

Jay just looked at her, smiling a little. Patiently.

'I don't see you staying here beyond a year.' Behind the scorn her voice was shaking. 'What are you going to do? Run the farm? You've hardly any money. You've blown it all on this place. What will you do when the money runs out?'

'I don't know.' His tone was cheery, indifferent. 'Do you care?'

'No!'

He shrugged. 'You'd better page your film crew and tell them to meet you somewhere else,' he told her quietly. 'There's no story for you here. Better try Le Pinot, just across the river. I'm sure you'll get something suitably upbeat and entertaining there.'

She stared at him, amazed. Just for a moment she thought she smelt something, a strange, vivid scent of sugar and apples and blackberry jelly and smoke. It was a nostalgic scent, and for a second she could almost understand why Jay loved this place so much, with its little vineyards and its apple trees and its roaming goats on the marsh flats. For that instant she was a little girl again, with her grandmother in the kitchen making pies and the wind from the coast making the telephone wires sing. Somehow, she felt the scent was a part of him, something which clung to him like old smoke, and as she looked at him for a moment he looked *gilded* somehow, as if lit from behind, filaments of brightness shooting from his hair, his clothes. Then the scent was gone, the light was gone, and there was nothing but the staleness of the unaired room and the dregs of the wine on the table in front of them. Kerry shrugged.

'It's your loss,' she said sullenly. 'Do what you like.'

He nodded. 'And the series?'

'I might just drive out to Le Pinot,' she said. 'Georges Clairmont tells me there was a production of *Clochemerle* filmed there recently. It might make a decent feature.'

He smiled. 'Good luck, Kerry.'

WHEN SHE HAD GONE HE WASHED AND PUT ON A CLEAN T-SHIRT and jeans. He considered for a moment what to do next. Even now there were no certainties. In life, the happy ending is never assured. Around us now the house was absolutely still. The buzz of energy which permeated the walls had vanished. No phantom scent of sugar and smoke remained. Even the cellar was quiet, the bottles of wine – new wine, Sauternes and Saint-Émilion and a dozen young Anjou – still and silent. Waiting.

64

AROUND NOON POPOTTE BROUGHT A PARCEL AND THE NEWS from the village. The film crew never arrived, she reported excitedly. The English lady interviewed no-one. Georges and Lucien were furious. *En tout cas*, she shrugged, it was probably for the best. Everyone knew that their plans never came to anything. Georges was already talking about a new venture, some kind of development plan in Montauban, which couldn't possibly fail. Lansquenet had already moved on.

THE PARCEL WAS POSTMARKED KIRBY MONCKTON. JAY OPENED IT alone, with care, unwrapping the stiff sheets of brown paper, untying the string. It was large and heavy. As he removed the packaging an envelope fell out. He recognized Joe's writing. There was a single sheet of faded letter paper inside.

Pog Hill Lane, 15th September.
Dear Jay,
    Sorry about the rush. I never was any cop at good-byes. I meant to stay on a bit longer, but you know what things are like. Bloody doctors won't tell you anything till the last minute. They think that because you're old you've got no idea. I'm sending you my collection – I reckon you'll know what to do with it. You should have learned something by the time you

330

get this. Make sure you get the soil right. Fondest regards, Joseph Cox.

Jay read the letter again. He touched the words on the page, written in black ink in that careful, shapeless hand. He even lifted the paper to his face to see if anything of him remained – a whiff of smoke, maybe, or the faint scent of ripe blackberries. But there was nothing. If there had been magic, it was elsewhere. Then he looked in the package. Everything was there. The contents of the seed chest, hundreds of tiny envelopes and twists of newspaper, dried bulbs, grains, corms, seed fluff no more substantial than a puff of dead dust – every one marked and numbered. Everything alight with the scent of those other places. *Tuberosa rubra maritima, tuberosa diabolica, tuberosa panax odarata*, thousands of potatoes, squash, peppers, carrots, over three hundred species of onion alone – Joe's entire collection. And, of course, the Specials. *Tuberosa rosifea* in all its glory, the true jackapple, the rediscovered original.

He looked at them for a long time. Later he would look at them all, placing each packet in the correct drawer of the old spice chest. Later there would be time for sorting, for labelling and numbering and cataloguing, until at last every one was in place again. But first there was one more thing he had to do. Someone to see. And something to find. Something in the cellar.

THERE WAS ONLY ONE POSSIBLE CHOICE. HE WIPED OFF THE familiar dust from the glass with a cloth, hoping time had not soured the contents. A bottle for a special occasion, he thought, the last of his own Specials – 1962, that good year; the first, he hoped, of many good years. He wrapped the bottle in tissue paper and put it in his jacket pocket. A peace offering.

She was sitting in the kitchen, shelling peas, when he arrived. She was wearing a white shirt over her jeans, and the sunlight was red on her autumn hair. Outside he could hear Rosa calling to Clopette.

'I brought you this,' he told her. 'I've been saving it for a special occasion. I thought maybe you and I could drink it together.'

She stared at him for a long time, her face unreadable. Her eyes were cool, verdigris, appraising. Finally she took the outstretched bottle and looked at the label.

'Fleurie 1962,' she said, and smiled. 'My favourite.'

THIS IS WHERE MY STORY ENDS. HERE, IN THE KITCHEN OF THE little farmhouse in Lansquenet. Here he pours me, releasing the scents of summers forgotten and places long past. He drinks to Joe and Pog Hill Lane; the toast is both a salute and a goodbye. Say what you will, there's nothing to beat the flavour of good grape. Blackcurrant aftertaste or not, I have my own magic, uncorked at last after thirty-seven years of waiting. I hope they appreciate that, both of them, mouths locked together and hands clasped. Now it is for them to do the talking. My part is at an end. I would like to think that theirs ends as happily. But that knowledge is beyond me now. I am subject to a different kind of chemistry. Evaporating blithely into the bright air, my own mystery approaches, and I see no phantoms, predict no futures, even the blissful present barely glimpsed – through a glass, darkly.

Postscript

From the *Lansquenet-gratuit*:

Obituaries

Mireille Annabelle Faizande, suddenly after a short illness. Leaves a nephew, Pierre-Emile, daughter-in-law, Marise, and granddaughter, Rosa.

Property Sales

To Mme. Marise d'Api, four hectares of cultivated and non-cultivated agricultural land between Rue des Marauds, Boulevard St-Espoir and the Tannes, including a farmhouse and outbuildings, from Pierre-Emile Foudouin, Rue Gene-vièvre, Toulouse.

From the *Courrier d'Agen*:
A local landowner has become the first known person since the seventeenth century to produce the *tuberosa rosifea* potato. This ancient species, thought to have been brought out of South America in 1643, is a large, sweet-scented pink tuber which thrives in our marshy, lime-rich soil. M. Jay Mackintosh, a former writer who emigrated from England eighteen months ago, plans to cultivate these and other rare species of vegetable on his farm in Lansquenet-sous-Tannes.

'I intend to reintroduce many of these old varieties for general consumption,' he told our reporter recently. 'It's only through luck that some of these species have not been lost for ever.' When questioned on the origins of these precious seeds, M. Mackintosh remains evasive. 'I'm just a collector,' he explains modestly. 'I have collected a large number of different seeds on my travels around the world.'

But, you may ask, what is so important about a few old seeds? Does it really matter what kind of potato we use for our *pommes frites*?

'Oh yes,' he says firmly. 'It does matter. Too many thousands of plant and animal species have already been lost for ever to modern farming methods and guidelines from Brussels. It's very important to keep the traditional varieties going. Plants have all kinds of properties which even now are not fully understood. Who knows, maybe in a few years' time scientists will be able to save lives using one of these rediscovered species.'

M. Mackintosh's unconventional methods have already spread beyond his own small farm. Local farmers have recently joined him in setting aside part of their land to the production of these old varieties. M. André Narcisse, M. Philippe Briançon and Mme. Marise d'Api have also decided to test the new seeds. And with *tuberosa rosifea* retailing at a hundred francs or more a kilo, the future looks rosy once again for the farmers of Lansquenet-sous-Tannes. As for M. Mackintosh, 36, of Château Cox, Lansquenet, overnight success has left him surprisingly modest. When asked to what he attributes this spectacular success he replies, 'Just luck.' He gives our reporter his mischievous smile. 'And, of course, a little magic.'

THE END

CHOCOLAT
Joanne Harris

'SENSUOUS AND THOUGHT-PROVOKING . . .
SUBTLE AND BRILLIANT'
Daily Telegraph

Try me . . . Test me . . . Taste me . . .

When an exotic stranger, Vianne Rocher, arrives in the French
village of Lansquenet and opens a chocolate boutique directly
opposite the church, Father Reynaud identifies her as a serious
danger to his flock – especially as it is the beginning of Lent,
the traditional season of self-denial. War is declared as the
priest denounces the newcomer's wares as the ultimate sin.

Suddenly Vianne's shop-cum-café means that there is
somewhere for secrets to be whispered, grievances to be aired,
dreams to be tested. But Vianne's plans for an Easter Chocolate
Festival divide the whole community in a conflict that escalates
into a 'Church not Chocolate' battle. As mouths water in
anticipation, can the solemnity of the Church compare with the
pagan passion of a chocolate éclair?

For the first time here is a novel in which chocolate enjoys
its true importance. Rich, clever and mischievous, *Chocolat* is
a literary feast for all the senses.

'MOODY AND ATMOSPHERIC . . . A RICHLY TEXTURED
TALE'
Independent

'MOUTHWATERING . . . A FEELGOOD BOOK OF THE
FIRST ORDER. AS YOU ARE LURED BY THE PLOT AND
THE WONDERFUL DESCRIPTIONS, YOUR SENSES ARE
LEFT REELING. READ IT'
Observer

'IS THIS THE BEST BOOK EVER WRITTEN? TRULY
EXCELLENT . . . HARRIS' ACHIEVEMENT IS NOT ONLY IN
HER STORY, IN HER INSIGHT AND HUMOUR AND THE
WONDERFUL PICTURE OF SMALL-TOWN LIFE IN RURAL
FRANCE, BUT ALSO IN HER WRITING'
Literary Review

0 552 99848 6

BLACK SWAN

A SELECTED LIST OF FINE WRITING
AVAILABLE FROM BLACK SWAN

99588 6	THE HOUSE OF THE SPIRITS	Isabel Allende	£7.99
99820 6	FLANDERS	Patricia Anthony	£6.99
99822 2	A CLASS APART	Diana Appleyard	£6.99
99842 7	EXCESS BAGGAGE	Judy Astley	£6.99
99619 X	HUMAN CROQUET	Kate Atkinson	£6.99
99853 2	LOVE IS A FOUR LETTER WORD	Claire Calman	£6.99
99687 4	THE PURVEYOR OF ENCHANTMENT	Marika Cobbold	£6.99
99767 6	SISTER OF MY HEART	Chitra Banerjee Divakaruni	£6.99
99836 2	A HEART OF STONE	Renate Dorrestein	£6.99
99587 8	LIKE WATER FOR CHOCOLATE	Laura Esquivel	£6.99
99770 6	TELLING LIDDY	Anne Fine	£6.99
99851 6	REMEMBERING BLUE	Connie May Fowler	£6.99
99760 9	THE DRESS CIRCLE	Laurie Graham	£6.99
99801 X	THE SHORT HISTORY OF A PRINCE	Jane Hamilton	£6.99
99848 6	CHOCOLAT	Joanne Harris	£6.99
99758 7	FRIEDA AND MIN	Pamela Jooste	£6.99
99737 4	GOLDEN LADS AND GIRLS	Angela Lambert	£6.99
99812 5	THE PHILOSOPHER'S HOUSE	Joan Marysmith	£6.99
99777 3	THE SPARROW	Mary Doria Russell	£6.99
99819 2	WHISTLING FOR THE ELEPHANTS	Sandi Toksvig	£6.99
99788 9	OTHER PEOPLE'S CHILDREN	Joanna Trollope	£6.99
99780 3	KNOWLEDGE OF ANGELS	Jill Paton Walsh	£6.99
99673 4	DINA'S BOOK	Herbjørg Wassmo	£6.99
99723 4	PART OF THE FURNITURE	Mary Wesley	£6.99
99834 6	COCKTAILS FOR THREE	Madeleine Wickham	£6.99
99651 3	AFTER THE UNICORN	Joyce Windsor	£6.99

Joanne Harris is the author of three previous novels, *Sleep, Pale Sister*, *The Evil Seed* and *Chocolat*. *Chocolat* was shortlisted for the 1999 Whitbread Novel of the Year Award and is also published by Black Swan. Her latest novel, *Five Quarters of the Orange*, is now available from Doubleday. Joanne Harris lives in Barnsley, Yorkshire, with her husband and small daughter.

Acclaim for *Blackberry Wine*:

'A lively and original talent'
Sunday Times

'Harris is at her best when detailing the sensual pleasures of taste and smell. As chocoholics stand advised to stock up on some of their favourite bars before biting into *Chocolat*, so boozers everywhere should get a couple of bottles in before opening *Blackberry Wine*'
Helen Falconer, *Guardian*

'Joanne Harris has the gift of conveying her delight in the sensuous pleasures of food, wine, scent and plants . . . [*Blackberry Wine*] has all the appeal of a velvety scented glass of vintage wine'
Lizzie Buchan, *Daily Mail*

'If Joanne Harris didn't exist, someone would have to invent her, she's such a welcome antidote to the modern preoccupation with the spare, pared down and non-fattening. Not for her the doubtful merits of an elegant and expensive sparkling water or an un-dressed rocket salad. In her previous novel, *Chocolat*, she invoked the scent and the flavour of rich, dark, sweet self-indulgence. In *Blackberry Wine* she celebrates the sensuous energy that can leap from a bottle after years of fermentation . . . Harris bombards the senses with the smells and tastes of times past . . . Harris's talent lies in her own grasp of the quality she ascribes to wine, "layman's alchemy, the magic of everyday things." She is fanciful and grounded at the same time – one moment shrouded in mystery, the next firmly planted in earth. Above all, she has wit'
Jenni Murray, *Sunday Express*

Also by Joanne Harris

SLEEP, PALE SISTER
THE EVIL SEED
CHOCOLAT
FIVE QUARTERS OF THE ORANGE